VIRGINIA

The OLD DOMINION *Edition*

OF THE WORKS OF

ELLEN GLASGOW.

Virginia.

Printed in GARDEN CITY, NEW YORK, *at the Country Life Press,* 1929.

DOUBLEDAY,
DORAN
&
COMPANY, INC.

To the
Radiant Spirit
Who Was My Sister
CARY GLASGOW
MCCORMACK

Preface

WHERE could the perfect flower of the Victorian ideal be studied to greater advantage than in the 1880's in Dinwiddie, Virginia? In this ancient town, Miss Priscilla Batte's Academy for Young Ladies still taught reading, penmanship ("up to the right, down to the left, my dear"), arithmetic, geography, history that was profane and yet proper, deportment, the fine arts, and the correct attitude of evasive idealism. Virginia Pendleton, prepared by the Academy for the perils of the actuality was the perfect wife as man invented her and as he imagined he cherished her. The pathos of it was that she was not a weak character, as several undiscerning critics have called her, but a woman whose energy of soul had been deflected by tradition and education into a single emotional centre. She was, indeed, the logical result of an inordinate sense of duty, the crowning achievement of the code of beautiful behaviour and the Episcopal Church. For she was an exquisite, if slightly fantastic, creation, and had the Victorian male been as pliant in nature, the moral experiment might have been pronounced a success.

A few weeks after finishing *Virginia,* I received a visit from one of the perpetual widows of the South, who ought to have served as the model for Mrs. Pendleton. Her reproachful face was as melancholy as a lost cause, and her

vii

mourning veil flowed to the hem of a skirt that was still modest in length.

"Do you really think, my dear," she asked with patient gentleness, for she had known my mother, "that a young girl could be inspired to do her duty in life by reading *Virginia?* I do not deny that there is truth in your book, but don't you feel that it is always a mistake when Southern writers stop writing about the war?" Then, sighing pensively, she added, "If only I had your gifts, I should devote them to proving to the world that the Confederacy was right. Of course, I know that even the best novelists are not so improving as they used to be; but I have always hoped in my heart that either you or Annie Cabell's son would write another *Surrey of Eagle's Nest.*"

That was in the year 1913, and the next time I saw my perpetual widow she was cutting out pajamas in the crowded rooms of a War Relief Association. Enthusiasm bloomed afresh in her pensive face; and if she had survived the need of pajamas, she would probably have devoted her ample gifts to proving to the world that still another war was "right" besides the one that celebrated the Confederacy. But she died, as she would have wished, in the midst of a righteous conflict, and even her type has vanished now as completely as the wasp waist, the sense of duty, or the code of beautiful behaviour. And yet no social history of Virginia could be authentic unless it enshrined her.

ELLEN GLASGOW.

Richmond, Virginia, August, 1929.

Contents

BOOK FIRST : THE DREAM

BOOK SECOND : THE REALITY

CONTENTS

Book First

THE DREAM

CHAPTER I

THE SYSTEM

TOWARD the close of a May afternoon in the year 1884, Miss Priscilla Batte, having learned by heart the lesson in physical geography she would teach her senior class on the morrow, stood feeding her canary on the little square porch of the Dinwiddie Academy for Young Ladies. The day had been hot, and the fitful wind, which had risen from the river, was just beginning to blow in soft gusts under the old mulberry trees in the street, and to scatter the loosened petals of syringa blossoms in a flowery snow over the grass. For a moment Miss Priscilla turned her flushed face to the scented air, while her eyes rested lovingly on the narrow walk, edged with pointed bricks and bordered by cowslips and wallflowers, which led through the short garden to the three stone steps and the tall iron gate. She was a shapeless yet majestic woman of some fifty years, with a large mottled face in which a steadfast expression of gentle obstinacy lingered beneath the evanescent ripples of thought or emotion. Her severe black silk gown, to which she had just changed from her morning dress of alpaca, was softened under her full double chin by a knot of lace and a cameo brooch bearing the profile of Pallas Athene. She wore a three-cornered cap trimmed with a ruching of organdie, and beneath it her thin gray hair was still streaked with faded yellow. Though she had never been handsome, her prodigious size had endowed her with an impressiveness which had passed in her youth, and among an indulgent people, for beauty. Only in the last few years had her fleshiness, owing to rich food which she could not resist and to lack of exercise for which she had an instinctive aversion, begun seriously to inconvenience her.

Beyond the wire cage, in which the canary spent his celibate life, an ancient microphylla rose-bush, with a single early bud blooming amid its glossy foliage, clambered over a green lattice to the gabled pediment of the porch, while the delicate shadows of the leaves rippled like lace-work on the gravel below. In the miniature garden, where the small spring blossoms strayed from the prim beds into the grass, there were syringa bushes, a little overblown; crêpe-myrtles not yet in bud; a holly tree veiled in bright green near the iron fence; a flowering almond shrub in late bloom against the shaded side of the house; and where a west wing put out on the left, a bower of red and white roses was steeped now in the faint sunshine. At the foot of the three steps ran the sunken moss-edged bricks of High Street, and across High Street there floated, like wind-blown flowers, the figures of Susan Treadwell and Virginia Pendleton.

Opening the rusty gate, the two girls tripped, with carefully held flounces, up the stone steps and between the cowslips and wallflowers that bordered the walk. Their white lawn dresses were made with the close-fitting sleeves and the narrow waists of the period, and their elaborately draped overskirts were looped on the left with graduated bows of light blue ottoman ribbon. They wore no hats, and Virginia, who was the shorter of the two, had fastened a Jacqueminot rose in the thick dark braid which was wound in a wreath about her head. Above her arched black eyebrows, which lent an expression of surprise and animation to her vivid oval face, her hair was parted, after

an earlier fashion, under its plaited crown, and allowed
to break in a mist of little curls over her temples. Even
in repose there was a joyousness in her look which seemed
less the result of an inward gaiety of mind than of some
happy outward accident of form and colour. Her eyes,
very far apart and set in black lashes, were of a deep,
soft blue, the blue of wild hyacinths after rain. By her
eyes, and by an old-world charm which she exhaled like
a perfume, it was easy to discern the feminine ideal of
the ages. To look at her was to think inevitably of love.
For that end, obedient to the powers of Life, the centuries
had formed and coloured her, as they had formed and
coloured the wild-rose with its whorl of delicate petals.
The air of a spoiled beauty which rested not ungracefully
upon her was sweetened by her expression of natural simplicity and goodness.

For an instant she stood listening in silence to the queru-
lous pipes of the bird and the earnest exhortations of the
teacher on the joys of cage life for both bird and lady.
Then plucking the solitary early bud from the microphylla
rose-bush, she tossed it over the railing of the porch on the
large and placid bosom of Miss Priscilla.

"Do leave Dicky alone for a minute!" she called in a
winning soprano voice.

At the sound, Miss Priscilla dropped the bit of cake
she held, and turned to lean delightedly over the walk,
while her face beamed like a beneficent moon through
the shining cloud of rose-leaves.

"Why, Virginia, I hadn't any idea that you and Susan
were here!"

Her smile included Virginia's companion, a tall, rather
heavy girl, with intelligent gray eyes and fair hair cut in
a straight fringe across her forehead. She was the daughter of Cyrus Treadwell, the wealthiest and therefore the

most prominent citizen of the town, and she was as intellectual as the early eighties and the twenty-one thousand inhabitants of Dinwiddie permitted a woman to be. Her friendship for Virginia had been one of those swift and absorbing emotions which come to women in their school-days. The stronger of the two, she dominated the other, as she dominated every person or situation in life, not by charm, but by the force of an energetic and capable mind. Though her dress matched Virginia's in every detail, from the soft folds of tulle at the neck to the fancy striped stockings beneath the *bouffant* draperies, the different shapes of the wearers imparted to the one gown an air of decorous composure and to the other a quaint and appealing grace. Flushed, ardent, expectant, both girls stood now at the beginning of womanhood. Life was theirs; it belonged to them, this veiled, radiant thing that was approaching. Nothing wonderful had come as yet; but to-morrow, the day after, or next year, the miracle would happen, and everything would be different! Experience floated in a luminous mystery before them. The unknown, which had borrowed the sweetness and the colour of their illusions, possessed them like a secret ecstasy, and shone, in spite of their shyness, in their startled and joyous look.

"Father asked me to take a message over to General Goode," Virginia explained, with a laugh as gay as the song of a bird, "but I couldn't go by without thanking you for the cherry bounce. I made mother drink some of it before dinner, and it almost gave her an appetite."

"I knew it was what she needed," Miss Priscilla answered, showing her pleasure by an increasing beam. "It was made right here in the house, and there's nothing better in the world, my poor mother used to say, to keep you

from running down in the spring. But why can't you and
Susan come in and sit a while?"

"We'll be back in a minute," Susan replied before Virginia could answer. "I've a piece of news I want to tell you
before anyone else does. Oliver came home last night."

"Oliver?" Miss Priscilla repeated, a little perplexed.
"You don't mean the son of your uncle Henry, who went
out to Australia? I thought your father had washed his
hands of him because he had started play-acting or something?" Curiosity, that devouring passion of the middle-
aged, worked in her bosom, and her placid face grew
almost intense in expression.

"Yes, that's the one," Susan replied. "They went to
Australia when Oliver was ten years old, and he's now
twenty-two. He lost both his parents about three years
ago."

"I know. His mother was my cousin," Miss Priscilla returned. "I lost sight of her after she left Dinwiddie, but
somebody was telling me the other day that Henry's investments all turned out badly and they came down to
real poverty. Sarah Jane was a pretty girl and I was
always very fond of her, but she was one of the improvi-
dent sort that couldn't make two ends meet without tying
them into a bowknot."

"Then Oliver must be just like her. After his mother's
death he went to Germany to study, and he gave away
the little money he had to some student he found starving
there in a garret."

"That was generous," Miss Priscilla commented
thoughtfully, "but I should hardly call it sensible. I hope
some day, Virginia, that your father will tell us in a sermon
whether there is biblical sanction for immoderate gen-
erosity or not."

"But what does he say?" Virginia asked softly, meaning not the rector, but the immoderate young man.

"Oh, Oliver says that there wasn't enough for both and that the other student is worth more to the world than he is," Susan answered. "Then, of course, when he got so poor that he had to pawn his clothes or starve, he wrote father an almost condescending letter and said that, as much as he hated business, he supposed he'd have to come back and go to work. 'Only,' he added, 'for God's sake, don't make it tobacco!' Wasn't that dreadful?"

"It was extremely impertinent," Miss Priscilla replied sternly, "and to Cyrus of all persons! I am surprised that he allowed him to come into the house."

"Oh, father doesn't take any of his talk seriously. He calls it 'starvation foolishness,' and says that Oliver will get over it as soon as he has a nice little bank account. Perhaps he will—he is only twenty-two, you know—but just now his head is full of new ideas he picked up somewhere abroad. He's as clever as he can be, there's no doubt of that, and he'd be really good-looking, too, if he didn't have the crooked nose of the Treadwells. Virginia has seen him only once in the street, but she's more than half in love with him already."

"Do come, Susan!" Virginia remonstrated, blushing as red as the rose in her hair. "It's past six o'clock, and the General will have gone if we don't hurry." And turning away from the porch, she ran between the flowering syringa bushes down the path to the gate.

Having lost his bit of cake, the bird began to pipe shrilly, while Miss Priscilla drew a straight wicker chair (she never used rockers) beside the cage, and, stretching out her feet in their large cloth shoes with elastic sides, counted the stitches in an afghan she was knitting in narrow blue and orange stripes. In front of her, the

street trailed between cool, dim houses which were filled
with quiet, and from the hall at her back there came a
whispering sound as the breeze moved like a ghostly foot-
step through an alcove window. With that strange power
of reflecting the variable moods of humanity which exist
in inanimate objects, the face of the old house had borrowed from the face of its mistress the look of cheerful
fortitude with which her generation had survived the
agony of defeat and the humiliation of reconstruction.
After nineteen years, the Academy still bore the scars of
war on its battered front. Once it had watched the spectre
of famine stalk over the grass-grown pavement, and had
heard the rattle of musketry and the roar of cannon borne
on the southern breeze which now wafted the sounds
of the saw and hammer from an adjacent street. Once
it had seen the flight of refugees, the overflow of the
wounded from hospitals and churches, the panic of liberated slaves, the steady conquering march of the army
of invasion. And though it would never have occurred to
Miss Priscilla that either she or her house had borne any
relation to history (which she regarded strictly as a branch
of study and pictured as a list of dates or as a king wearing his crown), she had, in fact, played a modest yet
effective part in the rapidly changing civilization of her
age. Events were powerless against the genial heroism in
which she was armoured, and it was characteristic of her,
as well as of her race, that, while she sat now in the midst
of encircling battlefields, with her eyes on the walk over
which she had seen the blood of the wounded drip when
they were lifted into her door, she should be brooding
not over the tremendous tragedies through which she had
passed, but over the lesson in physical geography she
must teach in the morning. Her lips moved gently, and
a listener, had there been one, might have heard her mur-

mur: "The four great alluvial plains of Asia—those of China and of the Amoo Daria in temperate regions; of the Euphrates and Tigris in the warm temperate; of the Indus and Ganges under the Tropic—with the Nile valley in Africa, were the theatres of the most ancient civilizations known to history or tradition——"

As she ended, a sigh escaped her, for the instruction of the young was a matter less of choice for her than of necessity. With the majority of maiden ladies left destitute in Dinwiddie after the war, she had turned naturally to teaching as the only nice and respectable occupation which required neither preparation of mind nor considerable outlay of money. The fact that she was the single surviving child of a gallant Confederate general, who, having distinguished himself and his descendants, fell at last in the Battle of Gettysburg, was sufficient recommendation in the eyes of her fellow-citizens. Had she chosen to paint portraits or to write poems, they would have rallied quite as loyally to her support. Few, indeed, were the girls born in Dinwiddie since the war who had not learned reading, penmanship ("up to the right, down to the left, my dear"), geography, history, arithmetic, deportment, and the fine arts, in the Academy for Young Ladies. The brilliant military record of the General still shed a legendary lustre upon the school, and it was earnestly believed that no girl, after leaving there with a diploma for good conduct, could possibly go wrong or become eccentric in her later years. To be sure, she might remain a trifle weak in her spelling (Miss Priscilla having, as she confessed, a poor head for that branch of study), but, after all, as the rector had once remarked, good spelling is by no means a necessary accomplishment for a lady; and it was certain that the moral education of a pupil of the Academy would be firmly rooted in such fundamental verities as the

superiority of man and the aristocratic supremacy of the
Episcopal Church. From charming Sally Goode, now
married to Tom Peachey, known familiarly as "honest
Tom," the editor of the Dinwiddie *Bee,* to lovely Virginia Pendleton, the mark of Miss Priscilla was efface-
ably impressed upon the daughters of the leading families.

Remembering this now, as she was disposed to do whenever she was knitting without company, Miss Priscilla
dropped her long wooden needles in her lap, and leaning
slightly forward gazed out upon the town with an expression of child-like confidence, of touching innocence. This
innocence, which belonged to the very essence of her soul,
had survived both the fugitive joys and the perennial disillusionment of her life. Experience could not shatter it,
for it was the product of a courage that feared nothing
except opinions. Just as the town had battled for a principle without understanding it, so she was capable of
dying for an idea, but not of conceiving one. She had suffered everything from the war, except the necessity of
thinking independently about it, and, though in later years
memory had become so sacred to her that she rarely
indulged in it, she still clung passionately to the habits of
her ancestors under the impression that she was clinging
to their ideals. Little things filled her days; the trivial
details of the classroom and the market, the small
domestic disturbances of her neighbours, the moral or
mental delinquencies of her two coloured servants; and
even her religious veneration for the Episcopal Church
had crystallized at last into a worship of customs.

To-day, at the beginning of the industrial awakening
of the South, she (who was but the embodied spirit of
her race) stood firmly rooted in all that was static, in all
that was obsolete and outgrown, in the Virginia of the
eighties. Though she felt as yet merely the vague un-

easiness with which her mind recoiled from the first stir-
rings of change, she was beginning dimly to realize that
the car of progress would move through the quiet streets
before the decade was over. The smoke of factories was
already succeeding the smoke of the battlefields, and from
the ashes of a vanquished idealism the spirit of commercial materialism was born. What was left of the old
was fighting valiantly but hopelessly against what had
come of the new. The two forces crowded the streets of
Dinwiddie. They were embodied in classes, in individuals,
in articles of faith, in ideals of manners. The symbol of
the one spirit was the memorial wreaths on the battlefields; of the other it was the prophetic smoke of the
factories. From where she stood in High Street, she could
see this incense to Mammon rising above the spires of
the churches, above the houses and the hovels, above the
charm and the provincialism which made the Dinwiddie
of the eighties. And this charm, as well as this provincialism, appeared to her to be so inalienable a part of the
old order, with its intrepid faith in itself, with its militant enthusiasm, with its courageous battle against industrial evolution, with its strength, its narrowness, its nobility, its blindness, that, looking ahead, she could discern
only the arid stretch of a civilization from which the last
remnant of beauty was banished for ever. Already she felt
the breaking of those bonds of sympathy which had held
the twenty-one thousand inhabitants of Dinwiddie, as they
had held the entire South, solidly knit together in a passive
yet effectual resistance to the spirit of change. Of the
world beyond the borders of Virginia, Didwiddians knew
merely that it was either Yankee or foreign, and therefore
to be pitied or condemned according to the Evangelical or
the Calvinistic convictions of the observer. Philosophy,

they regarded with the distrust of a people whose notable achievements have not been in the direction of the contemplative virtues; and having lived comfortably and created a civilization without the aid of science, they could afford, not unreasonably, to despise it. A quarter of a century had passed since "The Origin of Species" had changed the course of the world's thought, yet they had managed to evolve without being aware of it. To be sure, there was an old gentleman in Tabb Street whose title, "the professor," had been conferred in recognition of peaceful pursuits; but since he never went to church, his learning was chiefly effective when it was used to point a moral from the pulpit. There was, also, a tradition that General Goode had been seen reading Plato before the Battle of Seven Pines; and this picturesque incident had contributed the distinction of the scholar to the more effulgent glory of the soldier. But for purely abstract thought, for the thought that did not construct a heroic attitude or a concrete image, there was as little room in the newer industrial system as there had been in the aristocratic society that preceded it. The world still clung to the belief that the business of humanity was confined to institutions that existed in the present moment of history; and Dinwiddie was merely a quiet backwater into which opinions, like fashions, were borne on the current of some tributary stream of thought. Human nature in this town of twenty-one thousand inhabitants differed from human nature in London or in the Desert of Sahara mainly in the things that it ate and the manner in which it carried its clothes. The same passions stirred its heart, the same instincts moved its body, the same contentment with things as they are, and the same terror of things as they might be, warped its mind.

The canary fluted on, and from beyond the mulberry

trees there floated the droning voice of an aged negress, in tatters and a red bandanna turban, who persuasively offered strawberries to the silent houses.

"I'se got sw-eet straw-ber'-ies! I'se got swe-e-t str-aw-ber'-ies! Yes'm, I'se got sw-e-et straw-ber'ies jes' f'om de coun-try!"

Then, suddenly, out of nothing, it seemed to Miss Priscilla, a miracle occurred! The immemorial calm of High Street was broken by the sound of rapidly moving wheels (not the jingling rattle of market wagons nor the comfortable roll of doctors' buggies), and a strange new vehicle, belonging to the Dinwiddie Livery Stables, and containing a young man with longish hair and a flowing tie, turned the corner by Saint James' Church, and passed over the earthen roadbed in front of the green lattice. As the young man went by, he looked up quickly, smiled with the engaging frankness of a genial nature, and, lifting his hat with a charming bow, revealed to Miss Priscilla's eyes that his hair was thick and dark as well as long and wavy. While he looked at her, she noticed also that he had a thin, high-coloured face, lighted by a pair of eager dark eyes which lent a glow of impetuous energy to his features. The Treadwell nose, she recognized, but beneath the Treadwell nose there was a clean-shaven, boyish mouth which belied the Treadwell nature in every sensitive curve.

"I'd have known him anywhere from Susan's description," she thought, and added suspiciously, "I wonder why he peered so long round that corner? It wouldn't surprise me a bit if those girls were coming back that way."

Impelled by her mounting excitement, she leaned forward until the ball of orange-coloured yarn rolled from her short lap over the polished floor of the porch. Before she could stoop to pick it up, she was arrested by the reappearance of the two girls at the corner where Oliver had gazed so intently. Then, as they drew nearer, she saw that Virginia's face was pink and her eyes starry beneath their lowered lashes. An inward radiance shone in the girl's look, and bent her soul and body to its secret influence. Miss Priscilla, who had known her since the first day she came to school (with her lunch, from which she refused to be parted, tied up tightly in a red and white napkin), felt suddenly that she was a stranger. A quality she had never realized her pupil possessed had triumphed over the familiar attributes of her character. So swiftly does emotion separate the individual from the inherent soul of the race.

Susan, who was a little in advance, came rapidly up the walk, and the older woman greeted her with the words:

"My dear, I have seen him!"

"Yes, he passed us at the corner, and I wondered if you were looking. Do tell us what you think of him."

She sat down in a low chair by the teacher's side, while Virginia went over to the cage and stood gazing thoughtfully at the singing bird.

"Well, I don't think his nose spoils him," Miss Priscilla replied after a minute, "but there's something foreign looking about him, and I hope Cyrus isn't thinking seriously about putting him into the bank."

"That was the first thing that occurred to father," Susan answered, "but Oliver told me last night while we were unpacking his books—he has a quantity of books and he kept them even when he had to sell his clothes—that he didn't see to save his life how he was going to stand it."

"Stand what?" Miss Priscilla inquired, a trifle tartly; for after the vicissitudes of her life it was but natural that she should hesitate to regard so stable an institution as the Dinwiddie Bank as something to be "stood." "Why, I thought a young man couldn't do better than get a place in the bank. Virginia's father was telling me in the market last Saturday that he wanted his nephew John Henry to start right in there if they could find room for him."

"Oh, of course, it's just what John Henry would like," Virginia said, speaking for the first time.

"Then if it's good enough for John Henry, it's good enough for Oliver," Miss Priscilla rejoined. "Anybody who has mixed with beggars oughtn't to turn up his nose at a respectable bank."

"But he says it's because the bank is so respectable that he doesn't think he could stand it," Susan answered.

Virginia, who had been looking with her rapt gaze down the deserted street, quivered at the words as if they had stabbed her.

"But he wants to be a writer, Susan," she protested. "A great many very nice people are writers."

"Then why doesn't he go about it in a proper way, if he isn't ashamed of it?" asked the teacher, and she added reflectively after a pause, "I wish he'd write a good history of the war; one that doesn't deal so much with the North. I've almost had to stop teaching United States history because there is hardly one written now that I would let come inside my doors."

"He doesn't want to write histories," Susan replied. "Father suggested to him at supper last night that if he would try his hand at a history of Virginia, and be careful not to put in anything that might offend anybody, he could get it taught in every private school in the State. But he said he'd be shot first."

"Perhaps he's a genius," Virginia said in a startled

voice. "Geniuses are always different from other people, aren't they?"

"I don't know," Susan answered doubtfully. "He talks of things I never heard of before, and he seems to think they are the most important things in the world."

"What things?" Virginia asked breathlessly.

"Oh, I can't tell you because they are so new, but he seems on fire when he talks of them. He talks for hours about art and its service to humanity and about going down to the people and uplifting the masses."

"I hope he doesn't mean the negroes," Miss Priscilla commented suspiciously.

"He means the whole world, I believe," Susan responded. "He quotes all the time from writers I've never heard of, and he laughs at every book he sees in the house. Yesterday, he picked up one of Mrs. Southworth's novels on mother's bureau and asked her how she could allow such immoral stuff in her room. She had got it out of the bookcase to lend to Miss Willy Whitlow, who was there making my dress, but he scolded her so about it that at last Miss Willy went off with Mill's 'Essay on Liberty,' and mother burned all of Mrs. Southworth's she had in the house. Oliver has been so nice to mother that I believe she would make a bonfire of her furniture if he asked her to do it."

"Is he trying to unsettle Miss Willy's mind?" the teacher questioned anxiously. "How on earth could she go out sewing by the day if she didn't have her religious convictions?"

"That's just what I asked him," returned Susan, who, besides being dangerously clever, had a remarkably level head to keep her balanced. "But he answered that until people got unsettled they would never move, and when I wanted to find out where he thought poor little Miss

Willy could possibly move to, he only got impatient and said that I was trying to bury the principle under the facts. We very nearly quarrelled over Miss Willy, but of course she took the book to please Oliver and couldn't worry through a line of it to save her soul."

"Did he say anything about his work? What he wants to do, I mean?" Virginia asked, and her voice was so charged with feeling that it gave an emotional quality to the question.

"He wants to write," Susan replied. "His whole heart is in it, and when he isn't talking about reaching the people, he talks about what he calls 'technique.' "

"Are you sure it isn't poetry?" Miss Priscilla inquired, humming back like a bee to the tempting sweets of conjecture. "I've always heard that poetry was the ruination of Poe."

"No, it isn't poetry—not exactly at least—it's plays," Susan answered. "He talked to me till twelve o'clock last night while we were arranging his books, and he told me that he meant to write really great dramas, but that America wasn't ready for them yet and that was why he had had to sell his clothes. He looked positively starved, but he says he doesn't mind starving a while if only he can live up to his ideal."

"Well, I wonder what his ideal is?" Miss Priscilla remarked grimly.

"It has something to do with his belief that art can grow only out of sacrifice," Susan said. "I never heard anybody—not even Virginia's father in church—talk so much about sacrifice."

"But the rector doesn't talk about sacrifice for the theatre," the teacher retorted, and she added with crushing finality, "I don't believe there is a particle of sense in it. If he is going to write, why on earth doesn't he sit straight down and do it? Why, when little Miss Amanda Sheppard was left at sixty without a roof over her head, she began at once, without saying a word to anybody, to write historical novels."

"It does seem funny until you talk with him," Susan admitted. "But he is so much in earnest that when you listen to him, you can't help believing in him. He is so full of convictions that he persuades you in spite of yourself."

"Convictions about what?" Miss Priscilla demanded. "I don't see how a young man who refuses to be confirmed can have any convictions."

"Well, he has, and he feels just as strongly about them as we do about ours."

"But how can he possibly feel as strongly about a wrong conviction as we do about a right one?" insisted the older woman stubbornly; for she realized vaguely that they were approaching dangerous ground and set out to check their advance in true Dinwiddie fashion, which was strictly prohibitive.

"I like a man who has opinions of his own and isn't ashamed to stand up for them," Virginia said, with a resolution that made her appear suddenly taller.

"Not *false* opinions, Virginia!" Miss Priscilla rejoined, and her manner carried them with a bound back to the schoolroom. Her mental vision had seen in a flash the beribboned diploma for good conduct which her favourite pupil had borne away from the Academy on Commencement day two years ago, and a shudder seized her lest she should have left a single unprotected breach in the girl's mind through which an unsound idea might enter. Had she trusted too confidently to the fact that Virginia's father was a clergyman, and therefore spiritually armed for the defence and guidance of his daughter? Virginia, in spite of her gaiety, had been what Miss Priscilla called "a docile pupil," meaning one who deferentially submitted her opinions to her superiors, and to go through life perpetually submitting her opinions was, in the eyes of her parents and her teacher, the divinely appointed task of woman. Her education was founded upon the simple theory that the less a girl knew about life, the better prepared she would be to contend with it. Knowledge of any sort (except the rudiments of reading and writing, the geography of countries she would never visit, and the dates of battles in ancient history) was kept from her as rigorously as if it contained the germs of a contagious disease. And this ignorance of anything that could possibly be useful to her was supposed in some mysterious way to add to her value as a woman and to make her a more desirable companion to a man who, either by experience or by instinct, was expected "to know his world." Unlike Susan (who, in a community which offered few opportunities to women outside the nursery or the kitchen, had been born with the inquiring spirit and would ask questions), Virginia had, until to-day, accepted with humility the doctrine that a natural curiosity about the universe is the beginning of infidelity. The chief object of her upbringing, which differed in no essential particular from that of every other well-born and well-bred Southern woman of her day, was to paralyze her reasoning faculties so completely that all danger of mental "unsettling" or even movement was eliminated from her future. To solidify the forces of mind into the inherited mould of fixed beliefs was, in the opinion of the age, to achieve the definite end of all education. When the child ceased to wonder before the veil of appearances, the battle of orthodoxy with speculation was over, and Miss Priscilla felt that she could rest on her victory. With Susan she had failed, because the daughter of Cyrus Treadwell was one of those inexplicable variations from type over which the naturalists were still waging their merry war; but Virginia, with the blood of earnest theologians and saintly self-effacing women in her veins, offered as little resistance as some exquisite plastic material in the teacher's hands.

Now, as if the same lightning flash that illuminated the beribboned diploma in Miss Priscilla's mind passed to Virginia also, the girl bit back a retort that was trembling on her lips. "I wonder if she can be getting to know things?" the older woman thought, as she watched her, and she added half resentfully, "I've sometimes suspected that Gabriel Pendleton was almost too mild and easy-going for a clergyman. If the Lord hadn't made him a saint, Heaven knows what would have become of him!"

"Don't try to put notions into Virginia's head, Susan," she said, after a thoughtful pause. "If Oliver were the right kind of young man, he'd give up this nonsense and settle down to some sober work. The first time I get a chance I'm going to tell him so."

"I don't believe it will be any use," Susan responded. "Father tried to reason with him last night, and they almost quarrelled."

"Quarrelled with Cyrus!" the teacher gasped.

"At one time I thought he'd walk out of the house and never come back," Susan pursued. "He told father that his sordid commercialism would end by destroying all that was charming in Dinwiddie. Afterwards, he apologized for his rudeness, but when he did so, he said, 'I meant every word of it.'"

"Well, I never!" was Miss Priscilla's feeble rejoinder. "The idea of his daring to talk that way when Cyrus had to pay his fare down from New York."

"Of course, father brought it on," Susan returned judicially. "You know he doesn't like anybody to disagree with him, and when Oliver began to argue about its being unscrupulous to write history the way people wanted it, he lost his temper and said some angry things about the theatre and actors."

"I suppose a great man like your father may expect his family to bow to his opinions," the teacher replied; for so obscure was her mental connection between the past and the future, that she could honestly admire Cyrus Treadwell for possessing all the qualities her soul abhorred. The simple awe of financial success, which occupies in the American mind the vacant space of the monarchical cult, had begun already to generate the myth of greatness around Cyrus; and, like all other myths, this owed its origin less to the wilful conspiracy of the few than to the confiding superstition of the many.

"I hope Oliver won't do anything rash," Susan said, ignoring Miss Priscilla's tribute. "He is so impulsive and headstrong that I don't see how he can get on with father."

At this Virginia broke her quivering silence. "Can't you make him careful, Susan?" she asked, and without waiting for an answer, bent over and kissed Miss Priscilla on the cheek. "I must be going now or mother will worry," she added before she tripped ahead of Susan down the steps and along the palely shining path to the gate.

Rising from her chair, Miss Priscilla leaned over the railing of the porch, and gazed wistfully after the girls' vanishing figures.

"If there was ever a girl who looked as if she were cut out for happiness, it is Virginia Pendleton," she said aloud after a minute. A tear welled in her eye, and rolling over her cheek, dropped on her bosom. From some obscure corner of her memory, undevastated by war or by ruin, her own youth appeared to take the place of Virginia's. She saw herself, as she had seen the other an instant before, standing flushed and expectant before the untrodden road of the future. She heard again the wings of happiness rustling unseen about her, and she felt again the ardent challenge that youth flings to destiny. Life rose before her, not as she had found it, but as she had once believed it to be. The days when little things had not filled her thoughts returned in the fugitive glow of her memory—for she, also, middle-aged, obese, cumbered with trivial cares, had had her dream of a love that would change and glorify the reality. The heritage of woman was hers as well as Virginia's. And for the first time, standing there, she grew dimly conscious of the portion of suffering which Nature had allotted to them both from the beginning. Was it all waiting—waiting, as it had been while battles were fought and armies were marching? Did the future hold this for Virginia also? Would life yield nothing more to that radiant girl than it had yielded to her or to the other women whom she had known? Strange, how terrible innocence of youth had moved her placid middle-age as if it were sadness!

CHAPTER II

HER INHERITANCE

A BLOCK away, near the head of High Street, stood the old church of Saint James, and at its back, separated by a white paling fence from the squat pinkish tower and the solitary grave in the churchyard (which was that of a Southern soldier who had fallen in the Battle of Dinwiddie), was the oblong wooden rectory in which Gabriel Pendleton had lived since he had exchanged his sword for a prayer-book and his worn Confederate uniform for a surplice. The church, which was redeemed from architectural damnation by its sacred cruciform and its low ivied buttresses, where innumerable sparrows nested, cast its shadow, on clear days, over the beds of bleeding-hearts and lilies-of-the-valley in the neglected garden, to the quaint old house, with its spreading wings, its outside chimneys, and its sloping shingled roof, from which five dormer-windows stared in a row over the slender columns of the porch. The garden had been planned in the days when it was easy to put a dozen slaves to uprooting weeds or trimming flower-beds, and had passed in later years to the breathless ministrations of negro infants, whose experience varied from the doubtful innocence of the crawling age to the complete sophistication of six or seven years. Dandelion and wire-grass rioted, in spite of their earnest efforts, over the crooked path from the porch, and periwinkle, once an intruder from the churchyard, spread

24

now in rank disorder down the terraced hillside on the left, where a steep flight of steps fell clear to the narrow street. Directly in front of the porch, on either side of the path, grew two giant paulownia trees, royal at this season in a mantle of violet blossoms, and it was under their arching boughs that the girls stopped when they had entered the gardens. Ever since Virginia could remember, she had heard threats of cutting down the paulownias because of the litter the falling petals made in the spring, and ever since she could lisp at all she had begged her father to spare them for the sake of the enormous roots, into which she had loved to cuddle and hide.

"If I were ever to go away, I believe they would cut down these trees," she said now a little wistfully, but she was not thinking of the paulownias.

"Why should they, when the branches give such splendid shade? And, besides, they wouldn't do anything you didn't like for worlds."

"Oh, of course they wouldn't, but as soon as I was out of sight they might persuade themselves that I liked it," Virginia answered, with a tender laugh. Though she was not by nature discerning, there were moments when she surprised Susan by her penetrating insight into the character of her parents, and this insight, which was emotional rather than intelligent, had enabled her to dominate them almost from infancy.

Silence fell between them, while they gazed through the veil of twilight at the marble shaft above the grave of the Confederate soldier. Then, suddenly, Susan spoke in a constrained voice, without turning her head.

"Virginia, Oliver isn't one bit of a hero—not the kind of hero we used to talk about." It was with difficulty, urged by a vigorous and uncompromising conscience, that she uttered the words.

"And, besides," Virginia retorted merrily, "he is in love with Abby Goode."

"I don't believe that. They stayed in the same boarding-house once, and you know how Abby is about men."

"Yes, I know, and it's just the way men are about Abby."

"Well, Oliver isn't, I'm sure. I don't believe he's ever given her more than a thought, and he told me last night that he couldn't abide a bouncing woman."

"Does Abby bounce?"

"You know she does—dreadfully. But it wasn't because of Abby that I said what I did."

Something quivered softly between them, and a petal from the Jaqueminot rose in Virginia's hair fluttered like a crimson moth out into the twilight. "Was it because of him, then?" she asked in a whisper.

For a moment Susan did not answer. Her gaze was on the flight of steps, and drawing Virginia with her, she began to walk slowly toward the terraced side of the garden. An old lamplighter, carrying his ladder to a lamp-post at the corner, smiled up at them with his toothless mouth as he went by.

"Partly, darling," Susan said. "He is so—I don't know how to make you understand—so unsettled. No, that isn't exactly what I mean."

Her fine, serious face showed clear and pale in the twilight. From the high forehead, under the girlish fringe of fair hair, to the thin, firm lips, which were too straight and colourless for beauty, it was the face of a woman who could feel strongly, but whose affections would never blur the definite forms or outlines of life. She looked out upon the world with level, dispassionate eyes in which there was none of Virginia's uncritical softness. Her natural intelligence having overcome the defects of her education, she thought not vaguely, but with clearness and precision, and something of this clearness and precision was revealed in her manner and in her appearance, as if she had escaped at twenty years from the impulsive judgments and the troubled solicitudes of youth. At forty, she would probably begin to grow young again, and at fifty, it is not unlikely that she would turn her back upon old age for ever. Just now she was too earnest about life, which she treated quite in the large manner, to take a serious interest in living.

"Promise me, dear, that you'll never let anybody take my place," she said, turning when they had reached the head of the steps.

"You silly Susan! Why, of course, they shan't," replied Virginia, and they kissed ecstatically.

"Nobody will ever love you as I do."

"And I you, darling."

With arms interlaced they stood gazing down into the street, where the shadow of the old lamplighter glided like a ghost under the row of pale flickering lights. From a honeysuckle-trellis on the other side of the porch, a penetrating sweetness came in breaths, now rising, now dying away. In Virginia's heart, Love stirred suddenly, and blind, wingless, imprisoned, struggled for freedom.

"It is late, I must be going," Susan said. "I wish we lived nearer each other."

"Isn't it too dark for you to go alone? John Henry will stop on his way from work, and he'll take you—if you really won't stay to supper."

"No, I don't mind in the least going by myself. It isn't night, anyway, and people are sitting out on their porches."

A minute afterwards they parted, Susan going swiftly down High Street, while Virginia went back along the path to the porch, and passing under the paulownias, stopped beside the honeysuckle-trellis, which extended to the ruined kitchen garden at the rear of the house. Once vegetables were grown here, but, except for a square bed of mint which spread hardily beneath the back windows of the dining-room, the place was left now a prey to such barbarian invaders as burdock and moth mullein. On the brow of the hill, where the garden ended, there was a gnarled and twisted ailantus tree, and from its roots the ground fell sharply to a distant view of rear enclosures and grim smoking factories. Some clothes fluttered on a line that stretched from a bough of the tree, and turning away as if they offended her, Virginia closed her eyes and breathed in the sweetness of the honeysuckle, which mingled deliciously with the strange new sense of approaching happiness in her heart. The awakening of her imagination—an event more tumultuous in its effects than the mere awakening of emotion—had changed not only her inner life, but the ordinary details of the world in which she lived. Because a young man, who differed in no appreciable manner from dozens of other young men, had gazed into her eyes for an instant, the whole universe was altered. What had been until to-day a vague, wind-driven longing for happiness, the reaching out of the dream toward the reality, had assumed suddenly a fixed and definite purpose. Her bright girlish visions had wrapped themselves in a garment of flesh. A miracle more wonderful than any she had read of had occurred in the streets of Dinwiddie; in the very spot where she had walked, with blind eyes and deaf ears, every day since she could remember. Her soul blossomed in the twilight, as a flower blossoms, and shed its virginal sweetness. For the first time in her twenty years she felt that an unexplored region of happiness surrounded her. Life appeared so beautiful that she wanted to grasp and hold each fugitive sensation before it escaped her. "This is different from anything I've ever known. I never imagined it would be like this," she thought, and the next minute: "I wonder why no one has ever told me that it would happen? I wonder if it has ever really happened before, just like this, since the world began? Of all the ways I've dreamed of his coming, I never thought of this way—no, not for an instant. That I should see him first in the street like any stranger—that he should be Susan's cousin—that we should not have spoken a word before I knew it was he!" Everything about him, his smile, his clothes, the way he held his head and brushed his hair straight back from his forehead, his manner of reclining with a slight slouch on the seat of the cart, the picturesque blue dotted tie he wore, his hands, his way of bowing, the red-brown of his face, and above all the eager, impetuous look in his dark eyes—these things possessed a glowing interest which irradiated a delicious excitement over the bare round of living. It was enough merely to be alive and conscious that some day—to-morrow, next week, or the next hour, perhaps, she might meet again the look that had caused this mixture of ecstasy and terror in her heart. The knowledge that he was in the same town with her, watching the same lights, thinking the same thoughts, breathing the same fragrance of honeysuckle; this knowledge was of such tremendous importance that it dwarfed to insignificance all the proud historic past of Dinwiddie. Her imagination, seizing upon this bit of actuality, spun round it the iridescent gossamer web of her fancy. She felt that it was sufficient happiness just to stand motionless for hours and let this thought take possession of her. Nothing else mattered so long as this one thing was blissfully true.

Lights came out softly like stars in the house beyond the church-tower, and in the parlour of the rectory a lamp flared up and then burned dimly under a red shade. Look-

ing through the low window, she could see the prim set
of mahogany and horsehair furniture, with its deep,
heavily carved sofa midway of the opposite wall and the
twelve chairs that custom demanded arranged stiffly at
equal distances on the faded Axminster carpet.

For a moment, her gaze rested on the claw-footed mahogany table, bearing a family Bible and a photograph
album bound in morocco; on the engraving of the "Burial
of Latané" between the long windows at the back of the
room; on the cloudy, gilt-framed mirror above the mantel, with the two standing candelabra reflected in its surface; and all these familiar objects appeared to her as
vividly as if she had not lived with them from her infancy.
A new light had fallen over them, and it seemed to her
that this light released an inner meaning, a hidden soul,
even in the claw-footed table and the threadbare Axminster carpet. Then the door into the hall opened, and her
mother entered, wearing the patched black silk dress
which she had bought before the war and had turned and
darned ever since with untiring fingers. Shrinking back
into the dusk, Virginia watched the thin, slightly stooping
figure as it stood arrested there in the subdued glow of
the lamplight. She saw the pale oval face, so transparent
that it was like the face of a ghost, the fine brown hair
parted smoothly under the small net cap, the soft faded
eyes in their hollowed and faintly bluish sockets, and the
sweet, patient lips, with their expression of anxious sympathy, as of one who had lived not in her own joys and
sorrows, but in those of others. Vaguely, the girl realized
that her mother had had what is called "a hard life," but
this knowledge brought no tremor of apprehension for
herself, no shadow of disbelief in her own happiness. A
glorious certainty possessed her that her life would be different from anything that had ever been in the past.

The front door opened and shut; there was a step on the soft grass under the honeysuckle-trellis and her father came toward her, with his long black coat flapping about him. He always wore clothes several sizes too large for him under the impression that it was a point of economy and that they would last longer if there was no "strain" put upon them. He was a small, wiry man, with an amazing amount of strength for his build, and a keen, humorous face, ornamented by a pointed chin beard which he called his "goatee." His eyes were gray with a twinkle which rarely left them except at the altar, and the skin of his cheeks had never lost the drawn and parchment-like look he had brought from the war. One of the many martial Christians of the Confederacy, he had laid aside his surplice at the first call for troops to defend the borders, and had resumed it immediately after the surrender at Appomattox. It was still an open question in Dinwiddie whether Gabriel Pendleton, who was admitted to have been born a saint, had achieved greater distinction as a fighter or a clergyman; though he himself had accepted the opposite vocations with equal humility. Only in the dead of sweltering summer nights would he sometimes arouse his wife with a groan and the halting words, "Lucy, I can't sleep for thinking of those men I killed in the war." But with the earliest breeze of dawn, his remorse usually left him, and he would rise and go about his parochial duties with the serene and child-like faith that had once carried him into battle. A militant idealism had ennobled his fighting as it now exalted his preaching. He had never in his life seen things as they are because he had seen them always by the white flame of a soul on fire with righteousness. To reach his mind, impressions of persons or objects had first to pass through a refining atmosphere in which all baser substances were destroyed, and no fact had ever penetrated

this medium except in the flattering disguise of a sentiment. Having married at twenty an idealist only less ignorant of the world than himself, he had immediately
devoted his gifts to embellishing the actuality. Both
cherished the conviction that to acknowledge an
evil is in a manner to countenance its existence, and
both clung fervently to the belief that a pretty sham has
a more intimate relation to morality than has an ugly
truth. Yet, so unaware were they of weaving this elaborate tissue of illusion over the world they inhabited, that
they called the mental process by which they distorted
reality, "taking a true view of life." To "take a true
view" was to believe what was pleasant against what was
painful in spite of evidence: to grant honesty to all men
(with the possible exception of the Yankee army and a
few local scalawags known as Readjusters); to deny
virtue to no woman, not even to the New England Abo-
litionist; to regard the period before the war in Virginia
as attained perfection, and the present as falling short
of that perfection only inasmuch as it had occurred since
the surrender. As life in a small place, among a simple
and guileless class of gentlefolk, all passionately cherishing the same opinions, had never shaken these illusions,
it was but natural that they should have done their best to
hand them down as sacred heirlooms to their only child.
Even Gabriel's four years of hard fighting and scant ra-
tions were enkindled by so much of the disinterested idealism which had sent his State into the Confederacy, that
he had emerged from them with an impoverished body,
but an enriched spirit. Combined with his inherent inability to face the facts of life, there was an almost superhuman capacity for cheerful recovery from the shocks
of adversity. Since he had married by accident the one
woman who was made for him, he had managed to pre-

serve untarnished his innocent assumption that marriages
are arranged in Heaven; for the domestic infelicities of
many of his parishioners were powerless to affect a belief
that was founded upon a solitary personal experience.
Unhappy marriages, like all other misfortunes of society,
he was inclined to regard as entirely modern and owing
mainly to the decay of antebellum institutions. "I don't
remember that I ever heard of a discontented servant or
an unhappy marriage in my boyhood," he would say when
he was forced against his will to consider either of these
disturbing problems. Not progress, but a return to the
"ideals of our ancestors," was his sole hope for the future;
and in Virginia's childhood she had grown to regard this
phrase as second in reverence only to that other familiar
invocation: "If it be the will of God."

As he stood now in the square of lamplight that
streamed from the drawing-room window, she looked into
his thin, humorous face, so spiritualized by poverty and
self-sacrifice that it had become merely the veil for his
soul, and the thought came to her that she had never really
seen him as he was until to-day.

"You're out late, daughter. Isn't it time for supper?"
he asked, putting his arm about her. Beneath the simple
words, she felt the profound affection which he rarely
expressed, but of which she was aware whenever he
looked at her or spoke to her. Two days ago this affection, of which she never thought because it belonged to
her by right like the air she breathed, had been sufficient
to fill her life to overflowing; and now, in less than a
moment, the simplest accident had pushed it into the background. In the place where it had been there was a restless longing which seemed at one instant a part of the
universal stirring of the spring, and became the next an
importunate desire for the coming of the lover to whom

she had been taught to look as to the fulfilment of her womanhood. At times this lover appeared to have no connection wtih Oliver Treadwell; then the memory of his eager and searching look would flush the world with a magic enchantment. "He might pass here at any minute," she thought, and immediately every simple detail of her life was illuminated, as if a quivering rosy light had fallen aslant it. His drive down High Street in the afternoon had left a trail of glory over the earthen roadbed.

"Yes, I was just going in," she replied to the rector's question, and added: "How sweet the honeysuckle smells! I never knew it to be so fragrant."

"The end of the trellis needs propping up. I noticed it this morning," he returned, keeping his arm around her as they passed over the short grassy walk and up the steps to the porch. Then the door of the rectory opened, and the silhouette of Mrs. Pendleton, in her threadbare black silk dress with her cameo-like profile softened by the dark bands of her hair, appeared motionless against the lighted space of the hall.

"We're here, Lucy," the rector said, kissing her; and a minute later they entered the dining-room on the right of the staircase. The old mahogany table, scarred by a century of service, was laid with a simple supper of bread, tea, and sliced ham on a willow dish. At one end there was a bowl of freshly gathered strawberries, with the dew still on them, and Mrs. Pendleton hastened to explain that they were a present from Tom Peachey, who had driven out into the country in order to get them. "Well, I hope his wife has some also," commented the rector. "Tom's a good fellow, but he could never keep a closed fist, there's no use denying it."

Mrs. Pendleton, who had never denied anything in her life, except biblical sanction for the Thirteenth Amendment to the Constitution, shook her head gently and began to talk in the inattentive and anxious manner she had acquired at scantily furnished tables. Ever since the war, with the exception of the Reconstruction period, when she had lived virtually on charity, she had managed to exist with serenity, and numerous negro dependents, on the rector's salary of a thousand dollars a year. Simple and wholesome food she had supplied to her family and her followers, and for their desserts, as she called the sweet things of life, she had relied with touching confidence upon her neighbours. What they would be for the day, she did not know; but since poverty, not prosperity, breeds the generous heart, she was perfectly assured that when Miss Priscilla was putting up raspberries, or Mrs. Goode was making lemon pie, she should not be forgotten. During the terrible war years, it had become the custom of Dinwiddie housekeepers to remember the wife of the rector who had plucked off his surplice for the Confederacy, and among the older generation the habit still persisted, like all other links that bound them to a past which they cherished the more passionately because it enshrined a defeated cause. Like the soft apologetic murmur of Mrs. Pendleton's voice, which was meant to distract attention rather than to impart information, this impassioned memory of the thing that was dead sweetened the less romantic fact of the things that were living. The young were ignorant of it, but the old *knew*. Mrs. Pendleton, who was born a great lady, remained one when the props and the background of a great lady had crumbled around her; and though the part she filled was a narrow part, a mere niche in the world's history, she filled it superbly. From the dignity of possessions she had passed to the finer dignity of a poverty that can do without. All the intellect in her (for she was not clever) had been transmuted into char-

acter by this fiery passage from romance into reality, and
though life had done its worst with her, some fine invincible
blade in the depths of her being had never surrendered.
She would have gone to the stake for a principle as cheerfully as she had descended from her aristocratic niche into
unceasing poverty and self-denial, but she would have
gone wearing garlands on her head and with her faint,
grave smile, in which there was almost every quality,
except humour, touching her lips. Her hands, which
were once lovely, were now knotted and worn; for
she had toiled when it was necessary, though she had
toiled always with the manner of a lady. Even to-day this
dignity was so vital a factor in her life that there was none
of her husband's laughter at circumstances to lighten her
burden. To her the daily struggle of keeping an open
house on starvation fare was not a pathetic comedy, as
with Gabriel, but a desperately smiling tragedy. What to
Gabriel had been merely the discomfort of being poor
when everybody you respected was poor with you, had
been to his wife the slow agony of crucifixion. It was she,
not he, who had lain awake to wonder where to-morrow's
dinner could be got without begging; it was she, also,
who had feared to doze at dawn lest she should over-
sleep herself and not be downstairs in time to scrub the
floors and the furniture before the neighbours were stirring. Uncle Isam, whose knees were crippled with rheumatism, and Docia, who had a "stitch" in her side whenever
she stooped, were the only servants that remained with
her, and the nursing of these was usually added to the
pitiless drudgery of her winter. But the bitter edge to
all her suffering was the feeling which her husband spoke
of in the pulpit as "false pride," the feeling she prayed
over fervently yet without avail in church every Sunday,
and this was the ignoble terror of being seen on her knees

in her old black calico dress before she had gone upstairs again, washed her hands with cornmeal, powdered her face with her pink flannel starchbag, and descended in her breakfast gown of black cashmere or lawn, with a net scarf tied daintily round her thin throat, and a pair of exquisitely darned lace ruffles hiding her wrists.

As she sat now, calm and smiling, at the head of her table, there was no hint in her face of the gnawing anxiety behind the delicate blue-veined hollows in her temples. "I thought John Henry would come to supper," she observed, while her hands worked lovingly among the old white and gold teacups which had belonged to her mother, "so I gathered a few flowers."

In the centre of the table there was a handful of garden flowers arranged, with a generous disregard of colour, in a cut-glass bowl, as though all blossoms were intended by their Creator to go peaceably together. Only on formal occasions was such a decoration used on the table of the rectory, since the happiest adornment for a meal was supposed to be a bountiful supply of visible viands; but the hopelessly mended mats had pierced Mrs. Pendleton's heart, and the cut-glass bowl, like her endless prattle, was a pitiful subterfuge.

"Oh, I like them!" Virginia had started to answer, when a hearty voice called, "May I come in?" from the darkness, and a large, carelessly dressed young man, with an amiable and rather heavy countenance, entered the hall and passed on into the dining-room. In reply to Mrs. Pendleton's offer of tea, he answered that he had stopped at the Treadwells' on his way up from work. "I could hardly break away from Oliver," he added, "but I remembered that I'd promised Aunt Lucy to take her down to Tin Pot Alley after supper, so I made a bolt while he was convincing me that it's better to be poor with an

idea, as he calls it, than rich without one." Then turning
to Virginia, he asked suddenly: "What's the matter, little
cousin? Been about too much in the sun?"

"Oh, it's only the rose in my hair," Virginia responded,
and she felt that there was a fierce joy in blushing like this
even while she told herself that she would give everything
she possessed if she could only stop it.

"If you aren't well, you'd better not go with us, dear,"
Mrs. Pendleton said. "It was so sweet of John Henry to
remember that I'd promised to take Aunt Ailsey some
of the bitters we used to make before the war." Everything was "so sweet" to her, the weather, her husband's
sermons, the little trays that came continually from her
neighbours, and she lived in a perpetual state of thankfulness for favours so insignificant that a less impression-
able soul would have accepted them as undeserving of
more than the barest acknowledgment.

"I am perfectly well," Virginia insisted, a little angry
with John Henry because he had been the first to notice
her blushes.

Rising hurriedly from the table, she went to the door
and stood looking out into the spangled dusk under the
paulownias, while her mother wrapped the bottle in a
piece of white tissue paper and remarked with an animation which served to hide her fatigue from the unobservant eyes of her husband, that a walk would do her good
on such a "perfectly lovely night."

Gabriel, who loved her as much as a man can love a
wife who has sacrificed herself to him wisely and unwisely
for nearly thirty years, had grown so used to seeing her
suffer with a smile that he had drifted at last into the
belief that it was the only form of activity she enjoyed.
From the day of his marriage he had never been able to
deny her anything she had set her heart upon, not even

the privilege of working herself to death for his sake
when the opportunity offered.

"Well, well, if you feel like it, of course you must go,
my dear," he replied. "I'll step over and sit a minute with
Miss Priscilla while you are away. Never could bear the
house without you, Lucy."

While this protest was still on his lips, he followed her
from the house, and turned with Virginia and John Henry
in the direction of the Young Ladies' Academy. From the
darkness beyond the iron gate there came the soothing
flow of Miss Priscilla's voice entertaining a caller,
and when the rector left them, as if irresistibly drawn
toward the honeyed sound of gossip, Virginia walked
on in silence between John Henry and her mother.
At each corned a flickering street lamp burned with a thin
yellow flame, and in the narrow orbit of its light,
several shining moths circled swiftly like white
moons revolving about a sun. In the centre of the blocks,
where the darkness was broken only by small flakes of
light which fell in clusters through boughs of mulberry
or linden trees, there was the sound of whispering voices
and of rustling palm-leaf fans on the crowded porches
behind screens of roses or honeysuckle. Mrs. Pendleton,
whose instinct prompted her to efface herself whenever
she made a third at the meeting of man and maid (even
though the man was only her nephew John Henry), began
to talk at last after waiting modestly for her daughter to
begin the conversation. The story of Aunt Ailsey, of her
great age, and her dictatorial temper, which made living
with other servants impossible to her, started valiantly
on its familiar road, and tripped but little when the poor
lady realized that neither John Henry nor Virginia was
listening. She was so used to talking for the sake of the
sound she made rather than the impression she produced

that her silvery ripple had become almost as lacking in self-consciousness as the song of the canary.

But Virginia, walking so quietly at her side, was inhabiting at the moment a separate universe, a universe smelling of honeysuckle and filled with starry pathways to happiness. In this universe Aunt Aisley and her peculiarities, her mother's innocent prattle, and the solid body of John Henry touching her arm, were all as remote and trivial as the night moths circling dizzily round the lamps. Looking at John Henry from under her lowered lashes, she felt a sudden pity for him because he was so far—so very far indeed from being the right man. She saw him too clearly as he was; he stood before her in all the hard brightness of the reality, and first love, like beauty, depends less upon the truth of an outline than it does upon the softening quality of an atmosphere. There was no mystery for her in the simple fact of his being. There was nothing left to discover about his great stature, his excellent heart, and his safe, slow mind, which had been compelled to forego even the sort of education she had derived from Miss Priscilla. She knew that he had left school at the age of eight in order to become the support of a widowed mother, and she was pitifully aware of the tireless efforts he had made to remedy his ignorance. Never had she heard a complaint from him, never a regret for the sacrifice, never so much as an idle wonder why it should have been necessary. If the texture of his soul was not finely wrought, the proportions of it were heroic. In him the Pendleton idealism had left the skies and been transmuted into the common substance of clay. He was of a practical bent of mind and had developed a talent for his branch of business, which, to the bitter humiliation of his mother, was that of hardware, with a successful specialty in bathtubs. Until to-day Virginia had always believed that John Henry interested her, but now she wondered how she had ever spent so many hours listening to his talk about business. And with the thought her whole existence appeared to her as dull and commonplace as those hours. A single instant of experience seemed longer to her than all the years she had lived, and this instant had drained the colour and the sweetness from the rest of life. The shape of her universe had trembled suddenly and altered. Dimly she was beginning to realize that sensation, not time, is the true measure of life. Nothing and everything had happened to her since yesterday.

As they turned into Short Market Street, Mrs. Pendleton's voice trailed off at last into silence, and she did not speak again while they passed hurriedly between the crumbling houses and the dilapidated shops which rose darkly on either side of the narrow cinder-strewn walks. The scent of honeysuckle did not reach here, and when they stopped presently at the beginning of Tin Pot Alley, there floated out to them the sharp acrid odour of huddled negroes. In these squalid alleys, where the lamps burned at longer distances, the more primitive forms of life swarmed like distorted images under the transparent civilization of the town. The sound of banjo strumming came faintly from the dimness beyond, while at their feet the Problem of the South sprawled innocently amid tomato cans and rotting cabbage leaves.

"Wait here just a minute and I'll run up and speak to Aunt Aisley," Mrs. Pendleton remarked, with a dignity of a soul that is superior to smells; and without noticing her daughter's reproachful nod of acquiescence, she entered the alley and disappeared through the doorway of the nearest hovel. A minute later her serene face looked down at them over a patchwork quilt which hung airing from the window above. "But this is not life—it has nothing to do with life," Virginia thought, while the Pendleton blood in her rose in a fierce rebellion against all that was ugly and sordid in existence. Then her mother's tread was heard descending the short flight of steps, and the sensation vanished as quickly as it had come.

"I tried not to keep you waiting, dear," said Mrs. Pendleton, hastening toward them while she fanned herself rapidly with the small black fan she carried. Her face looked tired and worn, and before moving on, she paused a moment and held her hand to her thin fluttering breast, while deep bluish circles started out under the expression of pathetic cheerfulness in her eyes. This pathetic cheerfulness, so characteristic of the women of her generation, was the first thing, perhaps, that a stranger would have noticed in her face; yet it was a trait which neither her husband nor her child had ever observed. "I wonder if you would mind going on to Bolingbroke Street, so I may speak to Belinda Treadwell a minute?" she asked, as soon as she had recovered her breath. "I want to find out if she has engaged Miss Willy Whitlow for the whole week, or if there is any use my sending a message to her over in Botetourt. If she doesn't begin at once, Virginia, you won't have a dress to wear to Abby Goode's party."

Virginia's heart gave a single bound of joy and lay quiet. Not for worlds would she have asked to go to the Treadwells', yet ever since they had started, she had longed unceasingly to have her mother suggest it. The very stars, she felt, had worked together to bring about her desire.

"But aren't you tired, mother? It really doesn't matter about my dress," she murmured, for it was not in vain that she had wrested a diploma for deportment from Miss Priscilla.

"Why can't I take the message for you, Aunt Lucy? You look tired to death," John Henry urged.

"Oh, I shan't mind the walk as soon as we get out into the breeze," Mrs. Pendleton replied. "It's a lovely night, only a little close in this alley." And as she spoke she looked gently down on the Problem of the South, as the Southern woman had looked down on it for generations and would continue to look down on it for generations still to come, without seeing that it was a problem.

"Well, it's good to get a breath of air, anyway!" John Henry exclaimed with fervour, when they had passed out of the alley into the lighted street. Around them the town seemed to beat with a single heart, as if it waited, like Virginia, in breathless suspense for some secret that must come out of the darkness. Sometimes the sidewalks over which they passed were of flag-stones, sometimes they were of gravel or of strewn cinders. Now and then, an old stone house, which had once sheltered crinoline and lace ruffles, or had served as a trading station with the Indians before Dinwiddie had become a city, would loom between two small shops where the owners, coatless and covered with sweat, were selling flat beer to jaded and miserable customers. Up Bolingbroke Street a faint breeze blew, lifting the moist satin-like hair on Mrs. Pendleton's forehead. Already its ancient dignity had deserted the quarter in which the Treadwells lived, and it had begun to wear a forsaken and injured look, as though it resented the degradation of commerce into which it had fallen.

"I can't understand why Cyrus Treadwell doesn't move over to Sycamore Street," John Henry remarked after a moment of reflection in which he had appeared to weigh this simple sentence with scrupulous exactness. "He's rich enough, I suppose, to buy anything he wants."

"I've heard Susan say that it is her mother's old home

and she doesn't care to leave it," Mrs. Pendleton answered.

"I don't believe it's that a bit," broke in Virginia with characteristic impulsiveness. "The only reason is that Mr. Treadwell is stingy. With all his money, I know Mrs. Treadwell and Susan hardly ever have a dollar they can spend on themselves."

Though she spoke with her accustomed energy, she was aware all the time that the words she uttered were not the ones in her thoughts. What did Cyrus Treadwell's stinginess matter when his only relation to life consisted in his being the uncle of Oliver? It was as if a single shape moved alive through a universe peopled with shadows. Only a borrowed radiance attached itself now to the persons and objects that had filled the world for her yesterday. Yet she approached the crisis of her life so silently that those around her did not recognize it beneath the cover of circumstances. Like most great moments, it had come unheralded; and though the rustling of its wings brushed her soul, neither her mother nor John Henry heard a stir in the quiet air that surrounded them.

There were several blocks of Bolingbroke Street to walk before the Treadwells' house was reached, and as they sauntered slowly past decayed dwellings, Virginia's imagination ran joyously ahead of her to the meeting. Would it happen this time, as it had happened before when he looked at her, that something would pass between them which would make her feel that she belonged to him? So little resistance did she offer to the purpose of Life that she seemed to have existed from the beginning merely as an exquisite medium for a single emotion. It was as if the dreams of all the dead women of her race, who had lived only in loving, were concentrated into a single luminous centre of bliss; for the vibrations of centuries were in her soul when she trembled for the first time beneath the eyes of a lover. And yet all this blissful violence was powerless to change the most insignificant external fact in the universe. Though it was the greatest thing that could ever happen to her, it was nothing to the other twenty-one thousand human beings among whom she lived; it left no mark upon that procession of unimportant details which they called life.

They were in sight of the small old-fashioned brick house of the Treadwells, with its narrow windows set discreetly between outside shutters, and she saw that the little marble porch was deserted except for the two pink oleander trees, which stood in green tubs on either side of the curved iron railings. A minute later John Henry's imperative ring brought a young coloured maid to the door, and Virginia, who had lingered on the pavement, heard almost immediately an effusive duet from her mother and Mrs. Treadwell.

"Oh, do come in, Lucy, just for a minute!"

"I can't possibly, my dear; I only wanted to ask you if you have engaged Miss Willy Whitlow for the entire week, or if you could let me have her for Friday and Saturday? Virginia hasn't a rag to wear to Abby Goode's lawn party, and I don't know anybody who does quite so well for her as poor Miss Willy. Oh, that's so sweet of you! I can't thank you enough! And you'll tell her without my sending all the way over to Botetourt!"

By this time Susan had joined Virginia on the sidewalk, and the liquid honey of Mrs. Pendleton's voice dropped softly into indistinctness.

"Oh, Virginia, if I'd only known you were coming!" said Susan. "Oliver wanted me to take him to see you, and when I couldn't, he went over to call on Abby."

So this was the end of her walk winged with expectancy! A disappointment as sharp as her joy had been pierced her through as she stood there smiling into Susan's discomfited face. With the tragic power of youth to create its own torment, she told herself that life could never be the same after this first taste of its bitterness.

CHAPTER III

FIRST LOVE

THE next morning, so indestructible is the happiness of
youth, she awoke with her hope as fresh as if it had not
been blighted the evening before. As she lay in bed, with
her loosened hair making a cloud over the pillows, and
her eyes shining like blue flowers in the band of sunlight
that fell through the dormer-window, she quivered to the
early sweetness of honeysuckle as if it were the charmed
sweetness of love. She was only one of the many millions
of women who were awaking at the same hour to the same
miracle of Nature, yet she might have been the first woman
seeking the first man through the vastness and the mystery of an uninhabited earth.

Slipping out of bed, she threw her dressing-gown over
her shoulders, and kneeling beside the window, drank in
the flower-scented air of the May morning. During the
night, the paulownia trees had shed a rain of violet blossoms over the wet grass, where little wings of sunshine,
like golden moths, hovered above them. Beyond the bor-
der of lilies-of-the-valley she saw the squat pinkish tower
of the church, and beneath it, in the narrow churchyard,
rose the gleaming shaft above the grave of the Confederate soldier. On her right, in the centre of the crooked
path, three negro infants were prodding earnestly at roots
of wire-grass and dandelion; and brushing carelessly their
huddled figures, her gaze descended the twelve steps of

47

the almost obliterated terrace, and followed the steep
street down which a mulatto vegetable vendor was urg-
ing his slow-footed mule.

A wave of joy rose in her breast, and she felt that her
heart melted in gratitude for the divine beauty of life.
The world appeared to her a place filled with shining
vistas of happiness, and at the end of each of these vistas
there awaited the unknown enchanting thing which she
called in her thoughts "the future." The fact that it was
the same world in which Miss Priscilla and her mother
lived their narrow and prosaic lives did not alter by a
breath her ardent conviction that she herself was predestined for something more wonderful than they had imagined. "He may come this evening!" she thought, and
immediately the light of magic suffused the room, the
street outside, and every scarred roof in Dinwiddie.

At the head of her bed, wedged in between the candle-
stand and the window, there was a cheap little bookcase
of walnut which contained the only volumes she had ever
been permitted to own: the poems of Mrs. Hemans and
of Adelaide Anne Procter, a carefully expurgated edition
of Shakespeare, with an inscription in the rector's handwriting on the flyleaf; Miss Strickland's "Lives of the
Queens of England"; and several works of fiction belonging to the class which Mrs. Pendleton described as "sweet
stories." Among the more prominent of these were "Thad-
deus of Warsaw," a complete set of Miss Yonge's novels,
with a conspicuously tear-stained volume of "The Heir
of Redclyffe," and a romance or two by obscure but innocuous authors. That any book which told, however
mildly, the truth about life should have entered their
daughter's bedroom would have seemed little short of
profanation to both the rector and Mrs. Pendleton. The
sacred shelves of that bookcase (which had been cere-

moniously presented to her on her fourteenth birthday)
had never suffered the contaminating presence of realism.
The solitary purpose of art, in Mrs. Pendleton's eyes, was
to be "sweet," and she scrupulously judged all literature
by its success or failure in this particular quality. It seemed
to her as wholesome to feed her daughter's growing fancy
on an imaginary line of pious heroes, as it appeared to her
moral to screen her from all suspicion of the existence of
immorality. She did not honestly believe that any living
man resembled the "Heir of Redclyffe," any more than
she believed that the path of self-sacrifice leads inevitably
to happiness; but there was no doubt in her mind that she
advanced the cause of righteousness when she taught these
sanctified fallacies to Virginia.

As she rose from her knees, Virginia glanced at her
white dress, which was too crumpled for her to wear again
before it was smoothed, and thought regretfully of Aunt
Docia's heart, which invariably gave warning whenever
there was extra work to be done. "I shall have to wear
either my blue lawn or my green organdie this evening,"
she thought. "I wish I could have the sleeves changed. I
wonder if mother could run a tuck in them?"

It did not occur to her that she might smooth the dress
herself, because she knew that the iron would be wrested
from her by her mother's hands, which were so knotted and
worn that tears came to Virginia's eyes when she looked
at them. She let her mother slave over her because she had
been born into a world where the slaving of mothers was
a part of the natural order, and she was not independent
enough to question the morality of the commonplace.
At any minute she would gladly have worked, too,
but the phrase "spare Virginia" had been uttered so often
in her hearing that it had acquired at last almost a religious significance. To have been forced to train her daugh-

ter in any profitable occupation which might have lifted her out of the class of unskilled labour in which indigent gentlewomen by right belonged, would have been the final dregs of humiliation in Mrs. Pendleton's cup. On one of Aunt Docia's bad days, when Virginia had begged to be allowed to do part of the washing, she had met an almost passionate refusal from her mother. "It will be time enough to spoil your hands after you are married, darling!" And again, "Don't do that rough sewing, Virginia. Give it to me." From the cradle she had borne her part in this social custom of the sacrifice of generation to generation,—of the perpetual immolation of age on the flowery altars of youth. Like most customs in which we are nurtured, it had seemed natural and pleasant enough, until she had watched the hollows deepen in her mother's temples and the tireless knotted hands stumble at their work. Then a pang had seized her, and she had pleaded earnestly to be permitted to help.

"If only you knew how unhappy it makes me to see you ruining your pretty fingers, Virginia. My child, the one comfort I have is the thought that I am sparing you."

Sparing her! Always that from the first! Even Gabriel chimed in when it became a matter of Virginia. "Let me wash the dishes, Lucy," he would implore. "What? Will you trust me with other people's souls, but not with your china?"

"It's not a man's work, Mr. Pendleton. What would the neighbours think?"

"They would think, I hope, my dear, that I was doing my duty."

"But it would not be dignified for a clergyman. No, I cannot bear the sight of you with a dishcloth."

In the end she invariably had her way with them, for she was the strongest. Virginia must be spared, and Gabriel must do nothing undignified. About herself it made no difference unless the neighbours were looking; she had not thought of her own appearance, except in the indomitable failing of her "false pride," since her marriage, which had taken place in her twentieth year. A clergyman's wife might do menial tasks in secret, and nobody minded, but they were not for a clergyman.

For a minute, while she was dressing, Virginia thought of these things; of how hard life had been for her mother, of how pretty she must have been in her youth. What she did not think of was that her mother, like herself, was but one of the endless procession of women who pass perpetually from the sphere of pleasure into the sphere of service. It was as impossible for her to picture her mother as a girl of twenty as it was for her to imagine herself ever becoming a woman of fifty.

When she had finished dressing she closed the door softly after her as if she were afraid of disturbing the silence, and ran downstairs to the dining-room, where the rector and Mrs. Pendleton greeted her with subdued murmurs of joy.

"I was afraid I'd miss you, daughter," from the rector, as he drew her chair nearer.

"I was just going to carry up your tray, Virginia," from her mother. "I kept a nice breast of chicken for you that one of the neighbours sent me."

"I'd so much rather you'd eat it, mother," Virginia protested, on the point of tears.

"But I couldn't, darling, I really couldn't manage it. A cup of coffee and a bit of toast is all I can possibly stand in.the morning. I was up early, for Docia was threatened with one of her heart attacks, and it always gives me a little headache to miss my morning nap."

"Then you can't go to market, Lucy; it is out of the

question," the rector insisted. "After thirty years, you might as well make up your mind to trust me, my dear."

"But the last time you went, you gave away our shoulder of lamb to a beggar," replied his wife, and she hastened to add tenderly, lest he should accept the remark as a reproof, "it's sweet of you, dearest, but a little walk will be good for my head, if I am careful to keep on the shady side of the street. I can easily find a boy to bring home the basket, and I am sure it won't hurt me a bit."

"Why can't I go, mother?" Virginia implored. "Susan always markets for Mrs. Treadwell." And she felt that even the task of marketing was irradiated by this inner glow which had brightened the common aspect of life.

"Oh, Virginia, you know how you hate to feel the chickens, and one can never tell how plump they are by the feathers."

"Well, I'll feel them, mother, if you'll let me try."

"No, darling, but you may go with me and carry my sunshade. I'm so sorry Docia can't smooth your dress. Was it much crumpled?"

"Oh, dreadfully! And I did so want to wear it this evening. Do you think Aunt Docia could show me how to iron?"

Docia, who stood like an ebony image of Bellona behind her mistress's chair, waving a variegated tissue paper fly-brush over the coffee-urn, was heard to think aloud that "dish yer stitch ain' helt up er blessed minute sence befo' daylight." Not unnaturally, perhaps, since she was the most prominent figure in her own universe, she had come at last to regard her recurrent "stitch" as an event of greater consequence than Virginia's appearance in white muslin. An uncertain heart combined with a certain temper had elevated her from a servile position to one of absolute autocracy in the household. Everybody feared

her, so nobody had ever dared ask her to leave. As she had
rebelled long ago against the badge of cap and apron, she
appeared in the dining-room clad in garments of various
hues, and her dress on this particular morning was a purple
calico crowned majestically by a pink cotton turban. There
was a tradition still afloat that Docia had been an excellent
servant before the war; but this amiable superstition
had, perhaps, as much reason to support it as had Gabriel's
innocent conviction that there were no faithless husbands
when there were no divorces.

"I'm afraid Docia can't do it," sighed Mrs. Pendleton,
for her ears had caught the faint thunder of the war goddess behind her chair, and her soul, which feared neither
armies nor adversities, trembled before her former slaves.
"But it won't take me a minute, if you'll have it ready
right after dinner."

"Oh, mother, of course I wouldn't let you for anything.
I only thought Aunt Docia might be able to teach me how
to iron."

At this, Docia muttered audibly that she "ain' got no
time ter be sho'in' nobody nuttin'."

"There, now, Docia, you mustn't lose your temper,"
Gabriel observed as he rose from his chair. It was at such
moments that the remembered joys of slavery left a bitter
after taste on his lips. Clearly it was impossible to turn
into the streets even the poorest servant who had once
belonged to you!

When they were in the hall together, Mrs. Pendleton
whispered nervously to her husband that it must be "poor
Docia's heart that made her so disagreeable and that she
would feel better to-morrow."

"Wouldn't it be possible, my dear?" inquired the rector
in his pulpit manner, to which his wife's only answer was a
startled "Sh-sh-ush."

An hour later, the door of Gabriel's study opened softly, and Mrs. Pendleton entered with the humble and apologetic manner in which she always intruded upon her husband's pursuits. There was an accepted theory in the family, shared even by Uncle Isam and Aunt Docia, that whenever Gabriel was left alone for an instant, his thoughts naturally deflected into spiritual paths. In the early days of his marriage he had tried honestly to live up to this exalted idea of his character; then finding the effort beyond him, and being a man with an innate dislike for hypocrisy, he had earnestly endeavoured to disabuse his wife's imagination of the mistaken belief in his divinity. But a notion once firmly fixed in Mrs. Pendleton's mind might as well have been embedded in rock. By virtue of that gentle obstinacy which enabled her to believe in an illusion the more intensely because it had vanished, she had triumphed not only over circumstances but even over the truth.

"Are you busy with your sermon, dear?" she asked, pausing in the doorway, and gazing reverently at her husband over the small black silk bag she carried. Like other women of Dinwiddie who had lost relatives in the war, she had never laid aside her mourning since the surrender; and the frame of crape to her face gave her the pensive look of one who has stepped out of the pageant of life into the sacred shadows of memory.

"No, no, Lucy, I'm ready to start out with you," replied the rector apologetically, putting a box of fishing tackle he had been sorting back into the drawer of his desk. He was as fond as a child of a day's sport, and never quite so happy as when he set out with his rod and an old tomato can filled with worms, which he had dug out of the back garden; but owing to the many calls upon him and

his wife's conception of his clerical dignity, he was seldom
able to go fishing.

"Oh, father, please hurry!" called Virginia from the
porch, and rising obediently, he followed Mrs. Pendleton through the hall and out into the May sunshine, where
the little negroes stopped an excited chase of a black and
orange butterfly to return doggedly to their weeding.

"Are you sure you wouldn't rather I'd go to market,
Lucy?"

"Quite sure, dear," replied his wife, sniffing the scent
of lilies-of-the-valley with her delicate, slightly pinched
nostrils. "I thought you were going to see Mr. Treadwell about putting John Henry into the bank," she added.
"It is such a pity to keep the poor boy selling bathtubs.
His mother felt it so terribly."

"Ah, so I was—so I was," assented Gabriel, who,
though both of them would have been indignant at the
suggestion, was as putty in the hands of his wife. "Well,
I'll look into the bank on Cyrus after I've paid my sick
calls."

With that they parted, Gabriel going on to visit a bed-
ridden widow in the Old Ladies' Home, while Mrs. Pendleton and Virginia turned down a cross street that led
toward the market. At every corner, it seemed to Virginia,
middle-aged ladies, stout or thin, wearing crape veils and
holding small black silk bags in their hands, sprang out of
the shadows of mulberry trees, and barred their leisurely
progress. And though nothing had happened in Dinwiddie
since the war, and Mrs. Pendleton had seen many of these
ladies the day before, she stopped for a sympathetic chat
with each one of them, while Virginia, standing a little
apart, patiently prodded the cinders of the walk with the
end of her sunshade. All her life the girl had been taught

to regard time as the thing of least importance in the universe; but occasionally, while she listened in silence to the liquid murmur of her mother's voice, she wondered vaguely how the day's work was ever finished in Dinwiddie. The story of Docia's impertinence was told and retold a dozen times before they reached the market. "And you really mean that you can't get rid of her? Why, my dear Lucy, I wouldn't stand it a day! Now, there was my Mandy. Such an excellent servant until she got her head turned——" This from Mrs. Tom Peachey, an energetic little woman, with a rosy face and a straight gray "bang" cut short over her eyebrows. "But, Lucy, my child, are you doing right to submit to impertinence? In the old days, I remember, before the war——" This from Mrs. William Goode, who had been Sally Peterson, the beauty of Dinwiddie, and who was still superbly handsome in a tragic fashion, with a haunted look in her eyes and masses of snow-white hair under her mourning bonnet. Years ago Virginia had imagined her as dwelling perpetually with the memory of her young husband, who had fallen in his twenty-fifth year in the Battle of Cold Harbor; but she knew now that the haunted eyes, like all things human, were under the despotism of trifles. To the girl, who saw in this acquiescence in littleness merely the pitiful surrender of feeble souls, there was a passionate triumph in the thought that her own dreams were larger than the actuality that enmeshed her. Youth's scorn of the narrow details of life left no sympathy in her mind for the compromise that middle-age makes with necessity. While she waited dutifully, with her absent gaze fixed on the old mulberry trees, which whitened as the wind blew over them and then slowly darkened again, she wondered if servants and gossip were the only things that Oliver had met in his travels? Then she remembered that even in Dinwiddie men were less interested in such matters than they were in the industries of peanuts and tobacco. Was it only women, after all, who were in subjection to particulars?

When they turned into Old Street, John Henry hailed them from the doorway of a shop, where he stood flanked by a row of spotless bathtubs. He wore a loose pongee coat, which sagged at the shoulders, his straight flaxen hair had been freshly cut, and his crimson necktie had got a stain on it at breakfast; but to Virginia's astonishment, he appeared unaware of his bathtubs and his appearance. He was doubtless under the delusion that a pongee coat, being worn for comfort, was entirely successful when it achieved that end; and as for his business, it was beyond his comprehension that a Pendleton could have reason to blush for a bathtub, or for any other object that afforded him an honest livelihood.

He called to them at sight, and Mrs. Pendleton, following her instinct of fitness, left the conversation to youth.

"John Henry, father is going to see Mr. Treadwell about the place in the bank. Won't it be lovely if he gives it to you!"

"He won't," replied John Henry. "I'll bet you anything he's keeping it for his nephew."

Virginia's blush came quickly, and turning her head away, she gazed earnestly down the street to the octagonal market, which stood on the spot where slaves were offered for sale when she was born.

"Mr. Treadwell is crossing the street now," she said after a minute. "I wonder why he keeps his mouth shut so tight when he is alone?"

A covered cart, which had been passing slowly, moved up the hill, and from beyond it there appeared the tall spare figure of a man with iron-gray hair, curling a little on the temples, a sallow skin, splotched with red over the nose, and narrow colourless lips that looked as if they were cut out of steel. As he walked quickly up the street, every person he passed turned to glance after him.

"I wonder if it is true that he hasn't made his money honestly?" asked Virginia.

"Oh, I hope not!" Mrs. Pendleton exclaimed, who in her natural desire to believe only good about people was occasionally led into believing the truth.

"Well, I don't care," Virginia retorted, "he's mean. I know just by the way his wife dresses."

"O Virginia!" Mrs. Pendleton gasped, and glanced in embarrassment at her nephew, whose face, to her surprise, was beaming with enjoyment. The truth was that John Henry, who would have condemned so unreasonable an accusation had it been uttered by a full-grown male, was enraptured by the piquancy of hearing it on the lovely lips of his cousin. To demand that a pretty woman should possess the mental responsibility of a human being would have been an affront to his ideas of gallantry. His slow wit was enslaved by Virginia's audacity as completely as his kind ox-like eyes were enthralled by the young red and white of her beauty.

"But he's a great man. You can't deny that," he said, with the playful manner in which he might have prodded a kitten in order to make it claw.

"A great man! Just because he has made money!"

"Well, he couldn't have got rich, you know, if he hadn't had the sense to see how to do it," replied the young man with enthusiasm. Like most Southerners who had been forced without preparation into the hard school of industry, he had found that his standards followed inevitably the changing measure of his circumstances. From his altered point of view, the part of owning property appeared

so easy, and the part of winning it so difficult, that his respect for culture had yielded to his admiration for commerce. When the South came again to the front, he felt
instinctively that it would come, shorn of its traditional
plumage, a victor from the hard-fought industrial battlefields of the century; and because Cyrus Treadwell led the
way toward this triumph, he was ready to follow him.
Of the whole town, this grim, half legendary figure (passionately revered and as passionately hated) appeared to
him to stand alone not for the decaying past, but for the
growing future. The stories of the too rapid development
of the Treadwell fortune he cast scornfully aside as the
malicious slanders of failure. What did all this tittle-
tattle about a great man prove except his greatness? Suppose he *had* used his railroad to make a fortune—well,
but for him where would the Dinwiddie and Central be
to-day if not in the junk shop? Where would the lumber
market be? the cotton market? the tobacco market? For
around Cyrus, standing alone and solitary on his height,
there had gathered the great illusion that makes theft honest and falsehood truth; and simple John Henry Pendleton, who, after nineteen years of poverty and memory,
was bereft alike of classical pedantry and of physical
comfort, had grown a little weary of the endless lip-
homage to a single moment in history. Granted even that
it was the greatest moment the world had ever seen, still
why couldn't one be satisfied to let it take its place beside
the wars of the Spartans and the ancient Britons? Perpetual mourning was well enough for ladies in crape veils and
heroic gentlemen on crutches; but when your bread and
meat depended not upon the graves you had decorated, but
upon the bathtubs you had sold, surely something could
be said for the Treadwell point of view.

As Virginia could find no answer to this remark, the

three stood in silence, gazing dreamily, with three pairs of Pendleton eyes, down toward the site of the old slave market. Directly in their line of vision, an overladen mule with a sore shoulder was straining painfully under the lash, but none of them saw it, because each of them was morally incapable of looking an unpleasant fact in the face, if there was any honourable manner of avoiding it. What they beheld, indeed, was the most interesting street in the world, filled with the most interesting people, who drove happy animals that enjoyed their servitude and needed the sound of the lash to add cheer and liveliness to their labours. Never had the Pendleton idealism achieved a more absolute triumph over the actuality.

"Well, we must go on," Mrs. Pendleton murmured, withdrawing her visionary gaze from the hot street littered with fruit rinds and blood-stained papers from a neighbouring butcher shop. "It was lovely to have this glimpse of you, John Henry. What nice bathtubs you have!" Smiling her still lovely smile into the young man's eyes, she proceeded on her leisurely way, while Virginia raised the black silk sunshade over her head. In front of them they could see long rows of fishcarts and vegetable stalls around which hovered an army of eager housekeepers. The social hours in Dinwiddie were the early morning ones in the old market, and Virginia knew that she should hear Docia's story repeated again for the benefit of the curious or sympathetic listeners that would soon gather about her mother. Mrs. Pendleton's marketing, unlike the hurried and irresponsible sort of to-day, was an affair of time and ceremony. Among the greetings and the condolences from other marketers there would ensue lengthy conversations with the vendors of poultry, of fish, or of vegetables. Every vegetable must be carefully selected by her own hands and laid aside into her special basket, which was in the anxious charge of a small coloured urchin. While she felt the plump breasts of Mr. Dewlap's chickens, she would inquire with flattering condescension after the members of Mr. Dewlap's family. Not only did she remember each one of them by name, but she never forgot either the dates of their birthdays or the number of turkeys Mrs. Dewlap had raised in a season. If marketing is ever to be elevated from an occupation to an art, it will be by a return to Mrs. Pendleton's method.

"Mother, please buy some strawberries," Virginia begged.

"Darling, you know we never buy fruit, or desserts. Somebody will certainly send us something. I saw Mrs. Carrington whipping syllabub on her back porch as we passed."

"But they're only five cents a basket."

"Well, put a basket with my marketing, Mr. Dewlap. Yes, I'll take that white pullet if you're sure that she is plumper than the red one."

She moved on a step or two, while the white pullet was handed over by its feet to the small coloured urchin and destruction. If Mrs. Pendleton had ever reflected on the tragic fate of pullets, she would probably have concluded that it was "best" for them to be fried and eaten, or Providence, whose merciful wisdom she never questioned, would not have permitted it. So, in the old days, she had known where the slave market stood, without realizing in the least that men and women were sold there. "Poor things, it does seem dreadful, but I suppose it is better for them to have a change sometimes," she would have reasoned, no doubt, had the horror of the custom ever occurred to her; for her heart was so sensitive to pain that she could exist at all only by inventing a world of exquisite fiction around her.

"Aren't you nearly through, mother?" Virginia pleaded at last. "The sun will be so hot going home that it will make your head worse."

Mrs. Pendleton, who was splitting a pea-shell with her thumb in order to ascertain the size and quality of the peas, murmured soothingly, "Just a minute, dear"; and the girl, finding it impossible to share her mother's enthusiasm for slaughtered animals, fell back again into the narrow shade of the stalls. She revolted with a feeling of outrage against the side of life that confronted her, against the dirty floor, strewn with withered vegetables above which flies swarmed incessantly, and against the pathos of the small bleeding forms, which were related neither to the lamb in the arms of the Good Shepherd nor to the Sunday roast on the table. That evasive idealism, which enabled Mrs. Pendleton to see only the thing she wanted to see in every occurrence, was but partly developed as yet in Virginia; and while she stood there in the midst of her unromantic surroundings, the girl shuddered lest Oliver Treadwell should know that she had ever waited, hot, perspiring, with a draggled skirt, and a bag of tomatoes grasped in her hands, while her mother wandered from stall to stall in a tireless search for peas a few cents cheaper than those of Mr. Dewlap. Youth, with its ingenuous belief that love dwells in external circumstances, was protesting against the bland assumption of age that love creates its own peculiar circumstances out of itself. It was absurd, she knew, to imagine that her father's affection for her mother would alter because she haggled over the price of peas; yet the emotion with which she endowed Oliver Treadwell was so delicate and elusive that she felt that the sight of a soiled skirt and a perspiring face would blast it for ever. It appeared imperative that he should see her in white muslin, and she resolved that if it

cost Docia her life she would have the flounces of her dress
smoothed before evening. She, who was by nature almost
morbidly sensitive to suffering, became, in the hands of
this new and implacable power, as ruthless as Fate.

"Now I'm ready, Virginia dear. Are you tired waiting?"
asked Mrs. Pendleton, coming toward her with the coloured urchin in her train. "Why, there's Susan Treadwell. Have you spoken to her?"

The next instant, before the startled girl could turn, a
voice cried out triumphantly: "O Virginia!" and in front
of her, looking over Susan's shoulder, she saw the eager
eyes and the thin, high-coloured face of Oliver Treadwell.
For a moment she told herself that he had read her
thoughts with his penetrating gaze, which seemed to pierce
through her; and she blushed pink while her eyes burned
under her trembling lashes. Then the paper bag, containing the tomatoes, burst in her hands, and its contents
rolled, one by one, over the littered floor to his feet. Both
stooped at once to recover them, and while their hands
touched amid wilted cabbage leaves, the girl felt that
love had taken gilded wings and departed for ever!

"Put them in the basket, dear," Mrs. Pendleton could
be heard saying calmly in the midst of her daughter's
agony; for, having lived through the brief illumination of
romance, she had come at last into the steady glow that
encompasses the commonplace.

"This is my cousin Oliver, Virginia," remarked Susan,
as casually as if the meeting of the two had not been
planned from all eternity by the beneficent Powers.

"I'm afraid I've spoiled your nice red tomatoes," said
a voice that filled Virginia's whirling mind with a kind of
ecstatic dizziness. As the owner of the voice held out his
hand, she saw that it was long and thin like the rest of
him, with blue veins crossing the back, and slender, slightly

crooked fingers which hurt hers with the strength of their
pressure. "To confess the truth," he added gaily after an
instant, "my breath was quite taken away because, somehow, this was the last place on earth where I expected to
find you. It's a dreadful spot, don't you think so? If we've
got to be cannibals, why in Heaven's name make a show
and a parade of it?"

"What an extraordinary young man!" said Mrs. Pendleton's eyes; and Virginia found herself blushing again
because she felt that her mother had not understood him.
A delicious embarrassment, something different and more
vivid than any sensation she had ever known, held her
speechless while he looked at her. Had her life depended
on it, she could not have uttered a sentence, could barely
even have lifted her eyelids, which seemed suddenly to have
become so heavy that she felt the burden of them weighing over her eyes. All the picturesque phrases she had
planned to speak at their first meeting had taken wings
with perfidious romance; yet she would have given her
dearest possession to have been able to say something
really clever. "He thinks me a simpleton, of course," she
thought, perfectly unaware that Oliver was not thinking of her wits at all, but of the wonderful rose-pink of
her flesh. At one and the same instant, she felt that this
silence was the most marvellous thing that had ever happened to her and longed to break it with some speech so
brilliant that he would never forget it. Little thrills of
joy, like tiny flames, ran over her, and the light in her
eyes shone on him through the quivering dusk of her lashes.
Even when she looked away from him, she could still see
his expression of tender gaiety, as if he were trying in vain
to laugh himself free from an impulse that was fast growing too strong for him. What she did not know was that
the spring was calling to him through her youth, as it was

calling through the scented winds and the young buds on the trees. She was as ignorant that she offered herself to him with her velvet softness, with the glow in her eyes, with her quivering lips, as the flower is that it allures the bee by its perfume. So subtly did Life use her for its end that the illusion of choice in first love remained unimpaired. Though she was young desire incarnate, he saw in her only the unique and solitary woman of his dreams.

"Do you come here every day?" he asked, and immediately the blue sky and the octagonal market spun round at his voice.

As nothing but commonplace words would come to her, she was obliged at last to utter them. "Oh, no, not every day."

"I've always had a tremendous sympathy for women because they have to market and housekeep. I wonder if they won't revolt some time?"

This was so heretical a point of view that she tried earnestly to comprehend it; but all the time her heart was busy telling her how different he was from every other man, how much more interesting! how immeasurably superior! Her attention, in spite of her efforts at serious thought, would not wander from the charm of his voice, from the peculiar whimsical trick of his smile, which lifted his mouth at one corner and made odd little wrinkles come and go about his eyes. His manner was full of sudden nervous gestures which surprised and enchanted her. All other men were not merely as clay beside him; they were as straw! Seeing that he was waiting for a response, she made a violent endeavour to think of one, and uttered almost inaudibly: "But don't they like it?"

"Ah, that's just it," he answered as seriously as if she hadn't known that her speech bordered on imbecility. "Do they really like it? or have they been throwing dust in our eyes through the centuries?" And he gazed at her as eagerly as if he were hanging upon her answer. Oh, if she could only say something clever! If she could only say the sort of thing that would shock Miss Priscilla! But nothing came of her wish, and she was reduced at last to the pathetic rejoinder, "I don't know. I'm afraid I've never thought about it."

For a moment he stared at her as though he were enraptured by her reply. With such eyes and such hair, she might have been as simple as she appeared and he would never have known it. "Of course you haven't, or you wouldn't be you!" he responded; and by the time she came to her senses, she was following her mother and the negro urchin out of the market. Though she was in reality walking over cinders, she felt that her feet were treading on golden air.

CHAPTER IV

THE TREADWELLS

ABOVE the Dinwiddie of Virginia's girlhood, rising sharply out of the smoothly blended level of personalities, there towered, as far back as she could remember, the grim and yet strangely living figure of Cyrus Treadwell. From the intimate social life of the town he had remained detached; but from the beginning it had been impossible for that life to ignore him. Among a people knit by a common pulse, yet separated by a multitude of individual differences, he stood, aloof and indispensable, like one of the gaunt iron bridges of his great railway. He was at once the destroyer and the builder; the inexorable foe of the old feudal order and the beneficent source of the new industrialism. Though half of Dinwiddie hated him, the other half (hating him, perhaps, none the less) ate its bread from his hands. The town, which had lived, fought, lost, and suffered not as a group of individuals, but as a psychological unit, had surrendered at last less to the idea of readjustment than to the indomitable purpose of a single mind.

And yet nobody in Dinwiddie, not even Miss Willy Whitlow, who sewed out by the day, and knew the intimate structure of every skeleton in every closet of the town; nobody could tell the precise instant at which Cyrus had ceased to be an ordinary man and become a great one. A phrase, which had started as usual, "The Mr. Tread-

67

well, you know, who married poor Belinda Bolingbroke—"
swerved suddenly to "Cyrus Treadwell told me that,
and you must admit that *he* knows what he is talking
about"—and a reputation was made! His marriage to
"poor Belinda," which had at first appeared to be the
most conspicuous fact in his career, dwindled to insignificance beside the rebuilding of the tobacco industry and
his immediate elevation to the vacant presidency of one of
the Machlin railroads.

It was true that in the meantime he had fought irre-
proachably, but without renown, through a number of
battles; and returning to a vanquished and ruined city,
had found himself still young enough to go to school again
in matters of finance. Whether he had learned from An-
trum, the despised carpet-bagger for Machlin & Company, or had taken his instructions at first hand from the
great Machlin himself, was on open question in Dinwiddie
in the eighties. The choice was probably given to him to
learn or starve; and aided by the keen understanding and
the acute sense of property he had inherited from his
Scotch-Irish parentage, he had doubtless decided that to
learn was, after all, the easier way. Saving he had been always, and yet with such strange and sudden starts of gen-
erosity that he had been known to seek out obscure maiden
relatives and redeem the mortgaged roof over their heads.
His strongest instinct, which was merely an attenuated
shoot from his supreme feeling for possessions, was that
of race, though he had estranged both his son and his
daughter by his stubborn conviction that he was not doing
his duty by them except when he was making their lives
a burden. For, as with most men who have suffered in their
youth under oppression, his ambition was not so much to
relieve the oppressed as to become in his turn the oppres-
sor. Owing, perhaps, to his fine Scotch-Irish blood, which

ran a little muddy in his veins, he had never lost a certain primitive feeling of superstition, like the decaying root of a religious instinct; and he was as strict in his attendance upon church as he was loose in applying the principles of Christianity to his daily life. Sunday was vaguely associated in his mind with such popular fetiches as a frock coat and a roast of beef; and if the roast had been absent from dinner, he would have felt precisely the same discomfort that troubled him when the sermon was left out of the service. So completely did his outward life shape itself round the inner structure of his thought, that, except for the two days of the week which he spent with unfailing regularity in Wall Street, he might have been said to live only in his office. Once, when his doctor had prescribed exercise for a slight dyspepsia, he had added a few additional blocks to his morning and evening walk, and it was while he was performing this self-inflicted penance that he came upon Gabriel, who was hastening toward him in behalf of John Henry.

For an instant a gleam of light shone on Cyrus's features, and they stood out, palely illuminated, like the features of a bronze statue above which a torch suddenly flares. His shoulders, which stooped until his coat had curved in the back, straightened themselves with a jerk, while he held out his hand, on which an old sabre cut was still visible. This faded scar had always seemed to Gabriel the solitary proof that the great man was created of flesh and blood.

"I've come about a little matter of business," began the rector in an apologetic tone; for in Cyrus's presence he was never without an uneasy feeling that the problems of the spirit were secondary to the problems of finance.

"Well, I'm just going into the office. Come in and sit

down. I'm glad to see you. You bring back the four happiest years of my life, Gabriel."

"And of mine too. It's queer, isn't it, how the savage seems to sleep in the most peaceable of men? We were half starved in those days, half naked, and without the certainty that we'd live until sunset—but, dreadful as it sounds, I was happier then—God help me!—than I've ever been before or since."

Passing through an outer office, where a number of young men were bending over ledgers, they entered Cyrus's private room, and sat down in two plain pine chairs under the coloured lithograph of an engine which ornamented the largest space on the wall. The room was bare of the most ordinary comforts, as if its owner begrudged the few dollars he must spend to improve his surroundings.

"Well, those days are over, and you say it's business that you've come about?" Cyrus retorted, not rudely, but with the manner of a man who seldom wastes words and whose every expenditure either of time or money must achieve some definite result.

"Yes, it's business." The rector's tone had chilled a little, and he added in spite of his judgment, "I'm afraid it's a favour. Everybody comes begging to you, I suppose?"

"Then, it's the Sunday-school picnic, I reckon. I haven't forgotten it. Smithson!" An alert young man appeared at the door. "Make a note that Mr. Pendleton wants coaches for the Saint James' Church picnic on the twenty-ninth. You said twenty-ninth, didn't you, Gabriel?"

"If the weather's good," Gabriel replied meekly, and then as Smithson withdrew, he glanced nervously at the lithograph of the engine. "But it wasn't about the picnic I came," he said. "The fact is, I wanted to ask you to use your influence in the matter of getting John Henry a place in the bank. He has done very well at the night school, and I believe that you would find him satisfactory."

At the first mention of the bank, a look of distrust crept into Cyrus's face; a look, cautious, alert, suspicious, such as he wore at directors' meetings when there was a chance that something might be got out of him if for a minute he were to go off his guard.

"I feel a great responsibility for him," Gabriel resumed almost sternly, though he was painfully aware that his assurance had deserted him.

"Why don't you go to James? James is the one to see."

If the rector had spoken the thought in his mind, he would have answered, "Because James reminds me of a fish, and I can't abide him"; but instead, he replied simply, "I know James so slightly that I don't feel in a position to ask a favour of him."

The expression of suspicion left Cyrus's face, and he relaxed from the strained attitude in which he had sat ever since the Sunday-school picnic had been dismissed from the conversation. Leaning back in his chair, he drew two cigars from the pocket of his coat, and after glancing a little reluctantly at them both, offered one to the rector. "I believe he really wanted me to refuse it!" flashed through Gabriel's mind like an arrow, though the other's hesitation had been only a trick of manner which he had acquired during the long lean years when he had fattened chiefly by not giving away.

For a few minutes they smoked in silence. Then Cyrus remarked in his precise voice: "James is a clever fellow, a clever fellow."

"I've heard that he is as good as right hand to you. That's a fine thing to say of a son."

"Yes, I don't know what I should do without James.

He's a saving hand, and, I tell you, there are more for-
tunes made by saving than by gambling."

"Well, I don't think James need ever give you any
concern on that account," Gabriel replied, not without
gentle satire, for he recalled several unpleasant encoun-
ters with the younger Treadwell on the subject of charity.
"But I've heard different tales of that nephew of yours
who has just come back from God knows what country."

"He's Henry's son," Cyrus replied, with a frown. "You
haven't forgotten Henry?"

"Yes, I remember. Henry and George both went out
to Australia to open the tobacco market, and Henry died
poor while George lived and got rich, I believe?"

"George kept free of women and attended to his affairs," Cyrus returned, who was as frank about his family
as he was secretive about his business.

"But what about Henry's son? He's a promising chap,
isn't he?"

"That depends upon what you call promising. Before
he came I thought of putting him into the bank; but since
I've seen him, I can't, for the life of me, think of anything
to do with him. Unless, of course, you could see your way
toward taking him into the ministry," he concluded with
sardonic humour.

"His views on theology would prevent that, I fear,"
replied the rector, while all the kindly little wrinkles
leaped out round his eyes.

"Views? What do anybody's views matter who can't
make a living? But to tell the truth, there's something
about him that I don't trust. He isn't like Henry, so he
must take after that pretty fool Henry married. Now,
if he had James's temper, I could make something out
of him, but he's different. He's a fly-up-the-creek. He's as
flighty as a woman."

Gabriel, who had been a little cheered to learn that the young man, with all his faults, did not resemble James, hastened to assure Cyrus that there might be some good in the boy, after all, that he was only twenty-two, and that, in any case, it was too soon to pass judgment.

"I can't stand his talk," returned the other grimly. "I've never heard anybody but a preacher—I beg your pardon, Gabriel, nothing personal!—who could keep going so long when nobody was listening. A mere wind-bag, that's what he is, with a lot of nonsensical ideas about his own importance. If there wasn't a girl in the house, it would be no great matter, but that Susan of mine is so headstrong that I'm half afraid she'll get crazy and im-agine she's fallen in love with him."

This proof of parental anxiety touched Gabriel in his tenderest spot. After all, though Cyrus had a harsh sur-face, there was much good at the bottom of him. "I can enter into your feelings about that," he answered sym-pathetically, "though my Virginia, I am sure, would never allow herself to think seriously of a man without first ask-ing my opinion of him."

"Then you're fortunate," Cyrus commented dryly, "for I don't believe Susan would give a red cent for what I'd think if she once took a fancy. She'd as soon elope with that wild-eyed scamp as eat her dinner, if it once entered her head."

A knock came at the door, and Smithson entered and conferred with his employer over a telegram, while Gabriel rose to his feet.

"By the way," said Cyrus, turning abruptly from his secretary and stopping the rector as he was about to pass out of the door, "I was just wondering if you remembered the morning after Lee's surrender, when we started home on the road together?"

"Why, yes." There was a note of surprise in Gabriel's answer, for he remembered, also, that he had sold his watch a little later in the day to a Union soldier, and had divided the eighty dollars with Cyrus. For an instant, he almost believed that the other was going to allude for the first time to that incident.

"Well, I've never forgotten that green persimmon tree by the roadside," pursued the great man, "and the way you stopped under it and said, 'O Lord, wilt Thou not work a miracle and make persimmons ripen in the spring?'"

"No, I'd forgotten it," Gabriel rejoined coolly, for he was hurt by the flippancy and was thinking the worst of Cyrus again.

"You'd forgotten it? Well, I've a long memory, and I never forget. That's one thing you may count on me for," he added, "a good memory. As for John Henry—I'll see James about it. I'll see what James has to say."

When Gabriel had gone, accompanied as far as the outer door by the secretary, Cyrus turned back to the window, and stood gazing over a steep street or two, and past the gabled roof of an old stone house, to the new building of the Treadwell Tobacco Company. Around the skeleton structure he could see the workmen moving like ants, while in a widening circle of air the smoke of other factories floated slowly upward under a brazen sky. "There are too many of them," he thought bitterly. "It's competition that kills. There are too many of them."

So rapt was his look while he stood there that there came into his face an expression of yearning sentiment which made it almost human. Then his gaze wandered to the gleaming tracks of the two great railways which ran out of Dinwiddie toward the north, uncoiling their length like serpents between the broad fields sprinkled with the tender green of young crops. Beside them trailed the ashen country roads over which farmers were crawling with their covered wagons; but, while Cyrus watched from his height, there was as little thought in his mind for the men who drove those wagons through the parching dust as for the beasts that drew them. It is possible even that he did not see them; for just as Mrs. Pendleton's vision banished the sight of suffering because her heart was too tender to bear it, so he overlooked all facts except those which were a part of the dominant motive of his life. Nearer still, within the narrow board fences which surrounded the backyards of negro hovels, under the moving shadows of broad-leaved mulberry or sycamore trees, he gazed down on the swarms of mulatto children; though to his mind that problem, like the problem of labour, loomed vague, detached, and unreal, a thing that existed merely in the air, not in the concrete images that he could understand.

"Well, it's a pity Gabriel never made more of himself," he thought kindly. "Yes, it's a pity. I'll see what I can do for him."

At six o'clock that evening, when the end of his business day had come, he joined James at the door for his walk back to Bolingbroke Street.

"Have you done anything about Jones's place in the bank?" was the first question he asked after his abrupt nod of greeting.

"No, sir. I thought you were waiting to find out about Oliver."

"Then you thought wrong. The fellow's a fool. Look up that nephew of Gabriel Pendleton, and see if he is fit for the job. I am sorry Jones is dead," he added, with a touch of feeling. "I remember I got him that place the year after the war, and I never knew him to be ten minutes late in all the time that I worked with him."

"But what are we to do with Oliver?" inquired James after a pause. "Of course he wouldn't be much good in the bank, but——"

And without finishing his sentence, he glanced up in a tentative, non-committal manner into Cyrus's face. He was a smaller and somewhat imperfect copy of his father, naturally timid, and possessed of a superstitious feeling that he should die in an accident. His thin anæmic features lacked the strength of the Treadwells, though, in his cautious and taciturn way, he was very far indeed from being the fool people generally thought him. Since he had never loved anything with passion except money, he was regarded by his neighbours as a man of unimpeachable morality.

At the end of the block, while the long pointed shadows of their feet kept even pace on the stone crossing, Cyrus answered abruptly: "Put him anywhere out of my sight. I can't bear the look of him."

"How would you like to give him something to do on the road? Put him under Borrows, for instance, and let him learn a bit about freight?"

"Well, I don't care. Only don't let me see him—he turns my stomach."

"Then, as long as we've got to support him, I'll tell him he may try his hand at the job of assistant freight agent, if he wants to earn his keep."

"He'll never do that—just as well put him down under 'waste,' and have done with him," replied Cyrus, chuckling.

A little girl, rolling a hoop, tripped and fell at his feet, and he nodded to her kindly, for he had a strong physical liking for children, though he had never stopped to think about them in a human or personal way. He had, indeed, never stopped to think about anything except the absorbing problem of how to make something out of nothing. Everything else, even his marriage, had made merely a superficial impression upon him. What people called his "luck" was only the relentless pursuit of an idea; and in this pursuit all other sides of his nature had been sapped of energy. From the days when he had humbly accepted small commissions from the firm of Machlin & Company, to the last few years, when he had come to be regarded almost superstitiously as the saviour of sinking properties, he had moved quietly, cautiously, and unswervingly in one direction. The blighting panic of ten years before had scarcely touched him, so softly had he ventured, and so easy was it for him to return to his little deals and his diet of crumbs. They were bad times, those years, alike for rich and poor, for Northerner and Southerner; but in the midst of crashing firms and noiseless factories, he had cut down his household expenses to a pittance and had gone on as secretively as ever, waiting, watching, hoping, until the worst was over and Machlin & Company had found their man. Then, a little later, with the invasion of the cigarette, there went up the new Treadwell factory which the subtle minded still attributed to the genius of Cyrus. Even before George and Henry had sailed for Australia, the success of the house in Dinwiddie was assured. There was hardly a drug store in America in those days that did not offer as its favourite James's crowning triumph, the Magnolia cigarette. A few years later, competition came like a whirlwind; but in the beginning the Treadwell brand held the market alone, and in those few years Cyrus's fortune was made.

"Heard from George lately?" he inquired, when they had traversed, accompanied by their long and narrow shadows, another couple of blocks. The tobacco trade had been always for him merely a single pawn in the splendid game he was playing; but he had suspected recently that James felt something approaching a sentiment for the Magnolia cigarette, and true to the Treadwell scorn of romance, he was for ever trying to trick him into an admission of guilt.

"Not since that letter I showed you a month ago," James answered. "Too much competition, that's the story everywhere. They are flooding the market with cigarettes, and if it wasn't for the way the Magnolia holds on, we'd be swamped in little or no time."

"Well, I reckon the Claypole would pull us through," Cyrus commented. The Claypole was an old brand of plug tobacco with which the first Treadwell factory had started. "But you're right about competition. It's got to stop or we'll be driven clean out of the business."

He drew out his latchkey as he spoke, for they had reached the corner of Bolingbroke Street, and the small dingy house in which they lived was only a few doors away. As they passed between the two blossoming oleanders in green tubs on the sidewalk, James glanced up at the flat square roof, and observed doubtfully, "You'll be getting out of this old place before long now, I reckon."

"Oh, someday, someday," Cyrus answered. "There'll be time enough when the market settles and we can see where the money is coming from."

Once every year, in the spring, James asked his father this question, and once every year he received exactly the same answer. In his mind, Cyrus was always putting off the day when he should move into a larger house, for, though he got richer every week, he never seemed to get quite rich enough to commit himself to any definite change in his circumstances. Of course, in the nature of things, he knew that he ought to have left Bolingbroke Street long ago; there was barely a family still living there with whom his daughter associated, and she complained daily of having to pass saloons and barber shops whenever she went out of doors. But the truth was that, in spite of his answer to James's annual question, neither of them wanted to move away from the old home, and each hoped in his heart that he should never be forced into doing so. Cyrus had become wedded to a habit, and since the clinging to a habit was the only form of sentiment of which he was capable, he shrank more and more from what he felt to be the almost unbearable wrench of moving. A certain fidelity of purpose, the quality which had lifted him above the petty provincialism that crippled James, made the display of wealth as obnoxious to him as the possession of it was agreeable. So long as he was aware that he controlled the industrial future of Dinwiddie, it was a matter of indifference to him whether people supposed him to be a millionaire or a pauper. In time he would probably have to change his way of living, and put an end to his life-long practice of saving; but, meanwhile, he was quite content to go on year after year mending the roof and the chimneys of the old house into which he had moved the week after his marriage.

Entering the hall, he hung his hat on the walnut hat-rack in the dark corner behind the door, and followed the worn strip of blue and red oilcloth which ran up the narrow staircase to the floor above. Where the staircase bent sharply in the middle, the old-fashioned mahogany balustrade shone richly in the light of a gas-jet which jutted out on a brass stem from the wall. Although a window on the upper floor was opened wide to the sunset, the interior of the house had a close musty smell, as if it had been shut up, uninhabited, for months. Cyrus had never noticed the smell, for his senses, which were far from acute, had been rendered even duller than usual by custom.

At the top of the stairs, a coloured washerwoman, accompanied by a bright mulatto boy, who carried an empty clothes basket on his head, waited humbly in the shadow for the two men to pass. She was a dark glistening creature, with ox-like eyes, and the remains of a handsome figure, now running to fat.

"Howdy, Marster," she murmured under her breath as Cyrus reached her, to which he responded brusquely, "Howdy, Mandy," while he glanced with unseeing eyes at the mulatto boy at her side. Then, as he walked rapidly down the hall, with James at his heels, the woman turned back for a minute and gazed after him with an expression of animal submission and acquiescence. So little personal to Cyrus and so free from individual consciousness was this look, that it seemed less the casual glance from a servant to a master than the aspect of a primitive attitude toward life.

At the end of the hall, beyond the open door of the bedroom (which he still occupied with his wife from an inherited conviction that all respectable married persons slept together no matter how uncomfortable they might be), Cyrus discerned the untidy figure of Mrs. Treadwell reflected in a mirror before which she stood brushing her back hair straight up from her neck to a small round knot on the top of her head. She was a slender, flat-chested woman, whose clothes, following some natural bent of mind, appeared never to be put on quite straight or properly hooked and buttoned. It was as if she perpetually dressed in a panic, forgetting to fasten her placket, to put on her collar or to mend the frayed edges of her skirt. When she went out, she still made some spasmodic attempts at neatness; but Susan's untiring efforts and remonstrances had never convinced her that it mattered how one looked in the house, except indeed when a formal

caller arrived, for whom she hastily tied a scarf at the
neck of her dirty basque and flung a purple wool shawl
over her shoulders. Her spirit had been too long broken
to rebel consciously against her daughter's authority; but
her mind was so constituted that the sense of order was
missing, and the pretty coquetry of youth, which had
masqueraded once as the more enduring quality of self-
respect, was extinguished in the five and thirty penitential
years of her marriage. She had a small vacant face, where
the pink and white had run into muddiness, a mouth that
sagged at the corners like the mouth of a frightened child,
and eyes of a sickly purple, which had been compared by
Cyrus to "sweet violets," in the only compliment he ever
paid her. Thirty-five years ago, in one of those attacks
of indiscretion which overtake the most careful man in
the spring, Cyrus had proposed to her; and when she declined him, he had immediately repeated his offer, animated less by any active desire to possess her than by the
dogged male determination to override all obstacles,
whether feminine or financial. And pretty Belinda Bolingbroke, being alone and unsupported by other suitors at the
instant, had entwined herself instinctively round the nearest
male prop that offered. It had been one of those marriages
of opposites which people (ignoring the salient fact that
love has about as much part in it as it has in the pursuit
of a spring chicken by a hawk) speak of with sentiment
as "a triumph of love over differences." Even in the first
days of their engagement, there could be found no better
reason for their marriage than the meeting of Cyrus's
stubborn propensity to have his way with the terror of
spinsterhood which had seized Belinda in a temporary
lapse of suitors. Having married, they immediately proceeded, as if by mutual consent, to make the worst of it.
She, poor fluttering dove-like creature, had lost hope at

the first rebuff, and had let go all the harmless little sentiments that sweetened her life; while he, having married a dove by choice and because of her doveliness, had
never forgiven her that she did not develop into a brisk,
cackling hen of the barnyard. As usually happens in the
cases where "love triumphs over differences," he had
come at last to hate her for the very qualities which had
first caught his fancy. His ideal woman (though he was
perfectly unaware that she existed) was a managing
thrifty soul, in a starched calico dress, with a natural
capacity for driving a bargain; and life, with grim humour,
had rewarded this respectable preference, by bestowing
upon him feeble and insipid Belinda, who spent sleepless
nights trying to add three and five together, but who could
never, to save her soul, remember to put down the household expenses in the petty cash book. It was a case, he
sometimes told himself, of a man, who had resisted temptation all his life, being punished for one instant's folly
more harshly than if he were a practised libertine. No
libertine, indeed, could have got himself into such a scrape,
for none would have surrendered so completely to a single
manifestation of the primal force. To play the fool once,
he reflected bitterly, when his brief intoxication was over,
is, after all, more costly than to play it habitually. Had he
pursued a different pair of violet eyes every evening, he
would never have ended by embracing the phantom that
was Belinda.

But it was more than thirty years since Cyrus had
taken the trouble to turn his unhappiness into philosophy;
for, aided by time, he had become reconciled to his wife
as a man becomes reconciled to a physical infirmity. Except for that one eventful hour in April, women had occupied so small a place in his existence, that he had never

stopped to wonder if his domestic relations might have
been pleasanter had he gone about the business of selection
as carefully as he picked and chose the tobacco for his factory. Even the streak of sensuality in his nature did not
run warm as in the body of an ordinary mortal, and his
vices, like his virtues, had become so rarefied in the frozen
air of his intelligence that they had ceased to resemble the
common frailties of men.

"Ain't you dressed yet?" he inquired without looking
at his wife as he entered; for, having long ago lost his
pride of possession in her, he had ceased to regard her as
of sufficient importance to merit the ordinary civilities.

"I was helping Miss Willy whip one of Susan's
flounces," she answered, turning from the mirror, with
the hairbrush held out like a peace offering before her.
"We wanted to get through to-day," she added nervously,
"so Miss Willy can start on Virginia Pendleton's dress the
first thing in the morning."

If Cyrus had ever permitted himself the consolation of
doubtful language, he would probably have exclaimed
with earnestness, "Confound Miss Willy!"—but he came
of a stock which condemned an oath, or even an expletive,
on its face value, so this natural outlet for his irritation
was denied him. Instead, therefore, of replying in words,
he glanced sourly at the half-open door, through which
issued the whirring noise of the little dressmaker at her
sewing. Now and then, in the intervals when her feet left
the pedal, she could be heard humming softly to herself
with her mouth full of pins.

"Isn't she going?" Cyrus asked presently, while he
washed his hands at the washstand in one corner and
dried them on a towel which Belinda had elaborately embroidered in red. Peering through the crack of the door

as he put the question, he saw Miss Willy hurriedly pulling
basting threads out of a muslin skirt, and the fluttering
bird-like motions of her hands increased the singular
feeling of repulsion with which she inspired him. Though
he was aware that she was an entirely harmless person,
and, moreover, that her "days" supplied the only companionship his wife really enjoyed, he resented angrily the
weeks of work and gossip which the little seamstress spent
under his roof. Put two gabbling women like that together
and you could never tell what stories would be set going
about you before evening! A suspicion, unfortunately too
well founded, that his wife had whimpered out her heart
to the whirring accompaniment of Miss Willy's machine,
had caused him once or twice to rise in his authority and
forbid the dressmaker the house; but, in doing so, he
had reckoned without the strength which may lie in an
unscrupulous weakness. Belinda, who had never fought
for anything else in her life, refused absolutely to give up
her dressmaker. "If I can't see her here, I'll go to her
house," she had said, and Cyrus had yielded at last as
the bully always yields before the frenzied violence of his
victim.

After a hasty touch to the four round flat curls on her
forehead, Mrs. Treadwell turned from the bureau with
her habitually hopeless air, and slipped her thin arms into
the tight sleeves of a black silk basque which she took up
from the bed.

"Did you see Oliver when you came in?" she asked. "He
was in here looking for you a few minutes ago."

"No, I didn't see him, but I'm going to. He's got to
give up this highfaulting nonsense of his if he expects me
to support him. There's one thing the fellow's got to
understand, and that is that he can choose between his
precious stuff and his bread and meat. Before I give him

a job, he'll have to let me see that he is done with all this business of play-writing."

A frightened look came into his wife's face, and, indifferently glancing at her as he finished, he was arrested by something enigmatical and yet familiar in her features. A dim vision of the way she had looked in the early days of their marriage floated an instant before him.

"Do you think he wants to do that?" she asked, with a little sound as if she had drawn her breath so sharply that it whistled. What in thunder was the matter with the woman? he wondered irritably. Of course, she was a fool about the scamp—all the women, even Susan, lost their heads over him—but, after all, why should it make any difference to her whether he wrote plays or took freight orders, as long as he managed to feed himself?

"Well, I don't reckon it has come to a question of what he wants," he rejoined shortly.

"But the boy's heart is bound up in his ambition," Belinda urged, with an energy he had witnessed in her only once before in her life, and that was on the occasion of her historic defence of the seamstress.

For a moment Cyrus stared at her with attention, almost with curiosity. Then he opened his lips for a crushing rejoinder, but thinking better of his impulse, merely repeated dryly, "His heart?" before he turned toward the door. On the threshold he looked back and added, "The next time you see him, tell him I'd like a word with him."

Left alone in her room, Mrs. Treadwell sat down in a rocking-chair by the window, and clasped her hands tightly in her lap with a nervous gesture which she had acquired in long periods of silent waiting on destiny. Her mental attitude, which was one of secret, and usually passive, hostility to her husband, had stamped its likeness so indelibly upon her features, that, sitting there in the wan light, she resembled a woman who suffers from the effects of some slow yet deadly sickness. In the beginning she had asked so little of life that the denial of that little by Fate had appeared niggardly rather than tragic. A man, any man who would have lent himself gracefully as an object of worship, would have been sufficient material for happiness. Marriage, indeed, had appeared to her so desirable as an end in itself, entirely apart from the character of a husband, that she had awakened almost with surprise one morning to the knowledge that she was miserable. It was not so much that her romance had met with open disaster as that it had simply melted away. This gradual melting away of sentiment would have made perhaps only a trivial impression upon a soul to whom every other outlet into the world had not been closed by temperament or tradition. But love had been the one window through which light could enter her house of life; and when this darkened, her whole nature had sickened and grown morbid. Then at last all the corroding bitterness in her heart had gathered to a canker which ached ceaselessly, like a physical sore, in her breast.

"He saw I'd taken to Oliver—that's why he's anxious to spite him," she thought resentfully as she stared with unseeing eyes out into the gray twilight. "It's all just to worry me, that's why he is doing it. He knows I couldn't be any fonder of the boy if he had come of my own blood." And she, who had been a Bolingbroke, set her thin lips together with the only consciousness of superiority to her husband that she had ever known, the secret consciousness that she was better born. Out of the wreck of her entire life, this was the floating spar to which she still clung with a sense of security. Like its imposing symbol, the Saint Memin portrait of the great Archibald Bolingbroke, which lent distinction, by its very inappropriateness, to the drab wall on which it hung, this hidden triumph imparted a pathetic dignity to her manner.

"That's all on earth it is," she repeated with a kind of smothered fierceness. But, even while the words were on her lips, her face changed and softened, for in the adjoining room a voice, full of charm, could be heard saying: "Sewing still, Miss Willy? Don't you know that you are guilty of an immoral act when you work overtime?"

"I'm just this minute through, Mr. Oliver," answered the seamstress in fluttering tones. "As soon as I fold this skirt, I'm going to quit and put on my bonnet."

A few more words followed, and then the door opened wider and Oliver entered, with his ardent eyes, his irresolute mouth, and his physical charm, which brought an air of vital well-being into the depressing sultriness of the room.

"I missed you downstairs, Aunt Belinda. You haven't a headache, I hope," he said, and there was the same caressing kindness in his tone. It was as if his sympathy, like his charm, which cost him so little because it was one of the gifts of Nature, overflowed in every casual expression.

"No, I haven't a headache, dear," replied Mrs. Treadwell, putting up her hand to his cheek as he leaned over her. "Your uncle is waiting for you in the library, so you'd better go down at once," she added, catching her breath as she had done when Cyrus first spoke to her of Oliver.

"Have you any idea what it means? Did he tell you?"

"Yes, he wants to talk to you about business."

"The deuce he does! Well, if that's it, I'd be precious glad to get out of it. You don't suppose I could cut it, do you? Susan is going to take me to the Pendletons' after supper, and I'd like to run upstairs now and make a change."

"No, you'd better go down to him. He doesn't like to be kept waiting."

"All right, then—since you say so."

Meeting the dressmaker on the threshold, he forgot to answer her deprecating bow in his eagerness to have the conversation with Cyrus over and done with.

"I declare, he does startle a body when you ain't used to him," Miss Willy observed, with a bashful giggle. She was a diminutive, sparrow-like creature, with a natural taste for sick-rooms and death-beds, and an inexhaustible fund of gossip. As Mrs. Treadwell, for once, did not respond to her unspoken invitation to chat, she tied her bonnet strings under her sharp little chin, and taking up her satchel went out again, after repeating several times that she would be "back the very minute Mrs. Pendleton was through with her." A few minutes later, Belinda, still seated by the window, saw the shrunken figure ascend the area steps and cross the dusty street with a rapid and buoyant step, as if she, also, plain, overworked, and penniless, were feeling the delicious restlessness of the spring in her blood. "I wonder what on earth she's got to make her skip like that," Belinda thought, not without bitterness. "I reckon, she thinks she's just as important as anybody," she added after an instant, touching, though she was unaware of it, the profoundest truth of philosophy. "She's got nothing in the world but herself, yet, I reckon, to her that is everything, even if it doesn't make a particle of difference to anybody else whether she is living or dead."

Her eyes were still on Miss Willy, who stepped on briskly, swinging her bag joyously before her, when the sound of Cyrus's voice, raised high in anger, floated up to her from the library. A short silence followed; then a door opened and shut quickly, and rapid footsteps passed up the staircase and along the hall outside of her room. While she waited, overcome by the nervous indecision that attacked her like palsy whenever she was forced to take a definite stand, Susan ran up the stairs and called her name in a frightened voice.

"Oh, mother, father has quarrelled dreadfully with Oliver and ordered him out of the house!"

CHAPTER V

OLIVER, THE ROMANTIC

AN HOUR later, Oliver stood before the book-shelves in his room, wrapping each separate volume in newspapers. Downstairs in the basement, he knew, the family were at supper, but he had vowed, in his splendid scorn of material things, that he would never eat another morsel under Cyrus's roof. Even when his aunt, trembling in every limb, had brought him secretly a cup of coffee and a plate of waffles, he had refused to unlock his door and permit her to enter. "I'll come out when I am ready to leave," he had replied to her whispered entreaties.

It was a small room, furnished chiefly with book-shelves, which were still unfinished, and with a depressing view of red tin roofs and blackened chimneys. Above the chimneys a narrow band of sky, spangled with a few stars, was visible from where Oliver stood, and, now and then, he stopped in his work and gazed up at it with an exalted and resolute look. Sometimes a thin shred of smoke floated in from the kitchen chimney, and hung, as if arrested by some magnetic attraction, round the kerosene lamp on a corner of the washstand. The sultriness of the night, which was oppressive even in the street, was almost stifling in the little room with its scant western exposure.

But the flame burning in Oliver's breast had purged away such petty desires as those for material comforts. He had risen above the heat, above the emptiness of his pockets, above the demands of his body. It was a matter of complete indifference to him whether he slept in a house or out of doors, whether he ate or went hungry. His exaltation was so magnificent that while it lasted he felt that he had conquered the physical universe. He was strong! He was free! And it was characteristic of his sanguine intellect that the future should appear to him as something which existed not beyond him, but actually within his grasp. Anger had liberated his spirit as even art had not done; and he felt that all the blood in his body had rushed to his brain and given him the mastery over circumstances. He forgot yesterday as easily as he evaded to-day and subjugated to-morrow. The past, with its starved ambitions, its tragic failures, its blighting despondencies, melted away from him into obscurity; and he remembered only the brief alternating hours of ecstasy and accomplishment. With his wind-blown, flame-like temperament, oscillating in the heat of youth between the inclinations he miscalled convictions, he was still, though Cyrus had disowned him, only a romantic variation from the Treadwell stock. Somewhere, in the depths of his being, the essential Treadwell persisted. He hated Cyrus as a man hates his own weakness; he revolted from materialism as only a materialist in youth revolts.

A knock came at his door, and pausing, with a volume of Heine still unwrapped in his hand, he waited in silence until his visitor should retire down the stairs. But instead of Mrs. Treadwell's trembling tones, he heard, after a moment, the firm and energetic voice of Susan.

"Oliver, I must speak to you. If you won't unlock your door, I'll sit down on the steps and wait until you come out."

"I'm packing my books. I wish you'd go away, Susan."

"I haven't the slightest intention of going away until I've talked with you." And, then, being one of those persons who are born with the natural gift of their own way, she laid her hand on the door knob while Oliver impatiently turned the key in the lock.

"Since you are here, you might as well come in and help," he remarked none too graciously, as he made way for her to enter.

"Of course, I'll help you—but, oh, Oliver, what in the world are you going to do?"

"I haven't thought. I'm too busy, but I'll manage somehow."

"Father was terrible. I heard him all the way upstairs in my room. But," she looked at him a little doubtfully, "don't you think he will get over it?"

"He may, but I shan't. I'd rather starve than live under a petty tyranny like that!"

"I know," she nodded, and he saw that she understood him. It was wonderful how perfectly, from the very first instant, she had understood him. She grasped things, too, by intelligence, not by intuition, and he found this refreshing in an age when the purely feminine was in fashion. Never had he seen a finer example of young, buoyant, conquering womanhood, of womanhood freed from the consciousness and the disabilities of sex. "She's not the sort of girl a man would lose his head over," he reflected; "there's too little of the feminine about her—she's as free from coquetry as she is from the folderol of sentimentality. She's a free spirit, and God knows how she ever came out of the Treadwells." Her beauty even wasn't of the kind that usually goes by the name. He didn't suppose there were ten men in Dinwiddie who would turn to look at her; but, by Jove, if she hadn't beauty, she had the character that lends an even greater distinction. She looked as if she could ride life like a horse, could master and tame it and break it to the bridle.

"It's amazing how you know things, Susan," he said, "and you've never been outside of Dinwiddie."

"But I've wanted to, and I sometimes think wanting teaches one more than going."

He thought over this for an instant, and then, as if the inner flame which consumed him had leaped suddenly to the surface, he burst out joyously: "I've come to the greatest decision of my life in this last hour, Susan."

Her eyes shone. "You mean you've decided not to do what father asks, no matter what happens?"

"I've decided not to accept his conditions—no matter what happens," he answered.

"He was in earnest, then, about wanting you to give up writing?"

"So much in earnest that he would give me a job only on those terms."

"And you declined absolutely?"

"Of course, I declined absolutely."

"But how will you live, Oliver?"

"Oh, I can easily make thirty dollars a month by reviewing German books for New York papers, and I dare say I can manage to pull through on that. I'll have to stay in Dinwiddie, because I couldn't live anywhere else on nearly so little, and, besides, I shouldn't be able to buy a ticket away."

"That will be twenty dollars for your board," said the practical Susan, "and you will have to make ten dollars a month cover all your other expenses. Do you think you can do that?"

"I've got to. Better men have done worse things, haven't they? Better men have done worse things and written great plays while they were about them."

"I believe Mrs. Peachey would let you have a back room and board for that," Susan pursued. "But it will cost you something to get your books moved and the shelves put up there."

"As soon as I get through this I'll go over and see her. Oh, I'm free, Susan, I'm happy! Did you ever see an absolutely happy man before? I feel as if a weight had rolled off my shoulders. I'm tired—dog-tired of compromise and commercialism and all the rest of it. I've got something to say to the world, and I'll go out and make my bed in the gutter before I'll forfeit the opportunity of saying it. Do you know what that means, Susan? Do you know what it is to be willing to give your life if only you can speak out the thing that is inside of you?" The colour in his face mounted to his forehead, while his eyes grew black with emotion. In the smoky little room, Youth, with its fierce revolts, its impassioned egoism, its inextinguishable faith in itself, delivered its challenge to life. "I've got to be true to myself, Susan! A man who won't starve for his ambition isn't worth his salt, is he? And, besides, the best work is all done not in plenty, but in poverty—the most perfect art has grown from the poorest soil. If I were to accept Uncle Cyrus's offer, I'd grow soft to the core in a month, and be no more use than a rotten apple."

His conviction lent a golden ring to his voice, and so winning to Susan was the impetuous flow of his words, that she felt herself swept away from all the basic common sense of her character. She saw his ambition as clearly as he saw it; she weighed his purpose, as he weighed it, in the imaginary scales of his judgment; she accepted his estimate of his powers as passionately as he accepted it.

"Of course, you mustn't give up, Oliver; you couldn't," she said.

"You're right, I couldn't."

"If you can get steady reviewing, I believe you can
manage," she resumed. "Living in Dinwiddie costs really
so very little." Her voice thrilled suddenly. "It must be
beautiful to have something that you feel about like this.
Oh, I wish I were you, Oliver! I wish a thousand times I
were you!"

Withdrawing his eyes from the sky at which he had
been gazing, he turned to look at her as if her words had
arrested him. "You're a dear girl," he answered kindly,
"and I think all the world of you." As he spoke he thought
again what a fine thing it would be for the man who could
fall in love with her. "It would be the best thing that
could happen to any man to marry a woman like that,"
he reflected; "she'd keep him up to the mark and never let
him grow soft. Yes, it would be all right, if only one could
manage to fall in love with her—but I couldn't. She might
as well be a rose-bush for all the passion she'd ever arouse
in me." Then his charming egoism asserted itself, and he
said caressingly: "I believe I'd never stand Dinwiddie but
for you, Susan."

She smiled back at him, but there was a limpid clearness in her look which made him feel that she had seen
through him while he was thinking. This clearness, with
its utter freedom from affectation or sentimentality, embarrassed him by its unlikeliness to all the attributes he
mentally classified as feminine. To look straight seemed
to him almost as unwomanly as to throw straight, and
Susan would, doubtless, be quite capable of performing
either of these difficult feats. He liked her fine brow under
the short fringe, which he hated, and he liked the arched
bridge of her nose and the generous curve of her mouth.
Yet had he stopped to reflect, he would probably have said
that the woman spirit in her was expressed through char-

acter rather than emotion. Amid the cramping customs of
the period, she moved large, free, and simple, as though
she walked already in the purer and more bracing air of
the future.

"I wish I could help you," she said, stooping to pick
up a newspaper from a pile on the floor. "Here, let me
wrap that Spinoza. I'm afraid the back will come off if
you aren't careful."

"Of course a man has to work out his own career," he
replied, as he handed over the volume. "I doubt, when
it comes to that, if anybody can be of much help to another where his life's work is concerned. The main thing,
after all, is not to get in one's way, not to cripple one's
energy. I've got to be free—that's all there is to it. I've got
to belong to myself."

"And you know already just what you are going to do?
About your writing, I mean."

"Absolutely. I've ideas enough to fill fifty ordinary
lifetimes. I'm simply seething with them. Why, that box
over there in the corner is full of plays that would start
a national drama if the fool public had sense enough to
see what they are about. The trouble is that they don't
want life on the stage; they want a kind of theatrical
wedding-cake. And, by Jove, they get it! Any dramatist
who tries to force people to eat bread and meat when
they are crying for sugar plums may as well prepare to
starve until the public begins to suffer from acute indigestion. Then, if he isn't dead—or, perhaps, if he is—his hour
will come, and he will get his reward either here or in
heaven."

"So you'll go on just the same and wait until they're
ready for you?" asked Susan, laughing from sheer pride
in him. "You'll never, never cheapen yourself, Oliver?"

For the first time in her life she was face to face with an intellectual passion, and she felt almost as if she herself were inspired.

"Never. I've made my choice. I'll wait half a century if need be, but I'll wait. I know, too, what I am talking about, for I could do the other thing as easily as I could eat my dinner. I've got the trick of it. I could make a fortune to-morrow if I were to lose my intellectual honesty and go in simply for the making of money. Why, I am a Treadwell, after all, just as you are, my dear cousin, and I could commercialize the stage, I haven't a doubt, as successfully as your father has commercialized the railroad. It's in the blood—the instinct, you know—and the only thing that has kept it down in me is that I sincerely— yes, I sincerely believe that I am a genius. If I didn't, do you think I'd stick at this starvation business another fortnight? That's the whole story, ever blessed word of it, and I'm telling you because I feel expansive to-night—I'm such a tremendous egoist, you know, and because—well, because you are Susan."

"I think I understand a little bit how you feel," replied Susan. "Of course, I'm not a genius, but I've thought sometimes that I should almost be willing to starve if only I might go to college."

Checking the words on his lips, he looked at her with sympathy. "It's a shame you can't, but I suppose Uncle Cyrus won't hear of it."

"I haven't asked him, but I am going to do it. I am so afraid of a refusal—and, of course, he'll refuse—that I've lacked the courage to speak of it.

"Good God! Why is one generation left so absolutely at the mercy of another?" he demanded, turning back to the strip of sky over the roof. "It makes a man rage to think of the lives that are spoiled for a whim. Money, money—curse it!—it all comes to that in the end. Money makes us and destroys us."

"Do you remember what father said to you the other night—that you would come at last to what you called the property idea and be exactly like James and himself?"

"If I thought that, I'd go out and hang myself. I can understand a man selling his soul for drink, though I rarely touch a drop, or for women, though I've never bothered about them, but never, not even in the last extremity, for money."

A door creaked somewhere on the second floor, and a minute afterward the slow and hesitating steps of Mrs. Treadwell were heard ascending the stairs.

"Let her come in just a moment, Oliver," begged Susan, and her tone was full of the impatient, slightly arrogant affection she felt for her mother. There was little sympathy and less understanding between them; but on Susan's side there was a protective tenderness that was almost maternal. This tenderness was all her own, while the touch of arrogance in her manner belonged to the universal inability of youth to make allowances for age.

"Oh, well," Oliver assented indifferently; and going to the door, he opened it and stood waiting for Mrs. Treadwell to enter.

"I came up to ask if you wouldn't eat something, dear?" she asked. "But I suppose Susan has brought you your supper?"

"He won't touch a morsel, mother; it is useless to ask him. He is going away just as soon as we have finished packing."

"But where is he going? I didn't know that he had a place to go to."

"Oh, a man can always find a place somewhere."

"How can you take it so lightly, Susan?" protested Mrs. Treadwell, beginning to cry.

"That's the only sensible way to take it, isn't it, Oliver?" Susan asked, gaily.

"Don't get into a fidget about me, Aunt Belinda," Oliver said, pushing the pile of newspapers out of her way, while she sat down nervously on the end of a packing-case and wiped her eyes on the fringe of her purple shawl. The impulsive kindness with which he had spoken to her a few hours before had vanished from his tone, and left in its place an accent of irritation. His sympathy, which was never assumed, resulted so entirely from his mood that it was independent of the person or situation which appeared to inspire it. There were moments when, because of a sensation of mental or physical well-being, he overflowed with a feeling of tenderness for the beggar at the crossing; and there were longer periods, following a sudden despondency, when the suffering of his closest friend aroused in him merely a sense of personal outrage.

"But you don't mean that you are going for good?— that you'll never come back again to see Susan and me?" his aunt whimpered, while her sagging mouth trembled.

"You can't expect me to come back after the things Uncle Cyrus has said to me."

A look so bitter that it was almost venomous crept into Mrs. Treadwell's face. "He just did it to worry me, Oliver. He has done everything he could think of to worry me ever since he persuaded me to marry him. I sometimes believe," she added, gloating over the idea like a decayed remnant of the aristocratic spirit, "that he has always been jealous of me because I was born a Bolingbroke."

To Oliver, who had not, like Susan, become accustomed, through constant repetition, to Mrs. Treadwell's delu-

sion, this appeared so fresh a view of Cyrus's character
that it caught his interest even in the midst of his own
absorbing perplexities. Until he saw Susan's head shake
ominously over her mother's shoulder, it did not occur
to him that his aunt, whom he supposed to be without
imagination, had created this consoling belief out of her
own mental vacancy.

"Oh, he wanted to worry me all right, there's no doubt
about that," he replied.

"He hasn't spoken to me when he could help it for
twenty years," resumed his aunt, who was so possessed
by the idea of her own relation to her husband that she
was incapable of dwelling upon any other.

"I wouldn't talk about it, mother, if I were you," Susan
said, with resolute cheerfulness.

"I don't know why I shouldn't talk about it. It's all I've
got to talk about," Mrs. Treadwell returned peevishly;
and she added with smothered resentment, "Even my
children haven't been any comfort to me since they were
little. They've both turned against me because of the way
their father treats me. James hardly ever has so much as
a word to say to me."

"But I do, mother. How can you say such an unkind
thing to me?"

"You never do the things that I want you to. You know
I'd like you to go out and enjoy yourself and have attention as other girls do."

"You are disappointed because I'm not a belle like Abby
Goode or Virginia Pendleton," said Susan with the patience that is born of a basic sense of humour. "But I
couldn't help that, could I?"

"Any girl in my day would have felt badly if she wasn't
admired," Mrs. Treadwell retorted with the venom of

the embittered weak, "but I don't believe you'd care a particle if a man never looked at you twice."

"If one never looked at me once, I don't see why you should want me to be miserable about it," was Susan's smiling rejoinder; "and if the girls in your day couldn't be happy without admiration, they must have been silly creatures. I've a life of my own to live, and I'm not going to let my happiness depend on how many times a man looks at me." In the clear light of her ridicule, the spectre of spinsterhood, which was still an object of dread in the Dinwiddie of the eighties, dissolved into a shadow.

"Well, we've about finished, I believe," Oliver remarked, closing the case over which he was stooping, and devoutly thanking whatever beneficent Powers had not made him a woman. "I'll send for these sometime to-morrow, Aunt Belinda."

"You'd just as well spend the night," urged Mrs. Tread-well stubbornly. "He need never know of it."

"But I'd know of it—that's the great thing—and I'd never forget it."

Rising unsteadily from the box, she stood with the ends of her purple shawl clutched together over her flat bosom. "Then you'll wait just a minute. I've got something down-stairs I'd like to give you," she said.

"Why, of course, but won't you let me fetch it?"

"You'd never find it," she answered mysteriously, and hurried out while he held the door open to light her down the dark staircase.

When her tread was heard at last on the landing be-low, Susan glanced at the books that were still left on the shelves. "I'll pack the rest for you to-morrow, Oliver, and your clothes too. Have you any money?"

"A little left from selling my watch in New York. My clothes don't amount to much. I've got them all in that bag, but I'll leave my books in your charge until I can find a place for them."

"I'll take good care of them. Oh, Oliver," her face grew disturbed, "I forgot all about my promise to Virginia that I'd bring you to see her to-night."

"Well, I've no time to meet girls now, of course, but that doesn't mean that I'm not awfully knocked up about it."

"I hate so to disappoint her."

"She won't think of it twice, the beauty!"

"But she will. I'm sure she will. Hush! Mother is coming."

As he turned to the door, it opened slowly to admit his aunt, who was panting heavily from her hurried ascent of the stairs. Her ill-humour toward Susan had entirely disappeared, for the only resentment she had ever harboured for more than a few minutes was the lifelong one she cherished against her husband.

"It was not in the place where I had put it, so I thought one of the servants had taken it," she explained. "Mandy was alone in my room to-day while I was at dinner."

In her hand she held a small pasteboard box bearing a jeweller's imprint, and opening this, she took out a roll of money and counted out fifty dollars on the top of a packing-case. "I've saved this up for six months," she said. "It came from selling some silver forks that belonged to the Bolingbrokes, and I've always felt easier to think that I had a little laid away that he had nothing to do with. From the very day that I married him, he was always close about money," she added.

All the sordid tragedy, not of poverty, but of meanness, was in the gesture with which she gathered up the notes and pressed them into his shrinking hands. And yet Cyrus Treadwell was a rich man, the richest man in Dinwiddie!

Oliver understood now why she was crushed, why she had become the hopeless victim of the little troubles of life. "From the very day of our marriage, he was always close about money."

"I had three dozen forks and spoons in the beginning," she explained, as if there were no piercing significance in the fact she stated so simply, "but I've sold them all now, one or two at a time, when I needed a little money of my own. He has always paid the bills, but he never gave me a cent in my life to do as I pleased with."

"I can't take it from you, Aunt Belinda. It would burn my fingers."

"It's mine. I've got a right to do as I choose with it," she persisted almost passionately, "and I'd rather give it to you than buy anything in the world." Something in her face, the look of one who has risen to a generous impulse and finds happiness in the sacrifice, checked the hand with which he was thrusting the money away from him. He was deeply touched by her act; it was useless for him to pretend either to her or to himself that she had not touched him. The youth in him, unfettered, strong, triumphant, pitied her because she was no longer young; the artist in him pitied her because she was no longer beautiful. Without these two things, or at least one of these two, what was life worth to a woman?

"I'll take it on condition that you'll let me pay it back as soon as I get out of debt to Uncle Cyrus," he said in obedience to Susan's imploring nod.

To this she agreed after an ineffectual protest. "You needn't think about paying it back to me," she insisted; "I haven't anything to spend money on now, so it doesn't make much difference whether I have any or not. I can help you a little more after a while," she finished, with enthusiasm. "I'm raising a few squabs out in the back yard, and Meadows is going to buy them as soon as they are big enough to eat."

He felt at first merely a sense of physical revolt from the brutality of her self-revelation; from the nakedness to which she had stripped the horror of her marriage before the eyes of her daughter. Nothing, not even the natural impulse to screen one's soul from the gaze of the people with whom one lived, had prevented the appalling indignity of this exposure. The delusion that it is possible for a woman by mere virtue of being a woman to suffer in sweetness and silence, evaporated as he looked at her. He had believed her to be a nonentity, and she was revealing an inner life as intense, as real, as acutely personal as his own. A few words of casual kindness, and he had made a slave of her. He regretted it. He was embarrassed. He was sorry. He wished to heaven she hadn't brought him the money; and yet in spite of his regret and his embarrassment, he was profoundly moved. It occurred to him as he took it from her how easy it would have been for Cyrus to have subjugated and satisfied her in the beginning. All it needed was a little kindness, the cheapest virtue, and the tragedy of her ruined soul might have been averted. To make allowances! Ah, that was the philosophy of human relations! If men and women would only stop judging each other and make allowances!

"Well, I shan't starve just yet, thanks to you, Aunt Belinda," he said cheerfully enough, as he thrust the notes into his pocket. It was a small thing, after all, to make her happy by the sacrifice of his pride. Pride was not, he remembered, included among the Christian virtues, and, besides, as he told himself the next instant, trifling as the sum was, it would at least tide him over financially until he received the next payment for his reviewing. "I'd better

go, it's getting late," he said, with a return of his old
gaiety, while he bent over to kiss her. He was half
ashamed of the kiss, not because he was self-conscious
about kissing, since he had long since lost that mark of
provincialism, but because of the look of passionate gratitude that shone in her face. Gratitude always made him
uncomfortable. It was one of the things he was for ever
evading and yet for ever receiving. He hated it; he had
never in his life done anything to deserve it; but he could
never escape it.

"Good-bye, Susan." His lips touched hers, and though
he was moving only a few streets away, the caress contained all the solemnity of a last parting. Words wouldn't
come when he searched for them, and the bracing sense
of power he had felt half an hour before was curiously mingled now with an enervating tenderness. He was still
confident of himself; but he became suddenly aware
that these women were necessary to his happiness and his
success, that his nature demanded the constant daily tonic
of their love and service. He understood now the primal
necessity of woman, not as an individual, but as an incen-
tive to the dominant personality of man.

"Send for me if you need me," said Susan, resting her
loving eyes upon him; "and, Oliver, please promise me
to be very careful about money."

"I'll be careful, never fear!" he replied, with a laugh,
as he took up his bag and opened the door. A few minutes
later, when he was leaving the house, he reflected that the
fifty dollars in his pocket would keep life in him for a
considerable time in Dinwiddie.

CHAPTER VI

A TREADWELL IN REVOLT

YORK STREET, in which Mrs. Peachey lived and supplied the necessaries of life to a dozen boarders, ran like a frayed seam of gentility between the prosperous and the impoverished quarters of Dinwiddie; and in order to reach it, Oliver was obliged to pass the rectory, where, though he did not see her, Virginia sat in stiffly starched muslin on the old horsehair sofa. The fragrance of honeysuckle floated to his nostrils from the dim garden; but so absorbed was he in the engrossing problems of the moment that only after he had passed the tower of the church did he remember that the house behind him sheltered the girl who reminded him of one of the adorable young virgins of Perugino. For an instant he permitted himself to dwell longingly on the expression of gentle goodness that looked from her face; but this memory proved so disturbing that he put it away from him while he returned to the prudent consideration of the fifty dollars in his pocket.

The sultriness of the weather dampened his body, not his spirit, and while he walked on, carrying his heavy bag, along York Street, his consciousness of the tremendous importance of his decision exhilarated him like a tonic. He had freed himself from Cyrus and from commercialism at a single blow, and it had all been as easy as talking! The joke about starvation he had of course indulged in merely

for the pleasure of arousing Susan. He wasn't going to
starve; nobody was going to starve in Dinwiddie on thirty
dollars a month, and there was no doubt in the world of his
ability to make that much by his reviewing. It was all simple enough. What he intended to do was to write the national drama and to practise economy.

He had, indeed, provided for everything in his future,
he was to discover a little later, except the affable condescension of Mrs. Peachey toward the profession of letters. The hostility of Cyrus he had attributed to the crass
stupidity of the commercial mind; but it was a blow to encounter the same misconception, more discreetly veiled, in
a woman with the charm and character of Mrs. Peachey.
Bland, plump, and pretty, she received the avowal of his
occupation with the smiling skepticism peculiar to a race
whose genius has been military.

"I understand. It is very interesting," she observed
sweetly. "But what do you do besides—what do you do,
I mean, for a living?"

Here it was again, this fatuous intolerance! this complacent provincialism! And the terrible part of it was
that he had suddenly the sensation of being overwhelmed
by a weight, of being smothered under a mountain of preju-
dice. The flame of his anger against Cyrus went out
abruptly, leaving him cold. It was the world now against
which he rebelled. He felt that the whole world was pro-
vincial.

"I shall write reviews for a New York paper," he
answered, trying in vain to impress her by a touch of literary hauteur. At the moment it seemed to him that he
could cheerfully bear anything if they would only at least
pretend to take him seriously. What appalled him was
not the opposition, but the utter absence of comprehension. And he could never hope to convince them! Even if

he were to write great plays, they would still hold as obstinately by their assumption that the writing of plays did not matter, that what really mattered was to create and then to satisfy an inordinate appetite for tobacco. This was authentic success, and by no illegitimate triumph of genius could he persuade an industrial country that he was as great a man as his uncle. The smiling incredulity in Mrs. Peachey's face ceased to be individual and became a part of the American attitude toward the native-born artist. This attitude, he admitted, was not confined to Dinwiddie, since it was national. He had encountered it in New York; but never had the destructive force of it impressed him as it did on the ripe and charming lips of the woman before him. In that illuminating instant he understood why the American consciousness in literature was still unawakened, why the creative artist turned manufacturer, why the original thinker bent his knee in the end to the tin gods of commerce.

Her eyes, beautiful as the eyes of all happy women are, dwelt on him kindly while he struggled to explain his mission. All the dread of the unusual, all the inherited belief in the sanctity of fixed opinions, all the passionate distrust of ideas that have not stood the test of centuries;—these things, which make for the safety and the permanence of the race, were in the look of motherly indulgence with which she regarded him. She had just risen from a rocking-chair on the long porch, where honest Tom sat relating ponderous war anecdotes to an attentive group of boarders; and beyond her in the dimly lighted hall, he could see the wide old staircase climbing leisurely into the mysterious silence of the upper storeys.

"I have a small room at the back that I might rent to you," she said hesitatingly, after a pause. "I'm afraid you will find it warm in summer, as it is just under the

roof and has a western exposure, but I hardly think I
could do better for you at the price you are able to pay.
I understood that you intended to live with your uncle,"
she added in a burst of enthusiasm. "My husband has
always been one of his greatest admirers."

The mention of Cyrus was like a spur to Oliver's ambition, and he realized with gratitude that it was merely
his sensibility, not his resolution, which had been shaken.

"I'll take the room," he returned, ignoring what she
had said, as well as what she had implied, about Cyrus.
Then, as she tripped ahead of him, he entered the dis-
mantled hall, filled with broken pieces of fine old furniture, and ascended the stairs as far as the third floor.
When she turned a loosened doorknob and passed before
him into the little room at the back, he saw, first of all,
the narrow window, with its torn green shade, beyond
which clustered a blur of silvery foliage in the midst of
red roofs and huddled chimneys. From this hilltop, he
could look down unseen on that bit of the universal life
which was Dinwiddie. He could watch the town at work
and at play; he could see those twenty-one thousand souls
either moved as a unit by the secret forces which ignore
individuality, or separated and enclosed by that impenetrable wall of personality which surrounded each atom
among them. He could follow the division of class and
the still deeper divisions of race as they were symbolized
in the old brick walls, overgrown with young grasses,
which girdled the ancient gardens in High Street. From
the dazzling glimpses of white muslin under honeysuckle arbours, to the dusky forms that swarmed like
spawn in the alleys, the life of Dinwiddie loved, hated,
enjoyed, and suffered, beneath him. And over this love and
this hatred, this enjoyment and this suffering, there pre-
sided, an outward and visible sign of the triumph of in-

dustralism, the imposing brick walls of the new Treadwell tobacco factory.

A soft voice spoke in his ear, and turning, he looked
into the face of Mrs. Peachey, whom he had almost forgotten.

"You will find the sun warm in the afternoon, I am
afraid," she murmured, still with her manner of pleasantly humouring him which he found later to be an expression of her half maternal, wholly feminine, attitude
toward his sex.

"Oh, I dare say it will be all right," he responded. "I
shall work so hard that I shan't have time to bother
about the weather."

Leaving the window, he gazed round the little room
with an impulse of curiosity. Who had lived here before him? A clerk? A salesman? Perhaps one of the
numerous indigent gentlewomen who formed so large
and so important a part of the population of Dinwiddie?
The walls were smeared with a sickly blue wash, and in
several places there were the marks left from the pic-
tures of the preceding lodger. An old mahogany bureau,
black with age and ill usage, stood crosswise in the corner
behind the door, and reflected in the dim mirror he saw
his own face looking back at him. A film of dust lay over
everything in the room, over the muddy blue of the walls,
over the strip of discoloured matting on the floor, over
the few fine old pieces of furniture, fallen now into abject
degradation. The handsome French bed, placed con-
veniently between door and window, stood naked to the
eyes, with its cheap husk mattress rolled half back, and
its bare slats, of which the two middle ones were tied
together with rope, revealing its descent from elegance
into squalor. As he saw it, the room was the epitome of
tragedy; yet in the centre of it, on one of the battered and

broken-legged Heppelwhite chairs, sat Mrs. Peachey, rosy, plump, and pretty, regarding him with her quizzical smile. "Yes, life, of course, is sad if you stop to think about it," her smile seemed to assure him; "but the main thing, after all, is to be happy in spite of it."

"Do you wish to stay here to-night?" she asked, seeing that he had put down his bag.

"If you will let me. But I am afraid it will be inconvenient."

She shook her head. "Not if you don't mind the dust. The room has been shut up for weeks, and the dust is so dreadful in the spring. The servants have gone out," she added, "but I'll bring you some sheets for your bed, and you can fill your pitcher from the spout at the end of the passage. Only be careful not to stumble over the step there. It is hard to see when the gas is not lit."

"You won't object to my putting shelves round the walls?" he asked, while she pushed the mattress into place with the light and condescending touch of one who preserves the aristocratic manner not only in tragedy, but even in toil. It was, indeed, her peculiar distinction, he came to know afterwards, that she worked as gracefully as other women played.

"Couldn't you find room enough without them?" she inquired while her gaze left the mattress and travelled dubiously to the mantelpiece. "It seems a pity for you to go to any expense about shelves, doesn't it?"

"Oh, they won't cost much. I'll do the work myself, and I'll do it in the mornings when it won't disturb anybody. I'll have to push that bed round a bit in order to make space."

Something in his vibrant voice, so full of the richness and the buoyant energy of youth, made her look at him as she might have looked at one of her own children, or at that overgrown child whom she had married. And just as she had managed Tom all his life by pretending to let him have his way, so she proceeded now, by instinct, to manage Oliver. "You dear boy! Of course you may turn things upside down if you want to. Only wait a few days until you are settled and have seen how you like it."

Then she tripped out with her springy step, which had kept its elasticity through war and famine, while Oliver, gazing after her, wondered whether it was philosophy or merely a love of pleasure that sustained her? Was it thought or the absence of thought that produced her wonderful courage?

He heard her tread on the stairs; then the sound passed to the front hall; and a minute later there floated up the laughter with which the assembled boarders received her. Closing the door, which she had left open, he turned back to the window and stared from his hilltop down on the red roofs of Dinwiddie. White as milk, the moonlight lay on the brick wall at the foot of the garden, and down the gradual hill, rows of chimneys were outlined against the faintly dappled sky in the west. In the next yard, a hollow tree looked as if it were cut out of silver, and beneath its boughs, which drooped into the alley, he could see the huddled figure of an aged negress who had fallen asleep on a flagstone. So still was the night that the very smoke appeared to hang suspended above the tops of the chimneys, as though it were too heavy to rise and yet too light to float downward and rest upon the motionless trees. Under the pale beams the town lost its solidity and grew spectral. Nothing seemed to hold it to the earth except the stillness which held the fallen flowers of the syringa there also. Even the church towers looked as ephemeral as spires of thistledown, and the winding streets, which ran beside clear walls and dark shining gardens, trailed off from the

ground and vanished into the silvery air. Only the black
bulk of the Treadwell factory beside the river defied the
magic of the moon's rays and remained a solid reminder of
the brevity of all enchantment.

Gradually, while Oliver waited for Mrs. Peachey's return, he ceased to think of the furniture in his room; he
ceased to think even of the way in which he should manage
to do his work, and allowed his mind to dwell, almost
with a feeling of ecstasy, on the memory of Virginia. He
saw the mist of little curls on her temples, her blue eyes,
with their good and gentle expression, and the look of
radiant happiness which played like an edge of light over
her features. The beauty of the night acted as a spur to his
senses. He wanted companionship. He wanted the smile
and the touch of a woman. He wanted to fall in love with a
girl who had blue eyes and a mouth like a flower!

"It wouldn't take me ten minutes to become a fool about
her," he thought. "Confound this moonlight, anyhow.
It's making an idiot of me."

Like many persons of artistic sensibility, he had at
times the feeling that his imagination controlled his conduct, and under the sharp pressure of it now, he began
to picture what the end would be if he were to fling himself headlong in the direction where his desires were leading him. If only he could let himself go! If only he could
defy the future! If only he could forget in a single crisis
that he was a Treadwell!

"If I were the right sort, I suppose, I'd rush in and
make her fall in love with me, and then marry her and let
her starve," he thought. "But, somehow, I can't. I'm either
not enough of a genius or not enough of a Treadwell.
When it comes to starving a woman in cold blood, my
conscience begins to balk. There's only one thing it would
balk at more violently, and that is starving my work.

That's what Uncle Cyrus would like—nothing better. By Jove! the way he looked when he had the nerve to make that offer! And I honestly believe he thought I was going to accept it. I honestly believe he was surprised when I stood out against him. He's an idiot, that's what is the matter with him. Why, it would be a crime, nothing less than a crime, for me to give up, and go hunting after freight orders. Any ninny can do that. James can do that—but he couldn't see, he positively couldn't see that I'd be wasted at it."

The vision of Cyrus had banished the vision of Virginia, and leaving the window, Oliver began walking rapidly back and forth between the washstand and the bare bedstead. The fire of his ambition, which opposition had fanned into a blaze, had never burned more brightly in his heart than it did at that instant. He felt capable not only of renouncing Virginia, but of reforming the world. While he walked there, he dedicated himself to art as exclusively as Cyrus had dedicated himself to money: since Nature, who had made the individual, had been powerless to eradicate this dominant trait of the type. A Treadwell had always stood for success, and success meant merely seeing but one thing at a time and seeing that thing at every instant. It meant to Cyrus and to James the thought of money as absolutely as it meant to Oliver the thought of art. The way to it was the same, only the ideas that illumined the way were different. To Cyrus and to James, indeed, as to all Treadwells everywhere, the idea was scarcely an idea at all, since it had been crystallized by long usage into a fact. The word "success" (and what was success except another name for the universal Treadwell spirit?) invariably assumed the image of the dollar in the mind of Cyrus, while to Oliver, since his thinking was less precise, it was without shape or symbol. Pacing the dusty floor, with the pale moonlight brooding like a flock of white birds over the garden, the young man would have defined the word as embracing all the lofty aspirations in the human soul. It was the hour when youth scaled the heights and wrested the divine fire from the heavens. At the moment he was less an individual than the embodied age of two-and-twenty. He was intellect in adolescence; intellect finding its strength; intellect in revolt against the tyranny of industrialism.

The staircase creaked softly, and following a knock at the door, Mrs. Peachey entered with her arms full of bedclothes.

"I am so sorry I kept you waiting, Mr. Treadwell, but I was obliged to stop to speak to a caller. Oh, thank you. Do you really know how to make up a bed? How very clever of you! I'm sure Mr. Peachey couldn't do such a thing if his life depended upon it. Men are so helpless that it surprises me—it really does—when they know how to do anything. Oh, of course, you have lived about the world so much that you have had to learn how to manage. And you've been abroad? How very interesting! Some day when I have the time you must tell me about it. Not that I should ever care to go myself, but I love to hear other people talk about their travels. Professor Trimble—he lived over there a great many years—gave a talk before the Ladies' Aid Society of our church, and everybody said it was quite as instructive as going one's self. And then, too, we escaped all the misery of seasickness."

All the time she was busily spreading his bed, while he assisted her with what she described to her husband afterwards as "the most charming manner, just as if he enjoyed it." This charming manner, which was the outward expression of an inborn kindliness, won her entirely to his side before the bed-making was over. That any one so frank and pleasant, with such nice boyish eyes, and so rich a colour, should prove untrustworthy, was unbelievable to that part of her which ruled her judgment. And since this ruling part was not reason, but instinct, she possessed, perhaps, as infallible a guide to opinions as ever falls to the lot of erring humanity. "I know he's all right. Don't ask me *how* I know it, Mr. Peachey," she observed, while she brushed her hair for the night; "I don't know how I know it, but I do know it."

Oliver, meanwhile, had thrown off his coat, and settled down to work under the flickering gas, at the end of the mantelpiece. Inspiration had seized him while he helped Mrs. Peachey make his bed, and his "charming manner," which had at first been natural enough, had become at last something of an effort. He was writing the second act of a play in which he meant to supplant the pretty shams of the stage by the aspect of sober reality. The play dealt with woman, with the new woman who has grown so old in the last twenty years, with the woman whose past is a cross upon which she crucifies both herself and the public. Like most men of twenty-two, he was convinced that he understood all about women, and like most men of any age, he was under the impression that women acted, thought, and felt, not as individuals, but as a sex. The classic phrases, "women are like that," and "women think so queerly about things," were on his lips as constantly as if he were an average male and not an earnest-minded student of human nature. But while the average male applies general principles loosely, with Oliver the habit was the result of a distinctly formulated philosophy. He had, as he would probably have put it, a feeling for reality, and the stage appeared to him, on the whole, to be the most effective vehicle for revealing the universe to itself. If he was not a genius, he possessed the unconquerable individualism of genius; and he possessed, also, a cleverness which could assume the manner of genius without apparent endeavour. His ability, which no one but Cyrus had ever questioned, may not have been of the highest order, but at least it was better stuff than had ever gone into the making of American plays. In the early eighties profound darkness still hung over the stage, for the intellect of a democracy, which first seeks an outlet in statesmanship, secondly in commerce, and lastly in art and literature, had barely begun to express itself, with the immaturity of youth, in several of these latter fields. It was Oliver's distinction, as well as his misfortune, that he lived before his country was ready for him. Coming a quarter of a century later, he might have made a part of a national emancipation of intellect. Coming when he did, he stood merely for one of the spasmodic revolts against the dominant spirit. Unwritten history is full of such revolts, since it is by their accumulated vehemence that the world moves on its way.

But at the age of twenty-two, though he was assured that he understood both woman and the universe in which she belonged, he was pathetically ignorant of his own place in the extravagance of Nature. With the rest of us, he would have been astounded at the suggestion that he might have been born to be wasted. Other things were wasted, he knew, since those who called Nature an economist had grossly flattered her. Types and races and revolutions, were squandered with royal prodigality; but that he himself should be so misused was clearly incredible. Deep down in him there was the obstinate belief that his existence was a vital matter to the awful Power that ruled the universe; and while he worked that May evening on the second act of his great play, with the sweat raining from his brow in the breathless heat, it was impossible for him

to conceive of ultimate failure as it was for him to realize that he should ever cease to exist. The air was stagnant,
the light was bad, his stomach was empty, and he was tor-
mented by the stinging of the gnats that circled round the
flame; but he was gloriously happy with the happiness of a
man who has given himself to an idea.

CHAPTER VII

THE ARTIST IN PHILISTIA

AT DAWN, after a sleepless night, Oliver dressed himself and made a cup of coffee on the spirit lamp he carried in his bag. While he drank, a sense of power pervaded him like warmth. He was cheered, he was even exhilarated. A single cup of this miraculous fluid, and his depression was vanquished as no argument could have vanquished it. He remembered that he had eaten nothing for almost twenty-four hours (having missed yesterday's dinner), and this thought carried him downstairs, where he begged a roll from a yawning negro cook in the kitchen. Coming up to his room again, he poured out a second cup of coffee, added a dash of cream, which he had brought with him in a handleless pitcher, and leaning comfortably back in the worn horsehair covered chair by the window, relapsed into perfect contentment. His attitude toward the universe had been altered by a bubbling potful of brown liquid, and the tremendous result, so grotesquely out of proportion to its cause, appeared to him at the minute entirely right and proper. Everything was entirely right and proper, and he felt able, with a clear conscience and after the fashion of his day, to accept the universe.

Outside, the sunrise, which he could not see, was flooding the roofs of Dinwiddie with a dull golden light. The heat had given way before the soft wind, which smelt of flowers, and scattered tiny shreds of mist, like white rose-leaves, over the moist gardens. The look of unreality, which had been a fiction of the moonlight, faded gradually as the day broke, and left the harsh outlines and the blackened chimneys of the town unsoftened by any shadow of illusion. Presently, as the sunlight fell aslant the winding streets, there was a faint stir in the house; but since the day was Sunday, and Dinwiddie observed the Sabbath by sleeping late, this stir was slow and drowsy, like the movement of people but half awake. First, a dilapidated milk wagon rumbled through the alleys to the back gates, where dishevelled negro maids ran out with earthenware pitchers, which went back foaming around the brims. Then the doors of the houses opened slowly; the green outside shutters were flung wide; and an army of coloured servants bearing brooms appeared on the porches, and made expressive gestures to one another over the railings. Occasionally, when a maid lifted a doormat in order to beat the dust out of it, she would forget to put it down again while she stared after the milk cart. Nobody, not even the servants, seemed to regard the wasted hours as of any importance. It struck Oliver that the only use Dinwiddie made of time was to kill it.

He fell to work with enthusiasm, and he was still working when the reverberations of the breakfast bell thundered in his ears. Going downstairs to the dining-room, he found several thin and pinched looking young women, with their hats on and Sunday-school lessons beside their plates. Mrs. Peachey, still smiling her quizzical smile, sat at the head of the table, pouring coffee out of an old silver coffee-pot, which was battered in on one side as if it had seen active service in the war. When, after a few hurried mouthfuls, he asked permission to return to his work, she received his excuses with the same cheerful acquiescence with which she accepted the decrees of Providence. It is

doubtful, indeed, if her serenity, which was rooted in a
heroic hopelessness, could have been shaken either by the
apologies of a boarder or by the appearance of an earth-
quake. Her happiness was of that invulnerable sort which
builds its nest not in the luxuriant gardens of the emotions,
but in the bare, rock-bound places of the spirit. Courage,
humour, an adherence to conviction which is wedded to
the inability to respect any opinion except one's own;
loyalty which had sprung from a principle into a passion;
a fortifying trust, less in the Power that rules the universe
than in the peculiar virtues of the Episcopal prayer-book
bound in black; a capacity for self-sacrifice which had made
the South a nation of political martyrs; complacency, exaltation, narrowness of vision, and uncompromising devotion to an ideal:—these were the qualities which had
passed from the race into the individual and through the
individual again back into the very blood and fibre of the
race.

"Do you work on Sunday?" she inquired sweetly, yet
with the faintest tinge of disapproval in her tone.

He nodded. "Once in a while."

"Saint James' Church is only a few minutes' walk from
here; but I suppose you are a Presbyterian, like your
uncle?"

His respectability, he saw, hung in the balance—for to
have avowed himself a freethinker would have dyed him
socially only one shade less black than to have declared
himself a Republican—so, escaping without a further confession of faith, he ascended to his room and applied himself anew to the regeneration of the American drama. The
dull gold light that slept on the brick walls, began presently
to slant in long beams over the roofs, which mounted like
steps up the hillside, while, as the morning advanced, the
mellow sound of chimes floated out on the stillness, calling

Dinwiddians to worship, as it had called their fathers and
grandfathers and great-grandfathers before them. The
Sabbath calm, so heavy that an axe could have scarcely dis-
pelled it, filled the curving streets and the square gardens
like an invisible fog; a fog that dulled the brain and
weighed down the eyelids and made the grim walls of
the Treadwell tobacco factory look as if they were rising
out of a dream. Into this dream, under the thick boughs
of mulberry trees, there passed presently a thin file of
people, walking alone or in pairs. The men were mostly
old; but the women were of every age, and all except the
very young were clad in mourning and wore hanging veils
on their bonnets. Though Oliver did not know it, he was,
in reality, watching a procession of those who, having once
embraced a cause and lost it, were content to go on quietly
in a hush of memory for the rest of life. Passion had once
inflamed them; but they moved now in the inviolable peace
which comes only to those who have nothing left that they
may lose. At the end of the line, in the middle of the earthen
roadbed walked an old horse, with an earnest face, drawing a dump-cart, and in the cart were the boxes of books
that Susan had helped Oliver to pack the evening before.
"Who'd have thought she'd get them here so soon?" he
said to himself. "By George, she is a wonder! And Sunday too!"

The old horse, having reached the hilltop, disappeared
behind the next house, and ten minutes later Mrs. Peachey
escorted the smallest of his boxes into his bedroom.

"Your cousin is downstairs, but I didn't know whether
you wanted me to bring her up here or not?" she said.

"Of course, you do, don't you, Oliver?" asked Susan's
voice, and entering the room, she coolly presented her
cheek to him. This coolness, which impressed him almost
as much as her extraordinary capability, made him feel

sometimes as if she had built a stone wall between them.
Years afterwards he asked himself if this was the reason
his admiration had never warmed into love?

"Well, you're a good one!" he exclaimed, as she drew
back from the casual embrace.

"I knew you were here," she answered, "because John
Henry Pendleton" (was it his imagination or did the
faintest blush tinge her face?) "saw Major Peachey last
night and told me on his way home."

"You can't help me straighten up, I suppose? The room
looks a sight."

"Not now—I'm on my way to church, and I'll be late
if I don't hurry." She wore a gray cashmere dress, made
with a draped polonaise which accentuated her rather full
hips, and a hat with a steeple crown which did not suit
the Treadwell arch of her nose. He thought she looked
plain, but he did not realize that in another dress and hat
she might have been almost beautiful; that she was, indeed, one of those large-minded, passionately honest
women who, in their scorn of pretence or affectation,
rarely condescend to make the best of their appearances.
To have consciously selected a becoming hat would have
seemed to her a species of coquetry, and coquetry, even the
most innocent, she held in abhorrence. Her sincerity was
not only intellectual; it was of that rarer sort which has its
root in a physical instinct.

After she had gone, he worked steadily for a couple of
hours, and then opened one of the boxes Susan had brought
and arranged a few of his books in a row on the mantelpiece. It was while he stood still undecided whether to
place "The Origin of Species" or "The Critique of Pure
Reason" on the end nearest his bed, that a knock came at
his door, and the figure of Miss Priscilla Batte, attired in

a black silk dolman with bugle trimmings, appeared on the threshold.

"Sally Peachey just told me that you were here," she said, enfolding him in the embrace which seemed common to Dinwiddie, "so I thought I would speak to you on my way back from church. I don't suppose you've ever heard of me, but I am your cousin Priscilla Batte."

Though he was entirely unaware of it, the meeting was a momentous one in his career. The visit of Miss Priscilla may have seemed an insignificant matter to those who have not learned that the insignificant is merely the significant seen from another angle; but the truth is that it marked a decisive milestone in his emotional history. Even Mrs. Peachey, who had walked back from church with her, and who harboured the common delusion that Life selects only slim bodies for its secret agents, did not dream as she watched that enormous figure toil up the staircase that she was gazing upon the slow movement of destiny. Had Oliver been asked the dominant influence in shaping his career, he would probably have answered blindly, but sincerely, "The Critique of Pure Reason"; so far was he from suspecting that his philosophy had less control over his future than had the accident that his mother was the third cousin of Priscilla Batte.

He pushed a chair into the widest space he could find, and she seated herself as modestly as if she were not the vehicle of the invisible Powers. The stiff grosgrain strings of her bonnet stood out like small wings under her double chin, and on her massive bosom he saw the cameo brooch bearing the war-like profile of Athene. As she sat there, beaming complacently upon him, with her prayer-book and hymnal held at a proper angle in front of her, she seemed to Oliver to dominate the situation simply by the solid weight of her presence. In her single person she produced the effect of a majority. As a mere mass of humanity she carried conviction.

"I was sorry not to see you at church," she said, "but I suppose you went with Cyrus." As he shook his head silently, she added hastily, "I hope there's nothing wrong between you and him."

"Nothing except that I have decided not to go into the tobacco business."

"But what in the world are you going to do? How are you going to live if he doesn't provide for you?"

"Oh, I'll manage somehow. You needn't worry, Cousin Priscilla." He smiled at her across the unfinished page of his play, and this smile won her as it had won Mrs. Peachey. Like most spinsters she had remained a creature of sentiment, and the appeal of the young and masculine she found difficult to resist. After all, he was a charming boy, her heart told her. What he needed was merely some good girl to take care of him and convert him to the Episcopal Church. And, immediately, as is the way with women, she became as anxious to sacrifice Virginia to this possible redemption of the male as she had been alarmed by the suspicion that such a desire existed in Susan. Though it would have shocked her to hear that she held any opinion in common with Mohammed (who appeared in the universal history she taught only in a brief list of "false prophets"), there existed deep down in her the feeling that a man's soul was of greater consequence than a woman's in the eyes of God.

"I hope you haven't been foolish, Oliver," she said in a tone which conveyed an emotional sympathy as well as a moral protest.

"That depends upon what you mean by foolishness," he returned, still smiling.

"Well, I don't think you ought to quarrel with Cyrus.

He may not be perfect. I am not saying that he mightn't have been a better husband, for instance, though I always hold the woman to blame when a marriage turns out a failure; but when all's said and done, he is a great man, Oliver."

He shook his head impatiently. "I've heard that until I'm sick of it—forgive me, Cousin Priscilla."

"Everybody admires him; that is, everybody except Belinda."

"I should say she'd had excellent opportunities for forming an opinion. What's he ever done, anyhow, that's great," he asked almost angrily, "except accumulate money? It seems to me that you've gone mad over money in Dinwiddie. I suppose it's the reaction from having to do without it so long."

Miss Priscilla, whose native serenity drew strength from another's loss of temper, beamed into his flushed face as if she enjoyed the spectacle of his heightened colour.

"You oughtn't to talk like that, Oliver," she said. "How on earth are you going to fall in love and marry, if you haven't any money to keep a wife? What you need is a good girl to look after you. I never married, myself, but I am sometimes tempted to believe that even an unhappy marriage is better than none at all. At least it gives you something to think about."

"I have enough to think about already. I have my work."

"But work isn't a wife."

"I know it isn't, but I happen to like it better."

Her matchmaking instinct had received a check; but the placid determination which was the basis of her character was merely reinforced thereby to further efforts. It was for his good to marry (had not her mother and her grandmother instilled into her the doctrine that an early marriage was the single masculine safeguard, since, once married, a man's morality became not his own business, but his wife's), and marry him she was resolved to do, either with his cheerful coöperation, or, if necessary, without it. He had certainly looked at Virginia as if he admired her, and surely a girl like that—lovely, loving, unselfish to a fault, and trained from her infancy to excel in all the feminine virtues;—surely, this perfect flower of sex specialization could have been designed by Providence only for the delight and the improvement of man.

"Then, if that is the way your mind is made up I hope you will be careful not to trifle with the feelings of a girl like Virginia Pendleton," she retorted severely.

By a single stroke of genius, inspired by the diplomacy inherent in a sex whose chief concern has been the making of matches, she transfixed his imagination as skilfully as she might have impaled a butterfly on a bodkin. While he stared at her, she could almost see the iridescent wings of his fancy whirling madly round the idea by which she had arrested their flight. Trifle with Virginia! Trifle with that radiant vision of girlhood! All the chivalry of youth revolted from the suggestion, and he thought again of the wistful adoration in the eyes of a Perugino virgin. Was it possible that she could ever look at him with that angelic expression of meekness and surrender? The fire of first love, which had smouldered under the weight of his reason, burst suddenly into flame. His thoughts, which had been as clear as a geometrical figure, became suddenly blurred by the mystery upon which passion lives. He was seized by a consuming wonder about Virginia, and this wonder was heightened when he remembered the appealing sweetness in her face as she smiled up at him. Had he conquered by a look the exquisite modesty of her soul? With this thought the memory of her virginal shyness

stung his senses as if it were the challenge of sex. Chivalry,
love, vanity, curiosity;—all these circled helplessly round
the invisible axis of Miss Priscilla's idea.

"What do you mean? Surely you don't suppose—she
hasn't said anything——"

"You imagine that Virginia is the kind of girl who
would say anything, do you?" inquired Miss Priscilla.

"But there must be some reason why you should
have——"

"If there is, my dear boy, I'm not going to tell you," she
answered with a calmness which he felt, in his excited
state, to be positively infernal. "All I meant was to warn
you not to trifle with any girl as innocent of life as Virginia
Pendleton is. I don't want her to get her heart broken
before she has the chance to make some man happy."

"Do you mean to imply that I could break her heart if
I tried?"

"I don't mean to imply anything. I am only telling you
that she is just the kind of girl a man would want to marry.
She is her mother all over again, and I don't believe
Lucy has ever thought of herself a minute since she married."

"She looks like an angel," he said, "but——"

"And she isn't a bit the kind of girl that Susan is, though
they are so devoted. Now, I can understand a man not
wanting to marry Susan, because she is so full of ideas,
and has a mind of her own about things. But Virginia is
different."

Then, seeing that she had "unsettled" his mind sufficiently for her purpose, she rose and looked about the
room with the inordinate curiosity that kept her still young
in spite of her sixty years.

"You don't mean to tell me you brought all those books

with you, Oliver?" she asked. "Why on earth don't you get rid of some of them?"

"I can't spare any of them. I never know which one I may want next."

"What are those you're putting on the mantelpiece? Isn't Darwin the name of the man who said we were all descended from monkeys?"

As he made no answer to this except to press her hand and thank her for coming, she left the mantelpiece and wandered to the window, where her gaze rested, with a look of maternal satisfaction, on the roofs of Dinwiddie.

"It's a jolly view of the town, isn't it?" he said. "There's nothing like looking down from a hilltop to give one a sense of superiority."

"You can see straight into Mrs. Goode's backyard," she replied, "and I never knew before that she left her clothes hanging on the line on Sunday. That comes, I suppose, from not looking after her servants and gadding about on all sorts of charities. She told me the other day that she belonged to every charitable organization in Dinwiddie."

"Is she Abby's mother?"

"Yes, but you'd never imagine they were any relation. Abby gave me more trouble than any girl I ever taught. She never would learn the multiplication table, and I don't believe she knows it to this day. There isn't any harm in her except that she is a scatter-brain, and will make eyes or burst. I sometimes think it isn't her fault, that she was just born man-crazy."

"She's awfully good fun," he laughed.

"Are you going to her garden party on Wednesday?"

"I accepted before I quarrelled with Uncle Cyrus; but I'll have to get out of it now."

"Oh, I wouldn't. All the pretty girls in town will be there."

"Are there any plain ones? And what becomes of them?"

"The Lord only knows! Old Judge Bassett used to say that there wouldn't be any preserves and pickles in the world if all women were born good-looking. I declare, I never realized how small the tower of Saint James' Church is!"

For a moment he hesitated, and when he spoke his voice had taken a deeper tone. "Will Virginia Pendleton be at the party?" he asked.

"She wouldn't miss it for anything in the world. Miss Willy Whitlow was sewing there yesterday on a white organdie dress for her to wear. Have you ever seen Virginia in white organdie? I always tell Lucy the child looks sweet enough to eat when she puts it on."

He laughed again, but not as he had laughed at her description of Abby. "Ask her please to put blue bows on her flounces and a red rose in her hair," he said.

"Then you are going?"

"Not if I can possibly keep away. Oh, Cousin Priscilla, why didn't I inherit my soul from your side of the family?"

"Well, for my part I don't believe in all this talk about inheritance. Nobody ever heard of inheriting anything but money when I was a girl. You've got the kind of soul the good Lord wanted to put into you, and that's all there is about it."

When he returned from assisting her in her slow and difficult descent of the stairs, he sat down again before the unfinished act of his play; but his eyes wandered from the manuscript to the town, which lay as bright and still in the sunlight as if it were imprisoned in crystal. The wonder aroused in his mind by Miss Priscilla's allusion to

Virginia persisted as a disturbing element in the background of his thoughts. What had she meant? Was it possible that there was truth in the wildest imaginings of his vanity? Virginia's face, framed in her wreath of hair, floated beneath the tower of Saint James' Church at which he was gazing, and the radiant goodness in her look mounted like a draught of strong wine to his brain. Passion, which he had discounted in his plans for the future, appeared suddenly to shake the very foundations of life. Never before had the spirit and the flesh united in the appeal of a woman. Never before had the divine virgin of his dreams assumed the living red and white of young girlhood. He thought how soft her hair must be to the touch, and how warm her mouth would glow from his kisses. With a kind of wonder he realized that this was first love, that it was first love he had felt when he met her eyes under the dappled sunlight in High Street. The memory of her beauty was like a net which enmeshed his thoughts when he tried to escape it. Look where he would he saw always a cloud of dark hair and two deep blue eyes that shone as softly as wild hyacinths after a shower. Think as he would he met always the haunting doubt— "What did she mean? Can it be true that she already loves me?" So small an incident as Miss Priscilla's Sunday call had not only upset his work for the morning, but had changed in an instant the even course of his future. He decided suddenly that he must see Virginia again—that he would go to Abby Goode's party; and though the party was only three days off, it seemed to him that the waiting would be almost unbearable. Only after he had once seen her would it be possible, he felt, to stop thinking of her and to return comfortably to his work.

CHAPTER VIII

WHITE MAGIC

In the centre of her bedroom, with her back turned to the bookcase that was filled with sugared falsehoods about life, Virginia was standing very straight, while Miss Willy Whitlow knelt at her feet and sewed pale blue bows on her overskirt of white organdie. Occasionally, the door opened softly, and the rector or one of the servants looked in to see "Virginia" or "Miss Virginia dressed for the party," and when such interruptions occurred, Mrs. Pendleton, who sat on an ottoman at the dressmaker's right hand and held a spool of thread and pair of scissors in her lap, would say sternly, "Don't move, Virginia, stand straight or Miss Willy won't get the bows right." At these warning words, Virginia's thin shoulders would spring back and the filmy ruffles stir gently over her girlish bosom.

Through the open window, beyond the drooping boughs of the paulownia trees, a few wistful stars shone softly through the web of purple twilight. The night smelt of a thousand flowers. All the mingled sweetness of old gardens floated in on the warm wind and caressed the faded figure of Miss Willy as lovingly as it caressed the young and radiant vision of Virginia. Once or twice the kneeling seamstress had glanced up at the girl and thought: "I wonder how it feels to be as lovely as that?" Then she sighed as one who had missed her heritage, for she had been always plain, and went on patiently sewing the bows

on Virginia's overskirt. "You can't have everything in
this world, and I ought to be thankful that I've kept out
of the poorhouse," she added a minute later when a stab
of envy went through her at hearing the girl laugh from
sheer happiness.

"Am I all right, mother? Tell me how I look."

"Lovely, darling. There won't be any one there sweeter
than you are."

Maternal passion lit Mrs. Pendleton's eyes with splendour, and her worn face was illuminated as if a lamp had
been held suddenly close to it. All day, in spite of a neuralgia pain in her temples, she had worked hard hemming the
flounces for Virginia's dress, and into every stitch had
gone something of the divine ecstasy of martyrdom. Her
life centred so entirely in her affections that apart from
love she existed scarcely at all. In spite of her trials she
was probably the happiest woman in Dinwiddie, for she
had found her happiness in the only way it is ever won,
by turning her back on it. Never once had she thought of
it as an end to be pursued, never even as a flower to be
plucked from the wayside. It is doubtful if she had ever
stopped once in the thirty years of her marriage to ask
herself the questions: "Is this what I want to do?" or
"Does this make me happy?" Love meant to her not
grasping, but giving, and in serving others she had served
herself unawares. Even her besetting sin of "false pride"
she indulged not on her own account, but because she,
who could be humble enough for herself, could not bear
to associate the virtue of humility with either her husband
or her daughter.

The last blue bow was attached to the left side of the
overskirt, and while Miss Willy rose from her knees, Virginia crossed to the window and gazed up at the pale
stars over the tops of the paulownias. A joy so vibrant

that it was like living music swelled in her breast. She was young! She was beautiful! She was to be loved! Before this preternatural certainty of happiness the chilling disappointments of the last few days had melted as quickly as frost in the sunlight. Like all young and inexperienced creatures, she was possessed by the feeling that there exists a magnetic current of attraction between desire and the object that it desires. "Something told" her that she was meant for happiness, and the voice of this "something" was more convincing than the chaotic march of phenomena. Sorrow, decay, death—these appeared to her as things which must happen inevitably to other people, but from which she should be for ever shielded by some beneficent Providence. She thought of them as vaguely as she did of the remote tragedies of history. They bore no closer relation to her own life than did the French Revolution or the beheading of Charles the First. It was natural, if sad, that Miss Willy Whitlow should fade and suffer. The world, she knew, was full of old people, of weary people, of blighted people; but she cherished passionately the belief that these people were all miserable because, somehow, they had not chosen to be happy. There appeared something positively reprehensible in a person who could go sighing upon so kind and beautiful a planet. All things, even joy, seemed to her a mere matter of willing. It was impossible that any hostile powers should withstand the radiant energy of her desire.

Leaning there from the window, with her face lifted to the stars, and her mother's adoring gaze on her back, she thought of the "happiness" which would be hers in the future: and this "happiness" meant to her only the solitary experience of love. Like all the women of her race, she had played gallantly and staked her world upon a single chance. Whereas a man might have missed love and still have retained life, with a woman love and life were interchangeable terms. This one emotion represented not only her sole opportunity of joy, it constituted as well her single field of activity. The chasm between marriage and spinsterhood was as wide as the one between children and pickles. Yet so secret was this intense absorption in the thought of romance, that Mrs. Pendleton, forgetting her own girlhood, would have been startled had she penetrated that lovely head and discovered the ecstatic dreams that flocked through her daughter's brain. Though love was the single window through which a woman might look upon a larger world, she was fatuously supposed neither to think of it nor to desire it until it had offered itself unsolicited. Every girl born into the world was destined for a heritage of love or of barrenness; yet she was forbidden to exert herself either to invite the one or to avoid the other. For, in spite of the fiery splendour of Southern womanhood in the war years, to be feminine, in the eyes of the period, was to be morally passive.

"Your father has come to see your dress, dear," said her mother in the voice of a woman from whom sentiment overflowed in every tone, in every look, in every gesture.

Turning quickly, Virginia met the smiling eyes of the rector; those young and visionary eyes, which Nature, with a wistful irony, had placed beneath beetling brows in the creased and wrinkled face of an old man. The eyes were those of a prophet; of one who had lived his life in the light of a transcendent inspiration rather than by the prosaic rule of reason; but the face belonged to a man who had aged before his time under the accumulated stress of physical burdens.

"How do I look, father? Am I pretty?" asked Virginia, stretching out her thin young arms on either side of her, and waiting with parted lips to drink in his praise.

"Almost as beautiful as your mother, and she grows lovelier every day that she lives."

His admiring gaze, which held the spirit of beauty as a crystal holds the spirit of light, passed from the glowing features of Virginia to the lined and pallid face of his wife. In that gaze there had been no shadow of alteration for thirty years. It is doubtful even if he had seen any change in her since he had first looked upon her face, and thought it almost unearthly in its angelic fairness. From the physical union they had entered into that deeper union of souls in which the body dissolves as the shadow dissolves into the substance, and he saw her always as she had appeared to him on the first morning, as if the pool of sunlight in which she stood had never darkened around her. Yet to Virginia his words brought a startled realization that her mother—her own mother, with her faded face and her soft, anxious eyes—had once been as young and radiant as she herself. The love of her parents for each other had always seemed to her as natural and as far removed from the cloudless zone of romance as her own love for them; for, like most young creatures, she regarded love as belonging, with bright eyes and rosy cheeks, to the blissful period of youth.

"I hear John Henry's ring, darling. Are you ready?" Mrs. Pendleton asked.

"In a minute. Is the rose right in my hair?" Virginia replied, turning her profile toward her mother, while she flung a misty white scarf over her shoulders.

"Quite right, dear. I hope you will have a lovely time. I shall sit up for you, so you needn't bother to take a key."

"But you'll be so tired. Can't you make her go to bed, father?"

"I couldn't close my eyes till I knew you were safe

home, and heard how you'd enjoyed yourself," Mrs. Pendleton answered, as they slowly descended the staircase,
Virginia leading the way, and the rest following in a procession behind her. Turning at the gate, with her arm in
John Henry's, the girl saw them standing in the lighted
doorway, with their tender gaze following her, and the
faces of the little seamstress and the two coloured servants
staring over their shoulders. Trivial as the incident was,
it was one of the moments which stood out afterwards in
Virginia's memory, as if a white light had fallen across
it. Of such simple and expressive things life is woven,
though the years had not taught her this on that May
evening.

On the Goodes' lawn lanterns bloomed, like yellow
flowers among the branches of poplar trees, and beneath
them Mrs. Goode and Abby—a loud, handsome girl,
with a coarsened complexion and a "sporting" manner—
received their guests and waved them to a dancing platform which had been raised between a rose-crowned
summer-house and the old brick wall at the foot of the
garden. Ropes were stretched over the platform, from
the roof of the summer-house to a cherry tree at the end
of the walk, and on these more lanterns of red, blue, and
yellow paper were hanging. The air was scented with
honeysuckle, and from an obscure corner behind a trellis
the sound of a waltz floated. As music it was not of a
classic order, but this did not matter since nobody was
aware of it; and Dinwiddie, which developed quite a taste
for Wagner at the beginning of the next century, could
listen in the eighties with what was perhaps a sincerer
pleasure, to stringed instruments, a little rough but
played with fervour by negro musicians. As Virginia
drifted off in John Henry's arms for the first dance, which
she had promised him, she thought: "I wonder if he will

not come after all?" and a pang shot through her heart where the daring joy had been only a moment before. Then the music grew suddenly heavy while she felt her feet drag in the waltz. The smell of honeysuckle made her sad as if it brought back to her senses an unhappy association she could not remember; and it seemed to her that her soul and body trembled, like a bent flame, into an attitude of expectancy.

"Let me stop a minute. I want to watch the others," she said, drawing back into the scented dusk under a rose arbour.

"But don't you want to fill your card? If the men once catch sight of you, you won't have a dance left."

"No—no, I want to watch a while," she said, with so strange an accent of irritation that he stared at her in surprise. The suspense in her heart hurt her like a drawn cord in throbbing flesh, and she felt angry with John Henry because he was so dull that he could not see how she suffered. In the distance, under the waving gilded leaves of the poplars, she saw Abby laughing up into a man's face, and she thought: "Can he possibly be in love with Abby? Some men are mad about her, but I know he isn't. He could never like a loud woman, and, besides, he couldn't have looked at me that way if he hadn't cared." Then it seemed to her that something of the aching suspense in her own heart stole into Abby's laughing face while she watched it, and from Abby it passed onward into the faces of all the girls who were dancing on the raised platform. Suspense! Was that a woman's life, after all? Never to be able to go out and fight for what one wanted! Always to sit at home and wait, without moving a foot or lifting a hand toward happiness! Never to dare gallantly! Never even to suffer openly! Always to will in secret, always to hope in secret, always to triumph or to fail in secret. Never to be one's self; never to let one's soul or body relax from the attitude of expectancy into the attitude of achievement. For the first time, born of the mutinous longing in her heart, there came to her the tragic vision of life. The faces of the girls revolving in white muslin to the music of the waltz, became merged into one, and this was the face of all womanhood. Love, sorrow, hope, regret, wonder, all the sharp longing and the slow waiting of the centuries—above all the slow waiting—these things were in her brief vision of the single face that looked back at her out of the whirling dance. Then the music stopped, the one face dissolved into many faces, and from among them Susan passed under the swinging lanterns and came toward her.

"Oh, Virginia, where have you been hiding? I promised Oliver I would find you for him. He says he came only to look at you."

The music began joyously again; the young leaves, gilded by the yellow lantern-light, danced in the warm wind as if they were seized by the spirit of melody; and from the dusk of the trellis the ravished sweetness of honeysuckle flooded the garden with fragrance. With the vanished sadness in her heart there fled the sadness in the waltz and in the faces of the girls who danced to the music. Waiting no longer seemed pain to her, for it was enriched now by the burning sweetness of ecstasy.

Suddenly, for she had not seen him approach, she was aware that he was at her side, looking down at her beneath a lantern which was beginning to flicker. A sense of deep peace, of perfect contentment with the world as God planned it, took possession of her. Even the minutes of suspense seemed good because they had brought at last this swift rush of happiness. Every line of his face— of that face which had captured her imagination as though it had been the face of her dreams—was illumined by the quivering light that gilded the poplars. His eyes were so close to hers that she saw little flecks of gold on the brown, and she grew dizzy while she looked into them, as if she stood on a height and feared to turn lest she should lose her balance and fall. A delicious stillness, which began in her brain and passed to her throbbing pulses, enveloped her like a perfume. While she stood there she was incapable of thought, except the one joyous thought that this was the moment for which she had waited since the hour of her birth. Never could she be the same afterwards! Never could she be unhappy again in the future! For, like other mortals in other ecstatic instants, she surrendered herself to the intoxicating illusion of their immortality.

After that silence, so charged with emotion for them both, it seemed that when he spoke it must be to utter words that would enkindle the world to beauty; but he said merely: "Is this dance free? I came only to speak to you."

His look added, "I came because my longing had grown unbearable"; and though she replied only to his words, it was his look that made the honeysuckle-trellis, the yellow lanterns, and the sky, with its few soft stars, go round like coloured balls before her eyes. The world melted away from her, and the distance between her and the whirling figures in white muslin seemed greater than the distance between star and star. She had the sense of spiritual remoteness, of shining isolation, which joy brings to the heart of youth, as if she had escaped from the control of ordinary phenomena and stood in a blissful pause beyond time and eternity. It was the supreme moment of love; and to her, whose soul acknowledged no other supremacy, it was also the supreme moment of life.

His face, as he gazed down at her under the swinging leaves, seemed to her as different from all other faces as the exquisite violence in her heart was different from all other emotions she had ever known. She knew nothing more of him than that she could not be happy away from him. She needed no more infallible proof of his love than the look in his eyes when he smiled at her.

"I am glad you wore blue ribbons," he said suddenly.

Her lashes trembled and fell, but they could not hide the glow that shone in her eyes and the faint smile trembling like an edge of light on her lips.

"Will you come into the summer-house?" he asked when she did not speak, and she followed him under the hanging clusters of early roses to a bench in the dusk beside a little rustic table. Here, after a moment's silence, he spoke again recklessly, yet with a certain constraint of manner.

"I suppose I oughtn't to have come here to-night."

"Why not?" Their glances, bright as swords, crossed suddenly, and it seemed to her that the music grew louder. Had it been of any use, she would have prayed Life to dole the minutes out, one by one, like a miser. And all the time she was thinking: "This is the moment I've waited for ever since I was born. It has come. I am in the midst of it. How can I keep it for ever?"

"Well, I haven't any business thinking about anything but my work," he answered. "I've broken with my uncle, you know. I'm as poor as a church mouse and I'll never be better off until I get a play on the stage. For the next few years I've got to cut out everything but hard work."

"Yes." Her tongue was paralyzed; she couldn't say what she felt, and everything else seemed to her purposeless and ineffectual. She wondered passionately if he thought her a fool, for she could not look into his mind and discover how adorable he found her responses. The richness of her beauty combined with the poverty of her speech made an irresistible appeal to the strongest part of him, which was not his heart, but his imagination. He wondered what she would say if she were really to let herself go, and this wonder began gradually to enslave him.

"That's the reason I hadn't any business coming here," he added, "but the truth is I've wanted to see you again ever since that first afternoon. I got to wondering whether," he laughed in an embarrassed way, and added with an attempt at levity, "whether you would wear a red rose in your hair."

At his change of tone, she reached up suddenly, plucked the rose from her hair and flung it out on the grass. Her action, which belied her girlish beauty so strangely that only her mother would have recognized it as characteristic of the hidden force of the woman, held him for an instant speechless under her laughing eyes. Then turning away, he picked up the rose.

"I suppose you will never tell me why you did that?" he asked.

She shook her head. "I can't tell. I don't know. Something took me."

"Did you think I came just for the rose?"

"I didn't think."

"If I came for the rose, I ought to go. I wish I could. Do you suppose I'll be able to work again now that I've seen you? I've told myself for three days that if only I could see you again, I'd be able to stop thinking about you."

She was not looking at him; but in every line of her figure, in every quiver of her lashes, in every breath that she drew, he saw her response to his words. It was as if her whole palpitating loveliness had become the vehicle of an exquisite entreaty. Her soul seemed to him to possess the purity, not of snow, but of flame, and this flame, in whose light nothing evil could live, curved toward him as if blown by the wind. He felt suddenly that he was swept onward by some outside power which was stronger than his will. An enchantment had fallen over him, and at one and the same instant he longed to break the power of the spell and knew that life would cease to be worth living if he were ever to do so. He saw her eyes, like blue flowers in the soft dusk, and the mist of curls on her temples stirred gently in the scented breeze that blew over the garden. All the sweetness of the world was gathered into the little space that she filled. Every impulse of joy he had ever felt, —memories of autumn roads, of starlit mountains, of summer fields where bees drifted in golden clouds,—all these were packed like honey into that single minute of love. And with the awakening of passion, there came the exaltation, the sense of illimitable possibilities which passion brings to the young. Never before had he realized the power that was in him! Never until this instant had he seen his own soul in the making! He felt himself divided between an invincible brutality and an invincible tenderness. He would have fought with beasts for the sake of the gentle and passive creature beside him; yet he would have died rather than sully the look of angelic goodness with which she regarded him. To have her always gentle, always passive, never reaching out her hand, never descending to his level, but sitting for ever aloof and colourless, waiting eternally, patient, beautiful and unwearied, to crown the victory;—this was what the conquering male in him demanded.

"I ought to go," he said, so ineffectual was speech to convey the tumult within his brain. "I am keeping you from the others."

She had shrunk back into the dimness beyond the circle of lanterns, and he saw her face like a pale moon under the clustering rose-leaves. Her very breath seemed suspended, and there was a velvet softness in her look and in her timid gesture of protest. She was putting forth all her woman's power as innocently as the honeysuckle puts forth its fragrance. The white moths whirling in their brief passion over the lantern-flame were not more helpless before those inscrutable forces which we call Life. A strange stillness surrounded her—as though she were separated by a circle of bliss from the dancers beyond the rose-crowned walls of the summer-house—and into this stillness there passed, like an invisible current, the very essence of womanhood. The longing of all the dead women of her race flowed through her into the softness of the spring evening. Things were there which she could know only through her blood; all the mute patience, all the joy that is half fear, all the age-long dissatisfaction with the physical end of love; these were in that voiceless entreaty for happiness; and mingled with them, there were the inherited ideals of self-surrender, of service, pity, loyalty, and sacrifice.

"I wish I could help you," she said, and her voice thrilled with the craving to squander herself magnificently in his service.

"You are an angel, and I'm a selfish beast to bring you my troubles."

"I don't think you are selfish—of course you have to think of your work—a man's work means so much to him."

"It's wonderful of you to feel that," he replied; and, indeed, at the instant while he searched her eyes in the dusk, the words seemed to him to embody all the sympathetic understanding with which his imagination endowed her. How perfectly her face expressed the goodness and gentleness of her soul! What a companion she would make to a man! What a lover! What a wife! Always soft, exquisite, tender, womanly to the innermost fibre of her being, and confirmed in unselfishness as all womanly women are. How easy it would be to work if she were somewhere within call, ready to fly to him at a word! How glorious to go out into the world if he knew that she sat at home waiting; always waiting, with those eyes like wells of happiness, until he should return to her! A new meaning had entered swiftly into life. A feeling that was like a religious conversion had changed not only his spiritual vision, but the material aspect of nature. Whatever happened, he felt that he could never be the same man again.

"I shall see you soon?" he said, and the words fell like snow on the inner flame of his senses.

"Oh, soon!" she answered, bending a little toward him, while a sudden glory illumined her features. Her voice, which was vibrant as a harp, had captured the wistful magic of the spring, the softness of the winds, the sweetness of flowers, the mellow murmuring of the poplars.

She rose from the bench, moving softly as if she were under an enchantment which she feared to break by a gesture. An ecstasy as inarticulate as grief kept him silent, and it was into this silence that the voice of Abby floated, high, shrill, and dominant.

"Oh, Virginia, I've looked everywhere for you," she cried. "Mr. Carrington is simply dying to dance with you!"

She bounced, as only the solid actuality can bounce, into the dream, precipitating the unwelcome presence of Mr. Carrington—a young man with a golden beard and the manner of a commercial minor prophet—there also. A few minutes later, as Virginia drifted away in his arms to the music of the waltz, she saw, over the heads of the dancers, Oliver and Abby walking slowly in the direction of the gate. A feeling of unreality seized her, as though she were looking through an azure veil at the world. The dancers among whom she whirled, the anxious mothers sitting uneasily on chairs under the poplars, the flowering shrubs, the rose-crowned summer-house, the yellow lanterns with the clouds of white moths circling around them;—all these things had turned suddenly to shadows; and through a phantom garden, the one living figure moved beside an empty shape, which was Abby. Her feet had wings. She flew rather than danced in the arms of a shadow through the blue veil that enveloped her. Life burned within her like a flame in a porcelain vase, and this inner fire separated her, as genius separates its possessor, from the ordinary mortals among whom she moved.

Walking home with John Henry after the party was over, it seemed to her that she was lifted up and cradled in all the wonderful freshness of the spring. The sweet moist air fanned her face; the morning stars shone softly on her through the pearly mist; and the pale fingers of dawn were spread like a beneficent hand, above the eastern horizon. "To-morrow!" cried her heart, overflowing with joy; and something of this joy passed into the saddest hour of day and brightened it into radiance.

At the gate she parted from John Henry, and running eagerly along the path, opened the front door, which was unlocked, and burst into the dining-room, where her mother, wearied of her long watch, had fallen asleep beside the lamp, which was beginning to flicker.

"To-morrow!" still sang her heart, and the wild, sweet music of it filled the world. "To-morrow!"

CHAPTER IX

THE GREAT MAN MOVES

SEVERAL weeks later, at the close of a June afternoon, Cyrus Treadwell sat alone on the back porch of his house in Bolingbroke Street. He was smoking, and, between the measured whiffs of his pipe, he leaned over the railing and spat into a bed of miniature sunflowers which grew along the stone ledge of the area. For thirty years these flowers had sprung up valiantly every spring in that bleak strip of earth, and for thirty years Cyrus had spat among them while he smoked alone on the back porch on June afternoons.

While he sat there a great peace enfolded and possessed him. The street beyond the sagging wooden gate was still; the house behind him was still; the kitchen, in which appeared the ebony silhouette of a massive cook kneading dough, was still with the uncompromising stillness of the Sabbath. In the midst of this silence, his thoughts, which were usually as angular as lean birds on a bough, lost their sharpness of outline and melted into a vague and feathery mass. At the moment it was impossible to know of what he was thinking; but he was happy with the happiness that visits men of small parts and sterile imagination. By virtue of these limitations he had risen out of obscurity; for the spiritual law which decrees that to gain the world one must give up one's soul, was exemplified in him as in all his class. Success, the shibboleth of his kind, had controlled

his thoughts and even his impulses so completely for years
that he had come at last to resemble an animal less than he
resembled a machine; and Nature (who has a certain large
and careless manner of dispensing justice) had punished
him in the end by depriving him of the animal capacity for
pleasure. The present state of vacuous contentment was,
perhaps, as near the condition of enjoyment as he would
ever approach.

Half an hour before he had had an encounter with
Susan on the subject of her going to college, but even his
victory, which had been sharp and swift, was robbed of all
poignant satisfaction by his native inability to imagine
what his refusal must have meant to her. The girl had
stood straight and tall, with her commanding air, midway
between the railing and the weather-stained door of the
house.

"Father, I want to go to college," she had said quite
simply, for she was one who used words very much as
Cyrus used money, with a temperamental avoidance of
extravagance.

Her demand was a direct challenge to the male in
Cyrus, and though this creature was neither primitive nor
predatory, he was still active enough to defend himself
from the unprovoked assault of an offspring.

"Tut-tut," he responded. "If you want something to
occupy you, you'd better start about helping your mother
with her preserving."

"I put up seventy-five jars of strawberries."

"Well, the blackberries are coming along. I was always
partial to blackberries."

He sat there, bald, shrunken, yellow, as soulless as a
steam engine, and yet to Susan he represented a pitiless
manifestation of destiny; of those deaf, implacable forces
by which the lives of men and women are wrecked. He had

the power to ruin her life, and yet he would never see it because he had been born blind. That in his very blindness had lain his strength, was a fact which, naturally enough, escaped her for the moment. The one thought of which she was conscious was a fierce resentment against life because such men possessed such power over others.

"If you will lend me the money, I will pay it back to you as soon as I can take a position," she said, almost passionately.

Something that was like the ghost of a twinkle appeared in his eyes, and he let fall presently one of his rare pieces of humour.

"If you'd like a chance to repay me for your education," he said, "there's your schooling at Miss Priscilla's still owing, and I'll take it out in help about the housekeeping."

Then Susan went, because going in silence was the only way in which she could save the shreds of dignity which remained to her, and bending forward, with a contented chuckle, Cyrus spat benevolently down upon the miniature sunflowers.

In the half hour that followed he did not think of his daughter. From long discipline his mind had fallen out of the habit of thinking of people except in their relation to the single vital interest of his life, and this interest was not fatherhood. Susan was an incident—a less annoying incident, it is true, than Belinda—but still an incident. An inherent contempt for women, accentuated by his disillusioning marriage, made him address them always as if he were speaking from a platform. And, as is often the case with men of cold-blooded sensuality, women, from Belinda downward, had taken their revenge upon him.

The front door-bell jangled suddenly, and a little later he heard a springy step passing along the hall. Then the green lattice door of the porch opened, and the face of Mrs. Peachey, wearing the look of unnatural pleasantness that becomes fixed on the features of persons who spend their lives making the best of things, appeared in the spot where Susan had been half an hour before. She had trained her lips to smile so persistently that when, as now, she would have preferred to present a serious countenance to an observer, she found it impossible to relax the muscles of her mouth from their expression of perpetual cheerfulness. Cyrus, who had once remarked of her that he didn't believe she could keep a straight face at her own funeral, wondered, while he rose and offered her a chair, whether the periodical sprees of honest Tom were the cause or the result of the look of set felicity she wore. For an instant he was tempted to show his annoyance at the intrusion. Then, because she was a pretty woman and did not belong to him, he grew almost playful, with the playfulness of an uncertain tempered ram that is offered salt.

"It is not often that I am honoured by a visit from you," he said.

"The honour is mine, Mr. Treadwell," she replied, and she felt it. "I was on my way upstairs to see Belinda, and it just crossed my mind as I saw you sitting out here, that I'd better stop and speak to you about your nephew. I wonder Belinda doesn't plant a few rose-bushes along that back wall," she added.

"I'd pay you fifty dollars, ma'am, if you'd get Belinda to plant anything"—which was not delicately put, perhaps, but was, after all, spoken in the only language that Cyrus knew.

"I thought she was so fond of flowers. She used to be as a girl."

"Humph!" was Cyrus's rejoinder, and then: "Well,

what about my nephew, madam?" Clasping his bony hands over his knee, he leaned forward and waited, not without curiosity, for her answer. He did not admire Oliver; he even despised him; but when all was said, the boy had succeeded in riveting his attention. However poorly he might think of him, the fact remained that think of him he did. The young man was in the air as inescapably as if he were the measles.

"I'm worrying about him, Mr. Treadwell; I can't help myself. You know he boards with me."

"Yes'm, I know," replied Cyrus; for he had heard the fact from Miss Priscilla on his way home from church one Sunday.

"And he's not well. There's something the matter with him. He's so nervous and irritable that he's almost crazy. He doesn't eat a morsel, and I can hear him pacing up and down his room until daybreak. Once I got up and went upstairs to ask him if he was sick, but he said that he was perfectly well and was walking about for exercise. I am sure I don't know what it can be, but if it keeps up, he'll land in an asylum before the summer is over."

The look of satisfaction which her first words had brought to Cyrus's face deepened gradually as her story unfolded. "He's wanting money, I reckon," he commented, his imagination seizing upon the only medium in which it could work. As a philosopher may discern in all life different manifestations of the Deity, so he saw in all affliction only the wanting of money under varied aspects. Sorrows in which the lack of money did not bear a part always seemed to him to be unnecessary and generally self-inflicted by the sufferers. Of such people he would say impatiently that they took a morbid view of their troubles and were "nursing grief."

"I don't think it's that," said Mrs. Peachey. "He always

pays his bills promptly on the first day of the month, and I know that he gets checks from New York for the writing he does. I'm sometimes tempted to believe that he has fallen in love."

"Love? Pshaw!" said Cyrus, and dismissed the passion.

"But it goes hard with some people, and he's one of that kind," the little lady rejoined, with spirit, for in spite of her wholesome awe of Cyrus, she could not bear to hear the sentiment derided. "We aren't all as sensible as you are, Mr. Treadwell."

"Well, if he is in love, as you say, whom is he in love with?" demanded Cyrus.

"It's all guesswork," Mrs. Peachey answered. "He isn't paying attention to any girl that I know of—but, I suppose, if it's anybody, it must be Virginia Pendleton. All the young men are crazy about her."

She had been prepared for opposition; she had been prepared, being a lady, for anything, as she told Tom afterwards, short of an oath; but, to her amazement, the unexpected, which so rarely happened in the case of Cyrus, happened at that minute. Human nature, which she had treated almost as a science, proved suddenly that it was not even an art. One of those glaring inconsistencies that confute every theory and overturn all psychology was manifested before her.

"That's the daughter of old Gabriel, ain't it?" asked Cyrus, and his voice softened.

"Yes, she's Gabriel's daughter, and one of the sweetest girls that ever lived."

"Gabriel's a good man," said Cyrus. "I always liked Gabriel. We fought through the war together."

"A better man never lived, nor a better woman than Lucy. If she's got a fault on earth, it's that she's too unselfish."

"Well, if this girl takes after them, the young fool has shown more sense than I gave him credit for."

"I don't think he's a fool," Mrs. Peachey returned, reflecting how wonderfully she had "managed" the great man, "but, of course, he's queer. All writers are queer, aren't they?"

"He's kept it up longer than I thought, but I reckon he's about ready to give in," pursued Cyrus, ignoring her question as he did all excursions into the region of speculation. "If he'll start in to earn his living now, I'll let him have a job on the railroad out in Matoaca City. I meant to teach him a lesson, but I shouldn't like Henry's son to starve. I've nothing against Henry except that he was too soft. He was a good brother as brothers go, and I haven't forgotten it."

"Perhaps, if you'd talk to Oliver," Mrs. Peachey suggested. "I'm afraid I couldn't induce him to come to you, but——"

"Oh, I ain't proud—I don't need to be," Cyrus interrupted with a chuckle. "Only fools and the poor have any reason for pride. I'll look in upon him sometime along after supper, and see if he's come to his wits since I last talked to him."

"Then, I'm glad I came to you. Tom would be horrified almost to death if he knew of it; but I've always said that when an idea crosses my mind just like that," she snapped her thumb and forefinger, "there's something in it."

As she rose from her seat, she looked up at him with the coquetry which was so inalienable an attribute of her soul that, had the Deity assumed masculine shape before her, she would instinctively have used this weapon to soften the severity of His judgment. "It was so kind of you not to send me away, Mr. Treadwell," she said in honeyed accents.

"It is a pleasure to meet such a sensible woman," replied Cyrus, with awkward gallantry. Her flattery had warmed him pleasantly, and in the midst of the dried husks of his nature, he was aware suddenly that a single blade of living green still survived. He had ceased to feel old; he felt almost young again; and this rejuvenation had set in merely because a middle-aged woman, whom he had known since childhood, had shown an innocent pleasure in his society. Mrs. Peachey's traditional belief in the power of sex had proved its own justification.

When she had left him, Cyrus sat down again, and took up his pipe from the railing where he had placed it. "I'll go round and have some words with the young scamp," he thought. "There's no use waiting until after supper. I'll go round now while it is light."

Then, as if the softening impulse were a part of the Sabbath stillness, he leaned over the bed of sunflowers, and fixed his eyes on the pinkish tower of Saint James' Church, which he could see palely enkindled against the afterglow. A single white cloud floated like a dove in the west, and beneath it a rain of light fell on the shadowy roofs of the town. The air was so languorous that it was as if the day were being slowly smothered in honeysuckle. A vast melancholy, so vast that it seemed the effect less of a Southern summer than of a universal force residing in nature, was liberated, with the first cooling breath of the evening, from man and beast, from tree and shrub, from stock and stone. The very bricks, sun-baked and scarred, spoke of the weariness of heat, of the parching thirst of the interminable summers.

But to Cyrus the languor and the intense sweetness of

the air suggested only that the end of a hot day had come. "It's likely to be a drought," he was thinking while his upward gaze rested on the illuminated tower of the church. "A drought will go hard with the tobacco."

Having emptied his pipe, he was about to take down his straw hat from a nail on the wall, when the sound of the opening gate arrested him, and he waited with his eyes fixed on the winding brick walk, where the negro washer-woman appeared presently with a basket of clean clothes on her head. Beneath her burden he saw that there were some primitive attempts at Sunday adornment. She wore a green muslin dress, a little discoloured by perspiration, but with many compensating flounces; a bit of yellow ribbon floated from her throat; and in her hand she carried the festive hat which would decorate her head after the removal of the basket. Her figure, which had once been graceful, had grown heavy; and her face, of a light ginger-bread colour, with broad, not unpleasant features, wore a humble, inquiring look, the look of some trustful wild animal that man has tamed and only partly domesticated. Approaching the steps, she brought down the basket from her head, and came on, holding it with a deprecating swinging movement in front of her.

"Howdy, Marster," she said, as if uncertain whether to stop or to pass on into the doorway.

"Howdy, Mandy," Cyrus responded. "There's a hot spell coming, I reckon."

Lowering the basket to the floor of the porch, the woman drew a red bandanna handkerchief from her bosom and began slowly to wipe the drops of sweat from her face and neck. The acrid odour of her flesh reached Cyrus, but he made no movement to draw away from her.

"I'se been laid up wid er stitch in my side, Marster,

so I'se jes got dese yer close done dis mawnin'. Dar wan' noner de chillen at home ter tote um down yer, so I low I 'uz gwine ter drap by wid um on my way ter church."

As he did not reply, she hesitated an instant and over her features, which looked as if they had been flattened by a blow, there came an expression which was half scornful, half inviting, yet so little personal that it might have been worn by one of her treetop ancestors while he looked down from his sheltering boughs on a superior species of the jungle. The chance effect of light and shadow on a gray rock was scarcely less human or more primitive.

"I'se gittin' moughty well along, Marster," she said; "I reckon I'se gittin' on toward a hunnard."

"Nonsense, Mandy, you ain't a day over thirty-five. There's a plenty of life left in you yet."

"Go way f'om yer, Marster; you knows I'se a heap older 'n dat. How long ago was hit I done fust come yer ter you all?"

He thought a moment. A question of calculation always interested him, and he prided himself on his fine memory for dates.

"You came the year our son Henry died, didn't you? That was in '66—eighteen years ago. Why, you couldn't have been over fifteen that summer."

For the first time a look of cunning, of the pathetic cunning of a child pitted against a man, awoke in her face.

"En Miss Lindy sent me off befo' de year was up, Marster. My boy Jubal was born de mont' atter she done tu'n me out." She hesitated a minute, and then added, with a kind of savage coquetry, "I 'uz a moughty likely gal, Marster. You ain't done furgit dat, is you?"

Her words touched Cyrus like the flick of a whip on a sore, and he drew back quickly while his thin lips grew tight.

"You'd better take that basket into the house," he said sharply.

In the negress's face an expression of surprise wavered for a second and then disappeared. Her features resumed their usual passive and humble look; a look which said, if Cyrus could have read human nature as easily as he read finance, "I don't understand, but I submit without understanding. Am I not what you have made me? Have I not been what you wanted? And yet you despise me for being the thing you made."

"I didn't mean nuttin', Marster. I didn't mean nuttin'," she protested aloud.

"Then get into the house," Cyrus retorted harshly, "and don't stand gaping there. Any more of your insolence and I'll never let you set foot in this yard again."

"'Fo' de Lawd, I didn't mean nuttin'! Gawd a' moughty, I didn't mean nuttin'! I jes lowed as you mought be willin' ter gun me fo' dollars a mont' fur de washin'. My boy Jubal——"

"I'll not give you a red cent more. If you don't want it, you can leave it. Get out of here!"

All the primitive hostility of race, that instinct older than civilization, was in the voice with which he ordered her out of his sight. "It was downright blackmail. The fool was trying to blackmail me," he thought. "If I'd yielded an inch I'd have been at her mercy. It's a pretty pass things have come to when men have to protect themselves from negro women." The more he reflected on her impudence, the stronger grew his conviction that he had acted remarkably well. "Nipped it in the root. If I hadn't——" he thought.

And behind him in the doorway the washerwoman continued to regard him, over the lowered clothes basket, with her humble and deprecating look, which said, like the look of a beaten animal: "I don't understand, but I submit without understanding because you are stronger than I."

Taking down his hat, Cyrus turned away from her, and descended the steps. "I'll look up Henry's son before supper," he was thinking. "Even if the boy's a fool, I'm not one to let those of my own blood come to want."

CHAPTER X

OLIVER SURRENDERS

WHEN Cyrus's knock came at his door, Oliver crossed the room to let in his visitor, and then fell ba k, startled, at the sight of his uncle. "I wonder what has brought him here?" he thought inhospitably. But even if he had put the question, it is doubtful if Cyrus could have enlightened him; for the great man was so seldom visited by an impulse that when one actually took possession of him, he obeyed the pressure almost unconsciously. Like most men who pride themselves upon acting solely from reason, he was the abject slave of the few instincts which had managed to take root and thrive in the stony ground of his nature. The feeling for family, which was so closely entwined with his supreme feeling for property that the two had become inseparable, moved him to-day as it had done on the historic occasion when he had redeemed the mortgaged roof over the heads of his spinster relations. Perhaps, too, some of the vague softness of June had risen in him and made him gentler in his judgments of youth.

"I didn't expect you or I'd have straightened up a bit," Oliver said, not overgraciously, while he hastily pushed his supper of bread and tea to one end of the table. He resented what he called in his mind "the intrusion," and he had no particular objection to his uncle's observing his resentment. His temper, never of the most perfect equi-

librium, had been entirely upset by a June Sunday in Dinwiddie, and the affront of Cyrus's visit had become an indignity because of his unfortunate selection of the supper
hour. Some hidden obliquity in the Treadwell soul, which
kept it always at cross-purposes with life, prevented any
lessening of the deep antagonism between the old and the
young of the race. And so incurable was this obliquity in
the soul of Cyrus, that it forced him now to take a tone
which he had resolutely set his mind against from the moment of Mrs. Peachey's visit. He wanted to be pleasant,
but something deep down within him, some inherited tendency to bully, was stronger than his will.

"I looked in to see if you hadn't about come to your
senses," he began.

"If you mean come to your way of looking at things—
then I haven't," Oliver replied, and added in a more cour-
teous tone, "Won't you sit down?"

"No, sir, I can stand long enough to say what I came
to say," the other retorted, and it seemed to him that the
pleasanter he tried to make his voice, the harsher grew the
sound of it in his ears. What was it about the rascal that
rubbed him the wrong way only to look at him?

"As you please," Oliver replied quietly. "What in
thunder has he got to say to me?" he thought. "And why
can't he say it and have it over?" While Cyrus merely
despised him, he detested Cyrus with all the fiery intolerance of his age. "Standing there like an old turkey gob-
bler, ugh!" he said contemptuously to himself.

"So you ain't hungry yet?" the old man asked, and felt
that the words were forced out of him by that obstinate
cross-grain in his nature over which he had no control.

"I've just had tea."

"You haven't changed your mind since you last spoke
to me, eh?"

"No, I haven't changed my mind. Why should I?"

"Getting along pretty well, then?"

"As well as I expected to."

"That's good," Cyrus said mildly. "That's good. I just dropped in to make sure that you were getting along, that's all."

"Thank you," Oliver responded, and tried from the bottom of his soul to make the words sincere.

"If the time ever comes when you feel that you have changed your mind, I'll find a place out at Matoaca City for you. I just wanted you to understand that I'd do as much for Henry's son then as now. If you weren't Henry's son, I shouldn't think twice about you."

"You mean that you'll still give me the job if I stop writing plays?"

"Oh, I won't make a point of that as long as it doesn't interfere with your work. You may write in off hours as much as you want to. I won't make a point of that."

"You mean to be generous, I can see—but I don't think it likely that I shall ever make up my mind to take a regular job. I'm not built for it."

"You're not thinking about getting married, then, I reckon?"

A dark flush rose to Oliver's forehead, and turning away, he stared with unseeing eyes out of the window.

"No, I haven't any intention of that," he responded.

A certain craftiness appeared in Cyrus's face.

"Well, well, you're young yet, and you may be in want of a wife before you're many years older."

"I'm not the kind to marry. I'm too fond of my freedom."

"Most of us have felt like that at one time or another, but when the thought of a woman takes you by the throat, you'll begin to see things differently. And if you ever do, a good steady job at twelve hundred a year will be what you'll look out for."

"I suppose a man could marry on that down here," Oliver said, unaware that he was speaking aloud.

"I married on less, and I've known plenty of others that have done so. A good saving wife puts more into a man's pocket than she takes out of it."

As he paused, Oliver's attention, which had wandered off into a vague mist of feeling, became suddenly arrested by the appalling spectacle of his uncle's marriage. He saw the house in Bolingbroke Street, with the worn drab oil-cloth in the hall, and he smelled the odour of stale cooking that floated through the green lattice door at the back. All the sweetness of life, all the beauty, all the decency even, seemed strangled in that smell as in some malarial air. And in the midst of it, the unkempt, slack figure of Belinda, with her bitter eyes and her sagging skirt, passed perpetually, under the flickering gas-jet, up and down the dimly lighted staircase. This was how one marriage had ended; one marriage among many that had started out with passion and courage and the belief in happiness. Knowing but little of the April brevity of his uncle's mating impulse, he had embroidered the bare instinct with some of the idealism in which his own emotion was clothed. His imagination pictured Cyrus and Belinda starting as light-hearted adventurers to sail the chartless seas of romance. What remained of their gallant ship to-day except a stark and battered hulk wrecked on the pitiless rocks of the actuality? A month before that marriage had seemed merely ridiculous to him. Standing now beside the little window, where the wan face of evening, languid and sweet, looked in from the purple twilight, he was visited by one of those rare flashes of

insight which come to men of artistic sensibility after long
periods of spiritual warfare. Pity stabbed him as sharply
as ridicule had done a moment before, and with the first
sense of human kinship he had ever felt to Cyrus, he
understood suddenly the tragedy that underlies all comic
things. Could there be a deeper pathos, after all, than
simply being funny? This absurd old man, with his lean,
crooked figure, his mottled skin, and his bloodshot eyes,
like the eyes of an overgorged bird of prey, appeared now
as an object that moved one more to tears than laughter.
And yet because of this very quality that made him pitiable, this vulture-like instinct to seize and devour the
smaller, he stood to-day the most conspicuously envied
figure in Dinwiddie.

"I'm not the kind of man to marry," he repeated, but
his tone had changed.

"Well, perhaps you're wise," Cyrus said, "but if you
should ever wish to——" The confidence that had gone
out of Oliver had passed into him. With his strange power
of reading human nature—masculine human nature, for
the silliest woman could fool him hopelessly—he saw that
his nephew was already beginning to struggle against the
temptation to yield. And he was wise enough to know
that this temptation would become stronger as soon as
Oliver felt that the outside pressure was removed. The
young man's passion was putting forward a subtler argument than Cyrus could offer.

When his visitor had gone, Oliver turned back to the
window, and resting his arms on the sill, leaned out into
the velvet softness of the twilight. His wide vision had
deserted him. It was as if his gaze had narrowed down
to a few roofs and the single street without a turning;
but beyond them the thought of Virginia lay always like

an enclosed garden of sweetness and bloom. To think of her was to pass from the scorching heat of the day to the freshness of dew-washed flowers under the starlight.

"It is impossible," he said aloud, and immediately, as if in answer to a challenge, a thousand proofs came to him that other men were doing the impossible every day. How many writers—great writers, too—would have jumped at a job on a railway to insure them against starvation? How many had married young and faced the future on less than twelve hundred dollars a year? How many had let love lead them where it would without butting their heads for ever against the wall of expediency?

"It's impossible," he said again, and turning from the window, made himself ready to go out. While he brushed his hair and pulled the end of his necktie through the loop, his gaze wandered back over the roofs to where a solitary mimosa tree drooped against the lemon-coloured afterglow. The dust lay like gauze over the distance. Not a breath stirred. Not a leaf fell. Not a figure moved in the town, except the crouching figure of a stray cat that crawled, in search of food, along the brick wall under the dead tree.

"God! What a life!" he cried suddenly. And beyond this parching desert of the present he saw again that enclosed garden of sweetness and bloom, which was Virginia. His resolution, weakened by the long hot afternoon, seemed to faint under the pressure of his longing. All the burden of the day; the heat, the languor, the scorching thirst of the fields, the brazen blue of the sky, the stillness as of a suspended breath that wrapt the town;—all these things had passed into the intolerableness of his desire. He felt it like a hot wind blowing over him; and it seemed to him that he was as helpless as a leaf in the current of this wind which was sweeping him onward. Something older than his will was driving him; and this something had come to him from the twilight, where the mimosa trees drooped like a veil against the afterglow.

Taking up his hat, he left the room and descended the stairs to the wide hall where Tom Peachey sat, gasping for breath, midway of two open doors.

"I'll be darned if I can make a draught," muttered the old soldier irascibly, while he picked up his alpaca coat from the balustrade, and slipped into it before going out upon the front porch into the possible presence of ladies. His usually cheerful face was clouded, for his habitual apathy had deserted him, and he had reached the painful decision that when you looked things squarely in the face there was precious little that was worth living for; a conclusion to which he had been brought by the simple accident of an overdose of Kentucky rye in his mint julep after church. The overdose had sent him to sleep too soon after his Sunday dinner, and when he had awakened from his heavy and by no means quiet slumber, he had found himself confronting a world of gloom.

"I'm damned tired making the best of things, if you want to know what is the matter with me," he had remarked crossly to his wife.

"The idea, Mr. Peachey! You ought to be ashamed of yourself!" that sprightly lady had responded while she prepared herself for her victory over Cyrus.

"Well, I ain't," honest Tom had retorted. "I've gone on pretending for fifty years and I'm going to stop it. What good has it done, anyway? It hasn't put a roof on, has it?"

"I told you you oughtn't to go to sleep right on top of your dinner," she had replied soothingly. "I declare, you're perfectly purple. I never saw you so upset. Here, take this palm-leaf fan and go and see if you can't find a draught.

You know it's downright sinful to talk that way after the Lord has been so good to you."

But Philosophy, though she is unassailable when she clings to her safeguard of the universal, meets her match whenever she descends to an open engagement with the particular.

"W-what's He done for me?" honest Tom demanded.

Driven against that bleak rock of fact upon which so many shining generalizations have come to wreck, Mrs. Peachey had cast about helplessly for some floating spar of logic which might bear her to the firm ground of established optimism. "I declare, Tom, I believe you are out of your head!" she exclaimed, adding immediately, "You ought to be ashamed of yourself to be so ungrateful when the good Lord has kept you out of the poorhouse. If you weren't tipsy, I'd give you a hard shaking. Now, you take that palm-leaf fan and go right straight downstairs."

So Tom had gone, for his wife, who lacked the gift of argument, possessed the energy of character which renders such minor attributes unnecessary; and Oliver, passing through the hall a couple of hours later, found him still helplessly seeking the draught toward which she had directed him.

"Any chance of a breeze springing up?" inquired the young man, as they moved together to the porch.

The force which was driving him out of the house into the suffocating streets was in his voice when he spoke, but honest Tom did not hear it. After the four war years in which he had been almost sublime, the old soldier had gradually ceased even to be human, and that vegetable calm which envelops persons who have fallen into the habit of sitting still, had endowed him at last with the perfect serenity of a cabbage. The only active principle which ever moved in him was the borrowed principle of alcohol; for when that artificial energy subsided, he sank back, as he was beginning to do now, into the spiritual inertia which sustains those who have outlived their capacity for the heroic.

"I ain't felt a breath," he replied, peering southward where the stars were coming out in a cloudless sky. "I don't reckon we'll get it till on about eleven."

"Looks as if we were in for a scorching summer, doesn't it?"

"You never can tell. There's always a spell in June." And he who had been a hero sat down in his cane-bottomed chair and waved the palm-leaf fan feebly in front of him. He had had his day; he had fought his fight; he had helped to make the history of battles—and now what remained to him? The stainless memory of the four years when he was a hero; a smouldering ember still left from that flaming glory which was his soul!

In the street the dust lay thick and still, and the wilted foliage of the mulberry trees hung motionless from the great arching boughs. Only an aspen at the corner seemed alive and tremulous, while sensitive little shivers ran through the silvery leaves, which looked as if they were cut out of velvet. As Oliver left the house, the town awoke slowly from its lethargy, and the sound of laughter floated to him from the porches behind their screens of honeysuckle or roses. But even this laughter seemed to him to contain the burden of weariness that oppressed and disenchanted his spirit. The pall of melancholy spread from the winding yellow river at the foot of the hill to the procession of cedars which stood pitch-black against the few dim stars on the eastern horizon.

"What is the use?" he asked himself suddenly, uttering aloud that grim question which lies always beneath the vivid, richly clustering impressions in the imaginative

mind. Of his struggle, his sacrifice—of his art even—
what was the use? A bitter despondency, the crushing despondency of youth which age does not feel and has forgotten, weighed upon him like a physical burden. And
because he was young and not without a certain pride in
the intensity of his suffering, he increased his misery by
doggedly refusing to trace it back to its natural origin
in an empty stomach.

But the laws that govern the variable mind of man are
as inscrutable as the secret of light. Turning into a cross
street, he came upon the tower of Saint James' Church,
and grew suddenly cheerful. The quickening of his pulses
changed the aspect of the town as completely as if an
invigorating shower had fallen upon it. The supreme,
haunting interest of life revived.

He had meant merely to pass the rectory without stopping; but as he turned into the slanting street at the foot
of the twelve stone steps, he saw a glimmer of white on
the terrace, and the face of Virginia looked down at him
over the palings of the gate. Immediately it seemed to
him that he had known from the beginning that he should
meet her. A sense of recognition so piercingly sweet that
it stirred his pulses like wine was in his heart as he moved
toward her. The whole universe appeared to him to have
been planned and perfected for this instant. The languorous June evening, the fainting sweetness of flowers, the
strange lemon-coloured afterglow, and her face, shining
there like a star in the twilight; these had waited for him,
he felt, since the beginning of earth. That fatalistic reliance upon an outside Power, which assumed for him
the radiant guise of first love, and for Susan the stark
certainties of Presbyterianism, dominated him as completely as if he were the predestined vehicle of its expression. Ardent yet passive, Virginia leaned above him

on the dim terrace. So still she seemed that her breath left her parted lips as softly as the perfume detached itself from the opening rose-leaves. She made no gesture, she said no word; but suddenly he became aware that her stillness was stronger to draw him than any speech. All her woman's mystery was brooding there about her in the June twilight; and in this strange strength of quietness Nature had placed, for once, an invincible weapon in the weaker hands. Her appeal had become a part of the terrible and beneficent powers of Life.

Crossing the street, he went up the steps to where she leaned on the gate.

"It has been so long," he said, and the words seemed to him hideously empty. "I have not seen you but three times since the party."

She did not answer, and as he looked at her closer, he saw that her eyes were full of tears.

"Virginia!" he cried out sharply, and the next instant, at her first movement away from him, his arms were round her and his lips seeking hers.

The world stopped suddenly while a starry eternity enveloped them. All youth was packed into that minute, all the troubled sweetness of desire, all the fugitive ecstasy of fulfilment.

"I—I thought you did not care," she murmured beneath his kisses.

He could not speak; for it was a part of his ironic destiny that he, who was prodigal of words, should find himself stricken dumb in any crucial instant.

"You know—you know——" he stammered, holding her closer.

"Then it—it is not all a dream?" she asked.

"I adored you from the first minute—you saw that—

you knew it. I've wanted you day and night since I first looked at you."

"But you kept away. I couldn't understand."

"It was because I knew I couldn't be with you five minutes without kissing you. And I oughtn't to—it's madness in me—for I'm desperately poor, darling; I've no right to marry you."

A little smile shone on her lips. "As if I cared about that, Oliver."

"Then you'll marry me? You'll marry me, my beautiful?"

She lifted her face from his breast, and her look was like the enkindled glory of the sunrise. "Don't you see? Haven't you seen from the beginning?" she asked.

"I was afraid to see, darling—but, Virginia—oh, Virginia, let it be soon!"

While he went from her a little later, it seemed to him that all of life had been pressed down into the minute when he had held her against his breast; and as he walked through the dimly lighted streets, among the shadows of men who, like himself, were pursuing some shadowy joy, he carried with him that strange vision of a heaven on earth which has haunted mortal eyes since the beginning of love. Happiness appeared to him as a condition which he had achieved by a few words, by a kiss, in a minute of time, but which belonged to him so entirely now that he could never be defrauded of it again in the future. Whatever happened to him, he could never be separated from the bliss of that instant when he had held her.

He was going to Cyrus while his ecstasy ennobled even the prosaic fact of the railway. And just as on that other evening, when he had rushed in anger from the house of his uncle, so now he was exalted by the consciousness that he was following the lead of the more spiritual part of his nature; for the line of least resistance was so overgrown with exquisite impressions that he no longer recognized it. The sacrifice of art for love appeared to him to-day as splendidly romantic as the sacrifice of comfort for art had seemed to him a few months before. His desire controlled him so absolutely that he obeyed its different promptings under the belief that he was obeying the powers whose names he borrowed.

On the front steps, between the two pink oleanders, Cyrus was standing with his gaze fixed on a small grocery store across the street, and at the sight of his nephew a look of curiosity, which was as personal an emotion as he was in the habit of feeling, appeared on his lean yellow face. Behind him, the door into the hall stood open, and his stooping figure was outlined against the light of the gas-jet by the staircase.

"You see I've come," said Oliver; for Cyrus, who never spoke first unless he was sure of dominating the situation, had waited for him to begin.

"Yes, I see," the old man replied, not unkindly. "I expected you, but hardly so soon—hardly so soon."

"It's about the place on the railway. If you are still of the same mind, I'd like you to give me a trial."

"When would you want to start?"

"The sooner the better. I'd rather get settled there before the autumn. I'm going to be married sometime in the autumn—October, perhaps."

"Ah!" said Cyrus softly, and Oliver was grateful to him because he didn't attempt to crow.

"We haven't told any one yet; but I wanted to make sure of the job. It's all right, then, isn't it?"

"Oh, yes, it's all right, if you do your part. She's Gabriel Pendleton's girl, isn't she?"

"She's Virginia Pendleton. You know her, of course."

He tried honestly to be natural, but in spite of himself
he could not keep a note of constraint out of his voice.
Merely to discuss Virginia with Cyrus seemed, in some
subtle way, an affront to her. Yet he knew that the old
man wanted to be kind, and the knowledge touched him.

"Oh, yes, I know her. She's a good girl, and there
doesn't live a better man than Gabriel."

"I don't deserve her, of course. But, then, there never
lived a man who deserved an angel."

"Ain't you coming in?" Cyrus asked.

"Not this evening. I only wanted to speak to you. I
suppose I'd better go down to the office to-morrow and
talk to Mr. Burden, hadn't I?"

"Come about noon, and I'll tell him to expect you.
Well, if you ain't coming in, I reckon I'll close this door."

Looking up a minute later from the pavement, Oliver
saw his aunt rocking slowly back and forth at the window
of her room, and the remembrance of her fell like a blight
over his happiness.

By the time he reached High Street a wind had risen
beyond the hill near the river, and the scattered papers
on the pavement fled like gray wings before him into the
darkness. As the air freshened, faces appeared in the doors
along the way, and the whole town seemed to be drinking
in the cooling breeze as if it were water. On the wind
sped, blowing over the listless figure of Mrs. Treadwell;
blowing over the conquering smile of Susan, who was un-
binding her long hair; blowing over the joy-brightened
eyes of Virginia, who dreamed in the starlight of the life
that would come to her; blowing over the ghost-haunted
face of her mother, who dreamed of the life that had gone
by her; blowing at last, beyond the river, over the tired
hands of the little seamstress, who dreamed of nothing
more than the way to keep her living body out of the poor-

house and her dead body out of the potter's field. And over the town, with its twenty-one thousand souls, each of whom contained within itself a separate universe of joy and tragedy, of hope and disappointment, the wind passed as lightly it passed over the unquiet dust in the streets below.

Book Second
THE REALITY

CHAPTER I

VIRGINIA PREPARES FOR THE FUTURE

"MOTHER, I'm so happy! Oh, was there ever a girl so happy as I am?"

"I was, dear, once."

"When you married father? Yes, I know," said Virginia; but she said it without conviction. In her heart she did not believe that marrying her father—perfect old darling that he was!—could ever have caused any girl just the particular kind of ecstasy she was feeling. She even doubted whether such stainless happiness had ever before visited a mortal upon this planet. It was not only wonderful, it was not only perfect, but it felt so absolutely new that she secretly cherished the belief that it had been invented by the universe especially for Oliver and herself. It was ridiculous to imagine that the many million pairs of lovers that were marrying every instant had each experienced a miracle like this, and yet left the earth pretty much as if they had found it before they fell in love.

It was a week before her wedding, and she stood in the centre of the spare room in the west wing, which had been turned over to Miss Willy Whitlow. The little seamstress knelt now at her feet, pinning up the hem of a black silk polonaise, and turning her head from time to time to ask Mrs. Pendleton if she was "getting the proper length." For a quarter of a century, no girl of Virginia's class had married in Dinwiddie without the crowning benediction of a black silk gown, and ever since the announcement of Virginia's betrothal her mother had cramped her small economies in order that she might buy "grosgrain" of the best quality.

"Is that right, mother? Do you think I might curve it a little more in front?" asked the girl, holding her feet still with difficulty because she felt that she wanted to dance.

"No, dear, I think it will stay in fashion longer if you don't shorten it. Then it will be easier to make over the more goods you leave in it."

"It looks nice on me, doesn't it?" Standing there, with the stiff silk slipping away from her thin shoulders, and the dappled sunlight falling over her neck and arms through the tawny leaves of the paulownia tree in the garden, she was like a slim white lily unfolding softly out of its sheath.

"Lovely, darling, and it will be so useful. I got the very best quality, and it ought to wear for ever."

"I made Mrs. William Goode one ten years ago, and she's still wearing it," Miss Willy remarked, speaking with an effort through a mouthful of pins.

A machine, which had been whirring briskly by the side window, stopped suddenly, and the girl who sewed there (a sickly, sallow-faced creature of Virginia's age, who was hired by Mrs. Pendleton, partly out of charity because she supported an invalid father who had been crippled in the war, and partly because, having little strength and being an unskilled worker, her price was cheap) turned for an instant and stared wistfully at the black silk polonaise. All her life she had wanted a black silk dress, and though she knew that she should probably never have one, and should not have time to wear it if she ever had, she liked to linger over the thought of it, very much as Virginia lingered over the thought of her lover, or as little Miss Willy lingered over the thought of having a tombstone over her after she was dead. In the girl's face, where at first there had been only admiration, a change came gradually. A quiver, so faint that it was barely more than a shadow, passed over her drawn features, and her gaze left the trailing yards of silk and wandered to the blue October sky over the swinging leaves of the paulownia. But instead of the radiant autumn weather at which she was looking, she still saw that black silk polonaise which she wanted as she wanted youth and pleasure, and which she knew that she should never have.

"Everything is finished but this, isn't it, Miss Willy?" asked Virginia, and at the sound of her happy voice, that strange quiver passed again through the other girl's face.

"Everything except that organdie and a couple of nightgowns." There was no quiver in Miss Willy's face; for from constant consideration of the poorhouse and the cemetery, she had come to regard the other problems of life, if not with indifference, at least with something approaching a mild contempt. Even love, when measured by poverty or death, seemed to dwindle in magnitude.

"And I'll have enough clothes to last me for years, shan't I, mother?"

"I hope so, darling. Your father and I have done the best that we could for you."

"You've been angels. Oh, how I shall hate to leave you!"

"If only you weren't going away, Virginia!" Then she broke down, and dropping the tomato-shaped pincushion she had been holding, she slipped from the room, while

Virginia thrust the polonaise into Miss Willy's hands and fled breathlessly after her.

In the girl's room, with her head bowed on the top of the little bookcase, above those thin rows of fiction, Mrs. Pendleton was weeping almost wildly over the coming separation. She, who had not thought of herself for thirty years, had suddenly broken the constraint of the long habit. Yet it was characteristic of her, that even now her first feeling, when Virginia found her, should be one of shame that she had clouded for an instant the girl's happiness.

"It is nothing, darling. I have a little headache, and— oh, Virginia! Virginia!——"

"Mother, it won't be long. We are coming back to live just as soon as Oliver can get work. It isn't as if I were going for good, is it? And I'll write you every day— every single day. Mother, dearest, darling mother, I can't stay away from you——"

Then Virginia wept too, and Mrs. Pendleton, forgetting her own sorrow at sight of the girl's tears, began to comfort her.

"Of course, you'll write and tell me everything. It will be almost as if I were with you."

"And you love Oliver, don't you, mother?"

"How could I help it, dear—only I can't quite get used to your calling your husband by his name, Virginia. It would have horrified your grandmother, and somehow it does seem lacking in respect. However, I suppose I'm old-fashioned."

"But, mother, he laughs if I call him 'Mr. Treadwell.' He says it reminds him of his Aunt Belinda."

"Perhaps he's right, darling. Anyway, he prefers it, and I fancy your grandfather wouldn't have liked to hear

his wife address him so familiarly. Times have changed
since my girlhood."

"And Oliver has lived out in the world so much,
mother."

"Yes," Mrs. Pendleton assented, but her voice was without enthusiasm. The "world" to her was a vague and sinister shape, which resembled a bubble, and exerted a malig-
nant influence over those persons who lived beyond the
borders of Virginia. Her imagination, which seldom wandered farther afield than the possibility of the rector or of
Virginia falling ill, or the dreaded likelihood that her
market bills would overrun her weekly allowance, was
incapable of grasping a set of standards other than the
one which was accepted in Dinwiddie.

"Wherever you are, Virginia, I hope that you will never
forget the ideas your father and I have tried to implant
in you," she said.

"I'll always try to be worthy of you, mother."

"Your first duty now, of course, is to your husband.
Remember, we have always taught you that a woman's
strength lies in her gentleness. His will must be yours
now, and wherever your ideas cross, it is your duty to give
up, darling. It is the woman's part to sacrifice herself."

"I know, mother, I know."

"I have never forgotten this, dear, and my marriage has
been very happy. Of course," she added, while her forehead wrinkled nervously, "there are not many men like
your father."

"Of course not, mother, but Oliver——"

In Mrs. Pendleton's soft, anxious eyes the shadow
darkened, as if for the first time she had grown suspicious
of the wisdom she was imparting. But this suspicion was so
new and young that it could not struggle against her inher-

ited belief in the Pauline measure of her sex. It was characteristic of her, and indeed of most women of her generation, that she would have endured martyrdom in support of the consecrated doctrine of her inferiority to man.

"Even in the matter of religion you ought to yield to him, darling," she said, after a moment in which she had appealed to that orthodox arbiter, her conscience. "Your father and I were talking about what church you should go to, and I said that I supposed Oliver was a Presbyterian, like all the Treadwells."

"Oh, mother, I didn't tell you before because I hoped I could change him; but he doesn't go to any church. He says they all bore him equally. He has broken away from all the old ideas, you know. He is dreadfully—unsettled."

The anxiety, which had been until then merely a shadow in Mrs. Pendleton's eyes, deepened into a positive pain.

"Your father must have known, for he talked to him—but he wouldn't tell me," she said.

"I made father promise not to. I hoped so I could change Oliver, and maybe I can after we're married, mother."

"If he has given up the old spiritual standards, what has he in place of them?" asked Mrs. Pendleton, and she had suddenly a queer feeling as if fine needles were pricking her skin.

"I don't know, but he seems to have a great deal, more than any of us," answered Virginia, and she added passionately, "He is good, mother."

"I never doubted it, darling, but he is young, and his character cannot be entirely formed at his age. A man must be very strong in order to be good without faith."

"But he has faith, mother—of some kind."

"I am not judging him, my child, and neither your father nor I would ever criticize your husband to you.

Your happiness was set on him, and we can only pray
from our hearts that he will prove worthy of your love.
He is very lovable, and I am sure that he has fine, generous traits. Your father has been completely won over
by him."

"He likes me to be religious, mother. He says the church
has cultivated the loveliest type of woman the world has
ever seen."

"Then by fulfilling that ideal you will please him best."

"I shall try to be just what you have been to father—
just as unselfish, just as devoted."

"I have made many mistakes, Virginia, but I don't think
I have ever failed in love—not in love, at least."

Then the pain passed out of her eyes, and because it
was impossible for her to look on any fact in life except
through the evasive idealism with which the ages had endowed her, she became immediately convinced that everything, even the unsettling of Oliver's opinions, had been
arranged for the best. This assurance was the more solac-
ing because it was the result, not of external evidence, but
of that instinctive decision of temperament which breeds
the deepest conviction of all.

"Love is the only thing that really matters, isn't it,
mother?"

"A pure and noble love, darling. It is a woman's life.
God meant it so."

"You are so good! If I can only be half as good as you
are."

"No, Virginia, I'm not really good. I have had many
temptations—for I was born with a high temper, and it
has taken me a lifetime to learn to subdue it. I had—I
have still an unfortunate pride. But for your father's daily
example of humility and patience, I don't know how I
could have supported the trials and afflictions we have

known. Pray to be better than your mother, my child, if you want to become a perfect wife. What I am that seems good to you, your father has made me———"

"And father says that he would have been a savage but for you."

A tremor passed through Mrs. Pendleton's thin bosom, and bending over, she smoothed a fine darn in the skirt of her alpaca dress.

"We have loved each other," she answered. "If you and Oliver love as much, you will be happy whatever comes to you." Then choking down the hard lump in her throat, she took up her leather key-basket from the little table beside the bed, and moved slowly toward the door. "I must see about supper now, dear," she said in her usual voice of quiet cheerfulness.

Left to herself, Virginia opened the worn copy of the prayer-book she kept at her bedside, and read the marriage service from beginning to end, as she had done every day since her engagement to Oliver. The words seemed to her, as they seemed to her mother, to be almost divine in their nobility and beauty. She was troubled by no doubt as to the inspired wisdom of the canonical estimate of woman. What could be more beautiful or more sacred than to be "given" to Oliver—to belong to him as utterly as she had belonged to her father? What could make her happier than the knowledge that she must surrender her will to his from the day of her wedding until the day of her death? She embraced her circumscribed lot with a passion that glorified its limitations. The single gift the ages permitted her was the only one she desired. Her soul craved no adventure beyond the permissible adventure of being sought in marriage. Love was all that she asked of a universe that was overflowing with manifold aspects of life.

Beyond the window the tawny leaves of the paulownia were swinging in the October sunshine, and so gay they seemed that it was impossible to imagine them insensible to the splendour of the Indian Summer. Under the half-bared boughs, on the green grass in the garden, the leaves that had already fallen sped on, like a flock of frightened brown birds, toward the white paling fence of the church-yard.

While she sat there, with her prayer-book in her hand, and her eyes on the purple veil of the distance, it seemed to her that her joy was complete and there was nothing left even to hope for. All her life she had looked forward to the coming of what she thought of vaguely as "happiness," and now that it was here, she felt that it put an end to the tremulous expectancy which had filled her girlhood with wistful dreams. Marriage appeared to her (and indeed to Oliver, also) as a miraculous event, which would make not only herself but every aspect of life different. After that, there would be no vain longings, no spring restlessness, no hours of drab weariness, when the interests of living seemed to crumble from mere despondency. After that, they would be always happy, always eager, always buoyantly alive.

Leaving the marriage service, her thoughts brooded in a radiant stillness on the life of love that would begin for her on the day of her wedding. A strange light, the light that quivered like a golden wing over the autumn fields, shone also into the secret chambers of her soul, and illumined the things that had appeared merely dull and commonplace until to-day. Those innumerable little cares which fill the lives of most women were steeped in the magic glow of enchantment. She thought of the daily excitement of marketing, of the perpetual romance of mending his clothes, of the glorified monotony of pouring his coffee, as an adventurer on sunrise seas might dream of the rosy islands of hidden treasure. And then, so perfectly did she conform in spirit to the Victorian ideal of her sex, she ecstatically pictured herself in the immemorial attitude of woman. She saw herself waiting—waiting happily—but always waiting. She imagined the thrilling expectancy of the morning waiting for him to come home to his dinner; the hushed expectancy of the evening waiting for him to come home to his supper; the blissful expectancy of hoping he might be early; the painful expectancy of fearing he might be late. And it seemed to her divinely right and beautiful that, while he should have a hundred other absorbing interests in his life, her whole existence should perpetually circle round this single centre of thought. One by one, she lived in anticipation all the exquisite details of their life together, and in imagining them, she overlooked all possible changes that the years might bring, as entirely as she ignored the subtle variations of temperament which produce in each individual that fluid quantity we call character. She thought of Oliver, as she thought of herself, as though the fact of marriage would crystallize him into a shape from which he would never alter or dissolve in the future. And with a reticence peculiar to her type, she never once permitted her mind to stray to her crowning beatitude—the hope of a child; for, with that sacred inconsistency possible only to fixed beliefs, though motherhood was supposed to comprise every desire, adventure, and activity in the life of woman, it was considered indelicate for her to dwell upon the thought of it until the condition had become too obvious for refinement to deny.

The shadow of the church tower lengthened on the grass, and at the end of the cross street she saw Susan appear and stop for a minute to speak to Miss Priscilla, who was driving by in a small wagonette. Then the girl and the teacher parted, and ten minutes later there came Susan's imperative knock at Virginia's door.

"Miss Willy told mother that your wedding dress was finished, Virginia, and I am dying to see it!"

Going to the closet, which was built into one corner of the wall, Virginia unpinned a long white sheet scented with rose-leaves, and brought out a filmy mass of satin and lace. Her face as she looked down upon it was the face of girlhood incarnate. All her virginal dreams clustered there like doves quivering for flight. Its beauty was the beauty of fleeting things; of the wind in the apple blossoms at dawn. of the music of bees on an August afternoon.

"Mother wouldn't let me be married in anything but satin," she said, with a catch in her voice. "I believe it is the first time in her life she was ever extravagant, but she felt so strongly about it that I had to give in and not have white muslin as I wanted to do."

"And it's so lovely," Susan said. "I had no idea Miss Willy could do it. She's as proud, too, as if it were her own."

"She took a pleasure in every stitch, she told me. Oh, Susan, I sometimes feel that I haven't any right to be so happy. I seem to have everything and other women to have nothing."

For the first time Susan smiled, but it was a smile of understanding. "Perhaps they have more than you think, darling."

"But there's Miss Willy—what has she ever got out of life?"

"Well, I really believe she gets a kind of happiness out

of saving up the money to pay for her tombstone. It's a funny thing, but the people who ought to be unhappy, somehow never are. It doesn't seem to be a matter of what you have, but of the way you are born. Now, according to us, Miss Willy ought to be miserable, but the truth is that she isn't a bit so. Mother saw her once skipping for pure joy in the spring."

"But people who haven't things can't be as grateful to God as those who have. I feel that I'd like to spend every minute of my life on my knees thanking Him. I don't see how I can ever have a disappointed or a selfish thought again. I wonder if you can understand, you precious Susan, but I want to open my arms and take the whole world into them."

"Virginia," Susan said suddenly, "don't spoil Oliver."

"I couldn't—not if I tried every minute."

"I don't know, dear. He is very lovable, he has fine generous traits, he has the making of a big man in him; but his character isn't formed yet, you must remember. So much of him is imagination that he will take longer than most men to grow up to his stature."

"Oh, Susan!" Virginia exclaimed, and turned away.

"Perhaps I oughtn't to have said it, dear—but, no, I ought to tell you just what I think, and I don't regret it."

"Mother said the same thing to me," Virginia responded, looking as if she were on the point of tears; "but that is just because neither of you know him as I do."

"He is a Treadwell and so am I, and the chief characteristic of every Treadwell is that he is going to get the thing he wants most. It doesn't make any difference whether it is money or love or fame, the thing he wants most he will get sooner or later. So all I mean is that you needn't spoil Oliver by giving him the universe before he wants it."

"I can't give him the universe. I can only give him myself."

Stooping over, Susan kissed her.

"Happy, happy little Virginia!"

"There are only two things that trouble me, dear—one is going away from mother and father, and the other is that you are not so happy as I am."

"Some day I may get the thing I want like every other Treadwell."

"Do you mean going to college?"

"No," Susan said, "I don't mean that," and into her calm gray eyes a new light shone for an instant.

A clairvoyance deeper than knowledge came to Virginia while she looked at her.

"You darling!" she exclaimed. "I never suspected!"

"There's nothing to suspect. I was only joking."

"Why, it never crossed my mind that you would think of him for a minute."

"He hasn't thought of me for a minute yet."

"The idea! He'd be wild about you in ten seconds if he ever thought——"

"He was wild about you ten seconds ago, dear."

"He never was. It was just his fancy. Why, you are made for each other."

A laugh broke from Susan, but with that large and quiet candour which was characteristic of her, she did not seek to evade or deny Virginia's suspicion. That her friend should discover her feeling for John Henry seemed to her as natural as that she should be aware of it herself; for they were intimate with that full and perfect intimacy which exists only between two women who trust each other.

"There goes Miss Willy," Susan said, looking through the window to where the little dressmaker tripped down the stone steps to the street. "Mother wants to have early supper, so I must be running away."

"Good-bye, darling. Oh, Susan, I never loved you as I do now. It will be all right—I trust and pray that it will! And, just think, you will walk out of church together at my wedding!"

For a minute, standing on the threshold, Susan looked back at her with an expression of tender amusement in her eyes. "Don't imagine that I'm unhappy, dear," she said, "because I'm not—it isn't that kind—and, after all, even an unrequited affection may be simply an added interest in life, if we choose to take it that way."

When she had gone, Virginia lingered over her wedding dress, while she wondered what the wise Susan could see in the simple John Henry? Was it possible that John Henry was not so simple, after all? Or did Susan, forsaking the ancient tradition of love, care about him merely because he was good?

For a week the hours flew by with golden wings, and at last the most sacred day of her life dawned softly in a sunrise of rose and flame. When she looked back on it afterwards, there were three things that stood out unforgettably in her memory: the kiss her mother gave her when she turned to leave her girlhood's room for the last time; the sound of her father's voice as he spoke her name at the altar; and the look in Oliver's eyes when she put her hand into his. All the rest was enveloped in a shining mist which floated, like her wedding veil, between the old life and the new.

"It has been so perfect—so perfect—if only I can be worthy of this day and of you, Oliver," she said as the carriage started from the rectory gate to the station.

"You angel!" he murmured ecstatically.

Her eyes hung blissfully on his face for an instant, and then, moved by a sudden stab of reproach, she leaned from the window and looked back at her mother and father, who stood, with clasped hands, gazing after her over the white palings of the gate.

CHAPTER II

VIRGINIA'S LETTERS

MATOACA CITY, West Virginia. October 16, 1884.
DEAREST, DEAREST MOTHER:

We got here this morning after a dreadful trip—nine or ten hours late—and this is the first minute I've had when I could sit down and write to you. All the way on the train I was thinking of you and dear father, and longing for you so that I could barely keep back the tears. I don't see how I can possibly stay away from you for a whole year. Oliver says he wants to take me home for Christmas if everything goes right with us here and his work proves satisfactory to the manager. Oh, mother, he is the loveliest thing to me! I don't believe he has thought of himself a single minute since I married him. He says the only wish he has on earth is to make me happy—and he is so careful about me that I'm afraid I'll be spoiled to death before you see me again. He says he loves the little gray dress of shot silk, with the bonnet that makes me look like a Quaker. I wish now I'd got my other hat the bonnet shape as you wanted me to do—but perhaps, after all, it will be more useful and keep in fashion longer as it is. When I took out my clothes this morning, while Oliver was downstairs, and remembered how you had folded and packed everything, I just sat down on the floor in the midst of them and had a good cry. I never realized how much I loved you until I got into the carriage to come away. Then I wanted to jump out and put my arms around you and tell you that you are the best and dearest mother a girl ever had. My things were so beautifully packed that there wasn't a single crease anywhere—not even in the black silk polonaise that we were so afraid would get rumpled. I don't see how on earth you folded them so smoothly. By the way, I hardly think I shall have any need of my wedding dress while I am here, so you may as well put it away at home until I come back. This place seems to be just a mining town, with very few people of our class, and those all connected with the railroad. Of course, I may be mistaken, but from my first impressions I doubt if I'll ever want to have much to do with anybody I've seen. It doesn't make a bit of difference, because I shan't be lonesome a minute with the house to look after and Oliver's clothes to attend to; and, besides, I don't think a married woman ought to make many new friends. Her husband ought to be enough for her. Mrs. Payson, the manager's wife, was here to welcome me, but I hope I shan't see very much of her, because she isn't just exactly what I should call ladylike. Of course, I wouldn't breathe this to any other living soul, but I thought her entirely too free and easy in her manner, and she dresses in such very bright colours. Why, she had a red feather in her hat, and she must have been married at least fifteen years. Oliver says he doesn't believe she's a day under forty-five. He says he likes her well enough and thinks she's a good sort, but he is awfully glad I'm not that kind of woman. I feel sorry for her husband, for I'm sure no man wants his wife to make herself conspicuous, and they say she even makes speeches, when she is in the North. Maybe she isn't to blame, because she was brought up that way, but I am going to see just as little of her as I can.

And now I must tell you about our house, for I know you are dying to hear how we are fixed. It's the tiniest one you ever imagined, with a front yard the size of a pocket handkerchief, and it is painted the most perfectly hideous shade of yellow—the shade father calls bilious. I can't understand why they made it so ugly, but, then, the whole town is just as ugly as our house is. The people here don't seem to have the least bit of taste. All the porches have dreadful brown ornaments along the top of them, and they look exactly as if they were made out of gingerbread. There are very few gardens, and nobody takes any care of these. I suppose one reason is that it is almost impossible to get servants for love or money. There are scarcely any darkeys here, they say, and the few they have are perfectly worthless. Mrs. Midden—the woman who opened my house for me—hasn't been able to get me a cook, and we'll either have to take our meals at a boarding-house across the street, or I shall have to put to practise the lessons you gave me. I am so glad you made me learn how to housekeep and to cook, because I am certain that I shall have greater need of both these accomplishments than of either drawing or music. Oliver was simply horrified when I told him so. He said he'd rather starve than see me in the kitchen, and he urged me to get you to send us a servant from Dinwiddie—but things are so terribly costly here—you never dreamed of such prices—that I really don't believe we can afford to have one come. Then, Mrs. Midden says that they get ruined just as soon as they are brought here. Everybody tries it at first, she told me, and it has always proved a disappointment in the end. I am perfectly sure that I shan't mind cooking at all—and as for cleaning up this little house—why, it won't take me an hour—but Oliver almost weeps every time I mention it. He is afraid every instant he is away from me that I am lonesome or something has happened to me, and whenever he has ten minutes free he runs up here to see what I am doing. Do you know he has made me promise not to go out by myself until I am used to the place. Isn't that too absurd?

Dearest mother, I must stop now, and write some notes of thanks for my presents. The barrels of china haven't come yet, but the silver box got here almost as soon as we did. Freight takes a long time, Oliver says. It will be such fun unpacking all my presents and putting them away on the shelves. I was so excited those last few days that I hardly paid any attention to the things that came. Now I shall have time really to enjoy them, and to realize how sweet and lovely everybody has been to me. Wasn't it too dear of Miss Priscilla to give me that beautiful tea-set? And I was so touched by poor little Miss Willy spending her hard-earned money on that vase. I wish she hadn't. It makes me feel badly to think of it—but I don't see what I could do about it, do you? I think I'll try to send her a cloak or something at Christmas.

I haven't said half I want to—but I shall keep the rest for to-morrow.

With a dozen kisses and my dearest love to father,

Your ever, ever loving and grateful daughter,

VIRGINIA.

MATOACA CITY. December 25, 1884.

DEAREST MOTHER:

It almost broke my heart not to be able to go home for Christmas. It doesn't seem like Christmas at all away from you—though, of course, I try not to let Oliver see how I mind it. He has so much to bother him, poor dear, that I keep all of my worries, big and little, in the background. When anything goes wrong in the house I never tell him, because he has so many important things on his mind that I don't think I ought to trouble him about small ones. We have given up going to the boarding-house for our meals, because neither of us could eat a morsel of the food they had there—did you ever hear of such a thing as having pie and preserves for breakfast?—and Oliver says it used to make him sick to see me in the midst of all of those people. They came from all over the country, and scarcely anybody could speak a grammatical sentence. The man who sat next to me always said "he don't" and "I ain't feeling good to-day" and once even "I done it"—can you imagine such a thing? Every other word was "guess," and yet they had the impertinence to laugh at me when I said "reckon," which, I am sure father told me was Shakespearian English. Well, we stood it as long as we could, and then we started having our meals here, and it is so much nicer. Oliver says the change from the boarding-house has given him a splendid appetite, and he enjoys everything that I make so much—particularly the waffles by Aunt Aisley's recipe. Be sure to tell her. At first I had a servant, but she was so dreadful that I let her go at the end of the month, and I really get on ever so much better without her. She hadn't the faintest idea how to cook, and had never made a piece of light bread in her life. Besides, she was too untidy for anything, and actually swept the trash under the bed except once a week when she pretended to give a thorough cleaning. The first time she changed the sheets, I found that she had simply put on one fresh one, and was going to use the bottom one on top. She said she'd never heard of doing it any other way, and I had to laugh when I thought of how your face would have looked if you could have heard her. It really is the greatest relief to get rid of her, and I'd a hundred times rather do the work myself than have another of that kind. At first Oliver hated dreadfully to have me do everything about the house, but he is beginning to get used to it now, because, of course, I never let him see if anything happens to worry me or if I am tired when he comes home. It takes every minute of my time, but, then, there is nothing else here that I care to do, and I never leave the house except to take a little walk with Oliver on Sunday afternoon. Mrs. Midden says that I make a mistake to give a spring cleaning every day, but I love to keep the house looking perfectly spick and span, and I make hot bread twice a day, because Oliver is so fond of it. He is just as sweet and dear as he can be and wants to help about everything, but I hate to see him doing housework. Somehow, it doesn't seem to me to look manly. We have had our first quarrel about who is to get up and make the fires in the morning. Oliver insisted that he was to do it, but I wake so much earlier than he does, because I've got the bread on my mind, that I almost always have the wood burning before he gets up. The first few times he was really angry about it, and he didn't seem to understand why I hated so to wake him. He says he hates still worse to see my hands get rough—but I am so thankful that I am not one of those girls (like Abby Goode) who are for ever thinking of how they look. But Oliver made such a fuss about the fires that I didn't tell him I went down to the cellar one morning and brought up a basket of coal. The boy didn't come the day before, so there wasn't any to start the kitchen fire with, and I knew that by the time Oliver got up and dressed it would be too late to have hot muffins for breakfast. By the way, could you have a bushel of cornmeal sent to me from Dinwiddie? The kind they have here isn't the least bit like the water-ground sort we have at home, and most of it is yellow. Nobody ever has batterbread here. All the food is different from ours. I suppose that is because most of the people are from the North and West.

I have the table all set for our Christmas dinner, and in a few minutes I must put the turkey into the oven. I was so glad to get the plum pudding in the Christmas box, because I could never have made one half so good as yours, and the fruit cake will last me for ever—it is so big. I wrote you about the box yesterday just as soon as it came, but after I had sent my letter, I went back to it and found that rose point scarf of grandmother's wrapped in tissue paper in the bottom. Darling mother, it made me cry. You oughtn't to have given it to me. It always looked so lovely on your black silk, and it was almost the last thing you had left. I don't believe I shall ever make up my mind to wear it. I have on my little gray silk to-day, and it looks so nice. You must tell Miss Willy that it has been very much admired. Mrs. Payson asked me if it was made in Dinwiddie, and, you know, she gets all of her clothes from New York. That must have been why I thought her overdressed when I first saw her. By the way, I've almost changed my mind about her since I wrote you what I thought of her. I believe now that the whole trouble with her is simply that she isn't a Southern lady. She means well, I am sure, but she isn't what I should call exactly refined. There's something "horsey" about her —I can't think of any other way to express it—something that reminds me just a little bit of Abby—and, you remember, we always said Abby got that from being educated in the North. Tell dearest Susan I really think it is fortunate that she did not go to one of their colleges. Mrs. Payson is a college woman and it seems to me that she is always trying to appear as clever as a man. She talks in a way sometimes that sounds as if she believed in woman's rights and all that sort of thing. I told Oliver about it, and he laughed and said that men hated talk like that. He says all a man admires in a woman is her power of loving, and that when she begins to ape a man she loses her charm for him. I can't understand why Mr. Payson married his wife. He said such nice things to me the other day about my being so domestic and such a home lover that I really felt sorry for him. When I told him that I was so fond of staying indoors that I would never cross my threshold if Oliver didn't make me, he laughed and said that he wished I'd convert his wife to my way of thinking. Yet he seems to have the greatest admiration for her, and, do you know, I believe he even admires that red feather, though he doesn't approve of it. He never turns his eyes away from her when they are together, which isn't very much, as she goes about just as she pleases without him. Can you understand how a person can both admire and disapprove of a thing? Oliver says he knows how it is, but I must say that I don't. I hope and pray that our marriage will always be different from theirs. Oliver and I are never apart for a single minute except when he is at work in the office. He hasn't written a line since we came here, but he is going to begin as soon as we get settled, and then he says that I may sit in the room and sew if I want to. I can't believe that people really love each other unless they want to be together every instant, no matter what they are doing. Why, if Oliver went out to men's dinners without me as Mr. Payson does (though she doesn't seem to mind it) I should just sit at home by myself and cry my eyes out. I think love, if it is love, ought to be all in all. I am perfectly sure that if I live to be a hundred I shall never want any society but Oliver's. He is the whole world to me, and when he is not here I spend my time, unless I am at work, just sitting and thinking about him. My one idea is to make him as happy as I can, and when a woman does this for a man I don't think she has time to run around by herself as Mrs. Payson does. Tell dearest father that I so often think of his sermons and the beautiful things he said about women. The rector here doesn't compare with him as a preacher.

This is such a long letter it will take two stamps. I've just let myself run on without thinking what I was writing, so if I have made any mistakes in grammar or in spelling, please don't let father see them but read my letter aloud to him. I can shut my eyes and see you sitting at dinner, with Docia bringing in the plum pudding, and I know you will talk of me while you help to it. Write me who comes to dinner with you. I wonder if Miss Priscilla and John Henry are there as usual. Do you know whether John Henry ever goes to the Treadwells' or not? I wish you would ask him to take Susan to see his old mammy in Pink Alley. Now that I am not there to go to see her occasionally, I am afraid she will get lonesome.

Good-bye, dearest mother. I will write to you before New Year. I am so busy that I don't have time to write every day, but you will understand and so will father.

With my heart's fondest love to you both,

Your
VIRGINIA.

MATOACA CITY. June 6, 1885.

DARLING MOTHER:

The little patterns are exactly what I want—thank you a thousand times. I knew you would be overjoyed at the news, and you are the only person I've breathed it to —except, of course, dear Oliver, who is frightened to death already. He has made me stop everything at once, and whenever he sees me lift my hand, he begins to get nervous and begs me not to do it. Oh, mother, he loves me so that it is really pathetic to see his anxiety. And—can you believe it—he doesn't appear to be the least bit glad about it. When I told him, he looked amazed—as if he had never thought of its happening—and said, "Oh, Virginia, not so soon!" He told me afterwards that, of course, he'd always thought we'd have children after a while, before we were middle-aged, but that he had wanted to stay like this for at least five or ten years. When the baby comes, he says he supposes he'll like it, but that he can't honestly say he is glad. It's funny how frightened he is, because I am not the least bit so. All women must expect to have children when they marry, and if God makes them suffer for it, it must be because it is best that they should. Perhaps they wouldn't love their babies so much if they got them easily. I never think of the pain a minute. It all seems so beautiful and sacred to me that I can't understand why Oliver isn't enraptured just as I am. To think of a new life starting into the world from me—a life that is half mine and half Oliver's, and one that would never be at all except for our love. The baby will seem from the very first minute to be our love made into flesh. I don't see how a woman who feels this could waste a thought on what she has to suffer.

I am so glad you are going to send me a nurse from Dinwiddie, because I'm afraid I could never get one here that I could trust. The servant Oliver got me is no earthly account, and I still do as much of the cooking as I can. The house doesn't look nearly so nice as it used to, but the doctor tells me that I mustn't sweep, so I only do the light dusting. I sew almost all the time, and I've already finished the little slips. To-day I'm going to cut out the petticoats. I couldn't tell from the pattern you sent whether they fasten in front or in the back. There are no places for buttonholes. Do you use safety pins to fasten them with? The embroidery is perfectly lovely, and will make the sweetest trimming. I am using blue for the basket because Oliver and I both hope the baby will be a girl. If it is, I shall name her after you, of course, and I want her to be just exactly like you. Oliver says he can't understand why anybody ever wants a boy—girls are so much nicer. But then he insists that if she isn't born with blue eyes, he will send her to the orphanage.

I am trying to do just as you tell me to, and to be as careful as I possibly can. The doctor thinks I've stayed indoors too much since I came here, so I go out for a little walk with Oliver every night. I am so afraid that somebody will see me that I really hate to go out at all, and always choose the darkest streets I can find. Last night I had a bad stumble, and Oliver says he doesn't care if the whole town discovers us, he's not going to take me down any more unlighted alleys.

It has been terribly hot all day—not a breath of air stirring—and I never felt the heat so much in my life. The doctor says it's because of my condition—and last night, after Oliver went to sleep, I got up and sat by the window until daybreak. At first I was dreadfully frightened, and thought I was going to stifle—but poor Oliver had come home so tired that I made up my mind I wasn't going to wake him if I could possibly help it. This morning I didn't tell him a word about it, and he hasn't the least idea that I didn't sleep soundly all night. I suppose that's why I feel so dragged and worn out to-day, just as if somebody had given me a good beating. I was obliged to lie down most of the afternoon, but I am going to take a bath in a few minutes and try to make myself look nice and fresh before Oliver comes home. I have let out that flowered organdie—the one you liked so much—and I wear it almost every evening. I know I look dreadfully, but Oliver says I am more beautiful than ever. It seems to me sometimes that men are born blind where women are concerned, but perhaps God made it that way on purpose. Do you know Oliver really admires Mrs. Payson, and he thinks that red feather very becoming to her. He says she's much too good for her husband, but I have been obliged to disagree with him about that. Even if Mr. Payson does drink a little, I am sure it is only because he gets lonesome when he is left by himself, and that she could prevent it if she tried. Oliver and I never talk about these things because he sees that I feel so strongly about them.

Oh, darling mother, I shall be so glad to see you! I hope and pray that father will be well enough for you to come a whole month ahead. In that case you will be here in less than two months, won't you? If the baby comes on the twelfth of August, she (I am perfectly sure it will be a girl) and father will have the same birthday. I am so anxious that she shall be born on that day.

Well, I must stop now, though I could run on for ever. I never see a living soul from one day to another—Mrs. Payson is out of town—so when Oliver stays late at the office, and I am too tired to work, I get a little—just a little bit lonesome. Mr. Payson sent me a pile of novels by Oliver the other night—but I haven't looked into them. I always feel that it is a waste of time to read when there are things about the house that ought to be done. I wish everything didn't cost so much here. Money doesn't go half as far as it does in Dinwiddie. The price of meat is almost three times as much as it is at home, and chickens are so expensive that we have them only twice a week. It is hard to housekeep on a small allowance, and now that we have to save for the baby's coming, I have to count every penny. I have bought a little book like yours, and I put down all I spend during the day, and then add it up at night before going to bed. Oliver says I'm dreadfully frugal, but I am always so terribly afraid of running over my allowance (which is every cent that we can afford) and not having the money to pay the doctor's bills when they are due. Nobody could be more generous with money than Oliver is—I couldn't endure being married to a stingy man like Mr. Treadwell—and the other day when one of the men in the office died, he sent the most beautiful wreath that cost ten dollars. I am trying to save enough out of the housekeeping balance to pay for it, for Oliver always runs out of his pocket money before the middle of the month. I haven't bought anything for the baby because you sent me all the materials I needed, and I have been sewing on those ever since they came. Of course, my own clothes are still as good as new, so the only expense will be the doctor and the nurse and the extra things I shall be obliged to have to eat when I am sick.

Give dear father a dozen kisses from me, and tell him to hurry and get well so he can christen his granddaughter.

Your devoted and ever grateful
VIRGINIA.

MATOACA CITY. August 11, 1885.

DARLING MOTHER:

Just a line to say that I am so, so sorry you can't come, but that you mustn't worry a minute, because everything is going beautifully, and I am not the least bit afraid. The doctor says he never saw any one in a better frame of mind or so little nervous. Give my dear love to father. I am so distressed that he should suffer as he does. Rheumatism must be such terrible pain, and I don't wonder that you

are frightened lest it should go to his heart. I shall send
you a telegram as soon as the baby comes.

Your devoted daughter,
VIRGINIA.

MATOACA CITY. August 29, 1885.

MY PRECIOUS MOTHER:

This is the first time I have sat up in bed, and I am
trying to write a little note to you on a pillow instead of
a desk. My hand shakes so that I'm afraid you won't be
able to read it, but I felt that I wanted to send you a few
words of my very own, not dictated to the nurse or to
Mrs. Payson. I can't tell you how perfectly lovely Mrs.
Payson has been to me. She was here all that dreadful
night, and I believe I should have died without her. The
doctor said I had such a hard time because I'd let myself
get run down and stayed indoors too much. But I'm getting all right now—and the rest is over and doesn't matter.
As soon as I am strong again I shall be perfectly happy.

Oh, mother, aren't you delighted that the baby is a
girl, after all? It was the first question I asked when I
came back to consciousness the next morning, and when
they told me it was, I said, "Her name is Lucy Pendleton," and that was all. I was so weak they wouldn't let
me open my lips again, and Oliver was kept out of the
room for almost ten days because I would talk to him.
Poor fellow, it almost killed him. He is as white as a sheet
still, and looks as if he had been through tortures. It must
have been terrible for him, because I was really very, very
ill at one time.

But it is all over now, and the baby is the sweetest thing
you ever imagined. I believe she knows me already, and
Mrs. Payson says she is exactly like me, though I can
see the strongest resemblance to Oliver, even if she has

blue eyes and he hasn't. Wasn't it lovely how everything came just as we wanted it to—a girl, born on father's birthday, with blue eyes, and named Lucy? But, mother, darling, the most wonderful thing of all was that you seemed to be with me all through it. The whole time I was unconscious I thought you were here, and the nurse tells me that I was calling "Mother! Mother!" all that night. Nothing ever made me feel as close to you as having a baby of my own. I never knew before what you were to me, and how dearly, dearly I love you.

The nurse is taking the pencil away from me.

Your loving

VIRGINIA.

Isn't it funny that Oliver won't take any interest in the baby at all? He says she caused more trouble than she is worth. Was father like that?

MATOACA CITY. April 3, 1886.

DEAREST MOTHER:

My last letter was written an age ago, but I have been so busy since Marthy left that I've hardly had a moment in which to draw breath. It was a blow to me that she wouldn't stay for she was really an excellent nurse and the baby got on so well with her, but there aren't any coloured people of her kind here, and she got so homesick for Dinwiddie that I thought she would lose her mind if she stayed. You know how dependent they are upon company, and going out on Sunday afternoon and all that kind of thing, and there really wasn't any amusement for her except taking the baby out in the morning. She got so low spirited that it was almost a relief when she went, but of course I feel her loss dreadfully. I haven't let the baby out of my sight because I wouldn't trust Daisy with her for anything in the world. She is so terribly flighty.

I have the crib brought into my room (though Oliver hates it) and I take entire charge of her night and day. I should love to do it if only Oliver didn't mind it so much. He says I think more of the baby now than I do of him. Isn't that absurd? But, of course, she does take every single minute of my time, and I can't dress myself for him every evening as carefully as I used to do and look after all the housekeeping arrangements. Daisy is a very poor cook and she simply throws the things on the table, but it seems to me that my first duty is to the baby, so I try to put up with the discomforts. It is hard to eat what she cooks since everything tastes exactly alike, but I try to swallow as much as I can because the doctor says that if I don't keep up my strength I shall have to stop nursing the baby. Wouldn't that be dreadful? It almost breaks my heart to think of it, and I am sure we'd never get any artificial food to agree with her. She is perfectly well now, the sweetest, fattest thing you ever saw, and a real beauty, and she is so devoted to me that she cries whenever I go out of her sight. I am never tired of watching her, and even when she is asleep I sit sometimes for an hour by her crib just thinking how pretty she looks with her eyes closed and wishing you could see her. Oliver says I spoil her to death, but how can a baby of seven months be spoiled. He doesn't enjoy her half as much as I do, and sometimes I almost think that he gets impatient of seeing her always in my arms. At first he absolutely refused to have her crib brought into our room, but when I cried, he gave in and was very sweet about it. I feel so ashamed sometimes of the way the house looks, but there doesn't seem to be any help for it because the doctor says if I let myself get tired it will be bad for the baby. Of course, I wouldn't put my own health before his comfort, but I am obliged to think first of the baby, am I not? Last night, for instance, the poor little thing was very fretful and I was up and down with her until daybreak. Then this morning she woke early and I had to nurse her and give her her bath, and, added to everything else, Daisy's cousin died and she sent word she couldn't come. I slipped on a wrapper before taking a bath or fixing my hair and ran down to try and get Oliver's breakfast, but the baby began to cry and he came after me and said he wanted to make the coffee himself. Then he brought a cup upstairs to me, but I was so tired and nervous I couldn't drink it. He didn't seem to understand why, feeling as badly as I did, I wouldn't just put the baby back into her crib and make her stay there until I got some rest, but the little thing was so wide awake I hadn't the heart to do it. Besides, it is so important to keep regular hours with her, isn't it? I don't suppose a man ever realizes how a woman looks at these things, but you will understand, won't you, mother?

I am all alone in the house to-night because a play is in town that Oliver wanted to see and I made him go to it. He wanted to ask Mrs. Midden to sit downstairs (she has offered over and over again to do it) so that I might go too, but, of course, I wouldn't let him. I really couldn't have enjoyed it a minute for thinking of the baby, and besides I never cared for the theatre. Then, too, he doesn't know (for I never tell him) how very tired I am by the time night comes. Sometimes when Oliver comes home and we sit in the dining-room (we never use the drawing-room, because it is across the hall and I'm afraid I shouldn't hear the baby cry) it is as much as I can do to keep my eyes open. I try not to let him notice it, but one night when he read me the first act of a play he is writing, I went to sleep, and though he didn't say anything, I could see that he was very much hurt. He worries a good deal about my health, too, and he even went out one day and engaged a nurse without saying anything to me about it. After I had talked to her though, I saw that she would never do, so I sent her away before he came home. I wish I could get really strong and feel well again, but the doctor insists I never will until I get out of doors and use my muscles. But you stay in the house all the time and so did grandmother, so I don't believe there's a word of truth in what he says. Anyway, I go out every day now with the baby.

Thank you so much for the little bands. They are just what I wanted.

With dearest love,

Your devoted
VIRGINIA.

MATOACA CITY. June 10, 1886.

DEAREST MOTHER:

Daisy left a week ago and we couldn't find another servant until to-day. I must say I prefer coloured servants. They are so much more dependable. I didn't know until the evening before Daisy left that she was going, and I had to send Oliver straight out to see if he could find somebody to come in and help me. There wasn't a soul to be had until to-day, however, so for a week I was obliged to make Oliver get his dinner at the boarding-house. It doesn't make any difference what I have because I haven't a particle of appetite, and I'd just as soon eat tea and toast as anything else. Of course, but for the baby I could have managed perfectly well—but she has been so fretful of late that she doesn't let me put her down a minute. The doctor says her teeth are beginning to hurt her, and that I must expect to have trouble the first summer. She has been so well until now that he thinks it has been really remarkable. He tells me he never knew a healthier baby, but of course I am terribly anxious about her teething in the hot weather. If she grows much more fretful I'm afraid I shall have to take her to the country for July and August. It seems dreadful to leave Oliver all alone, but I don't see how I can help it if the doctor advises me to go. Oliver has gone to some musical comedy at the Academy to-night, and I am so tired that I am going to bed just as soon as I finish this letter. I hope and pray the baby will have a quiet night. Don't you think Daisy treated me very badly considering how kind I had been to her? Only a week ago when she was taken with pain in the night, I got up and made her a mustard plaster and sat by her bed until she felt easier. The next day I did all her work, and yet she has so little gratitude that she could leave me this way when she knows perfectly well that I am worried to death about the baby's first summer. I'd give anything if I could go home in July as you suggest, but it is such a long trip, and the heat will probably be quite as bad in Dinwiddie as here. Of course, it would make all the difference in the world to me to be where I could have you to advise me about the baby, and I'd go to-morrow if only it wasn't so far. Mrs. Midden has told me of a boarding-house in the country not more than twenty miles from here where Oliver could come down every evening, and we may decide to go there for a month or two. I can't help feeling very anxious, especially as Mrs. Scott's little boy—he is just the age of baby—was taken ill the other night, and they thought he would die before they could get a doctor.

This letter is full of my worries, but in spite of them I am the happiest woman that ever lived. Oliver is the best thing to me you can imagine, and the baby is so fascinating I enjoy every minute I am with her. It is the greatest fun to watch her in her bath. I know you would simply go into raptures over her—and she is so bright that she understands almost every word I say. She grows more like Oliver all the time, and the other day while I was watching her playing with her rubber doll, she looked so beautiful that it almost frightened me.

I am so glad dear father is well, and what you wrote me about John Henry's admiration for Susan interested me so much that I sat straight down and wrote to him. Why do you think it is only friendship and that he isn't in love with her? If he really thinks her the "finest girl in the world," I should imagine he was beginning to be pretty serious. I am delighted to hear that he is going to take her to the festival. Tell Susan from me that I shall never be satisfied until she is as happy as I am. Mr. Treadwell was right, I believe, not to let her go to college, though of course I want dear Susan to have whatever she sets her heart on. But, when all is said, you were wise in teaching me that nothing matters to a woman except love. More and more I am learning that if we only love unselfishly enough, everything else will work out for good to us. My little worries can't keep me from being so blissfully happy that I want to sing all the time. Work is a joy to me because I feel that I am doing it for Oliver and the baby. And with two such treasures to live for I should be the most ungrateful creature alive if I ever complained.

Your ever loving daughter,
VIRGINIA.

MATOACA CITY. July 1, 1886.

DEAREST MOTHER:

We are leaving suddenly for the country, and I'll send our address just as soon as we get there. The doctor thinks I ought to take the baby away from town, so I am going to the boarding-house I wrote you about. Oliver will come down every evening—it's only an hour's trip.

I am so tired from packing that I can't write any more.
Lovingly,
VIRGINIA.

MATOACA CITY. September 15, 1886.
DEAREST MOTHER:

Here we are back again in our home, and I was never so thankful in my life to get away from any place. I wrote you how dreadfully inconvenient it was, but it would take pages to tell you all my experiences in the last few days. Such people you never saw in your life! And the food got so uneatable that I lived on crackers for the last fortnight. Fortunately, I was still nursing the baby, but the doctor has just told me that I must stop. I am so distressed about it. Do you think it will go hard with her after the first year? She is as fat and well as she can be now, but I live in hourly terror of her getting sick. If anything should happen to her, I believe it would kill me.

Oliver sends love. He is working very hard at the office now, and he hates it.
Your loving
VIRGINIA.

I forgot to tell you that Mrs. Midden has found me such a nice servant. She is a very young coloured girl, but looks so kind and capable, and says she is perfectly devoted to children. Her name is Marthy, and I feel that she's going to be a great comfort to me.

MATOACA CITY. October 12, 1886.
MY DARLING MOTHER:

I was overjoyed to find your letter in the hall when I came out from breakfast. Has it really been two weeks since I wrote to you? That seems dreadful, but the days go by so fast that I hardly realize how long it is between my letters.

We are all well, and Marthy has become the greatest help to me. Of course, I don't let her do anything for the baby, but she is so careful and trustworthy that I am going to try having her take out the carriage in the morning. At first I shan't let her go off the block, so that I can have my eye on her all the time. Little Lucy took a fancy to her at once, and really enjoys playing with her. This makes it possible for me to do a little sewing, and I am working hard trying to make over one or two of my dresses. Oliver wants me to have a dressmaker do it, but we have so many extra expenses all the time that I don't feel we can afford to put out any sewing. We have spent a great deal on doctors since we were married, but of course with a young child we can't very well expect anything else.

And now, dearest mother, I have something to tell you, that no one knows—not even Oliver—except Doctor Marshall and myself. We are going to have another darling baby in March. I have kept it a secret because Oliver has had a good many business worries, and I knew it would make him miserable. It never seems to have entered his head that it might happen again so soon, and for his sake I do wish we could have waited until we got a little more money in the bank, but I suppose I oughtn't to say this because God would certainly not send children into the world unless it was right for them to be born. I try to remember what dear grandmamma said when somebody condoled with her at the time she was expecting her tenth child—that she hoped she was too good a Christian to dictate to the Lord as to how many souls He should send into the world. As for me, I should be perfectly delighted—it will be so much better for baby to have a little

brother or sister to play with when she gets bigger—but
I can't help worrying about Oliver's peculiar attitude of
mind. I am sure father wouldn't have felt that way,
and think how poor he has always been. Perhaps it comes
from dear Oliver having lived abroad so much and away
from the Christian influences, which have been the
greatest blessings of my life. I have put off telling him
every day just because I dread to think of the blow it will
be to him. He is the dearest and best husband that ever
lived, and I worship the ground he walks on, but, do you
know, things are always a surprise to him when they happen? He never looks ahead a single minute. I am sometimes afraid that he isn't the least bit practical, and it
makes him impatient when I talk to him about trying to
cut down expenses. Of course, I have to save as much as
I can and I count every single penny, or we'd never have
enough money to get through the month. I never buy a
stitch for either the baby or myself, though Oliver complains now and then that I don't dress as well as I used to
do. But how can I when I've worn the same things ever
since my marriage, besides making the baby's clothes out
of my old ones? You can understand from this how grateful I am for the check you sent—but, dearest mother, I
know that you oughtn't to have done it, and that you
sacrificed your own comfort and father's to give it to me.

I wish Oliver could get something to do in Dinwiddie.
He will never be happy here, and we could live on so much
less money at home—in a little house near the rectory.

Your loving child,

VIRGINIA.

CHAPTER III

THE RETURN

ON A February morning five years later, Mrs. Pendleton, who was returning from her daily trip to the market, met Susan Treadwell at the corner of Old Street.

"You are coming up to welcome Virginia, aren't you, Susan?" she asked. "The train gets in at four o'clock."

"Why, of course. I couldn't sleep a wink until I'd seen her. It has been seven years, and it seems a perfect eternity."

"She hasn't changed much—at least she hadn't six months ago when I was out there at the birth of her last baby. The little thing lived only two hours, you know, and I thought at first his death would kill her."

"It was a great blow; but she has been fortunate never to have had a day's sickness with the other three. I am dying to see them—especially the eldest. That's your namesake, isn't it?"

"Yes, that's Lucy. She's six years old now, and as good as an angel, but she hasn't fulfilled her promise of beauty. Virginia says she was the prettiest baby she ever saw."

"Everybody says that Jenny, the youngest, is a perfect. beauty."

"That's why her father makes so much of her. I told him when I was out there that he oughtn't to show such a difference between them. Do you know, Susan, I wouldn't say it to anybody else, but I don't believe Oliver has a real fondness for children. He gets tired of having them always about, and that makes him impatient. Now, Virginia is a born mother, just like her grandmother and all the women of our family."

"I should think Oliver would be crazy about the boy. He was named after his father too."

"Virginia felt she ought to name him Henry, but we call him Harry. No, Oliver hardly ever takes any notice of him. I don't mean, of course, that he isn't nice and kind to them; but he isn't wrapped up in them heart and soul as Virginia is. I really believe he is more absorbed in this play he has written than he is in the children."

"I am so glad to hear that two of his plays are going to be put on. That's splendid, isn't it?"

"He is coming back to Dinwiddie because of it. Now that he is assured of recognition, he says he is going to devote all his time to writing. Poor fellow, he did so hate the work out at Matoaca City, though I must say he was very faithful and persevering about it."

"You've taken that little house in Prince Street for them, where old Miss Franklin used to live, haven't you? The last time I saw you, you hadn't quite decided about it."

"I couldn't resist it because it is only three squares from the rectory. Mr. Pendleton set his heart on it from the first minute."

"Well, I'm so glad," Susan said, shifting the small basket of fruit she carried from one arm to the other, "and I'll certainly run in and see them this evening—I suppose they'll be at the rectory for supper?"

"Why, no. Virginia said she couldn't bear to be away from the children the first night, so we are all going there. I shall send Docia over to cook supper before they get here, and I've just been to market to see if I could find anything that Oliver would particularly like. He used to be so fond of sweetbreads."

"Mr. Dewlap has some very nice ones. I got one for mother. She hasn't been well for the last few days."

"I'm sorry to hear that. Give her my love and tell her I'll come down just as soon as I get Virginia settled. I've been so taken up getting the house ready that I haven't thought of another thing for three weeks."

"When will Oliver's play be put on in New York?" asked Susan, turning back after they had parted.

"In three weeks. He is going back again for the last rehearsals. I wish Virginia could go with him, but she wouldn't spend a night away from the children for anything on earth."

"Isn't it beautiful that her marriage has turned out so well?"

"Yes, she couldn't be any happier if she tried, and I must say that Oliver makes a much better husband than I ever thought he would. I never heard them disagree the whole time I was there. Of course, Virginia gives up to him in everything except where the children are concerned, but, then, a woman always expects to do that. One thing I'm certain of—he couldn't have found a better wife if he'd searched the world over. She never thinks of herself a minute, and you know how fond she used to be of pretty clothes and of fixing herself up. Now, she simply lives in Oliver and the children, and she is the proudest thing of his plays! The rector says she thinks he is Shakespeare and Milton rolled into one."

"Nothing could be nicer," Susan said, "and it is all such a happy surprise to me. Of course, I always thought Oliver very attractive—everybody does—but he seemed to me to be selfish and undisciplined, and I wasn't at all sure that Virginia was the kind of woman to bring out the best in him."

"You'll think so when you see them together."

Then they smiled and parted, Mrs. Pendleton hurrying back to the little house, while Susan turned down Old Street, in the direction of her home. She walked rapidly, with an easy swinging pace seldom seen in the women of Dinwiddie, and not heartily approved by the men. At twenty-seven she was far handsomer than she had been at twenty, for her figure had grown more shapely and her face had lost the look of intense preoccupation which had once marred its charm. Strong, capable, conquering, she still appeared; but in some subtle way she had grown softer. Mrs. Pendleton would probably have said that she had "settled."

At the first corner she met John Henry on his way to the bank, and turning, he walked with her to the end of the block, where they stood a moment discussing Virginia's return.

"I've just been to attend to some bills," he explained; "that's why I'm out at this hour. You never come into the bank now, I notice."

"Not often. Are you going to see Virginia this evening?"

"If you'll let me bring you home. I can't imagine Virginia with three children, can you? I'm half afraid to see her again."

"You mean you think she may have changed? Mrs. Pendleton says not."

"Oh, that's Aunt Lucy all over. If Virginia had got as fat as Miss Priscilla, she'd still believe she hadn't altered a particle."

"Well, she isn't fat, anyway. She weighs less than she ever did."

Her serious eyes dwelt on him under the green sun-shade she held, and it is possible that she wondered vaguely what it was about John Henry that had made her love him unsought ever since she could remember. He was certainly not handsome—though he was less stout and much better looking than he used to be: he was not particularly clever, even if he was successful with the work Cyrus had given him. She was under no delusion concerning him (being a remarkably clear-sighted young person), yet she knew that taking him just as he was, large, slow, kind, good, he aroused in her a tenderness that was almost absurd. She had waited patiently seven years for him to discover that he cared for her; a fact which had been perfectly evident to her long before his duller wit had perceived it.

"Do you want to be there to welcome Virginia?" he asked.

"I'd thought I'd go up about five, so I could get a glimpse of the children before they are put to bed."

"Then I'll meet you there and bring you home. I wouldn't take anything for meeting you, Susan. There's something about you that always cheers me."

She met his eyes frankly. "Well, I'm glad of that," she replied in her confident way, and held out her hand through the handle of the basket. An instant later, when she passed on into Bolingbroke Street, there was a smile on her face which made it almost pretty.

The front door was open, and as she entered the house, her mother came groping toward her out of the close-smelling dusk of the hall.

"I thought you'd never get back, Susan. I've had such a funny feeling."

"What kind of feeling, mother? It must be just nervousness. Here are some beautiful grapes I've brought you."

"I wish you wouldn't leave me alone. I don't like to be left alone."

"Well, I don't leave you any more than I'm obliged to, but if I stay shut up here I feel as if I'd smother. I've asked Miss Willy to come and sit with you this evening while I run up to welcome Virginia."

"Is she coming back? Nobody told me. Nobody tells me anything."

"But I did tell you. Why, we've been talking about it for weeks. You must have forgotten."

"I shouldn't have forgotten it. I'm sure I shouldn't have forgotten it if you had told me. But you keep everything from me. You are just like your father. You and James are both just like your father." Her voice had grown peevish, and an expression of fury distorted her usually passive features.

"Why, mother, what in the world is the matter?" asked Susan, startled by her manner. "Come upstairs and lie down. I don't believe you are well. You didn't eat a morsel of breakfast, so I'm going to fix you a nice little lunch. I got you a beautiful sweetbread from Mr. Dewlap."

Putting her arm about her, she led her up the long flight of steps to her room, where Mrs. Treadwell, pacified by the attention, began immediately to doze on the chintz-covered couch by the window.

"I don't see what on earth ever made me marry your father, Susan," she said, starting up half an hour later, when her daughter appeared with the tray. "Everybody knew the Treadwells couldn't hold a candle to my family."

"I wouldn't worry about that now, mother," Susan replied briskly, while she placed the tray on a little table at the head of the couch. "Sit up and eat these oysters."

"I'm obliged to worry over it," Mrs. Treadwell returned irritably, while she watched her daughter arrange the plate and pour out the green tea from the little Rebecca-at-the-well teapot. "I don't see what got into my head and made me do it. Why, his branch of the Treadwells had petered out until they were as common as dirt."

"Well, it's too late to mend matters, so we'd better turn in and try to make the best of them." She held out an oyster on the end of a fork, and her mother received and ate it obediently.

"If I could only once understand why I did it, I think I could rest easier, Susan."

"Perhaps you were in love with each other. I've heard of such a thing."

"Well, if I was going to fall in love, I reckon I could have found somebody better to fall in love with," Mrs. Treadwell retorted with the strange excitement in her manner. Then she took up her knife and fork and began to eat her lunch with relish.

At five o'clock that afternoon, when Susan reached the house in Prince Street, Virginia, with her youngest child in her arms, was just stepping out of a dilapidated landau from which a grinning negro driver handed a collection of baskets into the eager hands of the rector and Mrs. Pendleton, who stood on the pavement.

"Here's Susan!" Mrs. Pendleton called in her cheerful voice, rather as if she feared her daughter would overlook her friend in the excitement of homecoming.

"Oh, you darling Susan!" Virginia exclaimed, kissing her over the head of a sleeping child in her arms. "This is Jenny—poor little thing, she hasn't been able to keep her eyes open. Don't you think she is the living image of our Saint Memin portrait of great-grandmamma?"

"She's a cherub," said Susan. "Let me look at you first, Virginia. I want to see if you've changed."

"Well, you can't expect me to look exactly as I did before I had four babies!" Virginia returned, with a happy laugh. She was thinner, and there were dark circles of fatigue from the long journey under her eyes; but the Madonna dreams in her face were fulfilled, and it seemed to Susan that she was lovelier, if anything, than before. The loss of her girlish bloom was forgotten in the expression of love and goodness that irradiated her features. She wore a black cloth skirt, and a blouse of some ugly blue figured silk finished at the neck with the lace scarf Susan had sent her at Christmas. Her hat was a characterless black straw trimmed with a bunch of yellow daisies; and by its shape alone, Susan discerned that Virginia had ceased to consider whether or not her clothes were becoming. But she shone with an air of calm and radiant happiness in which all trivial details were transfigured as by a flood of light.

"This is Lucy. She is six years old, and to think that she has never seen her dear Aunt Susan," Virginia said, while she drew forward the little girl who was shyly clinging to her skirt. "And the other is Harry. Marthy, bring Harry here and let him speak to Miss Susan. He is nearly four, and so big for his age. Where is Harry, Marthy?"

"He's gone into the yard, ma'am, I couldn't keep him back," Marthy said. "As soon as he caught sight of that pile of bricks he wanted to begin building."

"Well, we'll go, too," Virginia replied. "That child is simply crazy about building. Has Oliver paid the driver, mother? And what has become of him? Susan, have you spoken to Oliver?"

No, Susan hadn't, but as they turned, he appeared on the porch and came eagerly forward. Her first impression was that he had grown handsomer than she had ever believed possible; and the next minute she asked herself how in the world he had managed to exercise his vitality in Matoaca City. He was one of those men, she saw, in whom the spirit of youth burned like a flame. Every year would pass as a blessing, not as a curse, to him, and already, because of her intenser emotions and narrower interests, Virginia was beginning to look older than he. There was a difference, too, in their dress, for he had the carefully finished and well-brushed appearance so rare in Dinwiddie, while Virginia's clothes might have been worn, with equal propriety, by Miss Priscilla Batte. She was still lovely, but it was a loveliness, Susan felt with a pang, that would break early.

"Why, there's Susan!" Oliver exclaimed, coming toward her with an eager pleasure in his face which made it more boyish than ever. "Well, well, it's good to see you, Susan. Are you the same old dear I left behind me?"

"The same," Susan said, laughing. "And so glad about your plays, Oliver, so perfectly delighted."

"By Jove, you're the first person to speak of them," he replied. "Nobody else seems to think a play is worth mentioning so long as a baby is in sight. That's a delusion of Virginia's too. I wish you'd convince her, Susan, that a man is of some use except as husband and father."

"But they are such nice babies, Oliver."

"Oh, nice enough as babies go. The boy's a trump. He'd be a man already, if his mother would let him. But babies ought to have their season like everything else under the sun. For God's sake, Susan, talk to me about something else!" he added in mock despair.

Virginia was already in the house, and when Oliver and Susan joined her, they found Mrs. Pendleton trying to persuade her to let Marthy carry the sleeping Jenny up to the nursery.

"Give me that child, Virginia," Oliver said, a trifle

sharply. "You know the doctor told you not to carry her upstairs."

"But I'm sure it won't hurt me," she responded, with angelic sweetness. "It will wake her to be changed, and the poor little thing has had such a trying day."

"Well, you aren't going to carry her, if she wakes twenty times," Oliver retorted. "Here, Marthy, if she thinks I'd drop her, suppose you try it."

"Why, bless you, sir, I can take her so she won't know it," Marthy returned reassuringly, and coming forward, she proved her ability by sliding the unconscious child from Virginia's arms into her own.

"Where is Harry?" Mrs. Pendleton asked anxiously. "Nobody has seen Harry since we got here."

"I is, ma'am," replied the cheerful Marthy over her shoulder, as she toiled up the stairs, with Virginia and little Lucy following noiselessly. "I've undressed him and I was obliged to hide his clothes to keep him from putting 'em on again. He's near daft with excitement."

"Perhaps I'd better go up and help get them to bed," said Mrs. Pendleton, turning from the rector to Oliver. "I'm afraid Virginia will be too tired to enjoy her supper. Harry is in such a gale of spirits I can hear him talking."

"You might as well, my dear," the rector rejoined mildly, as he stooped over to replace one of the baby's bottles in the basket from which it had slipped. "Don't you think we might get some of these things out of the way?" he added. "If you take that alcohol stove, Oliver, I'll follow with these caps and shawls."

"Certainly, sir," Oliver rejoined readily. He always addressed the rector as "sir," partly because it seemed to him to be appropriate, partly because he knew that the older man expected him to do so. It was one of Oliver's most engaging characteristics that he usually adapted himself

with perfect ease to whatever life or other people expected
of him.

While they were carrying the baskets into the passage
at the back of the dining-room, Mrs. Pendleton, whose
nervous longing had got at last beyond her control, deserted Susan, with an apology, and flitted up the stairs.

"Come up and tell Virginia good-night before you go,
dear," she added; "I'm afraid she will not get down again
to see you."

"Oh, don't worry about me," Susan replied. "I want
to say a few words to Oliver, and then I'm coming up to
see Harry. Harry appears to me to be a man of personality."

"He's a darling child," Mrs. Pendleton replied, a little
vaguely, "and Virginia says she never saw him so headstrong before. He is usually as good as gold."

"Well, well, it's a fine family," said the rector, beaming upon his son-in-law, when they returned from the
passage. "I never saw three healthier children. It's a pity
you lost the other one," he added in a graver tone, "but
as he lived such a little while, Virginia couldn't take it so
much to heart as if he had been older. She seems to have
got over the disappointment."

"Yes, I think she's got over it," Oliver said.

"It will be good for her to be back in Dinwiddie. I never
felt satisfied to think of her so far away."

"Yes, I'm glad we could come back," Oliver agreed
pleasantly, though he appeared to Susan's quick eye to
be making an effort.

"By the way, I haven't spoken of your literary work,"
the rector remarked, with the manner of a man who is
saying something very agreeable. "I have never been to
the theatre, but I understand that it is losing a great deal
of its ill odour. I always remember when anything is said

about the stage that, after all, Shakespeare was an actor. We may be old-fashioned in Dinwiddie," he pursued in the complacent tone in which the admission of this failing is invariably made, "but I don't think we can have any objection to sweet, clean plays, with an elevating moral tone to them. They are no worse, anyway, than novels."

Though Oliver kept his face under such admirable control, Susan, glancing at him quickly, saw a shade of expression, too fine for amusement, too cordial for resentment, pass over his features. His colour, which was always high, deepened, and raising his head, he brushed the smooth dark hair back from his forehead. Through some intuitive strain of sympathy, Susan understood, while she watched him, that his plays were as vital a matter in his life as the children were in Virginia's.

"I must run up and see Harry before he goes to sleep," she said, feeling that the conversation was becoming a strain.

At the allusion to his grandson, the rector's face lost immediately its expression of forced pleasantness and relapsed into its look of genial charm.

"You ought to be proud of that boy, Oliver," he observed, beaming. "There's the making of a fine man in him, but you mustn't let Virginia spoil him. It took all my strength and authority to keep Lucy from ruining Virginia, and I've always said that my brother-in-law Tom Bland would have been a first-rate fellow if it hadn't been for the way his mother humoured him. God knows, I like a woman to be wrapped up heart and soul in her household—and I don't suppose anybody ever accused the true Southern lady of lacking domesticity—but if they have a failing, which I refuse to admit, it is that they are almost too soft-hearted where their children—especially their sons—are concerned."

"I used to tell Virginia that she gave in to Harry too much when he was a baby," said Oliver, who was evidently not without convictions regarding the rearing of his offspring; "but she hasn't been nearly so bad about it since Jenny came. Jenny is the one I'm anxious about now. She is a headstrong little beggar and she has learned already how to get round her mother when she wants anything. It's been worse too," he added, "since we lost the last poor little chap. Ever since then Virginia has been in mortal terror for fear something would happen to the others."

"It was hard on her," said the rector. "We men can't understand how women feel about a thing like that, though," he added gently. "I remember when we lost our babies—you know we had three before Virginia came, but none of them lived more than a few hours—that I thought Lucy would die of grief and disappointment. You see they have all the burden and anxiety of it, and I sometimes think that a child begins to live for a woman a long time before a man ever thinks of it as a human being."

"I suppose you're right," Oliver returned in the softened tone which proved to Susan that he was emotionally stirred. "I tried to be as sympathetic with Virginia as I could, but—do you know?—I stopped to ask myself sometimes if I could really understand. It seemed to her so strange that I wasn't knocked all to pieces by the thing—that I could go on writing as if nothing had happened."

"I am not sure that it isn't beyond the imagination of a man to enter into a woman's most sacred feeling," the rector remarked, with a touch of the sentimentality in which he religiously shrouded the feminine sex. So ineradicable, indeed, was his belief in the inherent virtue of every woman, that he had several times fallen an easy victim in the financial traps of conscienceless Delilahs. But since his innocence was as temperamental a quality as was Virginia's maternal passion, experience had taught him nothing, and the fact that he had been deceived in the past threw no shadow of safeguard round his steps in the present. This endearing trait, which made him so successful as a husband, was probably the cause of his unmitigated failure as a reformer. In looking at a woman, it was impossible for him to see anything but perfection.

When Susan reached the top of the staircase, Mrs. Pendleton called to her, through the half open door of the nursery, to come in and hear how beautifully Lucy was saying her prayers. Her voice was full of suppressed excitement; there was a soft pink flush in her cheeks; and it seemed to Susan that the presence of her grandchildren had made her almost a girl again. She sat on the edge of a trundle-bed slipping a nightgown over the plump shoulders of little Lucy, who held herself very still and prim, for she was a serious child, with a natural taste for propriety. Her small plain face, with its prominent features and pale blue eyes, wore a look of earnest concentration, as if the business of getting to bed absorbed all her energies; and the only movement she made was to toss back the slender and very tight braid of brown hair from her shoulders. She said her prayer as if it were the multiplication table, and having finished, slid gently into bed, and held up her face to be kissed.

"Jenny wouldn't drink but half of her bottle, Miss Virginia," said Marthy, appearing suddenly on the threshold of Virginia's bedroom, for the youngest child slept in the room with her mother. "She dropped off to sleep so sound that I couldn't wake her."

"I hope she isn't sick, Marthy," Virginia responded in an anxious tone. "Did she seem at all feverish?"

"Naw'm, she ain't feverish, she's jest sleepy headed."

"Well, I'll come and look at her as soon as I can persuade Harry to finish his prayers. He stopped in the middle of them, and he refuses to bless anybody but himself."

She spoke gravely, gazing with her infinite patience over the impish yellow head of Harry, who knelt, in his little nightgown, on the rug at her feet. His roving blue eyes met Susan's as she came over to him, while his chubby face broke into a delicious smile.

"Don't notice him, Susan," Virginia said, in her lovely voice which was as full of tenderness and as lacking in humour as her mother's. "Harry, you shan't speak to Aunt Susan until you've been good and finished your prayers."

"Don't want to speak to Aunt Susan," retorted the monster of infant depravity, slipping his bare toes through a rent in the rug, and doubling up with delight.

"I never knew him to behave like this before," said Virginia, almost in tears from shame and weariness. "It must be the excitement of getting here. He is usually so good. Now, Harry, begin all over again. 'God bless dear papa, God bless dear mamma, God bless dear grandmamma, God bless dear grandpapa, God bless dear Lucy, God bless dear Jenny, God bless all our dear friends.' "

"God bless dear Harry," recited the monster.

"He has gone on like that ever since I started," said poor Virginia. "I don't know what to do about it. It seems dreadful to let him go to bed without saying his prayers properly. Now, Harry, please, please be good; poor mother is so tired, and she wants to go and kiss little Jenny good-night. 'God bless dear papa,' and I'll let you get in bed."

"God bless Harry," was the imperturbable rejoinder to this pleading.

"Don't you want your poor mother to have some supper, Harry?" Susan inquired severely.

"Harry wants supper," answered the innocent.

"I suppose I'll have to let him go," Virginia said, distractedly, "but Oliver will be horrified. He says I don't reason with them enough. Harry," she concluded sternly, "don't you understand that it is naughty of you to behave this way and keep mamma away from poor little Jenny?"

"Bad Jenny."

"If you don't say your prayers this minute, you shan't have any preserves on your bread to-morrow."

"Bad preserves."

"Well, if he won't, I don't see how I can make him," Virginia said. "Come, then, get into bed, Harry, and go to sleep. You have been a bad boy and hurt poor mamma's feelings so that she is going to cry. She won't be able to eat her supper for thinking of the way you have disobeyed her."

Jumping into bed with a bound, Harry dug his head into the pillows, gurgled, and then sat up very straight.

"God bless dear papa, God bless dear mamma, God bless dear grandmamma, God bless dear grandpapa, God bless dear Lucy, God bless dear Jenny, God bless our dear friends everywhere," he repeated in a resounding voice.

"Oh, you precious lamb!" Virginia exclaimed. "He couldn't bear to hurt poor mamma, could he?" and she kissed him ecstatically before hastening to the slumbering Jenny in the adjoining room.

"I like the little scamp," Susan said, when she reported the scene to John Henry on the way home, "but he manages his mother perfectly. Already his sense of humour is better developed than hers."

"I can't get over seeing Virginia with children," John Henry replied, as if the fact of Virginia's motherhood had just become evident to him. "It suits her, though. She looked happier than I ever saw her—and so, for that matter, did Aunt Lucy."

"It made me wonder how Mrs. Pendleton had lived away from them for seven years. Why, you can't imagine what she is. She doesn't seem to have any life at all until you see her with Virginia's children."

"It's a wonderful thing," John Henry said slowly, "and it taught me a lot just to look at them. I don't know why, but it seemed to make me understand how much I care about you, Susan."

"Hadn't you suspected it before?" Susan asked as calmly as he had spoken. Emotion, she knew, she would never find in John Henry's wooing, and, though she could not have explained the reason of it to herself, she liked the brusque directness of his courtship. It was part of that large sincerity of nature which had first attracted her to him.

"Of course, in a way I knew I cared more for you than for anybody else; but I didn't realize that you were more to me than Virginia had ever been. I had got so in the habit of thinking I was in love with her that it came almost as a surprise to me to find that it was over."

"I knew it long ago."

"Why didn't you make me see it?"

"Oh, I waited for you to find it out yourself. I was sure that you would some day."

"Do you think you could ever care for me, Susan?"

A smile quivered on Susan's lips as she looked up at him, but with the reticence which had always been hers, she answered simply:

"I think I could, John Henry."

His hand reached down and closed over hers, and in the long look which they exchanged under the flickering street lamp, she felt suddenly that perfect security which is usually the growth of happy years. Whatever the future brought to them, she knew that she could trust John Henry's love for her.

"And we've lost seven years, dearest," he said with a catch in his voice. "We've lost seven years just because I happened to be born a fool."

"But we've got fifty ahead of us," she replied with a joyous laugh.

As she spoke, her heart cried out, "Fifty years of the thing I want!" and she looked up into the kind, serious face of John Henry as if it were the face of incarnate happiness. A tremendous belief in life surged from her brain through her body, which felt incredibly warm and young. She thought exultantly of herself as of one who did not accept destiny but commanded it.

They walked the rest of the way in silence, but he held her hand pressed closely against his heart, and once or twice he turned in the deserted street and looked into her eyes as if he found there all the words that he needed.

"We shan't waste any more time, shall we, Susan?" he asked when they reached the house. "Let's be married in April."

"If mother is better by then. She hasn't been well, and I am anxious about her."

"We'll go to housekeeping at once. I'll begin looking about to-morrow. God bless you, darling, for what you are giving me."

She caressed his hand gently with her fingers, and he was about to speak again, when the door behind them opened and the head of Cyrus appeared like a desolate bird of prey.

"Is that you, Susan?" he inquired. "Where have you been all this time? Your mother was taken ill more than an hour ago, and the doctor says she has been paralyzed."

Breaking away from John Henry, Susan ran up the steps and past her father into the hall, where Miss Willy stood weeping.

"I was all by myself with her. There wasn't another living soul in the house," sobbed the little dressmaker. "She fell over just like that, with her face all twisted, while I was talking to her."

"Oh, poor mother, poor mother!" cried the girl as she ran upstairs. "Is she in her room, and who is with her?"

"The doctor has been there for over an hour, and he says that she'll never be able to move again. Oh, Susan, how will she stand it?"

But Susan had already outstripped her, and was entering the sick-room, where Mrs. Treadwell lay unconscious, with her distorted face turned toward the door, as if she were watching expectantly for some one who would never come. As the girl fell on her knees beside the couch, her happiness seemed to dissolve like mist before the grim facts of mortal anguish and death. It was not until dawn, when the night's watch was over and she stood alone beside her window, that she said to herself with all the courage she could summon:

"And it's over for me too. Everything is over for me too. Oh, poor, poor mother!"

CHAPTER IV

HER CHILDREN

"Poor Aunt Belinda was paralyzed last night, Oliver," said Virginia the next morning at breakfast. "Miss Willy Whitlow just brought me a message from Susan. She spent the night there and was on her way this morning to ask mother to go."

Oliver had come downstairs in one of his absent-minded moods, but by the time Virginia had repeated her news he was able to take it in, and to show a proper solicitude for his aunt.

"Are you going there?" he asked. "I am obliged to do a little work on my play while I have the idea, but tell Susan I'll come immediately after dinner."

"I'll stop to inquire on my way back from market, but I won't be able to stay, because I've got all my unpacking to do. Can you take the children out this afternoon so Marthy can help me?"

"I'm sorry, but I simply can't. I've got to get on with this idea while I have control of it, and if I go out with the children, I shan't be able to readjust my thoughts for twenty-four hours."

"I'd like to go out with papa," Lucy said, who sat carefully drinking her cambric tea, so that she might not spill a drop on the mahogany table.

"I want to go with papa," Harry remarked obstreper-

234

ously, while he began to drum with his spoon on the red tin tray which protected the table from his assaults.

"Papa can't go with you, darling, but if mamma finishes her unpacking in time, she'll come out into the park and play with you a little while. Be careful, Harry, you are spilling your milk. Let mamma take your spoon out for you."

Her coffee, which she had poured out a quarter of an hour before, stood untasted and tepid beside her plate; but from long habit she had grown to prefer it lukewarm. When the waffles were handed to her, she had absent-mindedly helped herself to one, while she watched Harry's reckless efforts to cut up his bacon, and it had grown sodden before she remembered that it ought to be buttered. She wore the black skirt and blue blouse in which she had travelled; for she had neglected to unpack her own clothes in her eagerness to get out the things that Oliver and the children might need. Her hair had been coiled hastily round her head, without so much as a glance in the mirror; but the expression of unselfish goodness in her face lent a charm even to the careless fashion in which she had put on her clothes. She was one of those women whose beauty, being essentially virginal, belongs, like the blush of the rose, to a particular season. The delicacy of her skin invited the mark of time or anxiety, and already fine little lines were visible, in the strong light of the morning, at the corners of her eyes and mouth. Yet nothing could destroy the look of angelic sweetness and love that illumined her features.

"Are you obliged to go to New York next week, Oliver?" she asked, dividing her attention between him and Harry's knife and fork. "Can't they rehearse 'The Beaten Road' just as well without you?"

"No, I want to be there. Is there any reason why I shouldn't?"

"Of course not. I was only thinking that Harry's birthday comes on Friday, and we should miss you."

"Well, I'm sorry, but he'll have to grow older without me. By the way, why can't you run on with me for the first night, Virginia? Your mother can look after the babies for a couple of days, can't she?"

But the absent-minded look of young motherhood had settled again on Virginia's face, for the voice of Jenny, raised in exasperated demand, was heard from the nursery above.

"I wonder what's the matter?" she said, half rising in her chair, while she glanced nervously at the door. "She was so fretful last night, Oliver, that I'm afraid she is going to be sick. Will you keep an eye on Harry while I run up and see?"

Ten minutes later she came down again, and began, with a relieved manner, to stir her cold coffee.

"What were you saying, Oliver?" she inquired so sweetly that his irritation vanished.

"I was just asking you if you couldn't let your mother look after the youngsters for a day or two and come on with me."

"Oh, I'd give anything in the world to see it, but I couldn't possibly leave the children. I'd be so terribly anxious for fear something would happen."

"Sometimes I get in a blue funk about that play," he said seriously. "I've staked so much on it that I'll be pretty well cut up, morally and financially, if it doesn't go."

"But, of course, it will go, Oliver. Anybody could tell that just to read it. Didn't Mr. Martin write you that he thought it one of the strongest plays ever written in America; and I'm sure that is a great deal for a manager to say. Nobody could read a line of it without seeing that it is a work of genius."

For an instant he appeared to draw assurance from her praise; then his face clouded, and he responded doubtfully:

"But you thought just as well of 'April Winds,' and nobody would look at that."

"Well, that was perfect too, of its kind, but of course they are different."

"I never thought much of that," he said, "but I honestly believe that 'The Beaten Road' is a great play. That's my judgment, and I'll stand by it."

"Of course it's great," she returned emphatically. "No, Harry, you can't have any more syrup on your buckwheat cake. You have eaten more already than sister Lucy, and she is two years older than you are."

"Give it to the little beggar. It won't hurt him," Oliver said impatiently, as Harry began to protest.

"But he really oughtn't to have it, Oliver. Well, then, just a drop. Oh, Oliver, you've given him a great deal too much. Here, take mamma's plate and give her yours, Harry."

But Harry made no answer to her plea, because he was busily eating the syrup as fast as he could, urged bv the fear that he might lose it all if he procrastinated.

"He'll be sick before night and you'll have yourself to blame, Oliver," Virginia said reproachfully.

Ever since the babies had come she had assumed naturally that Oliver's interest in the small details of his children's clothes or health was perpetually fresh and absorbing like her own, and her habit of not seeing what she did not want to see in life had protected her from the painful discovery that he was occasionally bored. Once he had even tried to explain to her that, although he loved

the children better than either his plays or the political
fate of nations, there were times when the latter questions interested him considerably more; but the humour
with which he veiled his protest had turned the point of
it entirely away from her comprehension. A deeper impression was made upon her by the fact that he had refused
to stop reading about the Presidential election long enough
to come and persuade Harry to swallow a dose of medicine. She, who seldom read a newspaper, and was innocent
of any desire to exert even the most indirect influence upon
the elections, had waked in the night to ask herself if it
could possibly be true that Oliver loved the children less
passionately than she did.

"I've got to get to work now, dear," he said, rising. "I
haven't had a quiet breakfast since Harry first came to the
table. Don't you think Marthy might feed him upstairs
again?"

"Oh, Oliver, it would break his heart. He would think
he was in disgrace."

"Well, I'm not sure that he oughtn't to be. Now, Lucy's
all right. She behaves like a lady; but if you consider
Harry an appetizing table companion, I don't."

"But, dearest, he's only a baby! And boys are different
from girls. You can't expect them to have as good manners."

"I can't remember that I ever made a nuisance of myself."

"Your father was very strict with you. But surely you
don't think it is right to make your children afraid of you?"

The genuine distress in her voice made him laugh.

"Oh, well, they are your children, darling, and you may
do as you please with them."

"Bad papa!" Harry said suddenly, chasing the last drop
of syrup round his plate with a bit of bread crumb.

"Oh, no, precious; good papa! You must promise papa to be a little gentleman or he won't let you breakfast with him any more."

It was Virginia's proud boast that Harry's smile would melt even his great-uncle, Cyrus, and she watched him now with breathless rapture as he turned in his high chair and tested the effect of this magic charm on his father. His baby mouth broadened deliciously, showing two rows of small irregular teeth; his blue eyes shone until they seemed full of sparkles; his roguish, irresistible face became an incarnation of infant entreaty.

"I want to bekfast wid papa, an' I want more 'lasses," he remarked.

"He's a fascinating little rascal, there's no doubt of that," Oliver observed, in response to Virginia's triumphant look. Then, bending over, he kissed her on the cheek, before he picked up his newspapers and went into his study at the back of the parlour.

Some hours later, at their early dinner, she reported the result of her visit to the Treadwells.

"It is too awful, Oliver. Aunt Belinda has not spoken yet, and she can't move the lower part of her body at all. The doctor says she may live for years, but he doesn't think she will ever be able to walk again. I feel so sorry for her and for poor Susan. Do you know, Susan became engaged to John Henry last night just before her mother was paralyzed, and they were to be married in April. But now she says she will give him up."

"John Henry!" Oliver exclaimed in amazement. "Why, what in the world does she see in John Henry?"

"I don't know. One never knows what people see in each other, but she has been in love with him all her life, I believe."

"Well, it's rough on her. Is she obliged to break with him now?"

"She says it wouldn't be fair to him not to. Her whole time must be given to nursing her mother. There's something splendid about Susan, Oliver. I never realized it as much as I did to-day. Whatever she does, you may be sure it will be because it is right to do it. She sees everything so clearly, and her wishes never obscure her judgment."

"It's a pity. She'd make a great mother, wouldn't she? But life doesn't seem able to get along without a sacrifice of the fittest."

In the afternoon Mrs. Pendleton came over; but the two women were so busy arranging the furniture in its proper place, and laying away Oliver's and the children's things in drawers and closets, that not until the entire house had been put in order, did they find time to sit down for a few minutes in the nursery and discuss the future of Susan.

"I believe John Henry will want to marry her and go to live at the Treadwells', if Susan will let him," Mrs. Pendleton remarked.

"How on earth could he get on with Uncle Cyrus?" Ever since her marriage Virginia had followed Oliver's habit and spoken of Cyrus as "uncle."

"Well, I don't suppose even John Henry could do that, but perhaps he thinks anything would be better than losing Susan."

"And he's right," Virginia returned loyally, while she got out her work-bag and began sorting the array of stockings that needed darning. "Do you know, mother, Oliver seems to think that I might go to New York with him."

"And leave the children, Virginia?"

"Of course, I've told him that I can't, but he's asked me two or three times to let you look after them for a day or two."

"I'd love to do it, darling; but you've never spent a night away from one of them since Lucy was born, have you?"

"No, and I'd be perfectly miserable—only I can't make Oliver understand it. Of course, they'd be just as safe with you as with me, but I'd keep imagining every minute that something had happened.

"I know exactly how you feel, dear. I never spent a night outside my home after my first child came until you grew up. I don't see how any true woman could bear to do it, unless, of course, she was called away because of a serious illness."

"If Oliver were ill, or you, or father, I'd go in a minute, unless one of the children was really sick; but just to see a play is different, and I'd feel as if I were neglecting my duty. The funny part is that Oliver is so wrapped up in this play that he doesn't seem to be able to get his mind off it, poor darling. Father was never that way about his sermons, was he?"

"Your father never thought of himself or of his own interests enough, Virginia. If he ever had a fault, it was that. But I suppose he approaches perfection as nearly as a man ever did."

Slipping the darning gourd into the toe of one of Lucy's little white stockings, Virginia gazed attentively at a small round hole while she held her needle arrested slightly above it. So exquisitely Madonna-like was the poise of her head and the dreaming, prophetic mystery in her face, that Mrs. Pendleton waited almost breathlessly for her words.

"There's not a single thing that I would change in Oliver, if I could," she said at last.

"It is so beautiful that you feel that way, darling. I suppose all happily married women do."

A week later, across Harry's birthday cake, which stood surrounded by four candles in the centre of the rectory table, Virginia offered her cheerful explanation of Oliver's absence, in reply to a mild inquiry from the rector. "He was obliged to go to New York yesterday about the rehearsal of 'The Beaten Road,' father. We were both so sorry he couldn't be here to-day, but it was impossible for him to wait over."

"It's a pity," the rector said gently. "Harry will never be just four years old again, will you, little man?" Even the fact that Oliver's play would, it was hoped, provide a financial support for his children, did not suffice to lift it from the region of the unimportant in the mind of his father-in-law.

"But he'll have plenty of other birthdays when papa will be here," Virginia remarked brightly. Though she had been a little hurt to find that Oliver had arranged to leave home the night before, and that he had appeared perfectly blind to the importance of his presence at Harry's celebration, her native good sense had not permitted her to make a grievance out of the matter. On her wedding day she had resolved that she would not be exacting of Oliver's time or attention, and the sweetness of her disposition had smoothed away any difficulties which had intervened between her and her ideal of wifehood. From the first love had meant to her the opportunity of giving rather than the privilege of receiving, and her failure to regard herself as of supreme consequence in any situation had protected her from the minor troubles and disillusionments of marriage.

"It is too bad to think that dear Oliver will have to be away for two whole weeks," Mrs. Pendleton said.

"Is he obliged to stay that long?" the rector asked, sympathetically. Never having missed an anniversary since the war, he could look upon Oliver's absence as a fit subject of condolence.

"He can't possibly come home until the play is produced, and that won't be for two weeks yet," Virginia replied.

"But I thought it rested with the actors now. Couldn't they go on just as well without him?"

"He thinks not, and, of course, it is such a great play that he doesn't want to take any risks with it."

"Of course he doesn't," assented Mrs. Pendleton, who had believed that the stage was immoral until Virginia's husband began to write for it.

"I know he'll come back the very first minute that he can get away," Virginia said with conviction, before she stooped to comfort Harry, who was depressed by the discovery that he was not expected to eat his entire cake, but instantly hopeful when he was promised a slice of sister Lucy's in the summer.

Late in the afternoon, when the children, warmly wrapped in extra shawls by Mrs. Pendleton, were led back through the cold to the house in Prince Street, one and all of the party agreed that it was the nicest birthday that had ever been. "I like grandmamma's cake better than our cake," announced Harry above his white muffler. "Why can't we have cake like that, mamma?"

He was trotting sturdily, with his hand in Virginia's, behind the perambulator, which contained a much muffled Jenny, and at his words Mrs. Pendleton, who walked a little ahead, turned suddenly and hugged him tight for an instant.

"Just listen to the darling boy!" she exclaimed, in a choking voice.

"Because nobody else can make such good cake as grandmamma's," answered Virginia, quite as pleased as her mother. "And she's going to give you one every birthday as long as you live."

"Can't I have another birthday soon, mamma?"

"Not till after sister Lucy's. You want sister Lucy to have one, don't you? and dear little Jenny?"

"But why can't I have a cake without a birthday, mamma?"

"You may, precious, and grandmamma will make you one," Mrs. Pendleton said, as she helped Marthy wheel the perambulator over the slippery crossing and into the front gate.

On the hall table there was a telegram from Oliver, and Virginia tore it open while her mother and Marthy unfastened the children's wraps.

"He's at the Hotel Bertram," she said joyously, "and he says the rehearsals are going splendidly."

"Did he mention Harry's birthday?" Mrs. Pendleton asked, trying to hide the instinctive dread which the sight of a telegram aroused in her.

"He must have forgotten it. Can't you come upstairs to the nursery with us, mother?"

"No, your father is all alone. I must be getting back," Mrs. Pendleton replied gently.

An hour or two later, when Virginia sat in her rocking-chair before the nursery fire, with Harry, worn out with his play and forgetful of the dignity of his four years, asleep in her lap, she opened the telegram again and re-read it hungrily while the light of love shone in her face. She knew intuitively that Oliver had sent the telegram because he had not written, and would not write, probably, until he had finished the hardest work of his play. It was an easy thing to do; it took considerably less time than a letter would have done; but she had inherited from her mother the sentimental vision of life that magnifies the meaning of trivial attentions. She looked through her emotions as through a prism on the simple fact of his telegraphing, and it became immediately transfigured. How dear it was of him to realize she would be anxious until she heard from him! How lonely he must be all by himself in that great city! How much he must have wanted to be with Harry on his birthday! Sitting there in the fire-lit nursery, her heart sent out waves of love and sympathy to him across the distance and the twilight. On the rug at her feet, Lucy rocked in her little chair, crooning to her doll with the beginning of the mother instinct already soft-ening her voice, and in the adjoining room Jenny lay asleep in her crib while the faithful Marthy watched by her side. Beyond the window, a fine icy rain had begun to fall, and down the long street the lamps flickered in revolving circles of frost. In the midst of the frozen streets, that little centre of red firelight separated her as completely from the other twenty-one thousand human beings among whom she lived as did the glow of personal joy that suffused her thoughts. From the dusk below she heard the tapping of a blind beg-gar's stick on the pavement, and the sound made, while it lasted, a plaintive accompaniment to the lullaby she was singing. "Two whole weeks," she thought, while her long-ing reached out to that unknown room in which she pic-tured Oliver sitting alone. "Two whole weeks. How hard it will be for him." In her guarded ignorance of the world she could not imagine that Oliver was suffering less from this enforced absence from all he loved than she herself would have suffered had she been in his place. Of course, men were different from women; that ancient dogma was embodied in her creed of life; but she had always understood that this difference vanished in some miraculous way after marriage. She knew that Oliver had to work, of course—how otherwise could he support his family?—but the idea that his work might ever usurp the place in his heart that belonged to her and the children would have been incomprehensible had it ever occurred to her. Jealousy was an alien weed which could not take root in the benign soil of her nature.

For a week there was no letter from Oliver, and at the end of that time a few lines scrawled on a sheet of hotel paper explained that he spent every minute of his time at the theatre.

"Poor fellow, it's dreadfully hard on him, isn't it?" Virginia said to her mother, when she showed her the imposing picture of the hotel at the head of his letter.

There was no hint of compassion for herself in her voice. Her pity was entirely for Oliver, constrained to be away for two whole weeks from his children, who grew more interesting and delightful every day that they lived. "Harry has gone into the first reader," she added, turning from the storeroom shelves on which she was laying strips of white oilcloth. "He will be able to read his lesson to Oliver when he comes home."

"I have always understood that your father could read his Bible at the age of four," remarked Mrs. Pendleton, who passionately treasured this solitary proof of the rector's brilliance.

"I am afraid Harry is backward. He hates his letters—especially the letter A—so much that it takes me an hour sometimes to get him to say it after me. My only comfort is that Oliver says he couldn't read a line until he was over seven years old. Would you scallop this oilcloth, mother, or leave it plain?"

"I always scallop mine. Mrs. Treadwell must be better, Virginia; Susan sent me a dessert yesterday."

"Yes, but she will never be able to move herself. Do you think that poor Susan will marry John Henry now?"

"I wonder?" Mrs. Pendleton replied vaguely. Then the sound of Harry's laughter floated in suddenly from the garden, and her eyes, following Virginia's, turned automatically to the pantry window.

"They've come home for a snack, I suppose?" she said. "Shall I fix some bread and preserves for them?"

"Oh, I'll do it," Virginia responded, while she reached for the crock of blackberry jam on the shelf at her side.

Another week passed and there was no word from Oliver, and Mrs. Pendleton came in at dusk one evening, with an anxious look on her face and a folded newspaper held tightly in her hand.

"Have you seen any of the accounts of Oliver's play, Virginia?" she asked.

"No, I haven't had time to look at the papers to-day. Harry has hurt his foot."

She spoke placidly, looking up from the nursery floor, where she knelt beside a basin of warm water at Harry's feet. "Poor little fellow, he fell on a pile of bricks," she added, "but he's such a hero he never even whimpered, did he, darling?"

"But it hurt bad," Harry said eagerly.

"Of course, it hurt dreadfully, and if he hadn't been a man he would have cried."

"Sister would have cried," the hero exulted.

"Indeed, sister would have cried. Sister is a girl," Virginia responded, smothering him with kisses over the basin of water.

But Mrs. Pendleton refused to be diverted from her purpose even by the heroism of her grandson.

"John Henry found this in a New York paper and brought it to me. He thought you ought to see it, though, of course, it may not be so serious as it sounds."

"Serious?" Virginia repeated, letting the soapy wash-rag fall back into the basin while she stretched out her moist and reddened hand for the paper.

"It says that the play didn't go very well," pursued her mother guardedly. "They expect to take it off at once, and—and Oliver is not well—he is ill in the hotel——"

"Ill?" Virginia cried, and as she rose to her feet the basin upset and deluged Harry's shoes and the rug on which she had been kneeling. Her mind, unable to grasp the significance of a theatrical failure, had seized upon the one salient fact that concerned her. Plays might succeed or fail, and it made little difference, but illness was another matter—illness was something definite and material. Illness could neither be talked away by religion nor denied by philosophy. It had its place in her mind not with the shadow, but with the substance of things. It was the one sinister force which had always dominated her, even when it was absent, by the sheer terror it aroused in her thoughts.

"Let me see," she said chokingly. "No, I can't read it—tell me."

"It only says that the play was a failure—nobody understood it, and a great many people said it was—oh, Virginia—*immoral!* There's something about its being foreign and an attack on American ideals—and they add that the author refused to be interviewed and they understood that he was ill in his room at the Bertram."

The charge of immorality, which would have crushed Virginia at another time, and which, even in the intense excitement of the moment, had been an added stab to

Mrs. Pendleton, was brushed aside as if it were the pes-
tiferous sting of an insect.

"I am going to him now—at once—when does the train
leave, mother?"

"But, Virginia, how can you? You have never been to
New York. You wouldn't know where to go."

"But he is ill. Nothing on earth is going to keep me
away from him. Will you please wipe Harry's feet while
I try to put on my clothes?"

"But, Virginia, the children?"

"You and Marthy must look after the children. Of
course I can't take them with me. Oh, Harry, won't you
please hush and let poor mamma dress? She is almost
distracted."

Something, a secret force of character which even her
mother had not suspected that she possessed, had arisen
in an instant and dominated the situation. She was no
longer the gentle and doting mother of a minute ago, but
a creature of fixed purpose and iron resolution. Even her
face appeared to lose its soft contour and hardened until
Mrs. Pendleton grew almost frightened. Never had she
imagined that Virginia could look like this.

"I am sure there is some mistake about it. Don't take
it so terribly to heart, Virginia," she pleaded, while she
knelt down, cowed and obedient, to wipe Harry's feet.

Virginia, who had already torn off her house dress,
and was hurriedly buttoning the navy blue waist in which
she had travelled, looked at her calmly without pausing
for an instant in her task.

"Will you bind up his foot with some arnica?" she
asked. "There's an old handkerchief in my work basket.
I want you and father to come here and stay until I get
back. It will be less trouble than moving all their things
over to the rectory."

"Very well, darling," Mrs. Pendleton replied meekly. "We'll do everything that we can, of course," and she added timidly, "Have you money enough?"

"I have thirty dollars. I just got it out of the bank to-day to pay Marthy and my housekeeping bills. Do you think that will be as much as I'll need?"

"I should think so, dear. Of course, if you find you want more, you can telegraph your father."

"The train doesn't leave for two hours, so I'll have plenty of time to get ready. It's just half-past six now, and Oliver didn't leave the house till eight o'clock."

"Won't you take a little something to eat before you go?"

"I couldn't swallow a morsel, but I'll sit with you and the children as soon as I've put the things in my satchel. I couldn't possibly need but this one dress, could I? If Oliver isn't really ill, I hope we can start home to-morrow. That will be two nights that I'll spend away. Oh, mother, ask father to pray that he won't be ill."

Her voice broke, but she fiercely bit back the sob before it escaped her lips.

"I will, dear, I promise you. We will both think of you and pray for you every minute. Virginia, are you sure it's wise? Couldn't we send some one—John Henry would go, I know—in your place?"

A spasm of irritation contracted Virginia's features. "Please don't, mother," she begged, "it just worries me. Whatever happens, I am going." Then she sobbed outright. "He wanted me to go with him at first, and I wouldn't because I thought it was my duty to stay at home with the children. If anything should happen to him, I'd never forgive myself."

She was slipping her black cloth skirt over her head as she spoke, and her terror-stricken face disappeared under the pleats before Mrs. Pendleton could turn to look at her. When her head emerged again above the belt of her skirt, the expression of her features had grown more natural.

"You'll go down in a carriage, won't you?" inquired her mother, whose mind achieved that perfect mingling of the practical and the sentimental which is rarely found in any except Southern women.

"I suppose I'll have to. Then I can take my satchel with me, and that will save trouble. You won't forget, mother, that I give Lucy a teaspoonful of cod-liver oil after each meal, will you? She has had that hacking cough for three weeks, and I want to break it up."

"I'll remember, Virginia, but I'm so miserable about your going alone."

Turning to the closet, Virginia unearthed an old black satchel from beneath a pile of toys, and began dusting it inside with a towel. Then she took out some underclothes from a bureau drawer and a few toilet articles, which she wrapped in pieces of tissue paper. Her movements were so methodical that the nervousness in Mrs. Pendleton's mind gave way slowly to astonishment. For the first time in her life, perhaps, the mother realized that her daughter was no longer a child, but a woman, and a woman whose character was as strong and as determined as her own. Vaguely, she understood, without analyzing the motives that moved Virginia, that this strength and this determination which so impressed her had arisen from those deep places in her daughter's soul where emotion and not thought had its source. Love was guiding her now as surely as it had guided her when she had refused to go with Oliver to New York, or when, but a few minutes ago, she had knelt down to wash and bandage Harry's little earth-stained feet. It was the only power to which she would ever surrender. No other principle could ever direct or control her.

Marthy, who appeared with Jenny's supper, was sent out to order the carriage and to bear a message to the rector, and Virginia took the little girl in her lap and began to crumble bread into the bowl of milk.

"Wouldn't you like me to do that, dear?" Mrs. Pendleton asked, with a submission in her tone which she had never used before except to the rector. "Don't you want to fix your hair over?"

"Oh, no, I'll keep on my hat till I go to bed, so it doesn't matter. I'd rather you'd finish my packing, if you don't mind. There's nothing more to go in except some collars and my bedroom slippers and that red wrapper hanging behind the door in the closet."

"Are you going to take any medicine?"

"Only that bottle of camphor and some mustard plasters. Yes, you'd better put in the brandy flask and the aromatic ammonia. You can never tell when you will need them. Now, my darlings, mother is going away and you must keep well and be as good as gold until she comes back."

To the amazement of Mrs. Pendleton (who reflected that you really never knew what to expect of children), this appeal produced an immediate and extraordinary result. Lucy, who had been fidgeting about and trying to help with the packing, became suddenly solemn and dignified, while an ennobling excitement mounted to Harry's face. Never particularly obedient before, they became, as soon as the words were uttered, as amenable as angels. Even Jenny stopped feeding long enough to raise herself and pat her mother's cheek with ten caressing, milky fingers.

"Mother's going away," Lucy said in a solemn voice, and a hush fell on the three of them.

"And grandma's coming here to live," Harry added after the silence had grown so depressing that Virginia had started to cry.

"Not to live, precious," Mrs. Pendleton corrected quickly. "Just to spend two days with you. Mother will be home in two days."

"Mother will be home in two days," Lucy repeated. "May I stay away from school while you're away, mamma?"

"And may I stop learning my letters?" Harry asked.

"No, darlings, you must do just as if I were here. Grandmamma will take care of you. Now promise me that you will be good."

They promised obediently, awed to submission.

"I don't see how I can possibly leave them—they are so good, and they behave exactly as if they realize how anxious I am," Virginia wept, breaking down when Marthy came to announce that the rector had come and the carriage was at the door.

"Suppose you give it up, Virginia. I—I'll send your father," Mrs. Pendleton pleaded, in desperation as she watched the tragedy of the parting.

But that strange force which the situation had developed in Virginia yielded neither to her mother's prayers nor to the last despairing wails of the children, who realized, at the sight of the black bag in Marthy's hands, that their providence was actually deserting them. The deepest of her instincts, the instinct at the root of all her mother love, was threatened, and she prepared for the conflict. The thing she loved best, she had learned, was neither husband nor child, but the one that needed her.

CHAPTER V

FAILURE

SHE had lain down in her clothes, impelled by the feeling that if there were to be a wreck she should prefer to appear completely dressed; so when the chill dawn came at last and the train pulled into Jersey City, she had nothing to do but adjust her veil and wait patiently until the porter came for her bag. His colour, which was black, inspired confidence, and she followed him trustfully to the platform, where he delivered her to another smiling member of his race. The cold was so penetrating that her teeth began to chatter as she turned to obey the orders of the second porter, who had assumed command of her. Never had she felt anything so bleak as the atmosphere of the station. Never in her life had she been so lonely as she was while she hurried down the long dim platform in the direction of a gate which looked as if it led into a prison. She was chilled through; her skin felt as if it had turned to india rubber; there was a sickening terror in her soul; and she longed above all things to sit down on one of the inhospitable tracks and burst into tears; but something stronger than impulse urged her shivering body onward and controlled the twitching muscles about her mouth. "In a few minutes I shall see Oliver. Oliver is ill and I am going to him," she repeated over and over to herself as if she were reciting a prayer.

Inside the station, she declined the offer of breakfast,

and was conducted to the ferry, where she was obliged
to run in order to catch the boat that was just leaving.
Seated on one of the long benches in the saloon, with her
bag at her feet and her umbrella grasped tightly in her
hand, she gazed helplessly at the other passengers, and
wondered if any one of them would tell her what to do
when she reached the opposite side. The women, she
thought, looked hard and harassed, and the men she could
not see because of the rows of newspapers behind which
they were hidden. Once her wandering gaze caught the
eyes of a middle-aged woman in rusty black, who smiled
at her above the head of a sleeping child.

"That's a pretty woman," a man said carelessly, as
he put down his paper, and she realized that he was talking about her to his companion. Then, as the terrible outlines of the city grew more distinct on the horizon, he
got up and strolled as carelessly past her to the deck. He
had spoken of her as indifferently as he might have spoken
of the weather.

As the tremendous battlements (which were not tremendous to any of the other passengers) emerged slowly
from the mist and cleft the sombre low-hanging clouds,
from which a few flakes of snow fell, her terror vanished
before the excitement which ran through her body. She
forgot her hunger, her loneliness, her shivering flesh, her
benumbed and aching feet. A sensation not unlike the one
with which the rector had marched into his first battle
fortified and exhilarated her. The fighting blood of her
ancestors grew warm in her veins. New York developed
suddenly from a mere spot on a map into a romance made
into brick; and when a ray of sunlight pierced the heavy
fog, and lay like a white wing aslant the few falling snow-
flakes, it seemed to her that the shadowy buildings lost
their sinister aspect and softened into a haunting and

mysterious beauty. Somewhere in that place of mystery and adventure Oliver was waiting for her! He was a part of that vast movement of life into which she was going. Then, youth, from which hope is never long absent, flamed up in her, and she was glad that she was still beautiful enough to cause strangers to turn and look at her.

But this mood also passed quickly, and a little later, while she rolled through the gray streets, into which the slant sunbeams could bring no colour, she surrendered again to that terror of the unknown which had seized her when she stood in the station. The beauty had departed from the buildings; the pavements were dirty; the little discoloured piles of snow made the crossings slippery and dangerous; and she held her breath as they passed through the crowded streets on the west side, overcome by the fear of "catching" some malign malady from the smells and the filth. The negro quarters in Dinwiddie were dirty enough, but not, she thought with a kind of triumph, quite so dirty as New York. When the cab turned into Fifth Avenue, she took her handkerchief from her nostrils; but this imposing street, which had not yet emerged from its evil dream of Victorian brownstone, impressed her chiefly as a place of a thousand prisons. It was impossible to believe that those frowning walls, undecorated by a creeper or the shadow of a tree, could really be homes where people lived and children were born.

At first she had gazed with childish interest and curiosity on the houses she was passing; then the sense of strangeness gave place to the exigent necessity of reaching Oliver as soon as possible. But the driver appeared indifferent to her timid taps on the glass at his back, while the horse progressed with the feeble activity of one who had spent a quarter of a century ineffectually making an effort. Her impatience, which she had at first kept under control, began to run in quivers of nervousness through her limbs. The very richness of her personal life, which had condensed all experience into a single emotional centre, and restricted her vision of the universe to that solitary window of the soul through which she looked, prevented her now from seeing in the city anything except the dreary background of Oliver's illness and failure. The artless wonder with which she had watched the gigantic outlines shape themselves out of the white fog, had faded utterly from her mind. She ached with longing to reach Oliver and to find him well enough to take the first train back to Dinwiddie.

At the hotel her bag and umbrella were wrested from her by an imperious attendant, and in what seemed to her an incredibly short space of time, she was following him along a velvet lined corridor on the tenth floor. The swift ascent in the elevator had made her dizzy, and the physical sensation reminded her that she was weak for food. Then the attendant rapped imperatively at a door just beyond a shining staircase, and she forget herself as completely as it had been her habit to do since her marriage.

"Come in!" responded a muffled voice on the inside, and as the door swung open, she saw Oliver, in his dressing-gown, and with an unshaved face, reading a newspaper beside a table on which stood an untasted cup of coffee.

"I didn't ring," he began impatiently, and then starting to his feet, he uttered her name in a voice which held her standing as if she were suddenly paralyzed on the threshold. "Virginia!"

A sob rose in her throat, and her faltering gaze passed from him to the hotel attendant, who responded to her unspoken appeal as readily as if it were a part of his duty.

Pushing her gently inside, he placed her bag and umbrella on an empty chair, took up the breakfast tray from the table, and inquired, with a kindness that strangely humbled her, if she wished to give an order. When she had helplessly shaken her head, he bowed and went out, closing the door softly upon their meeting.

"What in thunder, Virginia?" Oliver began, and she realized that he was angry.

"I heard you were sick—that the play had failed. I was so sorry I hadn't come with you——" she explained; and then, understanding for the first time the utter foolishness of what she had done, she put her hands up to her face and burst into tears.

He had risen from his chair, but he made no movement to come nearer to her, and when she took down her hands in order to wipe her eyes, she saw an expression in his face that frightened her by its strangeness. She had caught him when the guard that every human being, even a husband, wears, had fallen away, though in her ignorance it seemed to her that he had become suddenly another person. That she had entered into one of those awful hours of self-realization, when the soul must face its limitations alone and make its readjustments in silence, did not occur to her, because she, who had lived every minute of her life under the eyes of her parents or her children, could have no comprehension of the hunger for solitude which was devouring Oliver's heart. She saw merely that he did not want her, that she had not only startled, but angered him by coming; and the bitterness of that instant seemed to her more than she was able to bear. Something had changed him; he was older, he was harder, he was embittered.

"I—I am sorry," she stammered; and because even in the agony of this moment she could not think long of

herself, she added almost humbly, "Would you rather
that I should go back again?" Then, by the haggard look
of his face as he turned away from her toward the window, she saw that he also was suffering, and her soul
yearned over him as it had yearned over Harry when he
had had the toothache. "Oh, Oliver!" she cried, and
again, "Oh, Oliver, won't you let me help you?"

But he was in the mood of despairing humiliation when
one may support abuse better than pity. His failure, he
knew, had been undeserved, and he was still smarting
from the injustice of it as from the blows of a whip. For
twenty-four hours his nerves had been on the rack, and
his one desire had been to hide himself in the spiritual
nakedness to which he was stripped. Had he been obliged
to choose a witness to his suffering, it is probable that he
would have selected a stranger from the street rather than
his wife. The one thing that could have helped him, an
intelligent justification of his work, she was powerless to
give. In his need she had nothing but love to offer; and
love, she felt instinctively, was not the balm for his wound.

Afraid and yet passionately longing to meet his eyes,
she let her gaze fall away from him and wander timidly,
as if uncertain where to rest, about the disordered room,
with its dull red walls, its cheap Nottingham lace curtains
tied back with cords, its elaborately carved walnut furniture, and its litter of days-old newspapers upon the bed.
She saw his neckties hanging in an uneven row over the
oblong mirror, and she controlled a nervous impulse to
straighten them out and put them away.

"Why didn't you telegraph me?" he asked, after a
pause in which she had struggled vainly to look as if it
were the most natural thing in the world that he should
receive her in this way. "If I had known you were coming,
I should have met you."

"Father wanted to, but I wouldn't let him," she answered. "I—I thought you were sick."

In spite of his despair, it is probable that at the moment she was suffering more than he was, since a wound to love strikes deeper, after all, than a wound to ambition. Where she had expected to find her husband, she felt vaguely that she had encountered a stranger, and she was overwhelmed by that sense of irremediable loss which follows the discovery of terrible and unfamiliar qualities in those whom we have known and loved intimately for years. The fact that he was plainly struggling to disguise his annoyance, that he was trying as hard as she to assume a manner he did not feel, only added a sardonic humour to poignant tragedy.

"Have you had anything to eat?" he asked abruptly, and remembering that he had not kissed her when she entered, he put his arm about her and brushed her cheek with his lips.

"No, I waited to breakfast with you. I was in such a hurry to get here."

"By Jove!" he exclaimed, and going over to the bell, he touched it with the manner of a man who is delighted that anything so perfectly practical as food exists in the world.

While he was speaking to the waiter, she took off her hat, and washed the stains of smoke and tears from her face. Her hair was a sight, she thought, but while she gazed back at her stricken eyes in the little mirror over the washstand, she recalled with a throb of gratitude that the stranger on the boat had said she was pretty. She felt so humble that she clung almost with desperation to the thought that Oliver always liked to have people admire her.

When she turned from the washstand, he was reading

the newspaper again, and he put it aside with a forced cheerfulness to arrange the table for breakfast.

"Aren't you going to have something too?" she asked, looking disconsolately at the tray, for all her hunger had departed. If only he would be natural she felt that she could bear anything! If only he would stop trying to pretend that he was not miserable and that nothing had happened! After all, it couldn't be so very bad, could it? It wasn't in the least as if one of the children were ill.

She poured out a cup of coffee for him before drinking her own, and putting it down on the table at his side, waited patiently until he should look up again from his paper. A lump as hard as lead had risen in her throat and was choking her.

"Are the children well?" he asked presently, and she answered with an affected brightness more harrowing than tears, "Yes, mother is taking care of them. Lucy still has the little cough, but I'm giving her cod-liver oil. And, what do you think? I have a surprise for you. Harry can read the first lesson in his reader."

He smiled kindly enough, but from the vacancy in his face, she realized that he had not taken in a word she had said. His trouble, whatever it was, could absorb him so utterly that he had ceased even to be interested in his children. He, who had borne so calmly the loss of that day-old baby for whom she had grieved herself to a shadow, was plunged into this condition of abject hopelessness merely because his play was a failure! It was not only impossible for her to share his suffering; she realized, while she watched him, that she could not so much as comprehend it. Her limitations, of which she had never been acutely aware until to-day, appeared suddenly insurmountable. Love, which had seemed to her to solve all problems and smooth all difficulties, was helpless to enlighten her. It was not love; it was something else that she needed now, and of this something else she knew not even so much as the name.

She drank her coffee quickly, fearing that if she did not take food she should lose control of herself and anger him by a display of hysterics.

"I don't wonder you couldn't drink your coffee," she said, with a quivering little laugh. "It must have been made yesterday." Then, unable to bear the strain any longer, she cried out sharply: "Oh, Oliver, won't you tell me what is the matter?"

His look grew hard, while a spasm of irritation contracted his mouth.

"There's nothing you need worry about—except that I've borrowed money, and I'm afraid we'll have to cut down things a bit until I manage to pay it back."

"Why, of course we'll cut down things," she almost laughed in her relief. "We can live on a great deal less, and I'll market so carefully that you will hardly know the difference. I'll put Marthy in the kitchen and take care of the children myself. It won't be the least bit of trouble."

She knew by his face that he was grateful to her, though he said merely: "I'm a little knocked up, I suppose, so you mustn't mind. I've got a beast of a headache. Martin is going to take 'The Beaten Road' off at the end of the week, you know, and he doesn't think now that he will produce the other. There wasn't a good word for me from the critics, and yet, damn them, I know that the play is the best one that's ever come out of America. But it's real—that's why they fell foul of it—it isn't stuffed with sugar plums."

"Why, what in the world possessed them?" she returned indignantly. "It is a beautiful play."

She saw him flinch at the word, and the sombre irritation which his outburst had relieved for a minute, settled again on his features. Her praise, she understood, only exasperated him, though she did not realize that it was the lack of discrimination which offended his pride. At the moment, intelligent appreciation of his work would have been bread and meat to him, but her pitiful attempts at flattery were like bungling touches on raw flesh. Had he written the veriest rags of sentimental rubbish, he knew she would as passionately have defended their "beauty."

"I'll get dressed quickly and look after some business," he said, "and we'll go home to-night."

Her eyes shone, and she began to eat her eggs with a resolution born of the consoling memory of Dinwiddie. If only they could be at home again with the children, she felt that all this trouble and misunderstanding would vanish. With a strange confusion of ideas, it seemed to her that Oliver's suffering had been in some mysterious way produced by New York, and that it existed merely within the circumscribed limits of this dreadful city.

"Oh, Oliver, that will be lovely!" she exclaimed, and tried to subdue the note of joy in her voice.

"I shan't be able to get back to lunch, I'm afraid. What will you do about it?"

"Don't bother about me, dearest. I'll dress and take a little walk just to see what Fifth Avenue is like. I can't get lost if I go perfectly straight up the street, can I?"

"Fifth Avenue is only a block away. You can't miss it. Now, I'll hurry and be off."

She knew that he was anxious to be alone, and so firmly was she convinced that this mood of detachment would leave him as soon as he was in the midst of his family again, that she was able to smile brightly when he kissed her and, seizing his hat, rushed from the room. For a time after he had gone she amused herself putting his things in order and packing the little tin trunk he had brought with him; but the red walls and the steam heat in the room sickened her at last, and when she had bathed and dressed and there seemed nothing left for her to do but get out her work-bag and begin darning his socks, she decided that she would put on her hat and go out for a walk. It did not occur to her to feel hurt by the casual manner in which Oliver had shifted the responsibility of her presence, partly owing to her inability to take a selfish point of view about anything, and partly because of the habit of making allowances for the male in which she had been sedulously trained from her infancy.

At the door the porter directed her to Fifth Avenue, and she ventured cautiously as far as the flowing rivulet at the corner, where she would probably have stood until Oliver's return, if a friendly policeman had not observed her stranded helplessness and assisted her over. "How on earth am I to get back again?" she thought, smiling up at him; and this anxiety engrossed her so completely that for a minute she forgot to look at the amazing buildings and the curious crowds that hurried frantically in their shadows. Then a pale finger of sunlight pointed suddenly across the high roofs in front of her, and awed, in spite of her preoccupation, by the strangeness of the scene, she stopped and watched the moving carriages in the middle of the street and the never-ending stream of people that passed on the wet pavements. Occasionally, while she stood there, some of the passers-by would turn and look at her with friendly admiring eyes, as though they found something pleasant in her lovely wistful face and her old-fashioned clothes; and this pleased her so much that she lost her feeling of loneliness. It was a kindly crowd, and

because she was young and pretty and worth looking at,
a part of the exhilaration of this unknown life passed into
her, and she felt for a little while as if she belonged to it.
The youth in her responded to the passing call of the
streets, to this call which fluted like the sound of pipes in
her blood, and lifted her for a moment out of the narrow track of individual experience. It was charming to
feel that all these strangers looked kindly upon her, and
she tried to show that she returned their interest by letting
a little cordial light shine in her eyes. For the first time
in her life the personal boundaries of sympathy fell away
from her, and she realized, in a fleeting sensation, something of the vast underlying solidarity of human existence.
A humble baby in a go-cart waited at one of the crossings
for the traffic to pass, and bending over, she hugged him
ecstatically, not because he reminded her of Harry, but
simply because he was a baby.

"He is so sweet I just had to squeeze him," she said to
his mother, a working woman in a black shawl, who stood
behind him.

Then the two women smiled at each other in that free-
masonry of motherhood of which no man is aware, and
Virginia wondered why people had ever foolishly written
of the "indifference of a crowd." The chill that had lain
over her heart since her meeting with Oliver melted utterly in the glow with which she had embraced the baby
at the crossing. With the feeling of his warm little body
in her arms, everything had become suddenly right again.
New York was no longer a dreadful city, and Oliver's
failure appeared as brief as the passing pang of a toothache. Her sanguine spirit had returned like a rosy mist
to embellish and obscure the prosaic details of the situation. Like the cheerful winter sunshine, which transfigured

the harsh outlines of the houses, her vision adorned the reality in the mere act of beholding it.

Midway of the next block there was a jeweller's window full of gems set in intricate patterns, and stopping before it, she studied the trinkets carefully in the hope of being able to describe them to Lucy. Then a man selling little automatic pigs at the corner attracted her attention, and she bought two for Harry and Jenny, and carried them triumphantly away in boxes under her arm. She knew that she looked countrified and old-fashioned, and that nobody she met was wearing either a hat or a dress which in the least resembled the style of hers; but the knowledge of this did not trouble her, because in her heart she preferred the kind of clothes that were worn in Dinwiddie. The women in New York seemed to her artificial and affected in appearance, and they walked, she thought, as if they were trying to make people look at them. The bold way they laced in their figures she regarded as almost indecent, and she noticed that they looked straight into the eyes of men instead of lowering their lashes when they passed them. Her provincialism, like everything else that belonged to her and had become endeared by habit and association, seemed to her so truly beautiful and desirable that she would not have parted with it for worlds.

Turning presently, she walked down Fifth Avenue as far as Twenty-third Street, and then, confused by the crossing, she passed into Broadway, without knowing that it was Broadway, until she was enlightened by a stranger to whom she appealed. When she began to retrace her steps, she discovered that she was hungry, and she longed to go into one of the places where she saw people eating at little tables; but her terror of what she had heard of the high prices of food in New York restaurants restrained her. General Goode still told of paying six dollars and a half for a dinner he had ordered in a hotel in Fifth Avenue, and her frugal temperament, reinforced by anxiety as to Oliver's debts, preferred to take no unnecessary risks with the small amount in her pocketbook. Oliver, of course, would have laughed at her petty economies, and have ordered recklessly whatever attracted his appetite; but, as she gently reminded herself again, men were different. On the whole, this lordly prodigality pleased her rather than otherwise. She felt that it was in keeping with the bigness and virility of the masculine nature; and if there were pinching and scraping to be done, she immeasurably preferred that it should fall to her lot to do it and not to Oliver's.

At the hotel she found that Oliver had not come in, and after a belated luncheon of tea and toast in the dining-room, she went upstairs and sat down between the Nottingham lace curtains to watch for his return. From the terrific height, on which she felt like a sparrow, she could see a row of miniature puppets passing back and forth at the corner of Fifth Avenue. For hours she tried in vain to distinguish the figure of Oliver in the swiftly moving throng, and in spite of herself she could not repress a feeling of pleasant excitement. She knew that Oliver would think that she ought to be depressed by his failure, yet she could not prevent the return of a childlike confidence in the profound goodness of life. Everything would be right, everything was eternally bound to be right from the beginning. That evasive idealism, which had confused the pleasant with the true for generations, had become in her less a moral conviction than a fixed quality of soul. To dwell even for a minute on "the dark side of things" awoke in her the same instinct of mortal sin that she had felt at the discovery that Oliver was accustomed to "break" the Sabbath by reading profane literature.

When, at last, as the dusk fell in the room, she heard his hasty step in the corridor, a wave of joyful expectancy rose in her heart and trembled for utterance on her lips. Then the door opened; he came from the gloom into the pale gleam of light that shone in from the window, and with her first look into his face, her rising joy ebbed quickly away. A new element, for which neither her training nor her experience had prepared her, entered at that instant into her life. Not the external world, but the sacred inner circle in which they had loved and known each other was suddenly clouded. Everything outside of this was the same, but the fact confronted her there as grimly as a physical sore. The evil struck at the very heart of her love, since it was not life but Oliver that had changed.

CHAPTER VI

THE SHADOW

OLIVER had changed; for months this thought had lain
like a stone on her heart. She went about her life just as
usual, yet never for an instant during that long winter
and spring did she lose consciousness of its dreadful presence. It was the first thing to face her in the morning, the
last thing from which she turned when, worn out with
perplexity, she fell asleep at night. During the day the
children took her thoughts away from it for hours, but
never once, not even while she heard Harry's lessons or
tied the pink or blue bows in Lucy's and Jenny's curls,
did she ever really forget it. Since the failure of Oliver's
play, which had seemed to her such a little thing in itself,
something had gone out of their marriage, and this something was the perfect understanding that had existed
between them. There were times when her sympathy
appeared to her almost to infuriate him. Even her efforts
toward economy—for since their return from New York
she had put Marthy into the kitchen and had taken entire
charge of the children—irritated rather than pleased him.
And the more she irritated him, the more she sought
zealously, by innumerable small attentions, to please and
to pacify him. Instead of leaving him in the solitude he
sought, which might have restored him to his normal balance of mind, she became possessed, whenever he shut
himself in his study or went alone for a walk, with a

frenzied dread lest he should permit himself to brood
over the financial difficulties in which the wreck of his
ambition had placed them. She, who feared loneliness as
if it were the smallpox, devised a thousand innocent de-
ceptions by which she might break in upon him when he
sat in his study and discover whether he was actually reading the papers or merely pretending to do so. In her
natural simplicity, it never occurred to her to penetrate
beneath the surface disturbances of his mood. These engrossed her so completely that the cause of them was
almost forgotten. Dimly, she realized that this strange,
almost physical soreness, which made him shrink from her
presence as a man with weak eyes shrinks from the light,
was the outward sign of a secret violence of soul; yet she
ministered helplessly to each passing explosion of temper
as if it were the cause instead of the result of his suffering.
Introspection, which had lain under a moral ban in a
society that assumed the existence of an unholy alliance
between the secret and the evil, could not help her because
she had never indulged in it. Partly because of the ingenuous candour of the Pendleton nature, and partly owing
to the mildness of a climate which made it more comfortable for Dinwiddians to live for six months of the year
on their front porches and with their windows open, she
shared the ingrained Southern distrust of any state of
mind that could not cheerfully support the observation
of the neighbours. She knew that he had turned from his
work with disgust, and if he wasn't working and wasn't
reading, what on earth could he be doing alone unless he
had, as she imagined in desperation, begun wilfully to
nurse his despondency? Even the rector couldn't help her
here; for his knowledge of character was limited to the
types of the soldier and the churchman, and his son-in-law
did not belong, he admitted, in either of these noble

classifications. At the bottom of his soul the good man had always entertained for Oliver something of the kindly contempt with which his generation regarded a healthy male, who, it suspected, would decline either to preach a sermon or to kill a man in the cause of morality. But on one line of treatment father and daughter were passionately agreed: whatever happened, it was not good that Oliver should be left by himself for a minute. When he was in the bank, where Cyrus had found him a place as a clerk on an insignificant salary, it might be safely assumed that he was cheered by the unfailing company of his fellow-workers; but when he came home, the responsibility of his distraction and his cure rested upon Virginia and the children. And since her opinion of her own power to entertain was modest, she fell back with a sublime confidence on the unrivalled brilliancy and the infinite variety of the children's prattle. During the spring, as he grew more and more indifferent and depressed, she arranged that the children should be with him every instant while he was in the house. She brought Jenny's high chair to the table in order that the adorable infant might breakfast with her father; she kept Harry up an hour later at night so that he might add the gaiety of his innocent mirth to their otherwise long and silent evenings. Though she would have given anything to drop into bed as soon as the babies were undressed, she forced herself to sit up, without yawning, until Oliver turned out the lights, bolted the door, and remarked irritably that she ought to have been asleep hours ago.

"You aren't used to sitting up so late, Virginia; it makes you dark under the eyes," he said one June night as he came in from the porch where he had been to look up at the stars.

"But I can't go to bed until you do, darling. I get so worried about you."

"Why in heaven's name, should you worry about me? I am all right."

She saw her mistake, and with her unvarying sweetness, set out to rectify it.

"Of course, I know you are; but we have so little time together that I don't want to miss the evenings."

"So little!" he echoed, not unkindly, but in simple astonishment.

"I mean the children sit up late now, and we can't talk while they are playing in the room."

"Don't you think you might get them to bed earlier? They are becoming rather a nuisance, aren't they?"

He said it kindly enough, yet tears rushed to her eyes as she looked at him. It was impossible for her to conceive of any mood in which the children would become "rather a nuisance" to her, and the words hurt her more than he was ever to know. It was the last straw that she could not bear, said her heart as she turned away from him. She had borne the extra work without a complaint; she had pinched and scraped, if not happily, at least with a smile; she had sat up while her limbs ached with fatigue and the longing to be in bed: and all these things were as nothing to the tragic confession that the children had become "rather a nuisance." Of the many trials she had had to endure, this, she told herself, was the bitterest.

Though her feet burned and her muscles throbbed with fatigue, she lay awake for hours, with her eyes wide open in the moonlight. All the small harassing duties of the morrow, which usually swarmed like startled bees through her brain at night, were scattered now by this vague terror that assumed no definite shape. The delicacy of Lucy's chest, Harry's stubborn refusal to learn to spell, and even the harrowing certainty that the children's appetites were fast outstripping the frugal fare she provided; these

stinging worries had flown before a new anxiety which
was the more poignant, she felt, because she could not
give it a name. The Pendleton idealism was powerless to
dispel this malign shadow which corresponded so closely
to that substance of evil whose very existence the Pendleton idealism eternally denied. To battle with a delusion
was virtually to admit one's belief in its actuality, and this,
she reflected passionately, lying awake there in the darkness, was the last thing she was prepared at the moment to
do. Oliver was changed, and yet it was her duty to fortify
herself with the consoling assurance that, whatever happened, Oliver could never really change. Deep down in her
that essential fibre of her being which was her soul, which
drew its vitality from the race of which it was a part,
and yet which distinguished and separated her from every
other person and object in the universe;—this essential
fibre was compacted of innumerable Pendleton refusals
to face the reality. Even with Lucy's chest and Harry's
lessons and the cost of food, she had always felt a soothing conviction that by thinking hard enough about them she
could make them every one come out right in the morning.
As a normal human being in a world that was not designed
on altruistic principles, it was out of the question that she
should escape an occasional hour of despondency; but with
the narrow outlook of women who lead intense personal
lives, it would have been impossible for her to see anything really wrong in the universe while Oliver and all
the children were well. God was in His heaven so long as
the affairs of her household worked together for good.
"It can't be that he is different—I must have imagined it,"
she thought now, breathing softly lest she should disturb
the sleeping Oliver. "It is natural that he should be worried about his debts, and the failure of the play went very
hard with him, of course—but if he appears at times to

have grown bitter, it must be only that I have come to exact too much of him. I oughtn't to expect him to take the same interest in the children that I do——"

Then, rising softly on her elbow, she smoothed the sheet over Jenny's dimpled little body, and bent her ear downward to make sure that the child was breathing naturally in her sleep. In spite of her depression, that rosy face framed in hair like spun yellow silk, aroused in her a feeling of ecstasy. Whenever she looked at one of her children—at her youngest child especially—her maternal passion seemed to turn to flame in her blood. Even first love had not been so exquisitely satisfying, so interwoven of all imaginable secret meanings of bliss. Jenny's thumb was in her mouth, and removing it gently, Virginia bent lower and laid her hot cheek on the soft shining curls. Some vital power, an emanation from that single principle of Love which ruled her life, passed from the breath of the sleeping child into her body. Peace descended upon her, swift and merciful like sleep, and turning on her side, she lay with her hand on Jenny's crib, as though in clinging to her child she clung to all that was indestructible in the universe.

The next night Oliver telephoned from the Treadwells' that he would not be home to supper, and when he came in at eleven o'clock, he appeared annoyed to find her sitting up for him.

"You ought to have gone to bed, Virginia. You look positively haggard," he said.

"I wasn't sleepy. Mother came in for a few minutes, and we put the children to bed. Jenny wanted to say goodnight to you, and she cried when I told her you had gone out. I believe she loves you better than she does anybody in the world, Oliver."

He smiled with something of the gay defiance that had

first captivated her imagination. In spite of the melancholy which had clouded his charm of late, he had lost neither his glow of physical well-being nor the look of abounding intellectual energy which distinguished him from all other men whom she knew. It was this intellectual energy, she sometimes thought, which purified his character of that vein of earthiness which she had looked upon as the natural, and therefore the pardonable, attribute of the masculine point of view.

"If she keeps her looks, she'll leave her mother behind some day," he answered. "You need a new dress, Virginia. I hate that old waist and skirt. Why don't you wear the swishy blue silk I always liked on you?"

"I made it over for Lucy, dear. She had to have a dress to wear to Lily Carrington's birthday party, and I didn't want to buy one. It looks ever so nice on her."

"Doubtless, but I like it better on you."

"It doesn't matter what I wear, but Lucy is so fond of pretty things, and children dress more now than they used to do. What did Susan have to say?"

He had turned to bolt the front door, and while his back was toward her, she raised her hand to smother a yawn. All day she had been on her feet, except for the two hours when she had worked at her sewing-machine, while Harry and Jenny were taking their morning nap. She had not had time to change her dress until after supper, and she had felt so tired then that it had not seemed worth while to do so. There was, in fact, nothing to change to, since she had made over the blue silk, except an old black organdie, cut square in the neck, which she had worn in the months before Jenny's birth. As a girl she had loved pretty clothes; but there were so many other things to think about now; and from the day that her first child had come to her it had seemed to matter less

and less what she wore or how she appeared. Nothing had
really counted in life except the supreme privilege of giving herself, body and soul, in the service of love. All that
she was, all that she had, belonged to Oliver and to his
children, so what difference could it make to them, since
she gave herself so completely, whether she wore new
clothes or old?

When he turned to her, she had smothered the yawn,
and was smiling. "Is Aunt Belinda just the same?" she
asked, for he had not answered her question about Susan.

"To tell the truth, I forgot to ask," he replied, with a
laugh. "Susan seemed very cheerful, and John Henry was
there, of course. It wouldn't surprise me to hear any day
that they are to be married. By the way, Virginia, why
did you never tell me what a good rider you are? Abby
Goode says you would have been a better horsewoman than
she is if you hadn't given up riding."

"Why, I haven't been in the saddle for years. I stopped
when we had to sell my horse Bess, and that was before
you came back to Dinwiddie. How did Abby happen to
be there?"

"She stopped to see Susan about something, and then
we got to talking—the bunch of us. John Henry asked
me to exercise his horse for him when he doesn't go. I
rather hope I'll get a chance to go fox-hunting in the
autumn. Abby was talking about it."

"Has she changed much? I haven't seen her for years.
She is hardly ever in Dinwiddie."

"Well, she's fatter, but it's becoming to her. It makes
her look softer. She's a bit coarse, but she tells a capital
story. I always liked Abby."

"Yes, I always liked Abby too," Virginia answered,
and it was on the tip of her tongue to add that Abby had
always liked Oliver. "If he hadn't seen me, perhaps he

might have married her," she thought, and the remote
possibility of such bliss for poor defrauded Abby filled her
with an incredible tenderness. She would never have believed that bouncing, boisterous Abby Goode could have
aroused in her so tender a sympathy.

He appeared so much more cheerful than she had seen
him since his disastrous trip to New York, that, moved by
an unselfish impulse of gratitude toward the cause of it,
she put out her hand to him, while he raised his arm to
extinguish the light.

"I am so glad about the horse, dear," she said. "It will
be nice for you to go sometimes with Abby."

"Why couldn't you come too, Virginia?"

"Oh, I shouldn't have time—and, besides, I gave it up
long ago. I don't think a mother has any business on horseback."

"All the same I wish you wouldn't let yourself go to
pieces. What have you done to your hands? They used
to be so pretty."

She drew them hastily away, while the tears rose in a
mist to her eyes. It was like a man—it was especially like
Oliver—to imagine that she could clean up half a house
and take charge of three children, yet keep her hands as
white and soft as they had been when she was a girl and
did nothing but wait for a lover. In a flash of memory, she
saw the reddened and knotted hands of her mother, and
then a procession of hands belonging to all the mothers of
her race that had gone before her. Were her own but a
single pair in that chain of pathetic hands that had worked
in the exacting service of Love?

"It is so hard to keep them nice," she said; but her
heart cried, "What do my hands matter when it is for your
sake that I have spoiled them?" With her natural tendency
to undervalue the physical pleasure of life, she had looked

upon her beauty as a passing bloom which would attract her lover to the veiled wonders of her spirit. Beauty as an end in itself would have appeared to her as immoral a cult as the pursuit of wandering desire.

"I never noticed until to-night what pretty hands Abby has," he said, innocently enough, as he turned off the gas.

A strange sensation, so different from anything she had ever felt before that she could not give it a name, pierced her heart like an arrow. Then it fled as suddenly as it had come, and left her at ease with the thought: "Abby has had nothing to hurt her hands. Why shouldn't they be pretty?" But not for Abby's hands would she have given up a single hour when she had washed Jenny's little flannels or dug enchanted garden beds with Harry's miniature trowel.

"She used to have a beautiful figure," she said with perfect sincerity.

"Well, she's got it still, though she's a trifle too large for my taste. You can't help liking her; she's such jolly good company, but, somehow, she doesn't seem womanly. She's too fond of sport and all that sort of thing."

His ideal woman still corresponded to the type he had chosen for his mate; for true womanliness was inseparably associated in his mind with those qualities that had awakened for generations the impulse of selection in the men of his race. Though he enjoyed Abby, he refused stubbornly to admire her, since evolution, which moves rapidly in the social activities, had left his imagination still cherishing the conventions of the jungle in the matter of sex. He saw woman as dependent upon man for the very integrity of her being, and beyond the divine fact of this dependence, he did not see her at all. But there was nothing sardonic in his point of view, which had been strengthened by his marriage to Virginia, who shared it. It was one of those

mental attitudes, indeed, which, in the days of loose thinking and hazy generalizations, might have proved its divine
descent by its universality. Oliver, his Uncle Cyrus, the
rector, and honest John Henry, however they may have
differed in their views of the universe or of each other,
were one at least in accepting the historical dogma of the
supplementary being of woman.

And yet, so strange is life, so inexplicable are its contra-
dictions, there were times when Oliver's ideal appeared
almost to betray him, and the intellectual limitations of
Virginia bored rather than delighted him. Habit, which
is a sedative to a phlegmatic nature, acts not infrequently
as an irritant upon the temperament of the artist; and since
he had turned from his work in a passion of disgust at the
dramatic obtuseness of his generation, he had felt more
than ever the need of an outlet for the torrent of his
imagination. As a wife, Virginia was perfect; as a mental
companion, she barely existed at all. She was, he had come
to recognize, profoundly indifferent to the actual world.
Her universe was a fiction, except the part of it that concerned him or the children. He had never forgotten that
he had read his play to her one night shortly after Jenny's
birth, and she had learned forward with her chin on her
palm and a look in her face as if she were listening for a
cry which never came from the nursery. Her praise had
had the sound of being recited by rote, and had aroused
in him a sense of exasperation which returned even now
whenever she mentioned his work. In the days of his courtship the memory of her simplicities clung like an exquisite
bouquet to an intoxicating image; but in eight years of
daily intimacy the flavour and the perfume of mere innocence had evaporated. The quality that had first charmed
him was, perhaps, the first of which he had grown weary.
He still loved Virginia, but he had ceased to talk to her.

"If you go into the refrigerator, Oliver, don't upset Jenny's bottle of milk," she said, looking after him as he hurried toward the dining-room.

Her foot was already on the bottom step of the staircase, for she had heard, or imagined that she had heard, a sound from the nursery, and she was impatient to see if one of the children had awakened and got out of bed. All the evening, while she had changed the skin-tight sleeves of the eighties to the balloon ones of the nineties in an old waist which she had had before her marriage and had never worn because it was unbecoming, her thoughts had been of Harry, whom she had punished for some act of flagrant disobedience in the afternoon. Now, she was eager to comfort him if he were awake and unhappy, or merely to cuddle and kiss him if he were fast asleep in his bed.

At the top of the staircase she saw the lowered lamp in the nursery, and beside it stood Harry in his little night-gown, with a toy ship in his arms.

"Mamma, I'm tired of bed and I want to play."

"S—sush, darling, you will wake Jenny. It isn't day yet. You must go back to bed."

"But I'm tired of bed."

"You won't be after I tuck you in."

"Will you sit by me and tell me a story?"

"Yes, darling, I'll tell you a story if you'll promise not to talk."

Her eyes were heavy with sleep, and her limbs trembled from the exhaustion of the long June day; but she remembered the punishment of the afternoon, and as she looked at him her heart seemed melting with tenderness.

"And you'll promise not to go away until I'm fast asleep?—you'll promise, mamma?"

"I'll promise, precious. No, you mustn't take your ship to bed with you. That's a darling."

Then, as Oliver was heard coming softly up the stairs for fear of arousing the children, she caught Harry's moist hand in hers and stole with him into the nursery.

To Virginia, in the long torrid days of that summer, there seemed time for neither anxiety nor disappointment. Every minute of her eighteen waking hours was spent in keeping the children washed, dressed, and good-humoured. She thought of herself so little that it never occurred to her to reflect whether she was happy or unhappy—scarcely even whether she was awake or asleep. Twice a week John Henry's horse carried Oliver for a ride with Abby and Susan, and on these evenings he stayed so late that Virginia ceased presently even to make a pretence of waiting supper. Several times, on September afternoons, when the country burned with an illusive radiance as if it were seen through a mirage, she put on her old riding-habit, which she had hunted up in the attic at the rectory, and mounting one of Abby's horses, started to accompany them; but her conscience reproached her so bitterly at the thought that she was seeking pleasure away from the children, that she hurried homeward across the fields before the others were ready to turn. As with most women who are born for motherhood, that supreme fact had not only absorbed the emotional energy of her girlhood, but had consumed in its ecstatic flame even her ordinary capacities for enjoyment. While fatherhood left Oliver still a prey to dreams and disappointments, the more exclusive maternal passion rendered Virginia profoundly indifferent to every aspect of life except the intimate personal aspect of her marriage. She couldn't be happy, she couldn't even be at ease, while she remembered that the children were left to the honest, yet scarcely tender, mercies of Marthy.

"I shall never go again," she thought, as she slipped

from her saddle at the gate, and catching up her long riding-skirt, ran up the short walk to the steps. "I must be getting old. Something has gone out of me."

And there was no regret in her heart for this *something* that had fled out of her life, for the flashing desires and the old breathless pleasures of youth that she had lost. For a month this passive joy lasted; the joy of one whose days are full and whose every activity is in use. Then there came an October afternoon that she never forgot because it burned across her life like a prairie fire and left a scarred track of memory behind it. It had been a windless day, filled with glittering blue lights that darted like birds down the long ash-coloured roads, and spun with a golden web of air which made the fields and trees appear as thin and as insubstantial as dreams. The children were with Marthy in the park, and Virginia, attired in the old waist with the new sleeves, was leaning on the front gate watching the slow fall of the leaves from the gnarled mulberry tree at the corner, when Mrs. Pendleton appeared on the opposite side of the street and crossed the cobblestones of the road with her black alpaca skirt trailing behind her.

"I wonder why in the world mother doesn't hold up her skirt?" Virginia thought, swinging back the little wooden gate while she waited. "Mother, you are letting your train get all covered with dust!" she called, as soon as Mrs. Pendleton came near enough to catch her half-whispered warning.

Reaching down indifferently, the older woman caught up a handful of her skirt and left the rest to follow ignominiously in the dust. From the carelessness of the gesture, Virginia saw at once that her mother's mind was occupied by one of those rare states of excitement or distress in

which the preservation of her clothes had sunk to a matter
of secondary importance. When the small economies were
banished from Mrs. Pendleton's consciousness, matters
had assumed indeed a serious aspect.

"Why, mother, what on earth has happened?" Virginia
asked, hurrying toward her.

"Let me come in and speak to you, Virginia. I mean inside the house. One can never be sure that some of the
neighbours aren't listening," she said in a whisper.

Hastening past her daughter, she went in to the hall,
and, then turning, faced her with her hand on the doorknob. In the dim light of the hall her face looked white
and drawn, like the face of a person who has been suddenly
stricken with illness. "Virginia, I've just had a visit from
Mrs. Carrington—you know what a gossip she is—but I
think I ought to tell you that she says people are talking
about Oliver's riding so much with Abby."

A pain as sharp as if the teeth of a beast gnawed in her
heart, pierced Virginia while she stood there, barring the
door with her hands. Her peace, which had seemed indestructible a moment ago, was shattered by a sensation of
violent anger—not against Abby, not against Oliver, not
even against the gossiping old women of Dinwiddie—but
against her own blindness, her own inconceivable folly!
At the moment, the civilization of centuries was stripped
from her, and she was as simple, as primitive, as a female
of the jungle. On the surface she was still calm, but to her
own soul she felt that she presented the appalling spectacle
of a normal woman turned fury. It was one of those instants that are so expected, so entirely unnatural and out
of harmony with the rest of life, that they obliterate the
boundaries of character which separate the life of the individual from the ancient root of the race. Not Virginia,

but the primeval woman in her blood, shrieked out in protest as she saw her hold on her mate threatened. The destruction of the universe, so long as it left her house standing in its bit of ground, would have overwhelmed her less utterly.

"But what on earth can they say, mother? It was all my fault. I made him go. He never lifted his finger for Abby."

"I know, darling, I know. Of course, Oliver is not to blame, but people will talk, and I think Abby ought to have known better."

For an instant only Virginia hesitated. Then something stronger than the primitive female in her blood—the spirit of a lady—spoke through her lips.

"I don't believe Abby was to blame either," she said.

"But women ought to know better, Virginia, and Abby is nearly thirty."

"She always wanted me to go, mother. I don't believe she thought for a minute that she was doing anything wrong. Abby is a little coarse, but she's perfectly good. Nobody will make me think otherwise."

"Well, it can't go on, dear. You must stop Oliver's riding with her. And Mrs. Carrington says she hears that he is going to Atlantic City with them in General Goode's private car on Thursday."

"Abby asked me, too, but of course I couldn't leave the children."

"Of course not. Oliver must give it up. Oh, Virginia, a scandal, even where one is innocent, is so terrible. A woman —a true woman—would endure death rather than be talked about. I remember your cousin Jane Pendleton made an unhappy marriage, and her husband used to get drunk and beat her and even carry on dreadfully with the coloured servants; but she said that was better than the disgrace of a separation."

"But all that has nothing to do with me, mother. Oliver is an angel, and this is every bit my fault, not Abby's." The violence in her soul had passed, and she felt suddenly calm.

"Of course, darling, of course. Now that you see what it has led to, you can stop it immediately."

They were so alike as they stood there facing each other, mother and daughter, that they might have represented different periods of the same life: youth and age meeting together. Both were perfect products of that social order whose crowning grace and glory they were. Both were creatures trained to feel rather than think, whose very goodness was the result not of reason, but of emotion. And, above all, both were gentlewomen to the innermost cores of their natures. Passion could not banish for long that exquisite forbearance which the generations had developed from a necessity into an art.

"I can't stop his going with her, because that would make people think I believe the things they say; but I can go, too, mother, and I will. I'll borrow Susan's horse and go fox-hunting with them to-morrow."

"But the children, dear—and then, oh, Virginia, you might get hurt."

To her surprise Virginia laughed.

"I shan't get hurt, mother—and if I did——"

She left her sentence unfinished, but in the break there was the first note of bitterness that her mother had ever heard from her lips. Was it possible, after all, that there was "more in it" than she had let appear in her words? Was it possible that her passionate defence of Abby had been but a beautiful pretence?

"I'll go straight down to the Treadwells' to ask Susan for her horse," she added cheerfully, "and you'll come over very early, won't you, to stay with the children? Oliver always starts before daybreak."

"Yes, darling, I'll get up at dawn and come over—but, Virginia, promise me to be careful."

"Oh, I'll be careful," Virginia responded lightly, as she went out on the porch.

CHAPTER VII

THE WILL TO LIVE

"It's all horrid talk. There's not a word of truth in it," she thought, true to the Pendleton point of view, as she turned into Old Street on her way to the Treadwells'. Then the sound of horses' hoofs rang on the cobblestones, and, looking past the corner, she saw Oliver and Abby galloping under the wine-coloured leaves of the oak tree at the crossing. His face was turned back, as if he were looking over his shoulder at the red sunset, and he was laughing as she had not heard him laugh since that dreadful morning in the bedroom of the New York hotel. What a boy he was still! As she watched him, it seemed to her that she was old enough to be his mother, and the soreness in her heart changed into tenderness. Then he looked from the sunset to Abby, and, at the glance of innocent pleasure that passed between them, a stab of jealousy entered her heart like a blade. Before it faded, they had passed the corner, and were cantering wildly up Old Street in the direction of Abby's home.

"It is my fault. I am too settled. I am letting my youth go," she said, with a passionate determination to catch her girlhood and hold it fast before it escaped her for ever. "I am only twenty-eight, and I dress like a woman of forty." And it seemed to her that the one desirable thing in life was this fleet-winged spirit of youth, which passed like a breath, leaving existence robbed of all romance and beauty. An hour before she had not cared, and she would not care now if only Oliver could grow middle-aged and old at the moment when she did. Ah, there was the tragedy! All life was for men, and only a few radiant years of it were given to women. Men were never too old to love, to pursue and capture whatever joy the fugitive instant might hold for them. But women, though they were allowed only one experience out of the whole of life, were asked to resign even that one at the very minute when they needed it most. "I wonder what will become of me when the children grow big enough to be away all the time as Oliver is," she thought wistfully. "I wish one never grew too old to have babies."

The front door of the Treadwell house stood open, and in the hall Susan was arranging golden-rod and life-ever-lasting in a blue china bowl.

"Of course, you may have Belle to-morrow," she said in answer to Virginia's faltering request. "Even if I intended going, I'd be only too glad to lend her to you; but I can't leave mother anyway. She always gets restless if I stay out over an hour."

Mrs. Treadwell's illness had become one of those pain-ful facts which people accept as naturally as they accept the theological dogma of damnation. It was terrible, when they thought of it, but they seldom thought of it, thereby securing tranquillity of mind in the face of both facts and dogmas. Even Virginia had ceased to make her first question when she met Susan, "How is your mother?"

"But, Susan, you need the exercise. I thought that was why the doctor made Uncle Cyrus get you a horse."

"It was, but I only go for an hour in the afternoon. I begrudge every minute I spend away from mother. Oh, Virginia, she is so pathetic! It almost breaks my heart to watch her."

"I know, dearest," Virginia said; but at the back of her brain she was thinking, "They looked so happy together, yet he could never really admire Abby. She isn't at all the kind of woman he likes."

So preoccupied was she by this problem of her own creation, that her voice had a strangely far-off sound, as if it came from a distance. "I wish I could help you, dear Susan. If you ever want me, day or night, you know you have only to send for me. I'd let nothing except desperate illness stand in the way of my coming."

It was true, and because she knew that it was true, Susan stooped suddenly and kissed her.

"You are looking tired, Virginia. What is the matter?"

"Nothing except that I'm a sight in this old waist. I made it over to save buying one, but I wish now I hadn't. It makes me look so settled."

"You need some clothes, and you used to be so fond of them."

"That was before the children came. I've never cared much since. It's just as if life were a complete circle, somehow. There's nothing more to expect or to wait for—you'll understand what I mean some day, Susan."

"I think I do now. But only women are like that? Men are different——"

It was the classic formula again, but on Susan's lips the phrase assumed a new significance.

"And some women are different, too," Virginia replied. "Now there's Abby Goode—Susan, what do you honestly think of Abby?"

There was a wistful note in the question, and around her gentle blue eyes appeared a group of little lines, brought out by the nervous contraction of her forehead. Was it the wan, smoky light of the dusk?—Susan wondered, or was Virginia really beginning to break so soon?

"Why, I like Abby. I always did," she answered, trying to look as if she did not understand what Virginia had meant. "She's a little bit what John Henry calls 'loud,' but she has a good heart and would do anybody a kindness."

She had evaded answering, just as Virginia had evaded asking, the question that both knew had passed unuttered between them: was Abby to be trusted to keep inviolate the ancient unwritten pledge of honourable womanhood? Her character was being tested by the single decisive virtue exacted of her sex.

"I am glad you feel that way," Virginia said in a relieved manner, after a minute, "because I should hate not to believe in Abby, and some people don't understand her manner—mother among them."

"Oh, she's all right. I'm sure of it," Susan answered, with heartiness.

The wistful sound had passed out of Virginia's voice, while the little lines faded as suddenly from the corners of her eyes. She looked better already; only she ought not to wear such dowdy clothes, even though she was happily married, Susan reflected, as she watched her, a few minutes later, pass over the mulberry leaves, which lay, thick and still, on the sidewalk.

At the corner of Sycamore Street a shopkeeper was putting away his goods for the night, and in the window Virginia saw a length of hyacinth-blue silk, matching her eyes, which she had remotely coveted for weeks, never expecting to possess it, yet never quite reconciling herself to the thought that it might be worn by some other woman. That length of silk had begun to symbolize the last glimmer of girlish vanity which motherhood had not extinguished in her heart; and while she looked at it now, in her new recklessness of mood, a temptation, born of the perversity which rules human fate, came to her to go in and buy it while she was still desperate enough to act foolishly and not be afraid. For the first time in her life the spirit of adventure that lies buried under the dead leaves of civilization at the bottom of every human heart —with whose rearisen ghost men have moved mountains and ploughed jungles and charted illimitable seas—this imperishable spirit stirred restlessly in its grave and prompted her for once to be uncalculating and to risk the future. In the flickering motive that guided her as she entered the shop, one would scarcely have recognized the lusty impulse that had sent her ancestors on splendid rambles of knight-errantry; yet its hidden source was the same. The simple purchase of twelve yards of blue silk that she had wanted for weeks! To an outsider it would have appeared a small matter; yet in the act there was the intrepid struggle of a personal will to enforce its desire upon destiny. She would win back the romance and the beauty of living at the cost of prudence, at the cost of practical comforts, at the cost, if need be, of that womanly duty to which the centuries had trained her! For eight years she had barely thought of herself, for eight years she had worked and saved and planned and worried, for eight years she had given her life utterly and entirely to Oliver and the children; and the result was that he was happier with Abby—with Abby whom he didn't even admire—than he was with the wife whom he loved! The riddle not only puzzled, it enraged her. Though she was too simple to seek a psychological answer, the very fact that it existed became an immediate power in her life. She forgot the lateness of the evening, she forgot the children who were anxiously watching for her return. The forces of character, which she had always regarded as divinely fixed and established, melted and became suddenly fluid.

She wasn't what she had been the minute before; she wasn't even, she began dimly to realize, what she would probably be the minute afterwards. Yet the impulse that governed her now was as despotic as if it had reigned in undisputed authority since the day of her birth. She knew that it was a rebel against the disciplined and moderate rule of her conscience, but this knowledge, which would have horrified her had she been in a normal mood, aroused in her merely a breathless satisfaction at the spectacle of her audacity. The natural Virginia had triumphed for an instant over the Virginia whom the ages had bred.

At home she found Oliver waiting for supper, and the three children in tears for fear lest she should have decided to stay out for ever.

"Oh, mother, we thought you'd gone away never to come back," Lucy sobbed, throwing herself into her arms, "and what would little Jenny have done?"

"Where in the world have you been, Virginia?" Oliver asked, a trifle impatiently, for he was not used to having her absent from the house. "I was afraid somebody had been taken ill at the rectory, so I went round to inquire."

"No, nobody was ill," Virginia answered quietly. Though her resolution made her tremble all over, it did not occur to her that even now she might recede from it. As the rector had gone to the war, so she was going now to battle with Abby. She was afraid; but that quality which had made the Pendletons despise fear since the beginning of Dinwiddie's history, enabled her to control her quivering muscles and to laugh at the reproachful protests with which the children surrounded her. Through her mind shot the thought: "I have a secret from Oliver," and she felt suddenly guilty because for the first time since her marriage she was keeping something back from him. Then, following this, there came the knowledge, piercing her heart, that she must keep her secret because even if she told him, he would not understand. With the casualness of a man's point of view toward an emotion, he would judge its importance, she felt, chiefly by the power it possessed of disturbing the course of his life. Unobservant, and ever ready to twist and decorate facts as she was, it had still been impossible for her to escape the truth that men are by nature incapable of a woman's passion for nursing sentiment. To struggle to keep a feeling alive for no better reason than that it was a feeling, would appear as wastefully extravagant to Oliver as to the unimaginative majority of his sex. Such pure, sublime, uncalculating folly belonged to woman alone!

When, at last, supper was over and the children were safely in bed, she came downstairs to Oliver, who was smoking a cigar over a newspaper, and asked carelessly:

"At what time do you start in the morning?"

"I'd like to be up by five," he replied, without lowering his paper. "We're to meet the hounds at Croswell's store at a quarter to six, so I'll have to get off by five at the latest. I wanted my horse fresh for to-morrow, that's why I went only a few miles this afternoon," he added.

"Susan's to lend me Belle. I'm going with you," she said, after a pause in which he had begun to read his paper again. This habit of treating her as if she were not present when he wanted to read or work, was, she remembered, one of the things she had insisted upon in the beginning of her marriage.

"By Jove!" he exclaimed, and the paper dropped from his hands. "I'm jolly glad, but what will you do about the children?"

"Mother is coming to look after them. I'll be back in time to hear Harry's lessons, I suppose."

"Why, of course; but, look here, you'll be awfully sore.

You haven't ridden after the hounds since I knew you.
You might even get a fall."

"I used to go, though, a great deal—and it won't hurt
me to be stiff for a few days. Besides, I want to take
up hunting again."

Her motive was beyond him, perhaps because of her
nearness, which prevented his getting the proper perspec-
tive of vision. For all his keenness of insight, he failed
utterly to see into the mysterious mind of his wife. He
could not penetrate that subtle interplay of traditional
virtues and discover that she was in the clutch of the old-
est and most savage of passions.

"Then you'd better go to bed early and get some sleep,"
he said. "I suppose we'll have a cup of coffee before starting."

"I'll make it on the oil stove while I'm dressing. Marthy
won't be up then."

"Well, I'll come upstairs in ten minutes," he replied,
taking up his paper again. "I only want to finish this
article."

In the morning, when she opened the old green shutters
and looked out of the window, the horses, having been
saddled by candlelight, were standing under the mulberry
tree at the gate. Eight years ago, in her girlhood, she
would have awakened in a delicious excitement on the
morning of a fox-hunt, and have dressed as eagerly as if
she were going to a ball; but to-day, while she lit the oil-
stove in the hall-room and put on the kettle of water, she
was supported not by the hope of pleasure, but by a dull,
an almost indefinable sensation of dread. The instinct of
woman to adjust her personality to the changing desires of
the man she loves—this instinct older than civilization,
rooted in tragedy, and existing by right of an unconquerable necessity—rose superior at the moment to that more

stable maternal passion with which it has conflicted since
the beginning of motherhood. While she put on her riding-
habit and tied up the plait of her hair, the one thought in
Virginia's mind was that she must be, at all costs, the kind
of woman that Oliver wanted.

A little later, when they set out under the mulberry
trees, she glanced at him wistfully, as though she wanted
him to praise the way she looked in the saddle. But his
eyes were on the end of the street, where a little company
of riders awaited them, and before she could ask a question, Abby's high voice was heard exclaiming pleasantly
upon her presence. Not a particularly imposing figure, because of her short legs, when she was on the ground, it was
impossible for Virginia to deny that Abby was amazingly
handsome on horseback. Plump, dark, with a superb
bosom, and a colour in her cheeks like autumnal berries,
she had never appeared to better advantage than she did,
sitting on her spirited bay mare, under an arch of scarlet
leaves which curved over her head. Turning at their approach, she started at a brisk canter up the road, and as
Virginia followed her, the sound of the horn floated, now
loud, now faint, out of the pale mist that spun fanciful
silken webs over the trees and bushes.

"Remember to look out for the creeks. That's where
the danger comes," Oliver said, riding close to her, and
he added nervously, "Don't try to keep up with Abby."

Ahead of them stretched a deserted Virginian road,
with its look of brooding loneliness, as if it had waited
patiently through the centuries for a civilization that had
never come; and on the right of it, beyond a waste of
scarlet sumach and sassafras and a winding creek screened
by elder bushes, the dawn was breaking slowly under a
single golden-edged cloud. Somebody on Virginia's left—
a large, raw-boned, passionate huntsman, in an old plum-

coloured overcoat with a velvet collar—was complaining loudly that they had started too late and the fox would have gone to his lair before they reached the main party. Except for an oath, which he rapped out by way of an emphasis not intended for the ladies, he might have been conducting a religious revival, so solemnly energetic, so deeply moved, was his manner. The hunt, which observed the habits of a society that was ardently individualistic even in its sports, was one of the most informal, "go-as-you-please" affairs, in which the supreme joy of killing is not hampered by tedious regulations or unnecessary restrictions. The chief thing was to get a run: to start a rare red fox, if luck were good, because he was supposed to run straight by nature and not to move in circles after the inconsiderate manner of the commoner gray sort. But Providence, being inattentive to the needs of hunters in the neighbourhood of Dinwiddie, had decreed that the red fox should live there mainly in the vivid annals of old sportsmen.

"A gray fox with red ears. The best run I ever had. Tried to get in the crotch of a hickory tree at the end. Was so exhausted he couldn't stir a foot when the hounds got him." While they waited at the crossroads before a little country store, where the pack of hounds, lean, cringing, habitually hungry creatures, started from beneath an old field pine on the right, Virginia heard the broken phrases blown on the wind, which carried the joyous notes of the horn over the meadows. The casual cruelty of the words awoke no protest in her mind, because it was a cruelty to which she was accustomed. If the sport had been unknown to Dinwiddie, and she had read of it as the peculiar activity of the inhabitants of the British Islands, she would probably have condemned it as needlessly brutal and degrading. But, with that universal faculty of the human mind to adjust its morality to its inherited physical habits, she regarded "the rights of the fox" to-day with something of the humorous scorn of sentimental rubbish with which her gentler grandmother had once regarded "the rights of the slave." For centuries the hunt had been one of the cherished customs of Dinwiddians; and though she could not bear to see a moth caught in a flame, it would never have occurred to her to question the humanity of any sport in which her ancestors had delighted. In her girlhood the sound of the horn had called to her blood with all the intoxicating associations it awoke in the raw-boned, energetic rider in the plum-coloured coat; but to-day both the horn and the familiar landscape around her had grown strange and unhomelike. For the first time since her birth she and the country were out of harmony.

In the midst of the hounds, in the centre of the old field on the right, the huntsman, who was at the same time master and owner of the dogs, brandished a long raw-hide whip, flexible from the handle, which was pleasantly known in Dinwiddie as a "mule-skinner." His face, burned to the colour of ripe wheat, wore a rapt and exalted look, as though the chasing of a small animal to its death had called forth his latent spiritual ardours. Beyond him, like a low, smouldering fire, ran the red and gold of the abandoned field.

"Please be careful, Virginia," Oliver said again, as they left the road and cantered in the direction of a stretch of pine woods in a hollow beyond a rotting "snake" fence.

But she had seen his eyes on Abby a minute before, and had heard his laugh as he answered her. A wave of recklessness broke over her, and she felt that she despised fear with all her Pendleton blood, which loved a fight only less passionately than it loved a sermon. Whatever happened—if she broke her neck—she resolved that she

would keep up with Abby! With the drumming of the
blood in her ears, an almost savage joy awoke in her.
Deep down in her, so deep that it was buried beneath the
Virginia Pendleton whom she and her world knew, there
stirred faintly the seeds of that ancient lust of cruelty
from which have sprung the brutal pleasures of men. Part
of her, that small secret part which was primitive, answered
to the impulse of jealousy as it did to the rapturous baying
of the hounds out of the red and gold distance. A branch
grazed her cheek; her hat went as she raced down the high
banks of a stream; the thicket of elder tore the ribbon
from her head, and loosened her dark flying hair from its
braid. In that desolate country, in the midst of the October meadows, with the cries of the hounds rising, like the
voice of mortal tragedy, out of the tinted mist on the
marshes, the drama of human passions, which is the only
drama for the world's stage, was played out to an ending:
love, jealousy, cruelty, envy, desire, desperation, regret—   *   *   *

But when the hunt was over, and she rode home, with
a bedraggled brush, which had once been gray, tied to
her bridle, all the gorgeous pageantry of the autumnal
landscape seemed suddenly asking her: "What is the
use?" Her mood had altered, and she felt that her victory was as worthless as the mud-stained fox's brush that
swung mockingly back and forth from her bridle. The
excitement of the chase had ebbed away, leaving only the
lifeless satisfaction of the reward. She had neglected her
children, she had risked her life; and all for the sake of
wresting a bit of dead fur from Abby's grasp. A spirit
which was not her spirit, which was so old that she no
longer recognized that it had any part in her, which was
yet so young that it burned in her heart with the un-
quenchable flame of youth—this spirit, which was at the

same time herself and not herself, had driven her, as helpless as a fallen leaf, in a chase that she despised, toward a triumph that was worthless.

"By Jove, you rode superbly, Virginia! I had no idea you could do it," Oliver said, as they trotted into Din-widdie.

She smiled back at him, and her smile was tired, dust-stained, enigmatical.

"No, you did not know I could do it," she answered.

"You'll keep it up now, won't you?" he asked plead-ingly.

For an instant, looking away from him over the radiant fields, she pondered the question. The silence that had settled round her was unbroken by the thud of the horses' hoofs, by the laughter of the hunters, by the far-off soughing of the pine trees in the forest; and into this silence, which seemed to cover an eternity, the two Vir-ginias, the Virginia who desired and the Virginia who had learned from the ages to stifle her desire, wrestled for the first time together.

"Virginia!" Abby's breezy tones floated from the street behind her, and turning, she rode back to the Goodes' gate, where the others were dismounting. "Virginia, aren't you going to Atlantic City with us to-morrow?"

Again she hesitated. Almost unconsciously her gaze passed from Abby to Oliver, and she saw his pride in her in the smile with which he watched her.

"Yes, I'll go with you," she replied, after a minute.

She had, for once in her life, done the thing she wanted to do simply because she wanted to do it. She had won back what she was losing; she had fought a fair fight and she had triumphed; yet as she rode down the street to her gate, there was none of the exultation of victory, none of the fugitive excitement of pleasure even, in her heart.

Like other mortals in other triumphant instants, she was learning that the fruit of desire may be sweet to the eyes and bitter on the lips. She had sacrificed duty to pleasure, and suddenly she had discovered that to one with her heritage of good and evil the two are inseparable.

CHAPTER VIII

THE PANG OF MOTHERHOOD

IN THE night Harry awoke crying. He had dreamed, he said between his sobs, when Virginia, slipperless and in her nightgown, bent over him, that his mother was going away from him for ever.

"Only for two nights, darling. Here, lean close against mother. Don't you know that she couldn't stay away from her precious boy?"

"But two nights are so long. Aren't two nights almost for ever?"

"Why, my lamb, it was just two nights ago that grandmamma came over and told you the Bible story about Joseph and his brothers. That was only a teeny-weeny time ago, wasn't it?"

"But you were here then, mamma. And this morning was almost for ever. You stayed out so long that Lucy said you weren't coming back any more."

"That was naughty of Lucy because she is old enough to know better. Why do you choke that way? Does your throat hurt you?"

"It hurts because you are going away, mamma."

"But I'm going only to be with papa, precious. Don't you want poor papa to have somebody with him?"

"He's so big he can go by himself. But suppose the black man should come in the night while you are away, and I'd get scared and nobody would hear me."

"Grandmamma would hear you, Harry, and there isn't any black man that comes in the night. You must put that idea out of your head, dear. You're getting too big a boy to be afraid of the dark."

"Four isn't big, is it?"

"You're nearer five than four now, honey. Let me button your nightgown, and lie down and try to go to sleep while mamma sings to you. Does your throat really hurt you?"

"It feels as if it had teensy-weensy marbles in it. They came there when I woke up in the dark and thought that you were going away to-morrow."

"Well, if your throat hurts you, of course mamma won't leave you. Open your mouth wide now so I can look at it."

She lighted a candle while Harry, kneeling in the middle of his little bed, followed her with his blue eyes, which looked three times their usual size because of his flushed cheeks and his mounting excitement. His throat appeared slightly inflamed when she held the candle close to it, and after tucking him beneath the bedclothes, she poured a little camphorated oil into a cup and heated it on the small alcohol lamp she kept in the nursery.

"Mamma is going to put a nice bandage on your throat, and then she is going to lie down beside you and sing you to sleep," she said cheerfully, as she cut off a strip of flannel from an old petticoat and prepared to saturate it with the heated oil.

"Will you stay here all night?"

"All night, precious, if you'll be good and go fast asleep while I am singing."

Holding fast to her nightgown, Harry cuddled down between the pillows with a contented sigh. "Then I don't mind about the marbles in my throat," he said.

"But mamma minds, and she wants to cure them before morning. Now, lie very still while she wraps this good flannel bandage over the sore places."

"I'll lie very still, if you'll hold me, mamma."

Blowing out the candle, she crept into the little bed beside him, and lay singing softly until his hands released their desperate grasp, and he slipped quietly off to sleep. Even then, remembering her promise, she did not go back to her bedroom until daylight.

"I wonder what makes Harry so afraid of the dark?" she asked, when Oliver awoke and turned questioningly toward her. "He worked himself really sick last night just from pure nervousness. I had to put camphorated oil on his throat and chest, and lie beside him until morning. He is sleeping quietly now, but it simply frightens me to death when one of them complains of sore throat."

"You've spoiled him, that's what's the matter," Oliver replied, yawning. "As long as you humour him, he'll never outgrow these night terrors."

"But how can you tell whether the fright makes him sick or sickness brings on the fright? His throat was really red, there's no doubt about that, but I couldn't see last night that it was at all ulcerated."

"He gives you more trouble than both the other children put together."

"Well, he's a boy, and boys do give more trouble. But, then, you have less patience with him, Oliver."

"That's because he's a boy, and I like boys to show some pluck even when they are babies. Lucy and Jenny never raise these midnight rows whenever they awake in the dark."

"They are not nearly so sensitive. You don't understand Harry."

"Perhaps I don't, but I can see that you are ruining him."

"Oh, Oliver! How can you say such a cruel thing to me?"

"I didn't mean to be cruel, Virginia, and you know it, but all the same it makes me positively sick to see you make a slave of yourself over the children. Why, you look as if you hadn't slept for a week. You are positively haggard."

"But I have to be up with Harry when he is ill. How in the world could I help it?"

"You know he kicks up these rows almost every night, and you humour every one of his whims as if it were the first one. Don't you ever get tired?"

"Of course I do, but I can't let my child suffer even if it is only from fear. You haven't any patience, Oliver. Don't you remember the time when you used to be afraid of things?"

"I was never afraid of the dark in my life. No sensible child is, if he is brought up properly."

"Do you mean I am not bringing up my children——" Her tears choked her, and she could not finish the sentence.

"I don't mean anything except that you are making an old woman of yourself before your time. You've let yourself go until you look ten years older than——"

He checked himself in time, but she understood without his words that he had started to say, "ten years older than Abby." Yes, Abby did look young—amazingly young—but, then, what else had she to think of?

She lay down, but she was trembling so violently that she sat up quickly again in order to recover her self-possession more easily. It seemed to her that the furious beating of her heart must make him understand how he

had wounded her. It was the first discussion approaching
a quarrel they had had since their marriage; for she, who
was so pliable in all other matters, had discovered that
she could become as hard as iron where the difference
related to Harry.

"You are unjust, Oliver. I think you ought to see it,"
she said in a voice which she kept by an effort from breaking.

"I'll never see it, Virginia," and some dogged impulse
to hurt her more made him add, "It's for Harry's sake, as
well as yours, that I'm speaking."

"For Harry's sake? Oh, you don't mean—you can't
really mean that you think I'm not doing the best for my
child, Oliver?"

A year ago Oliver would have surrendered at once before the terror in her eyes; but in those twelve long months
of effort, of hope, of balked ambition, of bitter questioning, and of tragic disillusionment, a new quality had developed in his character, and the generous sympathy of
youth had hardened at thirty-four to the cautious cyni-
cism of middle age. It is doubtful if even he himself
realized how transient such a state must be to a nature
whose hidden springs were moved so easily by the mere
action of change, by the effect of any alteration in the
objects that surrounded him. Because the enthusiasm of
youth was exhausted at the minute, it seemed to him that
he had lost it for ever. And to Virginia, who saw but one
thing at a time and to whom that one thing was always
the present instant, it seemed that the firm ground upon
which she trod had crumbled beneath her.

"Well, if you want the truth," he said quietly (as if any
mother ever wanted the truth about such a matter), "I
think you make a mistake to spoil Harry as you do."

"But," she brought out the words with a pathetic

quiver, "I treat him just as I do the others, and you never say anything about my spoiling them."

"Oh, the others are girls. Girls aren't so easily ruined somehow. They don't get such hard knocks later on, so it makes less difference about them."

As she sat there in bed, propped up on her elbow, which trembled violently against the pillows, with her cambric nightgown, trimmed only with a narrow band of crocheted lace, open at her slender throat, and her hair, which was getting thin at the temples, drawn unbecomingly back from her forehead, she looked, indeed, as Oliver had thought, "at least ten years older than Abby." Though she was not yet thirty, the delicate, flower-like bloom of her beauty was already beginning to fade. The spirit which had animated her yesterday appeared to have gone out of her now. He thought how lovely she had been at twenty, when he saw her for the first time after his return to Dinwiddie; and a sudden anger seized him because she was letting herself break, because she was so needlessly sacrificing her youth and beauty.

An hour later she got up and dressed herself, with the feeling that she had not rested a minute during the night. Harry was listless and fretful when he awoke, and while she put on his clothes, she debated with herself whether or not she should summon old Doctor Fraser from round the corner. When his lesson hour came, he climbed into her lap and went to sleep, with his hot little head on her shoulder, and though he seemed better by evening, she was still so anxious about him that she forgot she had promised Abby to go with them to Atlantic City until Oliver came in at dusk and reminded her.

"Aren't you going, Virginia?" he inquired, as he hunted in the closet for his bag which she had not had time to pack.

"I can't, Oliver. Harry isn't well. He has been unlike himself all day, and I am afraid to leave him."

"He looks all right," he remarked, bending over the child in Virginia's lap. "Does anything hurt you, Harry?"

"He doesn't seem to know exactly what it is," Virginia answered, "but if he isn't well by morning, I'll send for Doctor Fraser."

"He's got a good colour, and I believe he's as well as he ever was," Oliver replied, while a curious note of hostility ruffled his voice. "There's nothing the matter with the boy," he added more positively after a minute. "Aren't you coming, Virginia?"

She looked up at him, with Harry in her arms, and as she did so, both became aware that the issue had broadened from a question of her going to Atlantic City into a direct conflict of wills. The only thing that could make her oppose him had happened for the first time since her marriage. The feminine impulse to yield was overmatched by the maternal impulse to protect. She would have surrendered her soul to him for the asking; but she could not surrender the mother love which had passed into her from out the ages before she had been, and which would pass through her into the ages to come.

"Of course, if the little chap were really suffering, I'd be as anxious about staying as you are," Oliver said impatiently; "but there's nothing the matter. You're all right, aren't you, Harry?"

"Yes, I'm all right," Harry repeated, yawning and snuggling closer to Virginia, "but I'm sleepy."

"He isn't all right," Virginia insisted obstinately. "There's something wrong with him. I don't know what it is, but he isn't in the least like himself."

"It's just your imagination. You've got the children on the brain, Virginia. Don't you remember the time you

woke me in the night and sent me after Doctor Fraser
because Jenny had a bad attack of the hiccoughs?"

"I know," Virginia acknowledged humbly. She could
be humble enough, but what good did that do when she
was, as he told himself irritably, "as stubborn as a mule"?
Her softness—she had seemed as soft as flowers when
he married her—had been her greatest charm for him
after her beauty; and now, at the end of eight years in
which she had appeared as delightfully invertebrate as
he could have desired, she revealed to his astonished eyes
a backbone that was evidently made of iron. She was immovable, he admitted, and because she was immovable
he was aware of a sharp unreasonable impulse to reduce
her to the pliant curves of her girlhood. After eight years
of an absolute supremacy, which had been far from good
for him, his will had been tripped up at last by so small
a thing as a mere whim of Virginia's.

"You told Abby you would go?" he urged, exasperated
rather than soothed by her humility. "And it's too late
now for her to ask any one else."

"I'm so sorry, dear, but I never once thought of it. I've
been worried all day."

He looked at the child, lying flushed and drowsy in
Virginia's arms, and his face hardened until a latent brutality crept out round his handsome, but loosely moulded,
lips. The truth was that Harry had never looked healthier
than he did at that instant in the firelight, and the whole
affair appeared to Oliver only another instance of what
he called Virginia's "sensational motherhood."

"Can't you see for yourself that he's perfectly well?"
he asked.

"I know he looks so, dear, but he isn't."

"Well, here's your mother. Leave it to her. She will
agree with me."

"Why, what is it, Virginia?" Mrs. Pendleton asked, laying her bundle on the couch (for she had come prepared to spend the night), and regarding Oliver with the indulgent eyes of the older generation.

"Virginia says at the last minute that she won't go with us," Oliver said, angry yet caressing, as he always was with his mother-in-law, to whom he was sincerely devoted. "She's got into her head that there's something wrong with Harry; but you can tell by looking at the child that he is perfectly well."

"But I was up with him last night, mother. His throat hurts him," broke in Virginia in a voice that was full of emotion.

"He certainly looks all right," Mrs. Pendleton remarked, "and I can take care of him, if anything should be wrong." Then she added very gravely, "If you can't go, of course Oliver must stay at home too, Virginia."

"I can't," Oliver said; "not just for a whim, anyway. It would break up the party. Besides, I didn't get a holiday all summer, and I'll blow up that confounded bank unless I have a change."

In the last quarter of an hour the trip had become of tremendous importance to him. From a trivial incident which he might have relinquished a week ago without regret, the excursion with Abby had attained suddenly the dignity and the power of an event in his life. Opposition had magnified inclination into desire.

"I don't think it will do for Oliver to go without you, Virginia," said Mrs. Pendleton, and the gravity of her face showed how carefully she was weighing her words.

"But I can't go, mother. You don't understand," Virginia replied, while her lips worked convulsively. No one could understand—not even her mother. Of the three of them, it is probable that she alone realized the complete significance of her decision.

"Well, it's too late now," Oliver remarked shortly. "You wouldn't have time to dress and catch the train even if you wanted to."

Taking up his bag, he kissed her carelessly, shook hands with Mrs. Pendleton, and throwing a "Good-bye, General!" to Harry, went out of the door.

As he vanished, Virginia started up quickly, called "Oliver!" under her breath, and then sat down again, drawing her child closer in her arms. Her face had grown gray and stricken like the face of an old woman. Every atom of her quivered with the longing to run after him, to yield to his wish, to promise anything he asked of her. Yet she knew that if he came back, they would only pass again through the old wearing struggle of wills. She had chosen not as she desired to, but as she must, and already she was learning that life forces one in the end to abide by one's choices.

"Oh, Virginia, I am afraid it was a mistake," Mrs. Pendleton said in an agonized tone. The horror of a scandal, which was stronger in the woman of her generation than even the horror of illness, still darkened her mind.

A shiver passed through Virginia and left her stiller and graver than before.

"No, it was not a mistake, mother," she answered quietly. "I did what I was obliged to do. Oliver could not understand."

As she uttered the words, she saw Oliver's face turned to Abby with the gay and laughing expression she had seen on it when the two rode down Old Street together, and a wave of passionate jealousy swept over her. She had let him go alone; he was angry with her; and for three days he would be with Abby almost every minute. And suddenly, she heard spoken by a mocking voice at the back of her brain: "You look at least ten years older than Abby."

"It does seem as if he might have stayed at home," Mrs. Pendleton remarked; "but he is so used to having his own way that it is harder for him to give up than for the rest of us. Your father says you have spoiled him."

She had spoiled him: this she saw clearly now, she who had never seen anything clearly until it was too late for sentimentality to work its harm. From the day of her marriage she had spoiled him because spoiling him had been for her own happiness as well as for his. She had yielded to him since her chief desire had been simply to yield and to satisfy. Her unselfishness had been merely selfishness cloaked in the familiar aspect of duty. Another vision of him, not as he looked when he was riding with Abby, but as he had appeared to her in the early days of their marriage, floated before her. He had been hers utterly then—hers with his generous impulses, his high ideals, his undisciplined emotions. And what had she done with him? What were her good intentions, what was her love even, worth, when her intentions and her love alike had been so lacking in wisdom? It was as if she condemned herself with a judgment which was not her own, as if her life-long habit of seeing only the present instant had suddenly deserted her.

"He has been so nervous and unlike himself ever since the failure of his play, mother," she said. "It's hard to understand, but it meant more to him than a woman can realize."

"I suppose so," Mrs. Pendleton returned sympathetically. "Your father says that he spoke to him bitterly the other day about being a failure. Of course, he isn't one in the least, darling," she added reassuringly.

"I sometimes think that Oliver's ambition was the greatest thing in his life," Virginia said musingly. "It meant to him, I believe, a great deal of what the children mean to me. He felt that it was himself, and yet in a way closer than himself. Until that dreadful time in New York, I never understood what his work may mean to a man."

"I wish you could have gone with him, Virginia."

"I couldn't," Virginia replied, as she had replied so often before. "I know Harry doesn't look sick," she went on, with that soft obstinacy which never attacked and yet never yielded a point, "but something tells me that he isn't well."

An hour later, when she put him to bed, he looked so gay and rosy that she almost allowed herself the weakness of a regret. Suppose nothing was wrong, after all? Suppose, as Oliver had said, she was merely "sensational"? While she undressed in the dark for fear of awaking Jenny, who was sleeping soundly in her crib on Virginia's side of the bed, her mind went back over the two harrowing days through which she had just lived, and she asked herself, not if she had triumphed for good over Abby, but if she had really done what was right for Oliver and the children. After all, the whole of life came back simply to doing the thing that was right. So unused was she to introspection that she thought slowly, from sheer lack of practice in the subtler processes of reasoning. Worry, the plain, ordinary sort of worry with which she was unhappily familiar, had not prepared her for the piercing anguish that follows the probing of the open wounds in one's soul. To lie sleepless over butchers' bills was different, somehow, from lying sleepless over the loss of Oliver's love. It was different, and yet, just as she had asked herself over and over again on those other nights if she had done right to run up so large an account at Mr. Dewlap's, so she questioned her conscience now in the hope of finding justification for Oliver. "Ought I to have gone on the hunt yesterday?" she asked kneeling, with sore and aching limbs, by the bedside. "Had I a right to risk my life when the children are so young that they need me every minute? It is true nothing happened. Providence watched over me; but, then, something might have happened, and I could have blamed only myself. I was jealous. For the first time in my life, I was jealous; and because I was jealous, I did wrong and neglected my duty. Yesterday, I sacrificed the children to Oliver, and to-day, I sacrificed Oliver to the children. I love Oliver as much, but I have made the children. They came only because I brought them into the world. I am responsible for them. I am responsible for them," she repeated passionately; and a moment later, she prayed softly: "O Lord, help me to want to do what is right!"

Through the night, tired and sore as she was, she hardly closed her eyes, and she was lying wide awake, with her hand on the railing of Jenny's crib, and her gaze on the half-bared bough of the old mulberry tree in the street, when a cry, or less than a cry, a small, choking whimper, from the nursery, caused her to spring out of bed with a start and slip into her wrapper which lay across the edge of the quilt.

"I'm coming, darling," she called softly, and the answer came back in Harry's voice: "Mamma, I'm afraid!"

Without waiting to put on her slippers, for one of them had slid under the bed, she ran across the carpet and through the doorway into the adjoining room.

"What is it, my lamb? Does anything hurt you?" she asked anxiously.

"I'm afraid, mamma."

"What are you afraid of? Mamma is here, precious."

His little hands were hot when she clasped them, and the pathetic wonder in his blue eyes made her heart stand still with a fear greater than Harry's. Ever since the children had come she had lived in terror of a serious illness attacking them.

"Where does it hurt you, darling? Can't you tell me?"

"It feels so funny when I swallow, mamma. It's all full of flannel."

"Will you open your mouth wide, then, and let mamma mop your throat with turpentine?"

But Harry hated turpentine even more than he hated the sore throat, and he protested with tears while she found the bottle in the bathroom and swathed the end of the wire mop in cotton. When she brought it to his bedside, he fought so strenuously that she was obliged at last to give up. His fever had excited him, and he sobbed violently while she applied the bandages to his throat and chest.

"Is it any better, dear?" she asked desperately, at the end of an hour in which he had lain, weeping and angry, in her arms.

"It feels funny. I don't like it," he sobbed, pushing her from him.

"Then I'll send for Doctor Fraser. He'll make you well."

But he didn't want Doctor Fraser, who gave the meanest medicines. He didn't want anybody. He hated everybody. He hated Lucy. He hated Jenny. When at last day came, and Marthy appeared to know what Virginia wanted for breakfast, he was still vowing passionately that he hated them all.

"Marthy, run at once for Doctor Fraser. Harry is quite sick," Virginia said, pale to the lips.

"But I won't see him, mamma, and I won't take his medicines. They are the meanest medicines."

"Perhaps he won't give you any, precious, and if he does, mamma will taste every single one for you."

Then Jenny began to beg to get up, and Lucy, who had been watching with dispassionate curiosity from the edge of her little bed, was sent to amuse her until Marthy's return.

"Suppose I had gone!" Virginia thought, while an overwhelming thankfulness swept the anxiety out of her mind. Not until the servant appeared, dragging the fat old doctor after her, did Virginia remember that she was still barefooted, and go into her bedroom to search for her slippers.

"You don't think he is seriously sick, do you, doctor? Is there any need to be alarmed?" she asked, and her voice entreated him to allay her anxiety.

The doctor, a benevolent soul in a body which had run to fat from lack of exercise, was engaged in holding down Harry's tongue with a silver spoon, while, in spite of the child's furious protests, he leisurely examined his throat. When the operation was over, and Harry, crying, choking, and kicking, rolled into Virginia's arms, she put the question again, vaguely rebelling against the gravity in the kind old face which was turned half away from her:

"There's nothing really the matter, is there, doctor?"

He turned to her, and laid a caressing, if heavy, hand on her shoulder, which shook suddenly under the thin folds of her dressing-gown. After forty years in which he had watched suffering and death, he preserved still his native repugnance to contact with any side of life that did not have a comfortable feeling to it.

"Oh, we'll get him all right soon, with some good nursing," he said gently, "but I think we're going to have a bit of an illness on our hands."

"But not serious, doctor? It isn't anything serious?"

She felt suddenly so weak that she could barely stand, and instinctively she reached out to grasp the large, protecting arm of the physician. Even then his bland professional smile, which had in it something of the serene detachment of the everlasting purpose, did not fade, scarcely changed even, on his features.

"Well, I think we'd better get the other children away. It might be serious if they all had it on our hands."

"Had it? Had what? Oh, doctor—not—diphtheria?"

She brought out the word with a face of such unutterable horror that he turned his eyes away, lest the memory of her look should interfere with his treatment of the next case he visited. There was something infernal in the sound of the thing which always knocked over the mothers of his generation. He had never seen one of them who could hear it without going to pieces on his hands; and for that reason he never mentioned the disease by name unless they drove him to it. They feared it as they might have feared the plague—and even more! If the medical profession would begin calling it something else, he wondered if the unmitigated terror of it wouldn't partly subside?

"Well, it looks like that now, Virginia," he said soothingly; "but we'll come out all right, never fear. It isn't a bad case, you know, and the chief thing is to get the other children out of danger."

At this she went over like a log on the bed, and it was only after he had found the bottle of camphor on the mantelpiece and held it to her nostrils, that she revived sufficiently to sit up again. But as soon as her strength came back, her courage surprised and rejoiced him. After that one sign of weakness, she became suddenly strong, and he knew by the expression of her face, for he had had great experience with mothers, that he could count on her not to break down again while he needed her.

"I'd like to get a tent made of some sheets and keep a kettle boiling under it," he said, for he was an old man and belonged to the dark ages of medicine. "But, first of all, I'll get the children over to your mother's. They'd better not come in here again. I'll ask the servant to attend to them."

"You'll find her in the dining-room," Virginia replied, while she straightened Harry's bed and made him more comfortable. The weakness had passed, leaving a numbed and hardened feeling, as if she had turned to wood; and when, a little later, she looked out of the door to wave good-bye to Lucy and Jenny, she was amazed to find that she felt almost indifferent. Even emotion, even her capacity for physical sensation, seemed to respond to the immediate need of her, to the incessant demands on her bodily strength and her courage. As long as there was anything to be done, she was sure now that she should be able to keep up and not lose control of herself.

"May we come back soon, mamma?" Lucy asked, standing on tiptoe to wave to her.

"Just as soon as Harry is well, darling. Ask grandpapa to pray that he will be well soon, won't you?"

"Jenny'll p'ay," the baby lisped, from Doctor Fraser's arms, where, with her cap on one side and her little feet kicking delightedly, she was beguiled by the promise of a birthday cake over at grandmamma's.

"I'll look in again in an hour or two," the doctor said in his jovial tones as he swung down the stairs. Then Lucy pattered after him, and in a few minutes the front door closed loudly behind them, and Virginia went back to the nursery, where Harry was coughing the strangling cough that tore at her heart.

By nightfall he had grown very ill, and when the next dawn came, it found her, wan, haggard, and sleepless, fighting beside the old doctor under the improvised tent of sheets which covered the little bed. The thought of self went from her so utterly that she only remembered she was alive when Marthy brought food and tried to force it between her lips.

"But you must swallow it, ma'am. You need to keep up your strength."

"How do you think he looks, Marthy? Does he feel quite so hot to you? He seems to breathe a little better, doesn't he?"

And during the long day, while the patch of sunlight grew larger, lay for an hour like yellow silk on the windowsill, and then slowly dwindled into the shadow, she sat, without moving, between the bed and the table, on which stood the bottles of medicine, a glass, and a pitcher of water. When the child slept, overcome by the stupor of fever, she watched him, with drawn breath, lest he should fade away from her if she were to withdraw her passionate gaze for an instant. When he awoke and lay moaning, while his little body shook with the long stifling gasps that struggled between his lips, she held him tightly clasped in her arms, with a woman's pathetic faith in the power of physical pressure to withstand the immaterial forces of death. A hundred times during the day he aroused himself, stirred faintly in his feverish sleep, and called her name in the voice of terror with which he used to summon her in the night.

"It isn't the black man now, darling, is it? Remember there is no black man, and mamma is close here beside you."

No, it wasn't the black man; he wasn't afraid of the darkness now, but he would like to have his ship. When she brought it, he played for a few minutes, and dozed off still grasping the toy in his hands. At twelve the doctor came, and again at four, when the patch of sunlight, by which she told the hours, had begun to grow fainter on the windowsill.

"He is better, doctor, isn't he? Don't you notice that he struggles less when he breathes?"

He looked at her with an expression of contemplative pity in his old watery eyes, and she gave a little cry and stretched out her hands, blindly groping.

"Doctor, I'll do anything—anything, if you'll only save him." An impulse to reach beyond him to some impersonal, cosmic Power greater than he was, made her add desperately: "I'll never ask for anything else in my life. I'll give up everything, if you'll only promise me that you will save him."

She stood up, drawing her thin figure, as tense as a cord, to its full height, and beneath the flowered blue dressing-gown her shoulder blades showed sharply under their fragile covering of flesh. Her hair, which she had not undone since the first shock of Harry's illness, hung in straight folds on either side of her pallid and haggard face. Even the colour of her eyes seemed to have changed, for their flower-like blue had faded to a dull gray.

"If we can pull through the night, Virginia," he said huskily, and added almost sternly, "you must bear up, so much depends on you. Remember, it is your first serious illness, but it may not be your last. You've got to take the pang of motherhood along with the pleasure, my dear——"

The pang of motherhood! Long after he had left her, and she had heard the street gate click behind him, she sat motionless, repeating the words, by Harry's little bed. The pang of motherhood—this was what she was suffering—the poignant suspense, the quivering waiting, the abject terror of loss, the unutterable anguish of the nerves, as if one's heart were being slowly torn out of one's body. She had had the joy, and now she was enduring the inevitable pang which is bound up, like a hidden pulse, in every mortal delight. Never pleasure without pain, never growth without decay, never life without death. The Law ruled even in love; and all the pitiful little sacrifices which one offered to Omnipotence, which one offered blindly to the Power that might separate, with a flaming sword, the cause from the effect, the substance from the shadow—what of them? While Harry lay there, wrapped in that burning stupor, she prayed, not as she had been taught to pray in her childhood, not with the humble and resigned worship of civilization, but in the wild and threatening lament of a savage who seeks to reach the ears of an implacable deity. In the last twenty-four hours the Unknown Power she entreated had changed, in her imagination, to an idol who responded only to the shedding of blood.

"Only spare my child and I will give up everything else!" she cried from the extremity of her anguish. The sharp edge of the bed hurt her bosom and she pressed frantically against it. Had it been possible to lacerate her body, to cut her flesh with knives, she might have found some pitiable comfort in the mere physical pain. Beside the agony in her mind, a pang of the flesh would have been almost a joy.

When at last she rose from her knees, Harry lay, breathing quietly, with his eyes closed and the toy ship on the blanket beside him. His childish features had shrunken in a day until they appeared only half their natural size, and a faint bluish tinge had crept over his face, wiping out all the sweet rosy colour. But he had swallowed a few spoonfuls of his last cup of broth, and the painful choking sound had ceased for a minute. The change, slight as it was, had followed so closely upon her prayers that, while it lasted, she passed through one of those spiritual crises which alter the whole aspect of life. An emotion, which was a curious mixture of superstitious terror and religious faith, swept over her, reviving and invigorating her heart. She had abased herself in the dust before God. She had offered all her life to Him if He would spare her child— and had He not answered? Might not Harry's illness, indeed, have been sent to punish her for her neglect? A shudder of abhorrence passed through her as she remembered the fox-hunt, and her passion of jealousy. The roll of blue silk, lying upstairs in a closet in the third storey, appeared to her now not as a temptation to vanity, but as a reminder of the mortal sin which had almost cost her the life of her child. And suppose God had not stopped her in time: suppose she had gone to Atlantic City as Oliver had begged her to do?

In the room the light faded softly, melting first like frost from the mirror in the corner beyond the Japanese screen, creeping slowly across the marble surface of the washstand, lingering, in little ripples, on the green sash of the windowsill. Out of doors, it was still day, and from where she sat by Harry's bed, she could see, under the raised tent, every detail of the street standing out distinctly in the gray twilight. Across the way the houses were beginning to show lights at the windows, and the old lamplighter was balancing himself unsteadily on his ladder at the corner. On the mulberry tree near the crossing the broad bronze leaves swung back and forth in the wind, which sighed restlessly round the house and drove the naked tendrils of a summer vine against the green shutters at the window. The fire had gone down, and after she had made it up very softly, she bent over Harry again, as if she feared that he might have slipped out of her grasp while she had crossed the room.

"If he only lives, I will let everything else go. I will think of nothing except my children. It will make no difference to me if I do look ten years older than Abby does. Nothing on earth will make any difference to me, if only God will let him get well."

And with the vow, it seemed to her that she laid her youth down on the altar of that unseen Power whose mercy she invoked. Let her prayer be heard, and she would demand nothing more of life; she would spend all her future years in the willing service of love. Was it possible that she had imagined herself unhappy thirty-six hours ago—thirty-six hours ago when her child was not threatened? As she looked back on her past life, it seemed to her that every minute had been crowded with happiness. Even the loss of her newborn baby appeared such a little thing—such a little thing beside the loss of Harry, her only son. Mere freedom from anxiety wore the aspect now of positive bliss.

Six o'clock struck, and Marthy knocked at the door with a cup of milk.

"Do you think he'll be able to swallow any of it?" she asked, and there were tears in her eyes.

"He is better, Marthy, I am sure he is better. Has mother been here this afternoon?"

"She stopped at the door, but she didn't like to come in on account of the children. They are both well, she says, and send you their love. Do you want any more water in the kettle, ma'am?"

The kettle, which was simmering away beside Harry's

bed, under the tent of sheets, was passed to Marthy through the crack in the door; and when, in a few minutes, the girl returned with fresh water, Virginia whispered to her that he had taken three spoonfuls of milk.

"And he let me mop his throat with turpentine," she said in quivering tones. "I am sure—oh, I am sure he is better."

"I am praying every minute," Marthy replied, weeping; and it seemed suddenly to Virginia that a wave of understanding passed between her and the ignorant mulatto girl, whom she had always regarded as of different clay from herself. With that miraculous power of grief to level all things, she felt that the barriers of knowledge, of race, of all the pitiful superiorities with which human beings have obscured the underlying spirit of life, had melted back into the nothingness from which they had emerged in the beginning. This feeling of oneness, which would have surprised and startled her yesterday, appeared so natural to her now, that, after the first instant of recognition, she hardly thought of it again.

"Thank you, Marthy," she answered gently, and closing the door, went back to her chair under the raised corner of the sheet. When the doctor came at nine o'clock she was sitting there, in the same position, so still and tense that she seemed scarcely to be breathing, so ashen gray that the sheet hanging above her head showed deadly white by contrast with her face. In those three hours she knew that the clinging tendrils of desire had relaxed their hold for ever on youth.

"If it doesn't get worse, we'll pull through," said the doctor, turning from his examination of Harry to lay his hand, which felt as heavy as lead, on her shoulder. "We've an even chance—if his heart doesn't go back on us." And he added, "Most mothers are good nurses, Virginia, but

I never saw a better one than you are—unless it was your
own mother. You get it from her, I reckon. I remember
when you went through diphtheria how she sent your
father to stay with one of the neighbours, and shut herself
up with old Ailsey to nurse you. I don't believe she undressed or closed her eyes for a week."

Her own mother! So she was not the only one who
had suffered this anguish; other women, many women,
had been through it before she was born. It was a part
of that immemorial pang of motherhood of which the
old doctor had spoken. "But, was I ever in danger? Was
I as ill as Harry?" she asked.

"For twenty-four hours we thought you'd slip through
our fingers every minute. 'Twas only your mother's nursing that kept you alive—I've told her that twenty times.
She never spared herself an instant, and, it may have been
imagination, but she never seemed to me to be the same
woman afterwards. Something had gone out of her."

Now she understood, now she knew, something had
gone out of her, also, and this something was youth. No
woman who had fought with death for a child could ever
be the same afterwards, could ever value again the small
personal joys, when she carried the memory of supreme
joy or anguish buried within her heart. She remembered
that her mother had never seemed young to her, not even
in her earliest childhood; and she understood now why
this had been so, why the deeper experiences of life rob
the smaller ones of all vividness, of all poignancy. It had
been so easy for her mother to give up little things, to
deny herself, to do without, to make no further demands
on life after the great demands had been granted her.
How often had she said unthinkingly in her girlhood,
"Mother, you never want anything for yourself." Ah, she
knew now what it meant, and with the knowledge a long-

ing seized her to throw herself into her mother's arms, to sob out her understanding and her sympathy, to let her feel before it was too late that she comprehended every step of the way, every throb of the agony!

"I'd spend the night with you, Virginia, if I didn't have to be with Milly Carrington, who has two children down with it," said the doctor; "but if there's any change, get Marthy to come for me. If not, I'll be sure to look in again before daybreak."

When he had gone, she moved the night lamp to the corner of the washstand, and after swallowing hastily a cup of coffee Marthy had brought to her before the doctor's visit, which had grown quite tepid and unpalatable, she resumed her patient watch under the raised end of the sheet. The whole of life, the whole of the universe even, had narrowed down for her into that faint circle of light which the lamp drew round Harry's little bed. It was as if this narrow circle beat with a separate pulse, divided from the rest of existence by its intense, its throbbing vitality. Here was concentrated for her all that the world had to offer of hope, fear, rapture, or anguish. The littleness and the terrible significance of the individual destiny were gathered into that faintly quivering centre of space, so small a part of the universe, and yet containing the whole universe within itself!

Outside, in the street, she could see a half-bared bough of the mulberry tree, arching against a square of window, from which the white curtains were drawn back; and in order to quiet her broken and disjointed thoughts, she began to count the leaves as they fell, one by one, turning softly at the stem, and then floating out into the darkness beyond. "One. Two. How long that leaf takes to loosen. He is better. The doctor certainly thought that he was better. If he only gets well. O God, let him get well, and

I will serve you all my life! Three—four—five— For twenty-four hours we thought you would slip through our fingers. Somebody said that—somebody—it must have been the doctor. And he was talking of me, not of Harry. That was twenty-six years ago, and my mother was enduring then all this agony that I am feeling to-night. Twenty-six years ago—perhaps at this very hour, she sat beside me alone as I am sitting now by Harry. And before that other women went through it. All the world over, wherever there are mothers—north, south, east, west—from the first baby that was born on the earth—they have every one suffered what I am suffering now—this pang of motherhood! To escape it one must escape birth, and escape the love that is greater than one's self."

And she understood suddenly that suffering and love are inseparable, that when one loves another more than one's self, one has opened the gate by which anguish will enter. She had forgotten to count the leaves, and when she remembered and looked again, the last one had fallen. Against the parted white curtains, the naked bough arched black and solitary. Even the small silent birds that had all day swayed dejectedly to and fro on the branches had flown off into the darkness. Presently, the light in the window went out, and as the hours wore on, a fine drizzling rain, as soft as tears, began to fall, from the starless sky over the mulberry tree. A sense of isolation greater than any she had ever known attacked her like a physical chill, and rising, she went over to the fire and stirred the pile of coal into a flame. She was alone in her despair, and she realized, with a feeling of terror, that one is always alone when one despairs, that there is a secret chamber in every soul where neither love nor sympathy can follow one. If Oliver were here beside her—if he were standing close to her in the throbbing circle about the bed—she would still be separated from him by the immensity of that inner space which is not measured by physical distances. "No, even if he were here, he could not reach me," she said, and an instant later, with one of those piercing illuminations that visit even perfectly normal women in moments of tragic intensity, she thought quickly, "If every woman told the truth to herself, would she say there is something in her that love has never reached?" Then, reproaching herself because she had left the bed for a minute, she went back again and bent over the unconscious child, her whole slender body curving itself passionately into an embrace. His face was ashen white, except where the skin around his mouth was discoloured with a faint bluish tinge. His flesh, even his bones, appeared to have shrunk almost away in twenty-four hours. It was impossible to imagine that he was the rosy, laughing boy, who had crawled into her arms only two nights ago. The disease held him like some unseen spiritual enemy, against which all physical weapons were as useless as the little toys of a child. How could one fight that sinister power which had removed him to an illimitable distance while he was still in her arms? The troubled stupor, which had in it none of the quiet and the restfulness of sleep, terrorized her as utterly as if it had been the personal spirit of evil. The invisible forces of Life and Death seemed battling in the quivering air within that small circle of light.

While she bent over him, he stirred, raised himself, and then fell back in a paroxysm of coughing. The violence of the spasm shook his fragile little body as a rough wind shakes a flower on a stalk. Over his face the bluish tinge spread like a shadow, and into his eyes there came the expression of wondering terror which she had seen before only in the eyes of young startled animals. For an instant it seemed almost as if the devil of disease were wrestling inside of him, as if the small vital force she called life would be beaten out in the struggle. Then the agony passed; the strangling sound ceased, and he grew quiet, while she wiped the poison from his mouth and nostrils, and made him swallow a few drops of milk from a teaspoon.

At the moment, while she fell on her knees by his bedside, it seemed to her that she had reached that deep place beyond which there is nothing.

*   *   *   *   *   *   *

"You've brought him through. We'll have him out of bed before many days now," the old doctor said at daybreak, and he added cheerfully, "By the way, your husband came in the front door with me. He wanted to rush up here at once, but I'm keeping him away because he is obliged to go back to the bank."

"Poor Oliver," Virginia said gently. "It is terrible on him. He must be so anxious." But, even while she uttered the words, she was aware of a curious sensation of unreality, as if she were speaking of a person whom she had known in another life. It was three days since she had seen Oliver, and in those three days she had lived and died many times.

CHAPTER IX

THE PROBLEM OF THE SOUTH

"FATHER, I want to marry John Henry," Susan said, just as she had said almost ten years ago, "Father, I want to go to college."

It was a March afternoon, ashen and windy, with flocks of small fleecy clouds hurrying across a changeable blue sky, and the vague, roving scents of early spring in the air. After his dinner, which he had taken for more than fifty years precisely at two o'clock, Cyrus had sat down for a peaceful pipe on the back porch before returning to the office. Between the sunken bricks in the little walled-in yard, blades of vivid green grass had shot up, seeking light out of darkness, and along the gray wooden ledge of the area the dauntless sunflowers were unfolding their small stunted leaves. On the railing of the porch a moth-eaten cat, the only animal for whom Cyrus entertained the remotest respect, was contentedly licking the shabby fur on her side.

"Father, I want to marry John Henry," Susan repeated, raising her voice to a higher key and towering like a flesh and blood image of Victory over the sagging cane chair in which he sat.

Taking his pipe from his mouth, he looked up at her; and so little had he altered in ten years, that the thought flashed through her mind that he had actually suffered

no change of expression since the afternoon when she
had asked him to send her to college. As a man he may
not have been impressive, but as a defeating force who
could say that he had not attained his fulfilment? It was
as if the instinct of patriarchal tyranny had entrenched
itself in his person as in a last stronghold of the disap-
pearing order. When he died many things would pass
away out of Dinwiddie; not only the soul and body of
Cyrus Treadwell, but the vanishing myth of the "strong
man," the rule of the individual despot, the belief in the
inalienable right of the father to demand blood sacrifices.
For, in common with other men of his type, he stood
equally for industrial advancement and domestic immobility. The body social might move, but the units that
formed the body social must remain stationary.

"Well, I don't think I'd worry about marrying, if I were
you," he replied, not unkindly, for Susan inspired him
with a respect against which he had struggled in vain.
"You are very comfortable now, ain't you? And I'll see
that you are well provided for after my death. John
Henry hasn't anything except his salary, I reckon."

Marriage as an economic necessity was perfectly com-
prehensible to him; but it was difficult for him to conceive of anybody indulging in it simply as a matter of
sentiment. That April afternoon was so far away that it
had ceased to exist even as an historical precedent.

"Yes, but I want to marry him, and I am going to,"
Susan replied decisively.

"What arrangements would you make about your
mother? It seems to me your mother needs your attention."

"Of course, I couldn't leave mother. If you agree to it,
John Henry is willing to come here to live so long as I
have to look after her. If not, I shall take her away with

me. I have spoken to her, and she is perfectly willing to go."

The ten years which had left Cyrus at a standstill had developed his daughter from a girl into a woman. She spoke with the manner of one who realizes that she holds the situation in her hands, and he yielded to this assumption of strength as he would have yielded ten years ago had she been clever enough to use it against him. It was his own manner in a more attractive guise, if he had only known it; and the Treadwell determination to get the thing it wanted most was asserting itself in Susan's desire to win John Henry quite as effectively as it had asserted itself in Cyrus's wish to possess the Dinwiddie and Central Railroad. Though the ends were different, the quality that moved father and daughter toward these different ends was precisely the same. In Cyrus, it was force degraded; in Susan, it was force refined; but the peculiar attribute that distinguished and united them was the power to command events.

"Take your mother away?" he repeated. "Why, where on earth would you take her?"

"Then you'll have to agree to John Henry's coming here. It won't make any difference to you, of course. You needn't see him except at the table."

"But what would James say about it?" he returned, with the cowardice natural to the habitual bully. The girl had character, certainly, and though he disliked character in a woman, he was obliged to admit that she had not failed to make an impression.

"James won't care, and besides," she added magnificently, "it is none of his business."

"And it's none of mine, either, I reckon," said Cyrus, with a chuckle.

"Well, of course, it's more of mine," Susan agreed, and her delicious laugh drowned his chuckle.

She had won her point, and, strange to say, she had pleased him rather than otherwise. He had suddenly a comfortable feeling in his digestive organs, as well as a sense of virtue in his soul. It was impossible not to feel proud of her as she towered there above him, with her superb body, as fine and as supple as the body of a race horse, and her splendid courage which made him wish, while he looked at her, that she, instead of James, had been born a male. She was not pretty—she had never been pretty—but he realized for the first time that there might be something better for a woman than beauty.

"Thank you, father," she said as she turned away, and he was glad again to feel that she had conquered him. To be conquered by one's own blood was different from being conquered by a business acquaintance.

"You mustn't disturb the household, you know," he said; but his voice did not sound as dry as he had endeavoured to make it.

"I shan't disturb anybody," Susan responded, with the amiability of a woman who, having gained her point, can afford to be pleasant. Then, wheeling about on the threshold, she added, "By the way, I forgot to tell you that Mandy was here three times this morning asking to see you. She is in trouble about her son. He was arrested for shooting a policeman over at Cross's Corner, you know, and the people down there are so enraged, she's afraid of a lynching. You read about it in the paper, didn't you?"

Yes, he had read about the shooting—Cross's Corner was only three miles away—but, if he had ever known the name of Mandy's son, he had forgotten it so completely that seeing it in print had suggested nothing to his mind.

"Well, she doesn't expect me to interfere, does she?"
he asked shortly.

"I believe she thinks you might go over and do something. I don't know what, help her engage a lawyer probably. She was very pitiable, but, after all, what can one
do for a negro that shoots a policeman? There's Miss
Willy calling me!"

She ran indoors, and taking his pipe, which was still
smoking, from his mouth, Cyrus leaned back in his chair
and stared intently at the small fleecy clouds in the west.
The cat, having cleaned herself to her satisfaction,
jumped down from the railing, and, after rubbing against
his thin legs, leaped gently into his lap.

"Tut-tut!" he remarked grimly; but he did not attempt
to dislodge the animal, and it may be that some secret
part of him was gratified by the attention. He was still
sitting there some minutes later, when he heard the warning click of the back gate, and the figure of Mandy appeared at the corner of the kitchen wall. Rising from his
chair, he shook the cat from his knees, and descending the
steps, met the woman in the centre of the walk, where a
few hardy dandelions were flattened like buttons between
the bricks.

"Howdy, Mandy. I'm sorry to hear that you're having
trouble with that boy of yours." He saw at once that she
was racked by a powerful emotion, and any emotion affected him unpleasantly as something extravagant and
indecent. Sweat had broken out in glistening clusters over
her face and neck, and her eyes, under the stray wisps of
hair, had in them an expression of dumb and uncomprehending submission.

"Ain't you gwineter git 'im away, Marster?" she began,
and stronger even than her terror was the awe of Cyrus
which subdued her voice to a tone of servile entreaty.

"Why did he shoot a policeman? He knew he'd hang for it," Cyrus returned sharply, and he added, "Of course, I can't get him away. He'll have to take his deserts. Your race has got to learn that when you break the law, you must pay for it."

At first he had made as if to push by her, but when she did not move, he thought better of it and waited for her to speak. The sound of her heavy breathing, like the growls of some crouching beast, awoke in him a curious repulsion. If only one could get rid of such creatures after their first youth was over! If only every careless act could perish with the impulse that led to it! If only the dried husks of pleasure did not turn to weapons against one! These thoughts—or disjointed snatches of thoughts like these—passed in a confused whirl through his brain as he stood there. For an instant, it was almost as if his accustomed lucidity deserted him; then the disturbance ceased, and with the renewal of order in his mind, his life-long habit of prompt decision returned to him.

"Your race has got to learn that when you break the law, you must pay for it," he repeated; for upon that sound principle of justice he felt that he must unalterably take his stand.

"He's all de boy I'se got, Marster," the negress rejoined, with an indifference to the matter of justice which had led others of her colour into those subterranean ways where abstract principles are not. "You ain' done furgot 'im, Marster," she added piteously. "He 'uz born jes two mont's atter Miss Lindy turnt me outer hyer—en he's jes ez w'ite ez ef'n he b'longed ter w'ite folks."

But she had gone too far; she had outraged that curious Anglo-Saxon instinct in Cyrus which permitted him to sin against his race's integrity, yet forbade him to

acknowledge, even to himself, that he bore any part in
the consequences of that sin. Illogical, he might have admitted, but there are some truths so poisonous that no
honest man could breathe the same air with them.

Taking out his pocket-book, he slowly drew a fifty-
dollar note from its innermost recesses, and as slowly unfolded it. He always handled money in that careful fashion; a habit which he had inherited from his father and
his grandfather before him, and of which he was entirely
unaware. Filtering down through so many generations,
the mannerism had ceased at last to be merely a physical
peculiarity, and had become strangely spiritual in its significance. The craving for possession, the singleness of
desire, the tenacity of grasp, the dread of relinquishment,
the cold-blooded determination to keep intact the thing
that it had cost so much to acquire—all that was bound
up in the spirit of Cyrus Treadwell, and would pass at
last with that spirit from off the earth, was expressed in
the gesture with which he held out the money. "Take this
—it is all I can do for you," he said, "and don't come whin-
ing around me any more. Black or white, the man that com-
mits a murder has got to hang for it."

From the negress there broke a sound that resembled a
human cry of grief less than it did the inarticulate moan
of an animal in mortal pain. Then it stopped suddenly,
strangled by that dull weight of usage beneath which the
primal impulse in her was crushed back into silence. Instinctively, as if in obedience to some reflex action, she
reached out and took the money from his hand, and still
instinctively, with the dazed look of one who performs in
delirium the customary movements of every day, she fell
back, holding her apron deprecatingly aside while he
brushed past her. And in her eyes as she gazed after him

there dawned the simple wonder of the brute that asks of
Life why it suffers.

Beyond the alley into which the gate opened, Cyrus
caught sight of Gabriel's erect figure hurrying down the
side street in the direction of the Old Ladies' Home, and
calling out to him, he scrambled over the ash heaps and
tomato cans, and emerged, irritated but smiling, into the
sunlight.

"I'm on my way to the bank. We'll walk down together," he remarked almost gently, for, though he dis-
approved of Gabriel's religious opinions and distrusted
his financial judgment, the war-like little rector represented the single romance of his life.

"I had intended stopping at the Old Ladies' Home, but
I'll go on with you instead," Gabriel responded. "I've just
had a message from one of our old servants calling me
down to Cross's Corner," he pursued, "so I'm in a bit of
a hurry. That's a bad thing, that murder down there yesterday, and I'm afraid it will mean trouble for the negroes.
Mr. Blylie, who came to market this morning, told me a
crowd had tried to lynch the fellow last night."

"Well, they've got to hang when they commit hanging
crimes," Cyrus replied stubbornly. "There's no way out
of that. It's just, ain't it?"

"Yes, I suppose so," Gabriel admitted, "though, for
my part, I've a feeling against capital punishment—except, of course, in cases of rape, where, I confess, my
blood turns against me."

"An eye for an eye and a tooth for a tooth—that's the
law of God, ain't it?"

"The old law, yes—but why not quote the law of Christ
instead?"

"It wouldn't do; not with the negroes," returned Cyrus,
who entertained for the Founder of Christianity all the

sentimental respect mingled with an innate distrust of His common sense with which he regarded His disciple.

"We can't condemn it until we've tried it," Gabriel said thoughtfully, and he went on after a moment:

"The terrible thing for us about the negroes is that they are so grave a responsibility—so grave a responsibility. Of course, we aren't to blame; we didn't bring them here; and yet I sometimes feel as if we had really done so."

This was a point of view Cyrus had never considered, and he felt an immediate suspicion of it. It looked, somehow, as if it were insidiously leading the way to an appeal for money.

"It's the best thing that could have happened to them," he replied shortly. "If they'd remained in Africa, they'd never have been civilized or—or Christianized."

"Ah, that is just where the responsibility rests on us. We stand for civilization to them; we stand even—or, at least, we used to stand—for Christianity. They haven't learned yet to look above or beyond us, and the example we set them is one that they are condemned, for sheer lack of any finer vision, to follow. The majority of them are still hardly more than uneducated children, and that very fact makes an appeal to one's compassion which becomes at times almost unbearable."

But this was more than Cyrus could stand even from the rector, whose conversation he usually tolerated because of the perverse, inexplicable liking he felt for the man. The charm that Gabriel exercised over him was almost feminine in its subtlety and in its utter defiance of any rational sanction. It may have been that his nature, incapable though it was of love, was not entirely devoid of the rarer capacity for friendship; or it may have been that, with the inscrutable irony which appears to control all human attractions, the caged brutality in his heart was

soothed by the flattery of the other's belief in him. Now,
however, he felt that Gabriel's highfaluting nonsense was
carrying him away. It was well enough to go on like that
in the pulpit; but on week days, when there was business to
think of and every minute might mean the loss of a dollar, there was no use dragging in either religion or sentiment. Had he put his thoughts plainly, he would probably
have said: "That's not business, Gabriel. The trouble with
you—and with most of you old-fashioned Virginians—
is that you don't understand the first principles of business." These words, indeed, were almost on his lips, when,
catching the rector's innocent glance wandering round to
him, he contented himself with remarking satirically:

"Well, you were always up in the clouds. It doesn't
hurt you, I reckon, though I doubt if it does much toward
keeping your pot boiling."

"I must turn off here," Gabriel said gently. "It's the
shortest way to Cross's Corner."

"Do you think any good will come of your going?"

"Probably not, but I couldn't refuse."

Much as he respected Cyrus, he was not sorry to part
from him, for their walk together had left him feeling
suddenly old and incompetent to battle with the problems
of life. He knew that Cyrus, even though he liked him,
considered him a bit of a fool, and with a humility which
was unusual in him (for in his heart he was absolutely
sure that his own convictions were right and that Cyrus's
were wrong) he began to ask himself if, by any chance,
the other's verdict could be secretly justified. Was he in
reality the failure that Cyrus believed him to be? Or was
it merely that he had drifted into that "depressing view"
of existence against which he so earnestly warned his
parishioners? Perhaps it wasn't Cyrus after all who had
produced this effect. Perhaps the touch of indigestion he

had felt after dinner had not entirely disappeared. Perhaps it meant that he was "getting on"—sixty-five his last birthday. Perhaps—but already the March wind, fresh and bud-scented, was blowing away his despondency. Already he was beginning to feel again that fortifying conviction that whatever was unpleasant could not possibly be natural.

Ahead of him the straight ashen road flushed to pale red where it climbed a steep hillside, and when he gained the top, the country lay before him in all the magic loveliness of early spring. Out of the rosy earth innumerable points of tender green were visible in the sunlight and invisible again beneath the faintly rippling shadows that filled the hollows. From every bough, from every bush, from every creeper that clung trembling to the rail fences, this wave of green, bursting through the sombre covering of winter, quivered, as delicate as foam, in the brilliant sunshine. On either side labourers were working, and where the ploughs pierced the soil they left narrow channels of darkness.

In the soul of Gabriel, that essence of the spring, which is immortally young and restless, awakened and gave him back his youth, as it gave the new grass to the fields and the longing for joy to the hearts of the ploughmen. He forgot that he was "getting on." He forgot the unnatural depression that had made him imagine for a moment the world was a more difficult place than he had permitted himself to believe; so difficult a place, indeed, that for some people there could be no solution of its injustice, its brutality, its dissonances, its inequalities. The rapture in the song of the bluebirds was sweeter than the voice of Cyrus to which he had listened. And in a meadow on the right, an old gray horse, scarred, dim-eyed, spavined, stood resting one crooked leg, while he gazed wistfully

over the topmost rail of the fence into the vivid green of
the distance; for into his aching old bones, also, there
had passed a little of that longing for joy which was born
of the miraculous softness and freshness of spring. To
him, as well as to Gabriel and to the ploughmen and to
the bluebirds flitting, like bits of fallen sky along the rail
fences, Nature, the great healer, had brought her annual
gift of the resurrection of hope.

"Cyrus means well," Gabriel thought, with a return of
that self-confidence without which no man can exist happily
and make a living. "He means well, but he takes a false
view of life." And he added after a minute: "It's odd how
the commercial spirit seems to suck a man dry when it once
gets a hold on him."

He walked on rapidly, leaving the old horse and the
ploughmen behind him, and around his energetic little figure the gray dust, as fine as powder, spun in swirls and
eddies before the driving wind, which had grown boisterous. As he moved there alone in the deserted road, with
his long black coat flapping against his legs, he appeared
so insignificant and so unheroic that an observer would
have scarcely suspected that the greatest belief on earth,
the belief in Life, in its universality in spite of its littleness, in its justification in spite of its cruelties—that this
belief shone through his shrunken little body as a flame
shines through a vase.

At the end of the next mile, midway between Dinwiddie
and Cross's Corner, stood the small log cabin of the
former slave who had sent for him, and as he approached
the narrow path that led, between oyster shells, from the
main road to the single flat brown rock before the doorstep, he noticed with pleasure how tranquil and happy
the little rustic home appeared under the windy brightness
of the March sky.

"People may say what they please, but there never were happier or more contented creatures than the darkeys," he thought. "I doubt if there's another peasantry in the world that is half so well-off or half so picturesque."

A large yellow rooster, pecking crumbs from the threshold, began to scold shrilly, and at the sound, the old servant, a decrepit negress in a blue gingham dress, hobbled out into the path and stood peering at him under her hollowed palm. Her forehead was ridged and furrowed beneath her white turban, and her bleared old eyes looked up at him with a blind and groping effort at recognition.

"I got your message, Aunt Mehitable. Don't you know me?"

"Is dat you, Marse Gabriel? I made sho' you wan' gwineter let nuttin' stop you f'om comin'."

"Don't I always come when you send for me?"

"You sutney do, suh. Dat's de gospel trufe—you sutney do."

As he looked at her standing there in the strong sunlight, with her palsied hand, which was gnarled and roughened until it resembled the shell of a walnut, curving over her eyes, he felt that a quality at once alien and enigmatical separated her not only from himself, but from every other man or woman who was born white instead of black. He had lived beside her all his life; and yet he could never understand her, could never reach her, could never even discern the hidden stuff of which she was made. He could make laws for her, but no child of a white mother could tell whether those laws ever penetrated that surface imitation of the superior race and reached the innate differences of thought, feeling, and memory which constituted her being. Was it development or mimicry that had brought her up out of savagery and clothed her in a blue gingham dress and a white turban, as in the outward covering of civilization?

Her look of crumbling age and the witch-like groping of her glance had cast a momentary spell over him. When it was gone, he said cheerfully:

"You mustn't be having troubles at your time of life, Aunt Mehitable," and in his voice there was the subtle recognition of all that she had meant to his family in the past, of all that his family had meant to her. Her claim upon him was the more authentic because it existed only in his imagination, and in hers. The tie that knit them together was woven of impalpable strands, but it was unbreakable while he and his generation were above the earth.

"Dar ain' no end er trouble, Marse Gabriel, ez long ez dar's yo' chillen en de chillen er yo' chillen ter come atter you. De ole ain' so techy—dey lets de hornet's nes' hang in peace whar de Lawd put hit—but de young dey's diff'rent."

"I suppose the neighbourhood is stirred up about the murder. What, in God's name, was that boy thinking of?"

The old blood crimes that never ceased where the white and the black races came together! The old savage folly and the new freedom! The old ignorance, the old lack of understanding, and the new restlessness, the new en-mity!

"He wan' thinkin' er nuttin', Marse Gabriel. We ole uns kin set down en steddy, but de young dey up en does wid dere brains ez addled ez de inside uv er bad aig. 'T wan' dat ar way in de old days w'en we all hed de say so ez ter w'at wuz en w'at wan't de way ter behave."

Like an institution left from the ruins of the feudal system, which had crumbled as all ancient and decrepit things must crumble when the wheels of progress roll over them, she stood there wrapped in the beliefs and customs of that other century to which she belonged. Her sentiments had clustered about the past, as his had done, until the border-line between the romance and the actuality had vanished. She could not help him because she, also, possessed the retrospective, not the constructive, vision. He was not aware of these thoughts; and yet, though he was unaware of them, they coloured his reflections while he stood there in the sunlight, which had begun to fall aslant the blasted pine by the roadside. The wind had lowered until it came like the breath of spring, bud-scented, caressing, provocative. Even Gabriel, whose optimism lay in his blood and bone rather than in his intellect, yielded for a moment to this call of the spring, as one might yield to the delicious melancholy of a vagrant mood. The long straight road, without bend or fork, had warmed in the paling sunlight to the colour of old ivory; in a neighbouring field a young maple tree rose in a flame of buds from the ridged earth where the ploughing was over; and against the azure sky in the south, a flock of wild geese drifted up, like blown smoke, from the marshes.

"Tell me your trouble, then," he said, dropping into the cane-seated chair she had brought out of the cabin and placed between the flat stone at the doorstep and the well-brink, on which the yellow rooster stood spreading his wings. But Aunt Mehitable had returned to the cabin, and when she reappeared she was holding out to him a cracked saucer on which there was a piece of preserved water-melon rind and a pewter spoon.

"Dish yer is de ve'y same sort er preserves yo' mouf use'n ter water fur w'en you wuz a chile," she remarked as she handed the sweet to him. Whatever her anxiety or affliction could have been, the importance of his visit had evidently banished it from her mind. She hovered over him as his mother may have done when he was in his cradle, while the cheerful self-effacement in which slavery had trained her lent a pathetic charm to her manner.

"How peaceful it looks," he thought, sitting there, with the saucer in his hand, and his eyes on the purple shadows that slanted over the ploughed fields. "You have a good view of the low-grounds, Aunt Mehitable," he said aloud, and added immediately, "What's that noise in the road? Do you hear it?"

The old woman shook her head.

"I'se got sorter hard er heahin', Marse Gabriel, but dar's al'ays a tur'able lot er fuss gwine on w'en de chillen begin ter come up f'om de fields. 'T wuz becase uv oner dem ar boys dat I sont fur you," she pursued. "He went plum outer his haid yestiddy en fout wid a w'ite man down yonder at Cross's Co'nder, en dar's gwine ter be trouble about'n hit jes ez sho' ez you live."

Seated on the flat stone, with her hands hanging over her knees, and her turbaned head swaying gently back and forth as she talked, she waited as tranquilly as the rock waited for the inevitable processes of decay. The patience in her look was the dumb patience of inanimate things; and her half-bared feet, protruding from the broken soles of her shoes, were encrusted with the earth of the fields until one could scarcely distinguish them from the ground on which they rested.

"It looks as if there was something like a fight down yonder by the blasted pine," the rector said, rising from his chair. "I'd better go and see what they're quarrelling about."

The negress rose also, and her dim eyes followed him while he went down the little path between the borders of oyster shells. As he turned into the open stretch of the road, he glanced back at her, and stopping for a moment,

waved his hand with a gesture that was careless and re-
assuring. The fight, or whatever it was that made the
noise, was still some distance ahead in the shadow of the
pine tree, and as he walked toward it he was thinking
casually of other matters: of the wretched condition of
the road after the winter rains, of the need of greater
thrift among the farmers, both white and black, of the
touch of indigestion that still troubled him. There was
nothing to warn him that he was approaching the supreme
event in his life, nothing to prepare him for a change beside
which all the changes of the past would appear as insubstantial as shadows. His soul might have been the soul in
the grass, so little did its coming or its going affect the
forces around him.

"If this shooting pain keeps up, I'll have to get a pre-
scription from Doctor Fraser," he thought, and the next
minute he cried out suddenly: "God help us!" and began
to run down the road in the direction of the blasted pine.
There was hardly a breath between the instant when he
had thought of his indigestion and the instant when he
had called out sharply on the name of God; yet that flash
of time had been long enough to change the ordinary man
into the hero. The spark of greatness in his nature flamed
up and irradiated all that had been merely dull and
common clay a moment before. As he ran on, with his
coat tails flapping round him, and his thin legs wobbling
from the unaccustomed speed at which he moved, he was
so unimposing a figure that only the Deity who judges
the motives, not the actions, of men would have been
impressed by the spectacle. Even the three hearty brutes
—and it took him but a glance to see that two of them
were drunk, and that the third, being a sober rascal, was
the more dangerous—barely ceased their merry torment

of the young negro in their midst when he came up with them.

"I know that boy," he said. "He is the grandson of Aunt Mehitable. What are you doing with him?"

A drunken laugh answered him, while the sober scoundrel, a lank, hairy ne'er-do-well, with a tendency to epilepsy, whose name he remembered to have heard, pushed him roughly to the roadside.

"You git out of this here mess, parson. We're goin' to teach this damn nigger a lesson, and I reckon when he's learned it in hell, he won't turn his grin on a white woman again in a jiffy."

"Fo' de Lawd, I didn't mean nuttin', Marster!" screamed the boy, livid with terror. "I didn't know de lady was dar—fo' de Lawd Jesus, I didn't! My foot jes slipped on de plank w'en I wuz crossin', en I knocked up agin' her."

"He jostled her," observed one of the drunken men judicially, "an' we'll be roasted befo' we'll let a damn nigger jostle a white lady—even if she ain't a lady—in these here parts."

In the rector's bone and fibre, drilled there by the ages that had shaped his character before he began to be, there was all the white man's horror of an insult to his womankind. But deeper even than this lay his personal feeling of responsibility for any creature whose fathers had belonged to him and had toiled in his service.

"I believe the boy is telling the truth," he said, and he added with one of his characteristic bursts of impulsiveness, "but whether he is or not, you are too drunk to judge."

There was going to be a battle, he saw, and in the swiftness with which he discerned this, he made his eternal choice between the preacher and the fighter. Stripping off

his coat, he reached down for a stick from the roadside;
then spinning round on the three of them he struck out
with all his strength, while there floated before him the
face of a man he had killed in his first charge at Manassas.
The old fury, the old triumph, the old blood-stained
splendour returned to him. He smelt the smoke again,
he heard the boom of the cannon, the long sobbing rattle
of musketry, and the thought stabbed through him, "God
forgive me for loving a fight!"

Then the fight stopped. There was a patter of feet in
the dust as the young negro fled like a hare up the road
in the direction of Dinwiddie. One of the men leaped the
fence and disappeared into the tangled thicket beyond;
while the other two, sobered suddenly, began walking
slowly over the ploughed ground on the right. Ten minutes later Gabriel was lying alone, with the blood oozing
from his mouth, on the trodden weeds by the roadside.
The shadow of the pine had not moved since he watched
it; on the flat rock in front of the cabin the old negress
stood, straining her eyes in the faint sunshine; and up
the long road the March wind still blew, as soft, as provocative, as bud-scented.

Book Third

THE ADJUSTMENT

CHAPTER I

THE CHANGING ORDER

"So THIS is life," Virginia thought, while she folded her mourning veil, and laid it away in the top drawer of her bureau. Like all who are suddenly brought face to face with tragedy, she felt at the moment that there was nothing else in existence. All the sweetness of the past had vanished so utterly that she remembered it only as one remembers a dream from which one has abruptly awakened. Nothing remained but this sense of the pitiful insufficiency of life, of the inexorable finality of death. It was a week since the rector's death, and in that week she had passed out of girlhood for ever. Of all the things that she had lived through, this alone had had the power to crush hope in her heart, and the odour of crape which floated through the crack of the drawer sickened her with its reminder of that agonized sense of loss which had settled over her at the funeral. She was only thirty—the best of her life should still be in the future—yet as she looked back at her white face in the mirror it seemed to her that she should never emerge from the leaden hopelessness which had descended like a weight on her body. Above the harsh black of her dress, which added ten years to her appearance, she saw the darkened circles rimming her eyes, the faded pallor of her skin, the lustreless wave of her hair, which had once had a satiny sheen on its ripples.

"Grief makes a person look like this," she thought. "I

shall never be a girl again—Oliver was right: I am the
kind to break early." Then, because to think of herself
in the midst of such sorrow seemed to her almost wicked,
she turned away from the mirror, and laid her crape-
trimmed hat on the shelf in the wardrobe. She was wearing a dress of black Henrietta cloth, which she had
borrowed from one of her neighbours who had worn
mourning, and the blouse and sleeves hung with an exaggerated fullness over her thin arms and bosom. All that
had distinguished her beauty, the radiance, the colour,
the flower-like delicacy of bloom and sweetness—these
were blotted out by her grief and by the voluminous
mourning dress of the nineties. A week had changed her,
as even Harry's illness had not changed her, from a girl
into a woman; and horrible beyond belief, with the exception of her mother, it had changed nothing else in the
universe! The tragedy that had ruined her life had left
the rest of the world, even the little world of Dinwiddie,
moving as serenely, as indifferently, on its way toward
eternity. On the morning of the funeral, she had heard
the same market wagons rumble over the cobblestones,
the same droning songs of the hucksters, the same casual
procession of feet on the pavement. A passionate indigna-
tion had seized her because life could be so brutal to death,
because the terror and the pity that flamed in her soul
shed no burning light on the town where her father had
worked and loved and fought and suffered and died. A little later, the ceaseless tread of visitors to the rectory door
had driven this thought from her mind; but through every
minute, while he lay in the closed room downstairs, while
she sat beside her mother in the slow crawling carriage
that went to the old churchyard, while she stood with
bowed head listening to the words of the service,—through
it all there had been the feeling that something must hap-

pen to alter a world in which such a thing had been possible, that life must stop, that the heavens must fall, that
God must put forth His hand and work a miracle in order
to show His compassion and His horror.

But nothing had changed. After the funeral her mother
had come home with her, and the others, many with tear-
stained faces, had drifted in separate ways back to eat
their separate dinners. For a few hours Dinwiddie had
been shaken out of its phlegmatic pursuit of happiness;
for a few hours it had attained an emotional solidarity
which swept it up from the innumerable bypaths of the
personal to a height where the personal rises at last into
the universal. Then the ebb had come; the sense of
tragedy had lessened slowly with the prolongation of feeling; and the universal vision had dissolved and crystallized
into the pitiless physical needs of the individual. After
the funeral a wave almost of relief had swept over the
town at the thought that the suspension and the strain
were at an end. The business of keeping alive, and the
moral compulsion of keeping abreast of one's neighbours,
reasserted their supremacy even while the carriages,
quickening their pace a trifle on the return drive, rolled out
of the churchyard. Now, at the end of a week, only
Virginia and her mother would take the time from living
to sit down and remember.

In the adjoining room, which was the nursery, Mrs.
Pendleton was sitting beside the window, with her Bible
open on her knees, and her head bent a little in the direction of Miss Priscilla, who was mending a black dress by
the table.

"It is so sweet of you, dear Miss Priscilla," she murmured in her vague and gentle voice as Virginia entered.
So old, so pallid, so fragile, she looked, that she might
have been mistaken by a stranger for a woman of eighty;

yet the impossibility of breaking the habit of a lifetime
kept the lines of her face still fixed in an expression of
anxious cheerfulness. For more than forty years she had
not thought of herself, and now that the opportunity had
come for her to do so, she found that she had almost
forgotten the way that one went about it. Even grief
could not make her selfish any more than it could make
her untidy. Her manner, like her dress, was so little a
matter of impulse, and so largely a matter of discipline
and of conscience, that it expressed her broken heart
scarcely more than did the widow's cap on her head or the
mourning brooch that fastened the crape folds of her
collar.

"Do you want anything, mother darling? What can
I do for you?" Virginia asked, stooping to kiss her.

"Nothing, dear. I was just telling Miss Priscilla that
I had had a visit from Mr. Treadwell, and that"—her
voice quivered a little—"he showed more feeling than I
should have believed possible. He even wanted to make
me an allowance."

Miss Priscilla drew out her large linen handkerchief,
which was like a man's, and loudly blew her nose. "I
always said there was more in Cyrus than people thought,"
she observed. "Here, I've shortened this dress, Virginia,
until it's just about your mother's length."

She tried to speak carelessly, for though she did not
concur in the popular belief that to ignore sorrow is to
assuage it, her social instinct, which was as strongly developed as Mrs. Pendleton's, encouraged her to throw
a pleasant veil over affliction.

"You're looking pale for want of air, Virginia," she
added, after a minute in which she had thought, "The
child has broken so in the last few days that she looks
years older than Oliver."

"I'm trying to make her go driving," Mrs. Pendleton said, leaning forward over the open page of her Bible.

"But I can't go, mother; I haven't the heart for it," Virginia replied, choking down a sob.

"I don't like to see you looking so badly, dear. You must keep up your strength for the children's sake, you know."

"Yes, I know," Virginia answered, but her voice had a weary sound.

A little later, when Miss Priscilla had gone, and Oliver came in to urge her to go with him, she shook her head again, still palely resolute, still softly obstinate.

"But, Virginia, it isn't right for you to let your health go," he urged. "You haven't had a breath of air for days and you're getting sallow."

His own colour was as fine as ever; he grew handsomer, if a trifle stouter, as he grew older; and at thirty-five there was all the vigour and the charm of twenty in his face and manner. In one way only he had altered, and of this alteration, he, as well as Virginia, was beginning faintly to be aware. Comfort was almost imperceptibly taking the place of conviction, and the passionate altruism of youth would yield before many years to the prudential philosophy of middle age. Life had defeated him. His best had been thrown back at him, and his nature, embittered by failure, was adjusting itself gradually to a different and a lower standard of values. Though he could not be successful, it was still possible, even within the narrow limits of his income and his opportunities, to be comfortable. And, like other men who had lived day by day with heroically unselfish women, he had fallen at last into the habit of thinking that his being comfortable was, after all, a question of supreme importance to the universe. Deeply as he had felt the rector's death, he, in common

with the rest of Dinwiddie, was conscious of breathing
more easily after the funeral was over. To his impression-
able nature, alternations of mood were almost an essential of being, and there was something intolerable to him
in any slowly harrowing grief. To watch Virginia nursing
every memory of her father because she shrank from the
subtle disloyalty of forgetfulness, aroused in him a curious mingling of sympathy and resentment.

"I wish you'd go, even if you don't feel like it—just
to please me, Virginia," he urged, and after a short
struggle she yielded to his altered tone, and got down her
hat from the shelf of the wardrobe.

A little later, as the dog-cart rolled out of Dinwiddie
into the country road, she looked through her black
grenadine veil on a world which appeared to have lost its
brightness. The road was the one along which she had
ridden on the morning of the fox-hunt; ahead of them
lay the same fields, sown now with the tender green of
the spring; the same creeks ran there, screened by the
same thickets of elder; the same pines wafted their tang
on the March wind that blew, singing, out of the forest.
It was all just as it had been on that morning—and yet
with what a difference!

"Put up your veil, Virginia—it's enough to smother
you."

But she only shook her head, shrinking farther down
into the shapeless borrowed dress as if she felt that it
protected her. Following the habit of persons whose choice
has been instinctive rather than deliberate, a choice of
the blood, not of the brain, they had long ago exhausted
the fund of conversation with which they had started.
There was nothing to talk about, since Virginia had never
learned to talk of herself, and Oliver had grown reticent
about the subjects that interested him. When the daily

anecdotes of the children had been aired between them with an effort at breeziness, nothing remained except the endless discussion of Harry's education. Even this had worn threadbare of late, and with the best intentions in the world, Virginia had failed to supply anything else of sufficient importance to take its place. An inherited habit, the habit that had made it possible for Mrs. Pendleton to efface her broken heart, prompted her to avoid any illusion to her grief in which she sat shrouded as in her mourning veil.

"The spring is so early this year," she remarked once, with her gaze on the rosy billows of an orchard. "The peach trees have almost finished blooming."

Then, as he made no answer except to flick at John Henry's bay mare with his whip, she asked daringly, "Are you writing again, Oliver?"

A frown darkened his forehead, and she saw the muscles about his mouth twitch as if he were irritated. For all his failure and his bitterness, he did not look a day older, she thought, than when she had first seen him driving down High Street in that unforgettable May. He was still as ardent, still as capable of inspiring first love in the imagination of a girl. The light and perfume of that enchanted spring seemed suddenly to envelop her, and moved by a yearning to recapture them for an instant, she drew closer to him, and slipped her hand through his arm.

"Oh, I'm trying my luck with some trash. Nothing but trash has any chance of going in this damned business."

"You mean it's different from your others? It's less serious?"

"Less serious? Well, I should say. It's the sort of ice-cream soda-water the public wants. But if I can get it put on, it ought to run, and a play that runs is obliged to make money. I doubt if there's anything much better than money, when it comes to that."

"You used to say it didn't matter."

"Did I? Well, I was a fool and I've learned better. These last few years have taught me that nothing else on earth matters much."

This was so different from what that other Oliver— the Oliver of her first love—might have said, that involuntarily her clasp on his arm tightened. The change in him, so gradual at first that her mind, unused to subtleties, had barely grasped it, was beginning to frighten her.

"You have such burdens, dear," she said, and he noticed that her voice had acquired the toneless sweetness of her mother's. "I've tried to be as saving as I could, but the children have been sick so much that it seems sometimes as if we should never get out of debt. I am trying now to pay off the bills I was obliged to make while Harry was ill in October. If I could only get perfectly strong, we might let Marthy go, now that Jenny is getting so big."

"You work hard enough as it is, Virginia. You've been awfully good about it," he answered; but his manner was almost casual, for he had grown to take for granted her unselfishness with something of the unconcern with which he took for granted the comfortable feeling of the spring weather. In the early days of their marriage, when her fresh beauty had been a power to rule him, she had taught him to assume his right to her self-immolation on the altar of his comfort; and with the taste of bitterness which sometimes follows the sweets of memory, she recalled that their first quarrel had arisen because she had insisted on getting out of bed to make the fires in the morning. Then, partly because the recollection appeared to reproach him, and partly because, not possessing the critical faculty, she had never learned to acknowledge the existence of a flaw in a person she loved, she edged closer to him, and replied cheerfully:

"I don't mind the work a bit, if only the children will keep well so we shan't have to spend any more money. I shan't need any black clothes," she added, with a trembling lip. "Mrs. Carrington has given me this dress, as she has gone out of mourning, and I've got a piece of blue silk put away that I am going to have dyed."

He glanced at the shapeless dress, not indignantly as he would once have done, but with a tinge of quiet amusement.

"It makes you look every day of forty."

"I know it isn't becoming, but at least it will save having to buy one."

In spite of the fact that her small economies had made it possible for them to live wholesomely, and with at least an appearance of decency, on his meagre salary, they had always aroused in him a sense of bitter exasperation. He respected her, of course, for her saving; yet in his heart he knew that she would probably have charmed him more had she been a spendthrift—since the little virtues are sometimes more deadly to the passion of love than are the larger vices. While he nodded, without disputing the sound common sense in her words, she thought a little wistfully how nice it would be to have pretty things if only one could afford them. Someday, when the children's schooling was over and Oliver earned a larger salary, she would begin to buy clothes that were becoming rather than durable. But that was in the future, and, meanwhile, how much better it was to grudge every penny she spent on herself so long as there were unpaid bills at the doctor's and the grocer's. All of which was, of course, perfectly reasonable; and like other women who have had a narrow experience of life, she cherished the delusion

that a man's love, as well as his philosophy, is rooted in
reason.

When they turned homeward, the bay mare, pricked
by desire for her stable, began to travel more rapidly,
and the fall of her hoofs, accompanied by the light roll
of the wheels, broke the silence which had almost imperceptibly settled upon them. Not until the cart drew up
at the gate did Virginia realize that they had scarcely
spoken a dozen words on the drive back.

"I feel better already, Oliver," she said, gratefully, as
he helped her to alight. Then hastening ahead of him, she
ran up the walk and into the hall, where her mother, looking wan and unnatural in her widow's cap, greeted her with
the question:

"Did you have a pleasant drive, dear?"

    *   *   *   *   *   *   *

For six months Mrs. Pendleton hid her broken heart
under a smile and went softly about the small daily duties
of the household, facing death, as she had faced life,
with a sublime unselfishness and the manner of a lady.
Her hopes, her joys, her fears even, lay in the past; there
was nothing for her to look forward to, nothing for her
to dread in the future. Life had given her all that it had
to offer of bliss or sorrow, and for the rest of her few
years she would be like one who, having finished her work
before the end of the day, sits waiting patiently for the
words of release to be spoken. As the months went on,
she moved like a gentle shadow about her daughter's
little home. So wasted and pallid was her body that at
times Virginia feared to touch her lest she should melt
like a phantom out of her arms. Yet to the last she never
faltered, never cried out for mercy, never sought to

hasten by a breath that end which was to her as the longing of her eyes, as the brightness of the sunlight, as the
sweetness of the springtime. Once, looking up from Lucy's
lesson which she was hearing, she said a little wistfully,
"I don't think, Virginia, it will be long now," and then
checking herself reproachfully, she added, "But God knows
best. I can trust Him."

It was the only time she had ever spoken of the
thought that was in her mind day and night, for when
she could no longer welcome her destiny, she had accepted it. Her faith, like her opinions, was child-like and
uncritical, the artless product of a simple and incurious
age. The strength in her had gone not into the building of
knowledge, but into the making of character, and she had
judged all thought as innocently as she had judged all literature, by its contribution to the external sweetness of
living. A child of ten might have demolished her theories,
and yet because of them, or in spite of them, she had
translated into action the end of all reasoning, the profoundest meaning in all philosophy. But she was born to
decorate instead of to reason. Though her mind had never
winnowed illusions from realities, her hands had patiently
woven both illusions and realities into the embroidered
fabric of Life.

For six months she went about the house and helped
Virginia with the sewing, which had become burdensome
since the children, and especially Harry, were big enough
to wear daily holes in their stockings. Then, when the
half year was over, she took to her bed one evening after
she had carefully undressed, folded her clothes out of sight,
and read a chapter in her Bible. In the morning she did not
get up, and at the end of a fortnight, in which she apologized for making extra work whenever food was brought
to her, she clasped her hands on her thin breast, smiled

once into Virginia's face, and died so quietly that there was barely a perceptible change in her breathing. She had gone through life without giving trouble, and she gave none at the end. As she lay there in her little bed in Virginia's spare room, to which she had moved after Gabriel's death in order that the rectory might be got ready for the new rector, she appeared so shadowy and unearthly that it was impossible to believe she had ever been a part of the restless striving and the sombre violence of life. On the candle-stand by her bed lay her spectacles, with steel rims because she had never felt that she could afford gold ones; and a single October rose, from which a golden petal had dropped, stood in a vase beside the Bible. On the foot of the bed hung her gray flannelette wrapper, with a patch in one sleeve over which Harry had spilled a bottle of shoe polish, while through the half-shuttered window the autumn sunshine fell in long yellow bars over the hemp rugs on the floor. And she was dead! Her mother was dead; no matter how much she needed her, she could never come back. Out of the vacancy around Virginia, some words of her own, spoken in her girlhood, returned to her. "There is only one thing I couldn't bear, and that is losing my mother." Only one thing! And now that one thing had happened, and she was not only bearing it, she was looking ahead to a future in which that one thing would be always beside her, always in her memory. Whatever the years brought to her, they could never bring her mother again; they could never bring her a love like her mother's.

Out of that same vacancy, which seemed to swallow and to hold everything, which seemed to exist both without and within, a multitude of forgotten images and impressions flashed into being. She saw the nursery fireside in the rectory, and her mother, with hair that still shone

like satin, rocking back and forth in the black wicker chair
with the sagging bottom. She saw her kneeling on the old
frayed red and blue drugget, her skirt pinned up at the
back of her waist, while she bathed her daughter's
scratched and aching feet in the oblong tin foot-tub. She
saw her, as beautiful as an angel, in church on Sunday
mornings, her worshipful eyes lifted to the pulpit, an
edge of tinted light falling on the open prayer-book in her
hand. She saw her, thin and stooping, a shadow of all that
she had once been—waiting—waiting—— She had always
been there. It was impossible to realize that a time could
ever come when she would not be there—and now she
was gone!

And behind all the images, all the impressions, the
stubborn thought persisted that this was life, that one
could never escape it, that whatever happened, one must
come back to it at the last. "I have my children still left—
but for my children I could not live!" she thought, dropping on her knees by the bedside, and hiding her face in
the gray wrapper.

*　　*　　*　　*　　*　　*　　*

After this it seemed to her that she ceased to live except
in the lives of her children, and her days passed so evenly,
so monotonously, that she only noticed their flight when
one of the old people in Dinwiddie remarked to her with
a certain surprise: "You've almost a grown daughter now,
Virginia," or "Harry will soon be getting as big as his
father. Have you decided where you will send him to
college?" She was not unhappy—had she ever stopped to
ask herself the question, she would have answered,
"If only mother and father were living, I should be
perfectly satisfied"; yet in spite of her assurances, there

existed deep down in her—so deep that her consciousness
had never fully grasped the fact of its presence—a dumb
feeling that something was missing from life, that the
actuality was a little less bright, a little less perfect than
it had appeared through the rosy glamour of her virgin
dreams. Was this "something missing" merely one of the
inevitable conditions of mortal existence? Or was there
somewhere on the earth that stainless happiness which
she had once believed her marriage would bring to her?
"I should be perfectly satisfied if only——" she would
sometimes say in the night, and then check herself before
she had ended the sentence. The lack, real as it was, was
still too formless to lend itself to the precision of words;
it belonged less to circumstances than to the essential
structure of life. And yet, as she put it to herself in her
rare moments of depression, she had so much to be thankful for! The children grew stronger as they grew older;
since Harry's attack of diphtheria, indeed, there had been
no serious illness in the family, and as she approached
middle age, her terror of illness increased rather than
diminished. The children made up for much; they ought
to have made up for everything; and yet did they? There
was no visible fault that she could attribute to them. With
her natural inability to see flaws, she was accustomed to
think of them as perfect children, as children whom she
would not change, had she the power, by so much as a hair
or an outline. They grew up, straight, fine, and fearless,
full of the new spirit, eager to test life, to examine facts,
possessed by that awakening feeling for truth which had
always frightened her a little in Susan. Vaguely, without
defining the sensation, she felt that they were growing
beyond her, that she could no longer keep up with them,
that, every year, they were leaving her a little farther
behind them. They were fond of her, but she understood

from something Jenny said one day, that they had ceased to be proud of her. It was while they were looking over an old photograph album of Susan's that, coming to a picture of Virginia, taken the week before her wedding, Jenny cried out: "Why, there's mother!" and slipped it out of the page.

"I never saw that before," Lucy said, leaning over with a laugh. "You were so young when you married, mother, and you wore such tight sleeves, and a bustle!"

"Would you ever have believed she was as pretty as that?" Jenny asked, with the unconscious brutality of childhood.

"If you are ever as beautiful as your mother was, you may thank your stars," Susan said dryly, and by the expression in her face Virginia knew that she was thinking, "If that were my child, I'd slap her!"

Harry, who had been stuffing fruitcake on the sofa— sweets were his weakness—rose suddenly and came over to the group.

"If you are ever as beautiful as she is now, you may thank your stars, Miss Yellow Frisk!" he remarked crushingly.

It was a little thing, so little that it seemed ridiculous to think of it as among the momentous happenings in a life; but with that extraordinary proneness of the little to usurp the significant places of memory, it had become one of the important milestones in her experience. At the end, when she forgot everything else, she would not forget Harry's foolish words, nor the look in his indignant boyish face when he uttered them. Until then she had not admitted to herself that there was a difference in her feeling for her children, but with the touch of his sympathetic, not over clean, hand on her shoulder, she knew that she should never again think of the three of them

as if they were in her interest and love. The girls
were good children, dear children—she would have let
herself be cut in pieces for either of them had it been
necessary—but between Harry and herself there was a
different bond, a closer and deeper dependence, which
strengthened almost insensibly as he grew older. Her
daughters she loved, but her son, as is the inexplicable
way of women, she adored blindly and without wisdom.
If it had been possible to ruin him, she would have done
so, but, unlike many other sons, he seemed, by virtue of
that invincible strength with which he had been born, to
be proof against both spoiling and flattery. He was a
nice boy even to strangers, even to Susan, with her serene
judgment of persons, he appeared a thoroughly nice boy!
He was not only a tall, lean, habitually towselled-headed
youngster, with a handsome sunburned face and a pair
of charming, slightly quizzical blue eyes, but he was, as
his teachers and his school reports bore witness, possessed
of an intellectual brilliancy which made study as easy,
and quite as interesting to him, as play. Unlike his father,
he had entered life endowed with a cheerful outlook upon
the world and with that temperament of success which
usually, but by no means inevitably, accompanies it. Whatever happened, he would make the best of it, he would
"get on," and it was impossible to imagine him in any
hole so deep that he could not, sooner or later, find the
way out of it. The Pendleton and the Treadwell spirits
had contributed their best to him. If he derived from
Cyrus, or from some obscure strain in Cyrus's ancestry,
a wholesome regard for material success, a robust determination to achieve results, combined with that hard,
clear vision of affairs which makes such achievement easy,
he had inherited from Gabriel his genial temper, his charm
of manner, and his faith in life, which, though it failed

to move mountains, had sweetened and enriched the mere fact of living. Though he was less demonstrative than Lucy, who had outgrown the plainness and the reticence of her childhood and was developing into a coquettish, shallow-minded girl, with what Miss Priscilla called "a glib tongue," Virginia learned gradually, in the secret way mothers learn things, that his love for her was, after his ambition, the strongest force in his character. Between him and his father there had existed ever since his babyhood a curious, silent, yet ineradicable, hostility. Whether the fault was Oliver's or Harry's, whether the father resented the energy and the initiative of his son, or the son resented the indifference and the self-absorption of his father, Virginia had never discovered. For years she fought against admitting the discord between them. Then, at last, on the occasion of a quarrel, when it was no longer possible to dissemble, she followed Oliver into his study, which had once been the "back parlour," and pleaded with him to show a little patience, a little sympathy with his son. "He's a boy any father would be proud of——" she finished, almost in tears.

"I know he is," he answered irritably, "but the truth is he rubs me the wrong way. I suppose the trouble is that you have spoiled him."

"But he isn't spoiled. Everybody says——"

"Oh, everybody!" he murmured disdainfully, with a shrug of his fine shoulders.

He looked back at her with the sombre fire of anger still in his eyes, and she saw, without trying to see, without even knowing that she did see, all the changes that years had wrought in his appearance. Physically, he was a finer animal than he had been when she married him; for time, which had sapped her youth and faded her too delicate bloom, had but added a deeper colour to the warm

brown of his skin, a steadier glow to his eyes, a more
silvery gloss to his hair. At forty, he was a handsomer
man than he had been at twenty-five, yet, in spite of this,
some virtue had gone out of him—here, too, as in life,
"something was missing." The generous impulses, the high
heart for adventure, the enthusiasm of youth, and youth's
white rage for perfection—where were these? It was as
if a rough hand had passed over him, coarsening here,
blotting out there, accentuating elsewhere. The slow,
insidious devil of compromise had done its work. Once
he had made one of that small band of fighters, who fight
not for advantage but for the truth; now he stood in
that middle place with the safe majority who are "neither
for God nor for His enemies." Life had done this to him
—life and Virginia.

He was buried in his work now, and there were months
during this year when she appeared hardly to see him,
so engrossed, so self-absorbed had he become. Sometimes
she would remember, stifling the pang it caused, the nights
when he had written his first plays in Matoaca City, and
how he had made her sit beside him with her sewing because he could not think if she were out of the room.
Now, he could write only when he was alone; he hated an
interruption so much that she often let the fire go out
rather than open his closed door to see if it were burning.
If she went in to speak to him, he laid his pen down and
did not take it up again while she was there. Yet this
change had come so stealthily that it had scarcely affected
her happiness. She had grown accustomed to the difference
before she had realized it sufficiently to suffer. Sometimes
she would say to herself a little wonderingly, "Oliver used
to be so romantic"; for with the majority of women whose
marriages have surrendered to an invasion of the commonplace, she accepted the comfortable theory that the altera-

tion was due less to circumstances than to the natural
drying of the springs of sentiment in her husband's heart.
Occasionally, she would remember with a smile her
three days' jealousy of Abby; but the brevity and the folly
of this had established her the more securely in her
impregnable position of unquestioning belief in him. She
had started life believing, as the women of her race had
believed for ages before her, that love is a divine gift
which comes but once in a lifetime, and which, coming
once, remained for ever indestructible. People, of course,
grew more practical and less intense as they left youth
farther behind them; and though this misty principle would
have dissolved at once had she applied it to herself (for
she became more sentimental as she approached middle
age), behind any suspicious haziness of generalization
there remained always the sacred formula, "Men are different." Once, when a sharp outbreak of the primal force
had precipitated a scandal in the home of one of her
neighbours, she had remarked to Susan that she was "devoutly thankful that Oliver did not have that side to his
nature."

"It must be a disagreeable side to live with," Susan,
happily married to John Henry, and blissfully expectant
of motherhood, had replied, "but, so far as I know, Oliver
never had a light fancy for a woman in his life—not even
before he was married. I used to tell him that it was because he expected too much. Physical beauty by itself
never seemed to attract him. It was the angel in you that
he first fell in love with."

A glow of pleasure flushed Virginia's sharpened features, mounting to the thin little curls on her forehead.
These little curls, to which she clung sentimentally in spite
of the changes in the fashions, were a cause of ceaseless
worry to Lucy, who had developed into a "stylish" girl,

and would have died sooner than reject the universal pompadour of the period. It was the single vanity that Virginia had ever permitted herself, this adhering at middle age to the quaint and rather coquettish hairdressing of her girlhood: and Fate had punished her by threading the little curls with gray, while Susan's stiff roll (she had adopted the newer mode) remained bravely flaxen. But Susan was one of those women who, lacking a fine fair skin and defying tradition, are physically at their best between forty and fifty.

"Oliver used to be so romantic," Virginia said, as she had said so often to herself, while the glow paled slowly from her cheeks, leaving them the colour of faded rose-leaves.

"Not so romantic as you were, Virginia."

"Oh, I am still," she laughed softly. "Lucy says I take more interest in her lovers now than she does," and she added after a minute, "Girls are so different to-day from what they used to be—they are so much less sentimental."

"But I thought Lucy was. She has enough flirtations for her age, hasn't she?"

"She has enough attention, of course—for the funny part is that, though she's only sixteen and not nearly so pretty as Jenny, the men are all crazy, as Miss Willy says, about her. But, somehow, it's different. Lucy enjoys it, but it isn't her life. As for Jenny, she's still too young to have taken shape, I suppose, but she has only one idea in her head and that is going to college. She never gives a boy a thought."

"That's queer, because she promises already to be the most beautiful girl in Dinwiddie."

"She is beautiful. I am quite sure that it isn't because she is my daughter that I think so. But, all the same, I'm afraid she'll never be so popular as Lucy is. She is so distant and overbearing to men that they are shy of her."

"And you'll let her go to college?"

"If we can afford it; and now that Oliver hopes to get one of his plays put on, we may have a little more money. But it seems such a waste to me. I never saw that it could possibly do a woman any good to go to college, though of course I always sympathized with your disappointment, dear Susan. Jenny is bent on it now, but I feel so strongly that it would be better for her to come out in Dinwiddie and go to parties and have attention."

"And does Oliver feel that too?"

"Oh, he doesn't care. Jenny is his favourite, and he will let her do anything he thinks she has set her heart on. But he has never put his whole life into the children as I have done."

"But if she goes, will you be able to send Harry?"

"Of course, Harry's education must come before everything else—even Oliver realizes that. Do you know, I've hardly bought a match for ten years that I haven't stopped to ask myself if it would take anything from Harry's education. That's why I've gone as shabby as this almost ever since he was born—that and my longing to give the girls a few pretty things."

"You haven't bought a dress for yourself since I can remember. I should think you would wear your clothes out making them over."

The look in Virginia's face showed that the recollection Susan had invoked was not entirely a pleasant one.

"I've done with as little as I could," she answered. "Only once was I really extravagant, and that was when I bought a light blue silk which I didn't have made up until years afterwards when it was dyed black. Dyed things never hold their own," she concluded pensively.

"You are too unselfish—that is your only fault," Susan

said impulsively. "I hope they appreciate all you have been to them."

"Oh, they appreciate me," Virginia returned with a laugh. "Harry does, anyhow."

"I believe Harry is your darling, Virginia."

"I try not to make any difference in my feeling—they are all the best children that ever lived—but—Susan, I wouldn't breathe this to anybody on earth but you— I can't help thinking that Harry loves me more than the others do. He—he has so much more patience with me. The girls sometimes laugh at me because I am old-fashioned and behind the times, and I can see that it annoys them because I am ignorant of things they seem to have been born knowing."

"But it was for their sake that you let yourself go. You gave up everything else for them from the minute they were born."

A tear shone in Virginia's eye, and Susan knew, without having it put into words, that a wound somewhere in that gentle heart was still hurting. "I'd like to slap them!" she thought fiercely, and then she said aloud with a manner of cheerful conviction:

"You are a great deal too good for them, Virginia, and some day they will know it."

A longing came over her to take the thin little figure in her arms and shake back into her something of the sparkle and radiance of her girlhood. Why did beauty fade? Why did youth grow middle-aged? Above all, why did love and sacrifice so often work their own punishment?

CHAPTER II

THE PRICE OF COMFORT

VIRGINIA knelt on the cushioned seat in the bay-window of her bedroom, gazing expectantly down on the pavement below. It was her forty-fifth birthday, and she was waiting impatiently for Harry, who was coming home for a few days before going abroad to finish his studies at Oxford. The house was a new, impeccably modern dwelling, produced by the utilitarian genius of the first decade of the twentieth century, and Oliver had bought it at a prodigious price a few years after his dramatic success had lifted him from poverty into comfort. The girls, charmed to have made the momentous passage into Sycamore Street, were delighted with the space and elegance of their new home, but Virginia had always felt as if she were missing. The drawing-room, and especially the butler's pantry, awed her. She had not dared to wash those august shelves with soda, nor to fasten her favourite strips of white oilcloth over their shining surface. The old joy of "fixing up" her storeroom had been wrested from her by the supercilious mulatto butler, who was imposing in the dining-room, but careless and extravagant in the pantry. Once when she had discovered a bucket of apple-parings tucked away under the sink, where it had stood for days, he had given "notice" so unexpectedly and so haughtily that she had been afraid ever since to look under dish-towels or into hidden places

373

while he was absent. Out of the problem of the South "the servant question" had arisen to torment and intimidate the housekeepers of Dinwiddie; and inferior service at high wages was regarded of late as a thing for which one had come to be thankful. Had they still lived in the little house, Virginia would gladly have done her work for the sake of the peace and cleanliness it would have ensured; but since the change in their circumstances, Oliver and the girls had grown so dependent upon the small luxuries of living that she put up with anything—even with the appalling suspicion that every mouthful she ate was not clean—rather than take the risk of having her three servants desert in a body. When she had unwisely complained to Oliver, he had remarked impatiently that he couldn't be bothered about the housekeeping, and Lucy had openly accused her of being "fussy."

After this she had said nothing more; but gathering suddenly all her energies, she had precipitated a scene with the servants (which ended to her relief in the departure of the magnificent butler) and had reorganized at a stroke the affairs of her household. For all her gentleness, she was not incapable of decisive action, and though it had always been easier for her to work herself than to direct others, her native talent for domesticity had enabled her to emerge triumphantly out of this crisis. Now, on her forty-fifth birthday, she could reflect with pride (the pride of a woman who has mastered her traditional *métier de femme*) that there was not a house in Dinwiddie which had better food or smoother service than she provided in hers. For more and more, as Oliver absorbed himself in his work, which kept him in New York many months of the year, and the children grew so big that they no longer needed her, did her life centre in the small monotonous details of cooking and cleaning. Only when,

as occasionally happened, the others of the family were
absent together, Oliver about his plays, Lucy on a visit
to Richmond, and Harry and Jenny at college, an awful
sense of futility descended upon her, and she felt that
both the purpose and the initiative were sapped from her
character. Sometimes, during such days or weeks of loneliness, she would think of her mother's words, uttered so
often in the old years at the rectory: "There isn't any
pleasure in making things unless there's somebody to make
them for."

Beyond the window, the November day, which had been
one of placid contentment for her, was drawing slowly to
its close. The pale red gleam of an autumn sunset lingered
in the west above the huddled roofs of the town, while the
mournful dusk of evening was creeping up from the earth.
A few chilled and silent sparrows hopped dejectedly along
the bared boughs of the young maple tree in front of the
house, and every now and then a brisk pedestrian would
pass on the concrete pavement below. Inside, a cheerful
fire burned in the grate, and near it, on one end of the
chintz-covered couch, lay Oliver's present to her—a set
of black bear furs, which he had brought down with him
from New York. Turning away from the window, she
slipped the neck-piece over her shoulders, and as she did
so, she tried to stifle the wonder whether he would have
bought them—whether even he would have remembered
the date—if Harry had not been with him. Last year he
had forgotten her birthday; and never before had he given
her so costly a present as this. They were beautiful furs,
but even she, with her ignorance of the subtler arts of
dress, saw that they were too heavy for her, that they
made her look shrunken and small and accentuated the
pallor of her skin, which had the colour and the texture
of withered rose-leaves. "They are just what Jenny has

always wanted, and they would be so becoming to her. I
wonder if Oliver would mind my letting her take them
back to Bryn Mawr after the holidays?"

If Oliver would mind! The phrase still remained after
the spirit that sanctified it had long departed. In her heart
she knew, though her happiness rested upon her passionate
evasion of the knowledge, that Oliver had not only ceased
to mind, that he had even ceased to notice whether she
wore his gifts or gave them to Jenny.

A light step flitted along the hall; her door opened without shutting again, and Lucy, in a street gown made in the
princess style, hurried across the room and turned a
slender back appealingly toward her.

"Oh, mother, please unhook me as fast as you can.
The Peytons are going to take me in their car over to
Richmond, and I've only a half hour in which to get
ready."

Then, as Virginia's hands fumbled a little at an obstinate
hook, Lucy gave an impatient pull of her shoulders, and
reached back, straining her arms, until she tore the offend-
ing fastenings from her dress. She was a small, graceful
girl, not particularly pretty, not particularly clever, but
possessing some indefinable quality which served her as
successfully as either beauty or cleverness could have done.
Though she was the most selfish and the least considerate
of the three children, Virginia was like wax in her hands,
and regarded her dashing, rather cynical, worldliness with
naïve and uncomprehending respect. She secretly disap-
proved of Lucy, but it was a disapproval tempered by admiration. It seemed miraculous to her that any girl of
twenty-two should possess so clearly formulated and critical a philosophy of life, or should be so utterly emanci-
pated from the last shackles of reverence. So far as her
mother could discern, Lucy respected nothing but her own

opinion. For authority she had as little reverence as a savage; yet she was not a savage, for she represented instead the perfect product of over-civilization. The world was bounded for her by her own personality. She was supremely interested in what she thought, felt, or imagined, and beyond the limits of her individuality, she was frankly bored by existence. The joys, sorrows, or experiences, of others failed even to arrest her attention. Yet the very sincerity of her egoism robbed it of offensiveness, and raised it from a trait of character to the dignity of a point of view. The law of self-sacrifice, which had guided her mother's life, was not only personally distasteful to her; it was morally indefensible. She was engaged not in illustrating precepts of conduct, but in realizing her independence; and this realization of herself appeared to her as the supreme and peculiar obligation of her being. Though she was less fine than Jenny, who in her studious way was a girl of much character, she was by no means as superficial as she appeared, and might in time, aided by fortuitous circumstances, make a strong and capable woman. Her faults, after all, were owing, in a large measure, to a training which had consistently magnified in her mind the space which she would ultimately occupy in the universe.

And she had charm. Without beauty, without intellect, without culture, she was still able to dominate her surroundings by charm alone. She was one of those women of whom people say, "It is impossible to tell what attracts men in a woman." She was indifferent, she was casual, she was even cruel; yet every male creature she met fell a victim before her. Her slightest gesture had a fascination for the masculine mind; her silliest words a significance. "I declare, men are the biggest fools where women are concerned," Miss Priscilla had remarked, watching her;

and the words had adequately expressed the opinion of the feminine half of Dinwiddie.

From sixteen to twenty-two she had remained as indifferent as a star to the impassioned moths flitting about her. Then, a month after her twenty-second birthday, she had coolly announced her engagement to a man whom she had seen but six times; a widower at that, twelve years older than herself, and the father of two children. The blow had fallen, without warning, upon Virginia, who had never seen the man, and did not like what she had heard of him. Unwisely, she had attempted to remonstrate, and had been met by the reply, "Mother, dear, you must allow me to decide what is for my happiness," and a manner which said, "After all, you know so much less of life than I do, how can you advise me?"

It was intolerable, of course, and the worst of it was that, rebel as she might against the admission, Virginia could not plausibly deny the truth either of the remark or the manner. On the face of it, Lucy must know best what she wanted, and as for knowledge of life, she was certainly justified in considering her mother a child beside her. Oliver, when the case was put before him, showed a sympathy with Virginia's point of view and a moral inability to coerce his daughter into accepting it. "She knows I never liked Craven," he said, "but, after all, what are we going to do about it? She's old enough to decide for herself, and you can't in this century put a girl on bread and water because she marries as she chooses."

Nothing about duty! nothing about consideration for her family! nothing about the awful responsibility of entering lightly into sacred relations! Lucy was evidently in love; if she hadn't been, why on earth should she have precipitated herself into an affair whose only reason was a lack of reason that was conclusive?—but she might have been engaging a chauffeur for all the solemnity she put into the arrangements. She had selected her clothes and planned her wedding with a practical wisdom which had awed and saddened her mother. All the wistful sentiments, the tender evasions, the consecrated dreams, that had gone into the preparations for Virginia's marriage, were buried somewhere under the fragrant past of the eighties—and the memory of them made her feel not forty-five, but a hundred. Yet the thing that troubled her most was a feeling that she was in the power of forces she could not understand; a sense that there were profound disturbances beneath the familiar surface of life.

When Lucy had gone out, with her dress open down the back and a glimpse of her smooth girlish shoulders showing between the fastenings, Virginia went over to the window again, and was rewarded by the sight of Harry's athletic figure crossing the street.

In a minute he came in, kissing her with the careless tenderness that was one of her secret joys.

"Halloo! little mother! All alone? Where are the others?" He was the only one of her children who appeared to enjoy her, and sometimes when they were alone together, he would turn and put his arms about her, or stroke her hands with an impulsive, protecting sympathy. There were moments when it seemed to her that he pitied her because the world had moved on without her; and others when he came to her for counsel about things of which she was not only ignorant, but even a little afraid. Once he had consulted her as to whether he should go on the football team at his college, and had listened respectfully enough to her timid objections. Respect, indeed, was the quality in which he had never failed her, and this, even more than his affection, had become a balm to her in recent years, when Lucy and Jenny occasionally lost patience and showed themselves openly amused by her old-fashioned opinions. She had never forgotten that he had once taken her part when the girls had tried to persuade her to brush back the little curls from her temples and wear her hair à la Pompadour.

"It would look so much more suitable for a woman of your age, mother dear," Lucy had remarked sweetly, with a condescending deference which had made Virginia feel as if she were a thousand.

"And it would be more becoming, too, now that your hair is turning gray," Jenny had added, with an intention to be kind and helpful which had gone wrong somehow and turned into officiousness.

"Shut up, and don't be silly geese," Harry had growled at them, and his rudeness in her behalf had given Virginia a delicious thrill, which was increased by the knowledge that his manners were usually excellent even to his sisters. "You let them fuss all they want to, mother," he concluded, "but your hair is a long sight better than theirs, and don't you let them nag you into making a mess of it."

All of which had been sweet beyond words to Virginia, though she was obliged to admit that his judgment was founded upon a deplorable lack of discrimination in the matter of hairdressing, since Lucy and Jenny both had magnificent hair, while her own had long since lost its gloss and grown thin from neglect. But if it had been really the truth, it could not have been half so sweet to her.

"Lucy is dressing to motor over to Richmond with the Peytons, and your father went out to ride. Harry, why won't you let me go on to New York to see you off?"

He was sailing the following week for England, and he had forbidden her to come to his boat, or even to New York, for a last glimpse of him.

"Oh, I hate having a scene at the boat, mother. It always makes me feel creepy to say good-bye. I never do it, if I can help."

"I know you don't, darling—you sneaked off after the holidays without telling me what train you were going by. But this is for such a long time. Two years, Harry."

Her voice broke, and turning away, she gazed through the window at the young maple tree as though her very soul were concentrated upon the leafless boughs.

He stirred uneasily, for like most men of twenty-one, he had a horror of sentiment.

"Oh, well, you may come over next summer, you know. I'll speak to father about it. If his play goes over to London, he'll have to be there, won't he?"

"I suppose so," she replied, choking down her tears, and becoming suddenly cheerful. "And you'll write to me once a week, Harry?"

"You bet! By the way, I've had nothing to eat since ten o'clock, and I feel rather gone. Have you some cake around anywhere?"

"But we'll have dinner in an hour, and there'll be turkey and cranberries. Hadn't you better wait?"

Her cheerfulness was not assumed now, for with the turn to practical matters, she felt suddenly that the universe had righted itself. Even Harry's departure was forgotten in the immediate necessity of providing for his appetite.

"Well, I'll wait, but I hope you've prepared for an army."

He snapped his jaws, and she laughed delightedly. For all his twenty-one years, and the scholarship which he had won so easily and which was taking him abroad, he was as boyish and as natural as he had been at ten. Even his love of sweets had not lessened with the increase of his dignity. To think of his demanding cake the minute after he had entered the house!

"Father's play made a great hit," he said presently, still steering carefully away from the reefs of emotion. "I suppose you read all about it in the papers?"

She shook her head, smiling. Though she tried her best to be as natural and as unemotional as he was, she could not keep her adoration out of her eyes, which feasted on him like the eyes of one who had starved for months. How handsome he was, with his broad shoulders, his fine sunburned face, and his frank, boyish smile. It was a pity he had to wear glasses; yet even his glasses seemed to her individual and charming. She couldn't imagine a single way in which he could be improved, and all the while she was perfectly sure that it wasn't in the least because she was his mother, that she wasn't a bit prejudiced in her judgment. It appeared out of the question that anybody, even a stranger, could have found fault with him. "No, I haven't had time to read the papers; I've been so busy getting ready for Lucy's wedding," she answered. "But your father told me about it. It must be splendid—only I wish he wouldn't speak so contemptuously of it," she added regretfully. "He says it's trash, and yet I'm sure everybody spoke well of it, and they say it is obliged to make a great deal of money. I can't understand why his success seems to irritate rather than please him."

"Well, he thinks, you know, that it is only since he's cheapened himself that he has had any hearing."

"Cheapened himself?" she repeated wistfully. "But his first plays failed entirely, so these last ones must be a great deal better if they are such splendid successes."

"Well, I suppose it's hard for us to understand his point of view. We talked about it one night in New York

when we were dining with Margaret Oldcastle. She takes
the leading part in 'Pretty Fanny,' you know."

"Yes, I know. What is she like?"

A strange, still look came into her face, as though she
waited with suspended breath for his answer.

"She's a charmer on the stage. I heard father tell her
that she made the play, and I'm not sure that he wasn't
right."

"But you saw her off the stage, didn't you?"

"Oh, yes, she asked me to dinner. She didn't look
nearly so young then, and she's not exactly pretty; but,
somehow, it didn't seem to matter. She has genius. You
couldn't be with her ten minutes without finding out that.
I never saw any one in my life so much alive. When she's
in a room, even if she doesn't speak, you can't keep your
eyes off her. She's like a bright flame that you can't stop
looking at; not even if there are a lot of prettier women
there too."

"Is she dark or fair?"

He stopped to think for a moment.

"To save my life I can't remember; but I think she's
dark—at least, her eyes are, though her hair may be light.
But you never think of her appearance when she's talking.
I believe she's the best talker I ever heard; better even
than father."

His enthusiasm had got the better of him, and it was
evident that Oliver's success had banished, for a time at
least, the secret hostility between father and son. That
passion for material results, which could not be separated
from the Treadwell spirit without robbing that spirit of its
vitality, had gradually altered the family attitude toward
Oliver's profession. Art, like business, must justify itself
by its results, and to a commercial age there could be no
justifiable results that could not bear translation into fig-

ures. Success was the chief end of man, and success could be measured only in terms of money.

"There's your father's step," said Virginia, whose face looked drawn and pallid in the dusk. "Let me light the lamp, darling. He hates to read his paper by anything but lamplight."

But he had jumped up before she had finished and was hunting for matches in the old place under the clock on the mantelpiece. She was such a little, thin, frail creature that he laughed as she tried to help him.

"So Lucy is going to marry that old rotter, is she?" he asked pleasantly as his father entered. "Well, father! I was just asking mother why she let Lucy marry that old rotter?"

"But the dear child has set her heart on him, and he is really very nice to us," Virginia replied hurriedly. Though she was disappointed in Lucy's choice, it seemed dreadful to her to speak of a man who was about to enter the family as a "rotter."

"You stop it, Harry, if you have the authority. I haven't," Oliver answered carelessly. "Is your neuralgia better, Virginia?"

"It's quite gone, dear. Doctor Powell gave me some aspirin and it cured it." She smiled gratefully at him, with a touching pleasure in the fact that he had remembered to ask. As she glanced quickly from father to son, eager to see them reconciled, utterly forgetful of herself, something of the anxious cheerfulness of Mrs. Pendleton's spirit appeared to live again in her look. Though her freshness had withered, she was still what is called "a sweet looking woman," and her expression of simple goodness lent an appealing charm to her features.

"Are you going back to New York soon, father?" asked Harry, turning politely in Oliver's direction. From his

manner, which had lost its boyishness, Virginia knew that
he was trying with all his energy to be agreeable, yet that
he could not overcome the old feeling of constraint and
lack of sympathy.

"Next week. 'The Home' is to be put on in February,
and I'm obliged to be there for the rehearsals."

"Does Miss Oldcastle take the leading part?"

"Yes."

Crossing the room, Oliver held out his hands to the fire,
and then turning, stretched his arms, with a stifled yawn,
above his head. The only fault that could be urged against
his appearance was that his figure was becoming a trifle
square, that he was beginning to look a little too well-fed,
a little too comfortable. For the rest, his hair, which had
gone quite gray, brought out the glow and richness of
his colour and lent a striking emphasis to his dark, shining
eyes.

"Do you think the new play is as good as 'Pretty
Fanny'?" asked Virginia.

"Well, they're both rot, you know," he answered with
a laugh.

"Oh, Oliver, how can you, when all the papers spoke so
admiringly of it?"

"Why shouldn't they? It is perfectly innocuous. The
kind of thing any father might take his daughter to see.
We shan't dispute that, anyhow."

His flippancy not only hurt, it confused her. It was
painful enough to have him speak so slightingly of his
success, but worse than this was the feeling it aroused in
her that he was defying authority. Even if her innate
respect for the printed word had not made her accept as
final the judgment of the newspapers, there was still the
incontestable fact that so many people had paid to see
"Pretty Fanny" that both Oliver and Miss Oldcastle had

reaped a small fortune. She glanced in a helpless way at Harry, and he said suddenly:

"Don't you think Jenny ought to come home to be with mother after Lucy marries? You are obliged to go to New York so often that she will be lonely."

"It's a good idea," Oliver agreed amicably, "but there's another case where you'll have to use greater authority than mine. When I stopped reforming people," he added gaily, "I began with my own family."

"The dear child would come in a minute if I suggested it," Virginia said, "but she enjoys her life at college so much that I wouldn't have her give it up for anything in the world. It would make me miserable to think that any of my children made a sacrifice for me."

"You needn't worry. We've trained them differently," Oliver said, and though his tone was slightly satirical, the satire was directed at himself, not at his wife.

'I am sure it is what I should never want," Virginia insisted almost passionately, while she smiled at Lucy, in trailing pink chiffon, on the threshold.

"Are you sure your coat is warm enough, dear?" she asked. "Wouldn't you like to wear my furs? They are heavier than yours."

"Oh, I'd love to, if you wouldn't mind, mother."

Raising herself on tiptoe, Lucy kissed Harry, and then ran to the mirror, eager to see if the black fur looked well on her.

"They're just lovely on me, mother. I feel gorgeous!" she exclaimed triumphantly, and indeed her charming girlish face rose like a white flower out of the rich dark furs.

In Virginia's eyes, as she turned to watch her, there was a radiant self-forgetfulness that illumined her features. For a moment she lived so completely in her daughter's youth that her body seemed to take warmth and colour from the emotion which transfigured her.

"I am so glad, darling," she said. "It gives me more pleasure to see you in them than it does to wear them myself." And though she did not know it, she embodied her gentle philosophy of life in that single sentence.

CHAPTER III

MIDDLE AGE

JENNY had promised to come home a week before Lucy's wedding; but at the last moment, while they waited supper for her, a telegram announced with serious brevity that she was "detained." Twenty-four hours later, a second telegram informed them that she would not arrive until the evening before the marriage, and at six o'clock on that day, Virginia, who had been packing Lucy's trunks ever since breakfast, looked out of the window at the sound of the door-bell, and saw the cab that had contained her second daughter standing beside the curbstone.

"Mother, have you the change to pay the driver?" asked a vision of stern loveliness floating into the room. With the winter glow in her cheeks and eyes and the bronze sheen on her splendid hair, which was brushed in rippling waves from her forehead and coiled in a severely simple knot on her neck, she might have been a wandering goddess, who had descended, with immortal calm, to direct the affairs of the household. Her white shirtwaist, with its starched severity, suited her austere beauty and her look of almost superhuman composure.

"Take off your hat, darling, and lie down on the couch while I finish Lucy's packing," Virginia said, when she had sent the servant downstairs to pay the cabman. Her soul was in her eyes while she watched Jenny remove her plain felt hat, with its bit of blue scarf around the crown;

a piece of millinery that presented a deceptive appearance of inexpensiveness, and pass the comb through the shining arch of her hair.

"I am so sorry, mother dear, I couldn't come before, but there were some important lectures I really couldn't afford to miss. I am specializing in biology, you know."

Her manner, calm, sweet, and gently condescending, was such as she might have used to a child whom she loved and with whom she possessed an infinite patience. One felt that while talking, she groped almost unconsciously for the simplest and shortest words in which her meaning might be conveyed. She did not lie down as Virginia had suggested, but straightened her short skirt, seated herself in an upright chair by the table and crossed her slender feet in their sensible, square-toed shoes. While she gazed at her, Virginia remembered, with a smile, that Harry had once said his sister was as flawless as a geometrical figure, and he couldn't look at her without wanting to twist her nose out of shape. In spite of her beauty, she was not attractive to men, whom she awed and intimidated by a candid assumption of superiority. For Lucy's conscienceless treatment of the male she had unmitigated contempt. Her sister, indeed, had she not been her sister, would have appeared to her as an object for frank condemnation: "one of those women who waste themselves in foolish flirtations." As it was, loving Lucy, and being a loyal soul, with modern ideas of her own responsibility for her sister, as well as for that abstract creature whom she classified as "the working woman," she thought of Lucy tenderly as a "dear girl but simple." Her mother, of course, was "simple, too"; but, then, what could one expect of a woman who had been educated at the Dinwiddie Academy for Young Ladies? To Jenny, education had usurped the place which the church had always occupied in the benighted mind of her mother. All the evils of our civilization, and these evils divided with the working woman the first right to her attention, she attributed to the fact that the former generations of women had had either no education at all, or worse even than that, had had the meretricious brand of education provided by an army of Miss Priscillas. For Miss Priscilla herself, entirely apart from the Academy, which she described frankly, to Virginia's horror, as a "menace," she cherished a sincere devotion, and this ability to detach her judgments from her affections made her appear almost miraculously wise to her mother, who had been born a Pendleton.

"No, I'm not tired. Is there anything I can help you about, mother?" she asked, for she was a good child and very helpful; the only drawback to her assistance being that when she helped she invariably commanded.

"Oh, no, darling, I'll be through presently, just as soon as I get this trunk packed. Lucy's things are lovely. I wish you had come in time to see them. Miss Willy and I spent all yesterday running blue ribbons in her underclothes, and though we began before breakfast, we had to sit up until twelve o'clock, so as to get through in time to begin on the trunks this morning."

Her eyes shone as she spoke, and she would have enjoyed describing all Lucy's clothes, for she loved pretty things, though she never bought them for herself, finding it impossible to break the habit of more than twenty years of economy; but Jenny, who was proud of her sincerity, looked so plainly bored that her mother checked her flowing descriptions.

"I hope you brought something beautiful to wear tomorrow, Jenny?" she ventured timidly, after a silence.

"Of course, I had to get a new dress, as I'm to be maid

of honour, but it seemed so extravagant, for I had two perfectly good white chiffons already."

"But it would have hurt Lucy, dear, if you hadn't worn something new. She even wanted me to order my dress from New York, but I was so afraid of wounding poor little Miss Willy—she has made my clothes ever since I could remember—that I persuaded the child to let her make it. Of course, it won't be stylish, but nobody will look at me anyway."

"I hope it is coloured, mother. You wear black too much. The psychological effect is not good for you."

With her knees on the floor and her back bent over the trunk into which she was packing a dozen pairs of slippers wrapped in tissue paper, Virginia turned her head and stared in bewilderment at her daughter, whose classic profile showed like marble flushed with rose in the lamplight.

"But at my time of life, dear? Why, I'm in my forty-sixth year."

"But forty-six is still young, mother. That was one of the greatest mistakes women used to make—to imagine that they must be old as soon as men ceased to make love to them. It was all because of the idea that men admired only schoolgirls, and that as soon as a woman stopped being admired she had stopped living."

"But they didn't stop living really. They merely stopped fixing up."

"Oh, of course. They spent the rest of their lives in the storeroom or the kitchen, slaving for the comfort of the men they could no longer amuse."

This so aptly described Virginia's own situation that her interest in Lucy's trousseau faded abruptly, while a wave of heartsickness swept over her. It was as if the sharp and searching light of truth had fallen suddenly upon all the frail and lovely pretences by which she had helped herself to live and be happy. A terror of the preternatural insight of youth made her turn her face away from Jenny's too critical eyes.

"But what else could they do, Jenny? They believed that it was right to step back and make room for the young," she said, with a pitiful attempt at justification of her exploded virtues.

"Oh, mother!" Jenny exclaimed still sweetly, "whoever heard of a man of that generation stepping back to make room for anybody?"

"But men are different, darling. One doesn't expect them to give up like women."

"Oh, *mother!*"—this time the sweetness had borrowed an edge of irony. It was Science annihilating tradition, and the tougher the tradition, the keener the blade that Science must apply.

"I can't help it, dear, it is the way I was taught. My darling mother felt like that"—a tear glistened in her eye—"and I am too old to change my way of thinking."

"Mother, mother, you silly pet!" Rising from her chair, Jenny put her arms about her and kissed her tenderly. "You can't help being old-fashioned, I know. You are not to blame for your ideas; it is Miss Priscilla." Her voice grew stern with condemnation as she uttered the name. "But don't you think you might try to see things a little more rationally? It is for your own sake I am speaking. Why should you make yourself old by dressing as if you were eighty simply because your grandmother did so?"

She was right, of course, for the trouble with Science is not its blindness, but its serene infallibility. As useless to reject her conclusions as to deny the laws and the principles of mathematics! After all manner of denials, the laws and the principles would still remain. Virginia, who had never argued in her life, did not attempt to do so with her own daughter. She merely accepted the truth of Jenny's inflexible logic; and, with that obstinate softness which is an inalienable quality of tradition, went on believing precisely what she had believed before. To have made them think alike, it would have been necessary to melt up the two generations and pour them into one; a task as hopeless as an endeavour to blend the Dinwiddie Young Ladies' Academy with a modern college. Jenny's clearly formulated and rather loud morality was unintelligible to her mother, whose conception of duty was that she should efface herself and make things comfortable for those around her. The obligation to think independently was as incomprehensible to Virginia as was that wider altruism which had swept Jenny's sympathies beyond the home into the factory and beyond the factory into the world where there were "evils." Her own instinct had been always the true instinct of the lady, to avoid "evil," not to seek it, to avoid it, honestly if possible, and, if not honestly—well, to avoid it at any cost. The love of truth for truth's sake is the last of the eternal verities to descend from philosophy into a working theory of life, and it had been unknown to Virginia until Jenny had returned, at the end of her first year, from college. To be sure, Oliver used to talk like that long ago; but it was so long ago that she had almost forgotten it.

"You are very clever, dear, much too clever for me," she said, rising from her knees. "I wonder if Lucy has anything else she wants to go into this trunk? It might be packed a little tighter."

In response to her call, the door opened, and Lucy entered breathlessly, with her hair, which she had washed and not entirely dried, hanging over her shoulders.

"What is it, mother? Oh, Jenny, you have come? I'm so glad!"

The sisters kissed delightedly. In spite of their lack of sympathy, they were very fond of each other.

"Do you want to put anything else into this trunk before I lock it, Lucy?"

"Could you find room for my blue flannel bathrobe? I'll want it on top where I can get it out without unpacking, and, oh, mother, won't you please put my alcohol stove and curling irons in my travelling bag?"

She was prettily excited, and during the last few days she had shown an almost child-like confidence in her mother's opinions about the trivial matters of packing.

"Mother, I don't want to come down yet; my hair isn't dry. Will you send dinner up to me? I'll dress about nine o'clock when Bertie and the girls are coming."

"Of course, I will, darling. I'll go straight downstairs and fix your tray. Is there anything you can think of that you would like?"

At this Jenny broke into a laugh: "Why, anybody would think she was dying instead of being married!"

"Just a cup of coffee. I really couldn't swallow a morsel," replied Lucy, whose single tribute to sentiment had been a complete loss of appetite. "You needn't laugh, Jenny. Wait until you are going to be married, and see if you are able to eat anything."

Putting the tray back into the trunk, Virginia closed it almost caressingly. For twenty-four hours, as Lucy's wedding began to draw nearer, she had been haunted by the feeling that she was losing her favourite child, and though her reason told her that this was not true—that Lucy was, in fact, less fond of her than either of the others, and far less dear to her heart than Harry—still she was unable wholly to banish the impression. It seemed only yesterday that she had sat waiting, month after month, week after week, day after day, for her to be born. Only yesterday that she had held her, a baby, in her arms, and now she was packing the clothes which that baby would carry away when she went off with her husband! Something of the hushed expectancy of those long months of approaching motherhood enveloped her again with the thought of Lucy's wedding to-morrow. After all, Lucy was her first child; neither of the others had been awaited with quite the same brooding ecstasy, with quite the same radiant dreams. To neither of the others had she given herself at the hour of birth with such an abandonment of soul and body. And she had been a good child; all day, with a lump in her throat, Virginia had assured herself again and again that no child could have been better. A hundred little charming ways, a hundred bright delicious tricks of expression and of voice, followed her from room to room, as though Lucy had indeed, as Jenny said, been dying upstairs instead of waiting to be married. And all the time, while she arranged the dinner-tray and attended to the making of the coffee so that it might be perfect, she was thinking, "Mother must have felt like this when I was married, and I never knew it, I never suspected." She saw her little bedroom at the rectory, with her own figure, in the floating tulle veil, reflected in the mirror, and her mother's face, that face from which all remembrance of self seemed to have vanished, looking at her over the bride's bouquet of white roses. If only she had told her then that she understood! If only she had ever really understood until to-night! If only it were not too late to turn back now and gather that plaintive figure, waiting with the white roses, into her arms!

The next morning she was up at daybreak, finishing the

packing, preparing the house before leaving for church,
making the final arrangements for the wedding breakfast.
When at last Lucy, with reddened eyes and tightly curled
hair, appeared in the pantry while her mother was helping
to wash a belated supply of glass and china which had
arrived from the caterer's, Virginia felt that the parting
was worse even than Harry's going to college.

"Mother, I've the greatest mind on earth not to do it."

"My pet, what is the matter?"

"I can't imagine why I ever thought I wanted to marry!
I don't want to do it a bit. I don't want to go away and
leave you and father. And, mother, I really don't believe
I love him!"

It was so like Lucy after months of cool determination,
of perfect assurance, of stubborn resistance to opposition;
it was so exactly like her to break down when it was too
late, and to begin to question whether she really wanted
her own way after she had won it. And it was so like Virginia that, at the first sign of weakness in her child, she
should grow suddenly strong and efficient.

"My darling, it is only nervousness. You will be better
as soon as you begin to dress. Come upstairs and I will
fix you a dose of aromatic ammonia."

"Do you really think it's too late to stop it?"

"Not if you feel you are going to regret it; but you
must be very sure that it isn't merely a mood, Lucy."

At the first sign that the step was not yet irrevocable,
the girl's courage returned.

"Well, I suppose I'll have to get married now," she
said, "but if I don't like it, I'm not going to live with
him."

"Not live with your husband! Why, Lucy!"

"It's perfectly absurd to think I'll have to live with a
man if I find I don't love him. Ask Jenny if it isn't."

Ask Jenny! This was her incredible suggestion! This was her reverence for authority, for duty, for the thundering admonition of Saint Paul! As far as Saint Paul was concerned, he might as well have been the ponderous anecdotal minister in the brick Presbyterian church on the corner.

"But Jenny is so—so——" Virginia murmured, and stopped because words failed her. Had Jenny been born in any family except her own, she would probably have described her as "dangerous"; but it was impossible to brand her daughter with so opprobrious an epithet. The word, owing to the metaphorical yet specific definition she had derived from the rector's sermons in her childhood, invariably suggested fire and brimstone to her imagination.

"Well, I'm not going to do it unless I want to," Lucy returned positively. "And you may look as shocked as you please, mother, but you needn't pretend that you wouldn't be glad to see me."

The difference between the two girls, as far as Virginia could see, was that Jenny really believed her dreadful ideas were right, and Lucy merely believed that they might help her the more effectively to follow her wishes.

"Of course, I'd be glad to see you, but, Lucy, it pains me so to hear you speak flippantly of your marriage. It is the most sacred day in your life, and you treat it as lightly as if it were a picnic."

"Do I? Poor little day, have I hurt its feelings?"

They were on the way upstairs, following a procession of wedding presents, which had just arrived by express, and glancing round over the heads of the servants, she made a laughing face at her mother. Clearly, she was incorrigible, and her passing fear, which was owing, as Virginia had suspected, to one of her rare attacks of nervousness, had entirely disappeared. In her normal

mood she was perfectly capable of taking care of herself
not only within the estate of matrimony, but in an African
jungle. She would in either situation inevitably get what
she wanted, and in order to get it she would shrink as
little from sacrificing a husband as from enslaving a savage.

And yet a few hours later, when she stood beneath her
bridal veil and gazed at her image in the cheval-glass in
her bedroom, she presented so enchanting a picture of
virgin innocence, that Virginia could scarcely believe she
harboured in her breast, under the sacred white satin of
her bride's gown, the heretical opinions she had uttered
downstairs in the pantry. Her charming face had attuned
its expression so perfectly to the dramatic values of the
moment that she appeared, in the words of that sentimental soul, Miss Priscilla, to be listening already to "The
Voice that Breathed o'er Eden."

"Doesn't mother look sweet?" she asked, catching sight
of Virginia's face in the mirror. "I love her in pale gray—
only she ought to have some flowers."

"I told father to order her a bunch of violets," Jenny
answered. "I wonder if he remembered to do it."

A look of pleasure, the first she had worn for days,
flitted over Virginia's face. She had all her mother's touching appreciation of insignificant favours, and, perhaps
because her pleasure was so excessive, people shrank a
little from arousing it. Like most persons who thought
perpetually of others, she was not accustomed to being
thought of very often in return.

But Oliver had remembered, and when the purple box
was brought up to her, and Jenny pinned the violets on
her dress, a blush mantled her thin cheeks, and she looked
for a moment almost as young and lovely as her daughters. Then Oliver came after Lucy, and gathering up her

train, the girl smiled at her mother and hurried out of
the room. At the last minute her qualms appeared suddenly to depart. Whatever happened in the months and
years that came afterwards, she had determined to get all
she could out of the excitement of the wedding. She had
cast no loving glance round the little room, where she was
leaving her girlhood behind her; but Virginia, lingering
for an instant after the others had gone out, looked with
tear-dimmed eyes at the small white bed and the white
furniture decorated in roses. She suffered in that minute
with an intensity and a depth of feeling that Lucy had
never known in the past—that she would probably never
know in the future; for it is given to mothers to live not
once, but twice or thrice or as many times as they have
children to live for. And the sunlight, entering through
the high window, fell very gently on the anxious love in
her eyes, on the fading white rose-leaves of her cheeks,
and on the silvery mist of curls framing her forehead.

*   *   *   *   *   *   *

That afternoon, when Lucy had motored off with her
husband, and Oliver and Jenny had gone riding together,
Virginia went back again into the room and put away the
scattered clothes the girl had left. On the bed was a little
pillow, with the embroidered slip over a cover of pink
satin Virginia had made, and taking it from the bed she
put it into one of the boxes which had been left open until
the last minute. As she did so, it was as if a miraculous
wand was waved over her memory, softening Lucy's
image until she appeared to her in all the angelic sweetness and charm of her childhood. Her egoism, her selfishness, her lack of consideration and reverence, all those
faults of an excessive individualism, vanished so com-

pletely that she forgot they had ever existed. Once again she felt in her breast the burning rapture of young mother-hood; once again she gathered her first-born child—hers alone, hers out of the whole world of children!—into her arms. A choking sensation rose in her throat, and dropping a handful of photographs she had started to put away, she hurried from the room, as if she were leaving dead there something that she loved.

Downstairs, the caterers and the florists were in pos-session, carting away glass and china, dismantling deco-rations, and ejecting palms as summarily as if they had come uninvited. The servants were busy sweeping floors and moving chairs and sofas back into place, and in the kitchen the negro cook was placidly beginning prepara-tions for supper. For a time, Virginia occupied herself re-turning the ornaments to the drawing-room mantelpiece, and the illustrated gift books to the centre table. When this was over, she looked about her with the nervous ex-pectancy of a person who has been overwhelmed for months by a multitude of exigent cares, and realized, with a start, that there was nothing for her to do. To-morrow, Oliver and Jenny were both going away, he to New York to attend the rehearsals of his play, and she back to finish her year at college; and Virginia would be left in an empty house, with all her pressing practical duties suddenly ended.

"You will have such a nice long rest now, mother dear," Lucy had said as she clung to her before stepping into the car, and Virginia had agreed unthinkingly that a rest for a little while would, perhaps, do her good. Now, turning away from the centre table, where she had laid the last useless volume in place, she walked slowly through the library to the dining-room, and then from the dining-room into the pantry. Here, the dishes were all washed, the cup-towels were drying in an orderly row beside the sink, and the two maids and the butler were "drawing a breath" in wooden chairs by the stove.

"There was enough chicken salad and ice cream left for dinner, wasn't there, Wotan?"

On being assured that there was enough for a week, she gave a few directions about the distribution of the other food left from the wedding breakfast, and then went out again and into Oliver's study. A feeling of restlessness more acute than any she had ever known kept her walking back and forth between the door and the window, which looked out into a square of garden, where a few lonely sticks protruded out of the discoloured snow on the grass. She had lived for others so long that she had lost the power of living for herself.

There was nothing to do to-day; there would be nothing to do to-morrow; and, unless Jenny came home to be married, there would be nothing to do next year or the years after that. While Oliver was in Dinwiddie, she had, of course, the pleasure of supplying his food and of watching him eat it; but beyond that, even when he sat in the room with her, there was little conversation between them. She herself loved to talk, for she had inherited her mother's ability to keep up a honeyed flow of sound about little things; but she had learned long ago that there were times when her voice, rippling on about nothing, only irritated him, and with her feminine genius for adaptability, she had made a habit of silence. He never spoke to her of his work, except in terms of flippant ridicule that pained her, and the supreme topic of the children's school reports had been absent now for many years. Companionship of a mental sort had been always lacking between them; yet so reverently did she still accept the traditional fictions of marriage, that she would have been astonished at the suggestion that a love which could survive the shocks of tragedy might at last melt away from a gradual decline of interest. Nothing had happened. There had been no scenes, no quarrels, no jealousies, no recriminations; merely a gentle yet deliberate withdrawal of personalities. He had worshipped her at twenty-two, and now, at forty-seven, there were moments when she realized with a stab of pain that she bored him; but beyond this she had felt no cause for unhappiness, and until the last year no cause even for apprehension. The libertine had always been absent from his nature; and during all the years of their marriage he had, as Susan put it, barely so much as looked at another woman. Whatever came between them, it would not be physical passion, but a far subtler thing.

Going to his desk, she took up a photograph of Margaret Oldcastle and studied it for a moment—not harshly, not critically, but with a pensive questioning. It was scarcely a beautiful face, but in its glowing intelligence, it was the face of a woman of power. So different was the look of noble reticence it wore from that of the conventional type of American actress, that while she gazed at it Virginia found herself asking vaguely, "I wonder why she went on the stage?" The woman was not a pretty doll; she was not a voluptuous enchantress; the coquetry of the one and the flesh of the other were missing. If the stories Virginia had heard of her were to be trusted, she had come out of poverty not by the easy steps of managers' favours, but by hard work, self-denial, and discipline. Though Virginia had never seen her, she felt instinctively that she was an "honest woman."

And yet why did this face, which had in it none of the charms of the seductress, disturb her so profoundly? She was too little given to introspection, too accustomed to

think always in concrete images, to answer the question;
but her intuition, rather than her thought, made her understand dimly that the things she feared in Margaret
Oldcastle were the qualities in which she herself was lacking. Whatever power the woman possessed drew its
strength and its completeness from a source that Virginia had never recognized as being necessary, or even
beneficent, to love. After all, was it not petty and unjust
in her to be hurt by Oliver's friendship for a woman who
had been of such tremendous assistance to him in his work?
Had he not said a hundred times that she had succeeded
in making his plays popular without making them at the
same time ridiculous?

Putting the photograph back in its place on the desk,
she turned away and began walking again over the strip
of carpet which led from the door to the window. In the
garden the dried stalks of last year's flowers looked so
lonely amid the dirty snow, that she felt a sudden impulse
of sympathy. Poor things, they had outlived their usefulness. The phrase occurred to her again, and she remembered how often her father had applied it to women whose
children had all married and left them.

"Poor Matilda! She is restless and dissatisfied, and she
doesn't understand that it is because she has outlived her
usefulness." At that time "poor Matilda" had seemed to
her an old woman—but, perhaps, she wasn't in reality
much over forty. How soon women grew old a generation
ago! Why, she felt as young to-day as she did the morning
on which she was married. She felt as young, and yet her
hair was graying, her face was wrinkled, and, like poor
Matilda, she had outlived her usefulness. While she stood
there that peculiar sensation which comes to women when
their youth is over, the sensation of a changed world, took
possession of her. She felt that life was slipping, slipping

past her, and that she was left behind like a bit of the
sentiment or the law of the last century. Though she still
felt young, it was not with the youth of to-day. She had
no part in the present; her ideals were the ideals of another period; even her children had outgrown her. She
saw now with a piercing flash of insight, so penetrating,
so impersonal, that it seemed the result of some outside
vision rather than of her own uncritical judgment, that
life had treated her as it treats those who give but never
demand. She had made the way too easy for others; she
had never exacted of them; she had never held them to
the austerity of their ideals. Then the illumination faded,
as if it had been the malicious act of a demon, and she
reproached herself for allowing such thoughts to enter
her mind.

"I don't know what can be the matter with me. I never
used to brood. I wonder if it can be my time of life that
makes me so nervous and apprehensive?"

For so long she had waited for some definite point of
time, for the children to begin school, for them to finish
school, for Harry to go off to college, for Lucy to be
married, that now, when she realized there was nothing to
expect, nothing to prepare for, her whole nature, with all
the multitudinous fibres that had held her being together,
seemed suddenly to relax from its tension. To be sure, Oliver would come home for a time at least after his rehearsals were over. Jenny would return for as much of the
holidays as her philanthropic duties permitted, and, if she
waited long enough, Harry would occasionally pay her a
visit. They all loved her; not one of them, she told herself,
would intentionally neglect her; but not one of them
needed her! She had outlived her usefulness!

The next afternoon, when Oliver and Jenny had driven
off to the station, she put on her street clothes, and went

out to call on Susan, who lived in a new house in High Street. Mrs. Treadwell, having worn out everybody's patience but Susan's, had died some five years before, and the incorrigible sentimentalists of Dinwiddie—there were many of them left—expressed publicly the belief that Cyrus had never been "the same man since his wife's death." As a matter of fact, Cyrus, who had retired from active finance in the same year that he lost Belinda, had missed his business considerably more than he had missed his wife, whose loss, if he had ever thought about it, would have resolved itself into the absence of somebody to bully. But on the very day that he had retired from work, he had begun to age rapidly, and now, standing on Susan's porch, he reminded Virginia of an orange from which every drop of juice had been squeezed. Of late he had taken to giving rather lavishly to churches, with a vague, superstitious hope, perhaps, that he might buy the salvation he had been too busy to work out in other ways. And so acute had become his terror of death, Virginia had heard, that after every attack of dyspepsia he dispatched a check to the missionary society of the church he attended.

Upstairs, in her bedroom, Susan, who had just come in, was taking off her hat, and she greeted Virginia with a delight that seemed, in some strange way, to be both a balm and a stimulant. One thing at least in her life had not altered with middle age, and that was Susan's devotion. She was a large, young, superbly vigorous woman of forty-five, with an abundant energy that overflowed outside of her household in a dozen different directions. She loved John Henry, but she did not love him to the exclusion of other people; she loved her children, but they did not absorb her. There was hardly a charity or a public movement in Dinwiddie in which she did not take a practical interest. She had kept her mind as alert as her body, and the number of books she read had always shocked Virginia a little, who felt that time for reading was obliged to be time subtracted from more important duties.

"I've thought of you so much, Virginia, darling. You mustn't let yourself begin to feel lonely."

Virginia shook her head with a smile, but in spite of her effort not to appear depressed, there was a touching wistfulness in her eyes.

"Of course, I miss the dear children, but I'm so thankful they are happy."

"I wish Jenny would come back home to stay with you."

"She would if I asked her, Susan"—her face showed her pleasure at the thought of Jenny's willingness for the sacrifice—"but I wouldn't have her do it for the world. She's so different from Lucy, who was quite happy as long as she could have attention and go to parties. Of course, it seems to me more natural for a girl to be like that, especially a Southern girl, but Jenny says that she is obliged to have something to think about besides men. I wonder what my dear father would have thought of her?"

"She'll take you by surprise some day, and marry as suddenly as Lucy did."

"That's what Oliver says, But Miss Priscilla is sure she'll be an old maid, because she's so fastidious. It's funny how much more women exact of men now than they used to. Don't you remember what a heroine the women of Miss Priscilla's generation thought Mrs. Tom Peachey was because she supported Major Peachey by taking boarders while he just drank himself into his grave? Well, somebody told that to Jenny the other day and she said it was 'disgusting.' "

"I always thought so," said Susan, "but, Virginia, I'm

more interested in you than I am in Mrs. Peachey. What are you going to do with yourself?" Almost unconsciously both had eliminated Oliver as the dominant figure in Virginia's future.

"I don't know, dear. I wish my children were as young as yours. Bessie is just six, isn't she?"

"You ought to have had a dozen children. Didn't you realize that Nature intended you to do it?"

"I know"—a pensive look came into her face—"but we were very poor, and after the three came so quickly, and the little one that I lost, Oliver felt that we could not afford to have any others. I've so often thought that I was never really happy except when I had a baby in my arms."

"It's a devilish trick of Nature's that she makes them stop coming at the very time that you want them most. Forty-five is not much more than half a lifetime."

"And when one has lived in their children as I have done, of course, one feels a little bit lost without them. Then, if Oliver were not obliged to be away so much——"

Her voice broke, and Susan, leaning forward impulsively, put her arms about her.

"Virginia, darling, I never saw you depressed before."

"I was never like this until to-day. It must be the weather—or my age. I suppose I shall get over it."

"Of course, you will get over it—but you mustn't let it grow on you. You mustn't be too much alone."

"How can I help it? Oliver will be away almost all winter, and when he is at home, he is so absorbed in his work that he sometimes doesn't speak for days. Of course, it isn't his fault," she added hastily; "it is the only way he can write."

"And you're alone now for the first time for twenty-five years. That's why you feel it so keenly."

The look of unselfish goodness that made Virginia's

face almost beautiful at times passed like an edge of light across her eyes and mouth. "Don't worry about me, Susan. I'll get used to it."

"You will, dear, but it isn't right. I wish Harry could have stayed in Dinwiddie. He would have been such a comfort to you."

"But I wouldn't have had him do it! The boy is so brilliant. He has a future before him. Already he has had several articles accepted by the magazines"—her face shone—"and I hope he will some day be as successful as Oliver has been without going through the long struggle."

"Can't you go to England to see him in the summer?"

"That's what I want to do." It was touching to see how her animation and interest revived when she began talking of Harry. "And when Oliver's play is put on in February, he has promised to take me to New York for the first night."

"I am glad of that. But, meanwhile, you mustn't sit at home and think too much. It isn't good for you. Can't you find an interest? If you would only take up reading again. You used to be fond of it."

"I know, but one gets out of the habit. I gave it up after the children came, when there was so much that was really important for me to do, and now, to save my life, I can't get interested in a book except for an hour or two at a time. I'm always stopping to ask myself if I'm not neglecting something, just as I used to do while the children were little. You see, I'm not a clever woman like you. I was made just to be a wife and mother, and nothing else."

"But you're obliged to be something else now. You are only forty-five. There may be forty more years ahead of you, and you can't go on being a mother every minute of your time. Even if you have grandchildren, they won't be like your own. You can't slave over them in the way you used to do over yours. The girls' husbands and Harry's wife would have something to say about it."

"Do you know, Susan, I try not to be little and jealous, but when you said 'Harry's wife' so carelessly just now it brought a lump to my throat."

"He will marry some day, darling, and you might as well accustom yourself to the thought."

"I know, and I want him to do it. I shall love his wife as if she were my daughter—but—but it seems to me at this minute as if I could not bear it!"

The gray twilight, entering through the high window above her head, enveloped her as tenderly as if it were the atmosphere of those romantic early eighties in which she belonged. The small aristocratic head, with its quaint old-fashioned clusters of curls on the temples, the delicate stooping figure, a little bent in the chest, the whole pensive, exquisite personality which expressed itself in that manner of gentle self-effacement;—these things spoke to Susan's heart, through the softness of the dusk, with all the touching appeal of the past. It was as if the inscrutable enigma of time waited there, shrouded in darkness, for a solution that would make clear the mystery and the blighted promises of life. She saw herself and Virginia on that May afternoon twenty-five years before, standing with eager hearts on the edge of the future; she saw them waiting, with breathless, expectant lips, for the miracle that must happen. Well, the miracle had happened, and like all other miracles, it had descended from the zone of the miraculous into the region of the ordinary. This was life, and looking back from middle age, she felt no impulse to regret the rapturous certainties of youth. Experience, though it contained an inevitable pang, was better than ignorance. It was good to have been young; it was good to be middle-aged; and it would be good to be old. For she was one of those who loved life, not because it was beautiful, but because it was life.

"I must go," Virginia said, rising in the aimless way of a person who is not moving toward a definite object.

"Stay and have dinner with us, Virginia. John Henry will take you home afterward."

"I can't, dear. The—the servants are expecting me." She kissed Susan on the cheek, and taking up her little black silk bag, turned to the door.

"Virginia, if I come by for you to-morrow, will you go with me to a board meeting or two? Couldn't you possibly take an interest in some charity?" It was a desperate move, but at the moment she could think of no other to make.

"Oh, I am interested, Susan—but I have no executive ability, you know. And—and, then, poor dear father used to have such a horror of women who were always running about to meetings. He would never even let mother do church work—except, of course, when there was a cake sale or a fair of the missionary society."

Susan's last effort had failed, and as she followed Virginia downstairs and to the front door, a look almost of gloom settled on her large cheerful face.

"Try to pay some calls every afternoon, won't you, dear?" she said at the door. "I'll come in to see you in the morning when we get back from market."

Then she added softly, "If you are ever lonesome and want me, telephone for me day or night. There's nothing on earth I wouldn't do for you, Virginia."

Virginia's eyes were wonderful with love and gratitude as they shone on her through the twilight. "We've been friends since we were two years old, Susan, and, do you know, there is nobody in the world that I would ask anything of as soon as I would of you."

A look of unutterable understanding and fidelity passed between them; then turning silently away, Virginia descended the steps and walked quickly along the path to the pavement, while Susan, after watching her through the gate, shut the door and went upstairs to the nursery.

The town lay under a thin crust of snow, which was beginning to melt in the chill rain that was falling. Raising her umbrella, Virginia picked her way carefully over the icy street, and Miss Priscilla, who was looking in search of diversion out of her front window, had a sudden palpitation of the heart because it seemed to her for a minute that "Lucy Pendleton had returned to life." So one generation of gentle shades after another had moved in the winter's dusk under the frosted lamps of High Street.

Through the windows of her house a cheerful light streamed out upon the piles of melting snow in the garden, and at the door one of her coloured servants met her with the news that a telegram was on the hall table. Before opening it she knew what it was, for Oliver's correspondence with her had taken this form for more than a year.

"Arrived safely. Very busy. Call on John Henry if you need anything."

She put it down and turned hastily to letters from Harry and Jenny. The first was only a scrawl in pencil, written with that boyish reticence which always overcame Harry when he wrote to one of his family; but beneath the stilted phrases she could read his homesickness and his longing for her in every line.

"Poor boy, I am afraid he is lonely," she thought, and caressed the paper as tenderly as if it had been the letter of a lover. He had written to her every Sunday since he had first gone off to college and several times, she knew, he had denied himself a pleasure in order to send her her weekly letter. Already, she had begun to trust to his "sense of responsibility" as she had never, even in the early days of her marriage, trusted to Oliver's.

Opening the large square envelope which was addressed in Jenny's impressive handwriting, she found four closely written pages entertainingly descriptive of the girl's journey back to college and of the urgent interests she found awaiting her there. In this letter there was none of the weakness of sentiment, there was none of the plaintive homesickness, she had read in Harry's. Jenny wrote regularly and affectionately because she felt that it was her duty to do so, for, unlike Lucy, who was heard from only when she wanted something, she was a girl who obeyed sedulously the promptings of her conscience. But if she loved her mother, she was plainly not interested in her. Her attitude toward life was masculine rather than feminine; and Virginia had long since learned that in the case of a man it is easier to inspire love than it is to hold his attention. Harry was different, of course; there was a feminine, or at least a poetic, streak in him which endowed him with the natural talent for the affections that is supposed to be womanly; but Jenny resembled Oliver in her preference for the active rather than the passive side of experience.

Going upstairs, Virginia took off her hat and coat, and, without changing her dress, came down again with a piece of fancy-work in her hands. Placing herself under the lamp in Oliver's study, she took a few careful stitches in the centrepiece she was embroidering for Lucy, and then letting her needle fall, sat gazing into the wood fire which crackled softly on the brass andirons. From the lamp on the desk an amber glow fell on the dull red of the leather-covered furniture, on the pale brown of the walls, on the rich blending of oriental colours in the rug at her feet.

It was the most comfortable room in the house, and for that reason she had fallen into the habit of using it when Oliver was away. Then, too, his personality had impressed itself so ineffaceably upon the surroundings which he had chosen and amid which he had worked, that she felt nearer to him while she sat in his favourite chair, breathing the scent of the wood fire he loved.

She thought of the "dear children," of how pleased she was that they were all well and happy, of how "sweet" Harry and Jenny were about writing to her; and so unaccustomed was she to thinking in the first person, that not until she took up her embroidery again and applied her needle to the centre of a flower, did she find herself saying aloud: "I must send for Miss Willy to-morrow and engage her for next week. That will be something to do."

And looking ahead, she saw days of endless stitching and basting, of endless gossip, accompanied by the cheerful whirring of the little dressmaker's machine. "I used to pitty Miss Willy because she was obliged to work," she thought, with surprise, "but now I almost envy her. I wonder if it is work that keeps her so young and brisk? She's never had anything in her life, and yet she is so much happier than some people who have had everything."

The maid came to announce supper, and, gathering up her fancy-work, Virginia laid it beside the lamp on the end of Oliver's writing table. As she did so, she saw that her photograph, taken the year of her marriage, which he usually carried on his journeys, had been laid aside and overlooked when he was packing his papers. It was the first time he had forgotten it, and a little chill struck her heart as she put it back in its place beside the bronze letter rack. Then the chill sharpened suddenly until it became an icy blade in her bosom, for she saw that the picture of Margaret Oldcastle was gone from its frame.

CHAPTER IV

LIFE'S CRUELTIES

THERE was a hard snowstorm on the day Oliver returned to Dinwiddie, and Virginia, who had watched from the window all the afternoon, saw him crossing the street through a whirl of feathery flakes. The wind drove violently against him, but he appeared almost unconscious of it, so buoyant, so full of physical energy was his walk. Never had he looked more desirable to her, never more lovable, than he did at that instant. Something, either a trick of imagination or an illusion produced by the flying whiteness of the storm, gave him back for a moment the glowing eyes and the eager lips of his youth. Then, as she turned toward the door, awaiting his step on the stairs, the mirror over the mantel showed her her own face, with its fallen lines, its soft pallor, its look of fading sweetness. She had laid her youth down on the altar of her love, while he had used love, as he had used life, merely to feed the flame of the unconquerable egoism that burned like genius within him.

He came in, brushing a few flakes of snow from his sleeve, and it seemed to her that the casual kindness of his kiss fell like ice on her cheek as he greeted her. It was almost three months since he had seen her, for he had been unable to come home for Christmas, but from his manner he might have parted from her only yesterday. He was kind

—he had never been kinder—but she would have preferred that he should strike her.

"Are you all right?" he asked gently, turning to warm
his hands at the fire. "Beastly cold, isn't it?"

"Oh, yes, I am all right, dear. The play is a great success, isn't it?"

His face clouded. "As such things go. It's awful rot,
but it's made a hit—there's no doubt of that."

"And the other one, 'The Home'—when is the first
night of that?"

"Next week. On Thursday. I must get back for it."

"And I am to go with you, am I not? I have looked
forward to it all winter."

At the sound of her anxious question, a contraction of
pain, the look of one who has been touched on the raw,
crossed his face. Though she was not penetrating enough
to discern it, there were times when his pity for her
amounted almost to a passion, and at such moments he
was swept by a blind anger against Life, as against
some implacable personal force, because it had robbed
him of the hard and narrow morality on which his ancestors leaned. The scourge of a creed that had kept even
Cyrus walking humbly in the straight and flinty road of
Calvinism, appeared to him in such rare instants as one
of the spiritual luxuries a rationalistic age had destroyed; for it is not granted to man to look into the heart
of another, and so he was ignorant alike of the sanctities
and the passions of Cyrus's soul. What he felt was merely
that the breaking of the iron bonds of the old faith had
weakened his powers of resistance as inevitably as it had
liberated his thought. The sound of his own rebellion was
in his ears, and filled with the noise of it, he had not
stopped to reflect that the rebellion of his ancestors had
seemed less loud only because it was inarticulate. Was it

really that his generation had lost the capacity for endurance, the spiritual grace of self-denial, or was it simply that it had lost its reticence and its secrecy with the passing of its inflexible dogmas?

"Why, certainly you must go if you would care to," he answered.

"Perhaps Jenny will come over from Bryn Mawr to join us. The dear child was so disappointed that she couldn't come home for Christmas."

"If I'd known in time that she wasn't coming, I'd have found a way of getting down just for dinner with you. I hope you weren't alone, Virginia."

"Oh, no, Miss Priscilla came to spend the day with me. You know she used to take dinner with us every Christmas at the rectory."

A troubled look clouded his face. "Jenny ought to have been here," he said, and asked suddenly, as if it were a relief to him to change the subject: "Have you had news of Harry?"

The light that the name of Harry always brought to her eyes shone there now, enriching their faded beauty. "He writes to me every week. You know he hasn't missed a single Sunday letter since he first went off to school. He is wild about Oxford, but I think he gets a little homesick sometimes, though, of course, he'd never say so."

"He'll do well, that boy. The stuff is in him."

"I'm sure he's a genius, if there ever was one, Oliver. Only yesterday Professor Trimble was telling me that Harry was far and away the most brilliant pupil he had ever had."

"Well, he's something to be proud of. And now what about Lucy? Is she still satisfied with Craven?"

"She never writes about anything else except about her house. Her marriage seems to have turned out beautifully. You remember, I wrote you she was perfectly delighted with her stepchildren, and she really appears to be as happy as the day is long."

"You never can tell. I thought she'd be back again before two months were up."

"I know. We all prophesied dreadful things—even Susan."

"That reminds me—I came down on the train with John Henry, and he said that Uncle Cyrus was breaking rapidly."

"He has never been the same since his wife's death," replied Virginia, who was a victim of this sentimental fallacy. "It's strange—isn't it?—because we used to think they got on so badly."

"I wonder if it is really that? Well, is there any other news? Has anything else happened?"

With his back to the fire, he stood looking down on her with kindly, questioning eyes. He had done his best; from the moment when he had entered the room and met the touching brightness in her face, he had struggled to be as natural, to be as affectionate even, as she desired. At the moment, so softened, so self-reproachful, was his mood, he would willingly have cut off his arm for her could the sacrifice in any manner have secured her happiness. But there were times when it seemed easier to give his life for her than to live it with her; when to shed his blood would have cost less than to make conversation. He yearned over Virginia, but he could not talk to her. Some impregnable barrier of personality separated them as if it were a wall. Already they belonged to different generations; they spoke in the language of different periods. At forty-seven, that second youth, the Indian summer of the emotions, which lingers like autumnal sunshine in the lives of most men and of a few women, was again enkindling his heart. And with this return of youth, he felt the awakening of an infinite promise, of the ancient ineradicable belief that happiness lies in possession. Love, which had used up her spirit and body in its service, had left him untouched by its exactions. While she, having fulfilled her nature, was content to live anew not in herself, but in her children, the force of personal desire was sweeping over him again, with all the flame and splendour of adolescence. The "something missing" waited there, just a little beyond, as he had seen it waiting in that enchanted May when he fell in love with Virginia. And between him and his vision of happiness there interposed merely his undisciplined conscience, his variable, though honest, desire to do the thing that was right. Duty, which had controlled Virginia's every step, was as remote and aloof from his life as was the creed of his fathers. Like his age, he was adrift among disestablished beliefs, among floating wrecks of what had once been rules of conduct by which men had lived. And the widening responsibilities, the deepening consciousness of a force for good greater than creed or rules, all the awakening moral strength which would lend balance and power to his age, these things had been weakened in his character by the indomitable egoism that had ordered his life. There was nothing for him to fall back upon, nothing that he could place above the restless surge of his will.

Sitting there in the firelight, with her loving eyes following his movements, she told him, bit by bit, all the latest gossip of Dinwiddie. Susan's eldest girl had developed a beautiful voice and was beginning to take lessons; poor Miss Priscilla had had a bad fall in Old Street while she was on the way to market, and at first they feared she had broken her hip, but it turned out that she was only dreadfully bruised; Major Peachey had died very suddenly and she had felt obliged to go to his funeral; Abby Goode had been home on a visit and everybody said she didn't look a day over twenty-five, though she was every bit of forty-four. Then, taking a little pile of samples from her work basket which stood on the table, she showed him a piece of black brocaded satin. "Miss Willy is making me a dress out of this to wear in New York with you. I don't suppose you noticed whether or not they were wearing brocade."

No, he hadn't noticed, but the sample was very pretty, he thought. "Why don't you buy a dress there, Virginia? It would save you so much trouble."

"Poor little Miss Willy has set her heart on making it, Oliver. And, besides, I shan't have time if we go only the day before."

A flush had come to her face; at the corners of her mouth a tender little smile rippled; and her look of faded sweetness gave place for an instant to the warmth and animation of girlhood. But the excitement of girlhood could not restore to her the freshness of youth. Her pleasure was the pleasure of middle age; the wistful expectancy in her face was the expectancy of one whose interests are centred on little things. That inviolable quality of self-sacrifice, the quality which knit her soul to the enduring soul of her race, had enabled her to find happiness in the simple act of renouncement. The quiet years had kept undiminished her capacity for enjoyment, the exaggerated appreciation of trivial favours, which had filled Mrs. Pendleton's life with a flutter of thankfulness; and while Virginia smoothed the piece of black brocade on her knee, she might have been the rearisen pensive spirit of her mother. Of the two, perhaps because she had ceased to wish for anything for herself, she was happier than Oliver.

All through dinner, while her soft anxious eyes dwelt on him over the bowl of pink roses in the centre of the table, he tried hard to throw himself into her narrow life, to talk only of things in which he felt that she was interested. Slight as the effort was, he could see her gratitude in her face, could hear it in the gentle silvery sound of her voice. When he praised the dinner, she blushed like a girl; when he made her describe the dress Miss Willy was making, she grew as excited as if she had been speaking of the sacred white satin she had worn as a bride. So little was needed to make her happy—that was the pathos! She was satisfied with the crumbs of life, and yet they were denied her. Though she had been alone ever since Lucy's wedding, she accepted his belated visit as thankfully as if it were a gratuitous gift. "It is so good of you to come down, dear, when you are needed every minute in New York," she murmured, with a caressing touch on his arm, and, looking at her, he was reminded of Mrs. Pendleton's tremulous pleasure in the sweets that came to her on little trays from her neighbours. Once she had said eagerly, "It will be so nice to see Miss Oldcastle, Oliver," and he had answered in a constrained tone which he tried to make light and casual, "I am not sure that the part is going to suit her."

Then he had changed the subject abruptly by rising from the table and asking her to let him see her latest letter from Harry.

The next morning he went out after breakfast to consult Cyrus about some investments, while Virginia laid out the lengths of brocade on the bed in the spare room, and sat down to wait for the arrival of the dressmaker. Outside, the trees were still white from the storm, and the wind, blowing through them, made a dry crackling sound, as if it were rattling thorns in a forest. Though it was intensely cold, the sunshine fell in golden bars over the pavement and filled the town with a dazzling brilliance through which the little seamstress was seen presently making her way. Alert, birdlike, consumed with her insatiable interest in other people, she entered, after she had removed her bonnet and wraps, and began to spread out her patterns. It was twenty-odd years since she had made the white satin dress in which Virginia was married, yet she looked scarcely a day older than she had done when she knelt at the girl's feet and envied her happiness while she pinned up the shining train. Failing love, she had filled her life with an inextinguishable curiosity; and this passion, being independent of the desires of others, was proof alike against disillusionment and the destructive processes of time.

"So Mr. Treadwell has come home," she remarked, with a tentative flourish of the scissors. "I declare, he gets handsomer every day he lives. It suits him somehow to fill out, or it may be I'm partial to fat like my poor mother before me."

"He does look well, but I'd hardly call him fat, would you?"

"Well, he's stouter than he used to be, anyway. Did he say when he was going to take you back with him?"

"Next Wednesday. We'll have to hurry to get this dress ready in time."

"I'll start right in at it. Have you made up your mind whether you'll have it princess or a separate waist and skirt?"

"I'm a little too thin for a princess gown, don't you think? Hadn't I better have it made like that black poplin everybody thought looked so well on me?"

"But it ain't half so stylish as the princess. You just let me put a few cambric ruffles inside the bust and you'll stand out a plenty. I was reading in a fashion sheet only yesterday that they are trying to look as flat as they can manage in Paris."

"Well, I'll try it," Virginia murmured uncertainly; for her standards of dress were so vague that she was thankful to be able to rely on Miss Willy's self-constituted authority.

"You just leave it to me," was the dressmaker's reply, while she thrust the point of the scissors into the gleaming brocade on the bed.

The morning passed so quickly amid cutting, basting, and gossip, that it came as a surprise to Virginia when she heard the front door open and shut and Oliver's rapid step mounting the stairs. Meeting him in the hall, she led the way into her bedroom, and asked with the caressing, slightly conciliatory manner which expressed so perfectly her attitude toward life:

"Did you see Uncle Cyrus?"

"Yes, and he was nicer than I have ever known him to be. By the way, Virginia, I've transferred enough property to you to bring you in a separate income. This was really what I went down about."

"But what is the matter, dear? Don't you feel well? Have you had any worries that you haven't told me?"

"Oh, I'm all right, but it's better so in case something should happen."

"But what could possibly happen? I never saw you look better. Miss Willy was just saying so."

He turned away, not impatiently, but as one who is seeking to hide an emotion that has become too strong. Then without replying to her question, he muttered something about "a number of letters to write before lunch," and hurried out of the room and downstairs to his study.

"I wonder if he has lost money," she thought, vaguely troubled, as she instinctively straightened the brushes he

had disarranged on the bureau. "Poor Oliver! He seems
to think about nothing but money now, and he used to be
so romantic."

He used to be so romantic! She repeated this to Susan
that evening when, after Miss Willy's departure for the
night, she took her friend into the spare room to show
her the pattern of the princess gown.

"Do you remember that we used to call him an incurable Don Quixote?" she asked. "And now he has become
so different that at times it makes me smile to think of
him as he was when I first knew him. I suppose it's better
so, it's more normal. He used to be what Uncle Cyrus
called 'flighty,' bent on reforming the world and on improving people, you know, and now he doesn't seem to
care whether outside things are good or bad, just as long
as his plays go well and he can give us all the money we
want."

"It's natural, isn't it?" Susan asked. "One can't stay
young for ever, you see."

"And yet in some ways he doesn't appear to be a bit
older. I like his hair being gray, don't you? It makes his
colour look even richer than before."

"Yes," Susan said, "I like his hair and I like him. Only
I wish he didn't have to leave you by yourself so much
of the time."

"He is going to take me back with him on Wednesday.
Miss Willy is making this dress for me to wear. I want
to look nice because, of course, everybody will be noticing Oliver."

"It's lovely, and I'm sure you'll look as sweet as the
angel that you are, Virginia," Susan answered, stooping to
kiss her.

By Tuesday night the dress was finished, and Virginia
was stuffing the sleeves with tissue paper before packing

it into her trunk, when Oliver came into the room and stood watching her in silence.

"I do hope it won't get crumpled," she said anxiously, as she spread a towel over the tray. "Miss Willy is so proud of it, and I'm sure I couldn't have got anything prettier in New York."

"Virginia," he said suddenly, "you've set your heart on going to-morrow, haven't you?"

Turning from the trunk, she looked up at him with a tender, inquiring smile. Above her head the electric light, with which Oliver and the girls had insisted on replacing the gas-jets that she preferred, cast a hard glitter over the hollowed lines of her face and over the thinning curls which she had striven to brush back from her temples. Her figure, unassisted as yet by Miss Willy's ruffles, looked so fragile in the pitiless glare that his heart melted in one of those waves of sentimentality which, because they were impotent to affect his conduct, cost him so little. As she stood there, he realized more acutely than he had ever done before how utterly stationary she had remained since he married her. With her sweetness, her humility, her old-fashioned courtesy and consideration for others, she belonged still in the honey-scented twilight of the eighties. While he had moved with the world, she, who was confirmed in the traditions of another age, had never altered in spirit since that ecstatic moment when he had first loved her. The charm, the grace, the virtues, even the look of gentle goodness, that had won his heart, were all there just as they had been when she was twenty. Except for the fading flesh, the woman had not changed; only the needs and the desires of the man were different. Only the resurgent youth in him was again demanding youth for its mate.

"Why, my trunk is all packed," she replied. "Has anything happened?"

"Oh, no, I was only wondering how you would manage to amuse yourself. You know, I shall be at the theatre most of the time."

"But you mustn't have me on your mind a minute, Oliver. I won't go a step unless you promise me not to worry about me a bit. It's all so new to me that I shall enjoy just sitting in the hotel and watching the people."

"Then we'd better go to the Waldorf. That might interest you more."

His eagerness to provide entertainment for her touched her as deeply as if it had been a proof of his love instead of his anxiety, and she determined in her heart that if she were lonesome a minute he must never suspect it. Ennui, having its roots in an egoism she did not possess, was unknown to her.

"That will be lovely, dear. Lucy wrote me when she was there on her wedding trip that she used to sit for hours in the corridor looking at the people that went by, and that it was as good as a play."

"That settles it. I'll telegraph for rooms," he said cheerfully, relieved to find that she fell in so readily with his suggestion.

She was giving a last caressing pat to the tray before closing the trunk, and the look of her thin hands, with their slightly swollen knuckles, caused him to lean forward suddenly and wrest the keys away from her.

"Let me do that. I hate to see you stooping," he said.

The telegram was sent, and late the next evening, as they rolled through the brilliant streets toward the hotel, Virginia's interest was as effervescent as if she were indeed the girl she almost felt herself to have become. The sound of the streets excited her like martial music, and little gasps of surprise and pleasure broke from her lips as the taxicab turned into Broadway. It was all so different from her other visit when she had come alone to find Oliver, sick with failure, in the dismal bedroom of that hotel. Now it seemed to her that the city had grown younger, that it was more awake, that it was brighter, gayer, and that she herself had a part in its brightness and gaiety. The crowds on Broadway seemed keeping step to some happy tune, and she felt that her heart was dancing with them, so elated, so girlishly irresponsible, was her mood.

"Why, Oliver, there is a sign of your play with a picture of Miss Oldcastle on it!" she exclaimed delightedly, pointing to an advertisement before a theatre they were passing. Then, suddenly, it appeared to her that the whole city was waving this advertisement. Wherever she turned "The Home" stared back at her, an orgy of red and blue, surrounding the smiling effigy of the actress. And this proof of Oliver's fame thrilled her as she had not been thrilled since the telegram had come announcing that Harry had won the scholarship which would take him to Oxford. The woman's power of sinking her ambition, and even her identity, into the activities of the man was deeply interwoven with all that was essential and permanent in her soul. Her keenest joys, as well as her sharpest sorrows, had never belonged to herself, but to others. It was doubtful, indeed, if, since the day of her marriage, she had been profoundly moved by any feeling which was centred merely in a personal desire. She had wanted things for Oliver and for the children, but for herself there had been no separate existence apart from them.

"Oliver, I never dreamed that it would be like this. The play will be a great success—even a greater one than the last, won't it, dear?" Her face, with its exquisite look of exaltation, of self-forgetfulness, was turned eagerly toward the crowd of feverish pleasure-seekers that passed on, pursuing its little joys, under the garish signs of the street.

"Well, it ought to be," he returned; "it's bad enough anyway."

His eyes, like hers, were fixed on the thronging streets, but, unlike hers, they reflected the restless animation, the pathetic hunger, which made each of those passing faces the medium of an insatiable craving for life. Handsome, well preserved, a little overcoloured, a little square of figure, with his look of worldly importance, of assured material success, he stood to-day, as Cyrus had stood the quarter of a century before, as an imposing example of that Treadwell spirit from which his youth had revolted.

That night, when they had finished dinner, and Oliver, in response to a telephone message, had hurried down to the theatre, Virginia went upstairs to her room, and, after putting on the lavender silk dressing-gown which Miss Willy had made for the occasion, sat down to write her weekly letter to Harry.

My Darling Boy.

I know you will be surprised to see from this letter that I am really in New York at last—and at the Waldorf! It seems almost like a dream to me, and whenever I shut my eyes, I find myself forgetting that I am not in Dinwiddie—but, you remember, your father had always promised me that I should come for the first night of his new play, which will be acted to-morrow. You simply can't imagine till you get here how famous he is and how interested people are in everything about him, even the smallest trifles. Wherever you look you see advertisements of his plays (he has three running now) and coming up Broadway for only a block or two last night, I am sure that I saw Miss Oldcastle's picture a dozen times. I should think she would hate dreadfully to have to make herself so conspicuous—for she has a nice, refined face—but Oliver says all actresses have to do it if they want to get on. He takes all the fuss they make over him just as if he despised it, though I am sure that in his heart he can't help being pleased. While we were having dinner, everybody in the dining-room was turning to look at him, and if I hadn't known, of course, that not a soul was thinking of me, I should have felt badly because I hadn't time to change my dress after I got here. All the other women were beautifully dressed (I never dreamed that there were so many diamonds in the world. Miss Willy would simply go crazy over them), but I didn't mind a bit, and if anybody thought of me at all, of course, they knew I had just stepped off the train. After dinner your father went to the theatre, and I sat downstairs alone in the corridor for a while and watched the people coming and going. It was perfectly fascinating at first. I never saw so many beautiful women, and their hair was arranged in such a lovely way, all just alike, that it must have taken hours to do each head. The fashions that are worn here are not in the least like those of Dinwiddie, though Miss Willy made my black brocade exactly like one in a fashion plate that came directly from Paris, but I know that you aren't as much interested in this as Lucy and Jenny would be. The dear girls are both well, and Lucy is carried away with her stepchildren. She says she doesn't see why every woman doesn't marry a widower. Isn't that exactly like Lucy? She is always so funny. If only one of you were here with me, I should enjoy every minute, but after I'd sat there for a while in the midst of all those strangers, I began to feel a little lonely, so I came upstairs to write you this letter. New York is a fascinating place to visit, but I am glad I live in Dinwiddie where everybody knows me.

And now, my dearest boy, I must tell you how perfectly overjoyed I was to get your last letter, and to know that you are so delighted with Oxford. I think of you every minute, and I pray for you the last thing at night before I get into bed. Try to keep well and strong, and if you get a cold, be sure not to let it run on till it turns to a hacking cough. Remember that Doctor Fraser always used to say that every cough, no matter how slight, is dangerous. I hope you aren't studying too hard or overdoing athletics. It is so easy to tax one's strength too much when one gets excited. I am sure I don't know what to think of the English students being "stand-offish" with Americans. It seems very foolish of them not to be nice and friendly, especially to Virginians, who were really English in the beginning. But I am glad that you don't mind, and that you

would rather be a countryman of George Washington than a
countryman of George the Third. Of course England is the greatest country in the world—you remember your grandfather always
said that—and we owe it everything that we have, but I think it
very silly of English people to be stiff and ill-mannered.

I hope you still read your Bible, darling, and that you find time
to go to church once every Sunday. Even if it seems a waste of time
to you, it would have pleased your grandfather, and for his sake I
hope you will go whenever you can possibly do so. It was so sweet
of you to write in Addison's Walk because you did not want to
miss my Sunday letter and yet the day was too beautiful not to be
out of doors. God only knows, my boy, what a comfort you are to
me. There was never a better son, nor one who was loved more
devotedly.

YOUR MOTHER.

In the morning, with the breakfast tray, there arrived
a bunch of orchids from one of Oliver's theatrical friends,
who had heard that his wife was in town; and while Virginia laid the box carefully in the bathtub, her eyes shone
with the grateful light which came into them whenever
some one did her a small kindness or courtesy.

"They will be lovely for me to wear to-night, Oliver.
It was so nice of him to send them, wasn't it?"

"Yes, it was nice," Oliver replied, looking up from
his paper at the pleased sound of her voice. Ever since
his return at a late hour last night, she had noticed
the nervousness in his manner and had sympathetically
attributed it to his anxiety over the fate of his play. It
was so like Oliver to be silent and self-absorbed when he
was anxious.

Through the day he was absent, and when he returned,
in the evening, to dress for the theatre, she was standing
before the mirror fastening the bunch of orchids on the
front of her gown. As he entered, she turned toward him
with a look of eager interest, of pleasant yet anxious

excitement. She had never in her life, except on the morning of her wedding day, taken so long to dress; but it seemed to her important that as Oliver's wife she should look as nice as she could.

"Am I all right?" she asked timidly, while she cast a doubtful glance in the mirror at the skirt of the black brocade.

"Yes, you're all right," he responded, without looking at her, and the suppressed pain in his voice caused her to move suddenly toward him with the question, "Aren't you well, Oliver?"

"Oh, I'm well, but I'm tired. I had a headache on the way up and I haven't been able to shake it off."

"Shall I get something for it?"

"No, it will pass. I'd like a nap, but I suppose it's time for me to dress."

"Yes, it's half-past six, and we've ordered dinner for seven."

He went into the dressing-room, and turning again to the mirror, she changed the position of the bunch of orchids, and gave a little dissatisfied pat to the hair on her forehead. If only she could bring back some of the bloom and the freshness of youth! The glow had gone out of her eyes; the winged happiness, which had given her face the look of one flying toward life, had passed, leaving her features a little wan and drawn, and fading her delicate skin to the colour of withered flowers. Yet the little smile, which lingered like autumn sunshine about her lips, was full of that sweetness which time could not destroy, because it belonged not to her flesh, but to an unalterable quality of her soul; and this sweetness, which she exhaled like a fragrance, would cause perhaps one of a hundred strangers to glance after her with the thought, "How lovely that woman must once have been!"

"Are you ready?" Oliver asked, coming out of his dressing-room, and again she started and turned quickly toward him, because it seemed to her that she was hearing his voice for the first time. So nervous, so irritable, so quivering with suppressed feeling, was the sound of it, that she hesitated between the longing to offer sympathy and the fear that her words might only add to his suffering.

"Yes, I am quite ready," she answered, without adding that she had been ready for more than an hour; and picking up her wrap from the bed, she passed ahead of him through the door which he had opened. As he stopped to draw the key from the lock, her eyes rested with pride on the gloss of his hair, which had gone gray in the last year, and on his figure, with its square shoulders and its look of obvious distinction, as of a man who had achieved results so emphatically that it was impossible either to overlook or to belittle them. How splendid he looked! And what a pity that, after all his triumphs, he should still be so nervous on the first night of a play!

In the elevator there was a woman in an ermine wrap, with Titian hair under a jewelled net; and Virginia's eyes were suffused with pleasure as she gazed at her. "I never saw any one so beautiful!" she exclaimed to Oliver, as they stepped out into the hall; but he merely replied indifferently: "Was she? I didn't notice." Then his tone lost its deadness. "If you'll wait here a minute, I'd like to speak to Cranston about something," he said, almost eagerly. "I shan't keep you a second."

"Don't worry about me," she answered cheerfully, pleased at the sudden change in his manner. "Stay as long as you like. I never get tired watching the people."

He hurried off, while, dazzled by the lights, she drew back behind a sheltering palm, and stood a little screened from the brilliant crowd in which she took such innocent

pleasure. "How I wish Miss Willy could be here," she
thought, for it was impossible for her to feel perfect
enjoyment while there existed the knowledge that another
person would have found even greater delight in the scene
than she was finding herself. "How gay they all look—
and there are not any old people. Everybody, even the
white-haired women, dress as if they were girls. I wonder
what it is that gives them all this gloss, as if they had
been polished, the same gloss that has come on Oliver
since he has been so successful? What a short time he
stayed. He is coming back already, and every single person
is turning to look at him."

Then a voice beyond the palm spoke as distinctly as if
the words were uttered into her ear. "That's Treadwell
over there—a good-looking man, isn't he?—but have you
seen the dowdy, middle-aged woman he is married to? It's
a pity that all great men marry young—and now they
say, you know, that he has fallen in love with Margaret
Oldcastle——"

CHAPTER V

BITTERNESS

IN THE night, after a restless sleep, she awoke in terror. A hundred incidents, a hundred phrases, looks, gestures, which she had thought meaningless until last evening, flashed out of the darkness and hung there, blazing, against the background of the night. Yesterday, these things had appeared purposeless; and now it seemed to her that only her incredible blindness, only her childish inability to face any painful fact until it struck her between the eyes, had kept her from discovering the truth before it was thrust on her by the idle chatter of strangers. A curious rigidity, as if she had been suddenly paralyzed, passed from her heart, which seemed to have ceased beating, and crept through her limbs to her motionless hands and feet. Though she longed to call out and awaken Oliver, who, complaining of insomnia, spent the night in the adjoining room, this immobility, which was like the graven immobility of death, held her imprisoned there as speechless and still as if she lay in her coffin. Only her brain seemed on fire, so pitilessly, so horribly alive had it become.

From the street beyond the dim square of the window, across which the curtains were drawn, she could hear the ceaseless passing of carriages and motor cars; but her thoughts had grown so confused that for a long while, as she lay there, chill and rigid under the bedclothes, she could not separate the outside sounds from the tumult

433

within her brain. "Now that I know the truth I must decide what is best to do," she thought quite calmly. "As soon as this noise stops, I must think it all over and decide what is best to do." But round this one lucid idea the discordant roar of the streets seemed to gather force until it raged with the violence of a storm. It was impossible to think clearly until this noise, which, in some strange way, was both in the street outside and within the secret chambers of her soul, had subsided and given place to the quiet of night again. Then, gradually, the tempest of sound died away, and in the midst of the stillness that followed it she lived over every hour, every minute, of that last evening when it had seemed to her that she was crucified by Oliver's triumph. She saw him, as he came toward her down the shining corridor, easy, brilliant, impressive, a little bored by his celebrity, yet with the look of vital well-being, of second youth, which separated and distinguished him from the curious gazers among whom he moved. She saw him opposite to her during the long dinner, which she could not eat; she saw him beside her in the car that carried them to the theatre; and clearer than ever, as if a burning iron had seared the memory into her brain, she saw him lean on the railing of the box, with his eyes on the stage, where Margaret Oldcastle, against the lowered curtain, smiled her charming smile at the house. It had been a wonderful night, and through it all she had felt the iron nails of her crucifixion driven into her soul.

Breaking away from that chill of terror with which she had awakened, she left the bed and went over to the window, where she drew the heavy curtains aside. In Fifth Avenue the electric lights sparkled like frost on the pavement, while beyond the roofs of the houses the first melancholy glow of a winter's sunrise was suffusing the sky with red. While she watched it, a wave of unutterable loneliness swept over her, of that profound spiritual loneliness which comes to one at dawn in a great city, when knowledge of the sleeping millions within reach seems only to intensify the fact of individual littleness and isolation. She felt that she stood alone, not merely in the world, but in the universe; and the thought that Oliver slept there in the next room made more poignant this feeling, as though she were solitary and detached in the midst of limitless space. Even if she called him and he came to her, she could not reach him. Even if he stood at her side, the immeasurable distance between them would not lessen.

When the morning came, she dressed herself in her prettiest gown, a violet cloth, with ruffles of old lace at the throat and wrists; but this dress, of which she had been so proud in Dinwiddie that she had saved it for months in order to have it fresh for New York, appeared somehow to have lost its charm and distinction, and she knew that last evening had not only destroyed her happiness, but had robbed her of confidence in the taste and the workmanship of Miss Willy. Knowledge, she saw now, had shattered the little beliefs of life as well as the large ones.

Oliver liked to breakfast in his dressing-gown, fresh from his bath and eager for the papers, so when he came hurriedly into the sitting-room, the shining tray was already awaiting him, and she sat pouring his coffee in a band of sunlight beside the table. This sunlight, so merciful to the violet gown, shone pitilessly on the darkened hollows the night had left under her eyes, and on the little lines that had gathered round her bravely smiling mouth.

"It was a wonderful success, all the papers say so, Oliver," she said, when he had seated himself at the other end of the table and taken the coffee from her hand, which shook in spite of her effort.

"Yes, it went off well, there's no doubt of it," he answered cheerfully, so cheerfully that for a minute a blind hope shot trembling through her mind. Could it all have been a dream? Was there some dreadful mistake? Would she presently discover that she had imagined the night of useless agony through which she had passed?

"The audience was so sympathetic. I saw a number of women crying in the last act when the heroine comes back to her old home."

"It caught them. I thought it would. It's the kind of thing they like."

He opened a paper as he spoke, and seeing that he wanted to read the criticisms, she broke his eggs for him, and then turning to her own breakfast tried in vain to swallow the piece of toast she had buttered. But it was useless. She could not eat; she could not even drink her coffee, which had stood so long that it had grown tepid. A feeling of spiritual nausea, beside which all physical sensations were as trivial and meaningless as the stinging of wasps, pervaded her soul and body, and choked her, like unshed tears, whenever she tried to force a bit of food between her trembling lips. All the casual interests with which she filled her days, those seemingly small yet actually tremendous interests without which daily life becomes almost unlivable, flagged suddenly and died while she sat there. Nothing mattered any longer, neither the universe nor that little circle of it which she inhabited, neither life nor death, neither Oliver's success nor the food that she was trying to eat. This strange sickness that had fallen upon her affected not only her soul and body, but everything that surrounded her, every person or object at which she looked, every stranger in the street

below, every roof she could see sharply outlined
against the glittering blue of the sky. Something had
passed out of them all, some essential quality that united
them to reality, some inner secret of being without which
the animate and the inanimate alike became no better than
phantoms. The spirit that made life vital had gone out
of the world. And she felt that this would always be so,
that the next minute and the next year and all the years
that came afterwards would bring to her merely the effort
of living: since Life, having used her for its dominant purpose, had no further need of her. Once only the thought
occurred to her that there were women who might keep
their own even now by fighting against the loss of it, by
passionately refusing to surrender what they could no
longer hold as a gift. But with the idea there came also
that self-knowledge which told her that she was not one
of these. The strength in her was the strength of fortitude;
she could endure, but she could not battle. Long ago, as
long ago as the night on which she had watched in the
shadow of death beside Harry's bed, she had lost that
energy of soul which had flamed up in her with her
three days' jealousy of Abby. It was her youth and beauty
then that had inspirited her, and she was wise enough to
know that the passions which become youth appear ridiculous in middle age.

Having drunk his coffee, Oliver passed his cup to her,
and laid down his paper.

"You look tired, Virginia. I hope it hasn't been too
much for you?"

"Oh, no. Have you quite got over your headache?"

"Pretty much, but those lights last night were trying.
Don't put any cream in this time. I want the stimulant."

"Perhaps it has got cold. Shall I ring for fresh?"

"It doesn't matter. This will do quite as well. Have you any shopping that you would like to do this morning?"

Shopping! When her whole world had crumbled round her! For an instant the lump in her throat made speech impossible; then summoning that mild yet indestructible spirit, which was as the spirit of all those generations of women who lived in her blood, she answered gently:

"Yes, I had intended to buy some presents for the girls."

"Then you'd better take a taxicab for the morning. I suppose you know the names of the shops you want to go to?"

"Oh, yes. I know the names. Are you going to the theatre?"

"I've got to change a few lines in the play, and the sooner I go about it the better."

"Then don't bother about me, dear. I'll just put on my long coat over this dress and go out right after breakfast."

"But you haven't eaten anything," he remarked, glancing at her plate.

"I wasn't hungry. The fresh air will do me good. It has turned so much warmer, and the snow is all melting."

As she spoke, she rose from the table and began to prepare herself for the street, putting on the black hat with the ostrich tip and the bunch of violets on one side, which didn't seem just right since she had come to New York, and carefully wrapping the ends of her fur neckpiece round her throat. It was already ten o'clock, for Oliver had slept late, and she must be hurrying if she hoped to get through her shopping before lunch. While she dressed, a wan spirit of humour entered into her, and she saw how absurd it was that she should rush about from shop to shop, buying things that did not matter in order to fill a life that mattered as little as they did. To her, whose mental outlook had had in it so little humour, it seemed suddenly that the whole of life was ridiculous. Why should she have sat there, pouring Oliver's coffee and talking to him about insignificant things, when her heart was bursting with this sense of something gone out of existence, with this torturing realization of the irretrievable failure of love?

Taking up her muff and her little black bag from the bureau, she looked back at him with a smile as she turned toward the door.

"Good-bye. Will you be here for lunch?"

"I'm afraid I can't. I've an appointment downtown, but I'll come back as early as I can."

Then she went out and along the hall to the elevator, in which there was a little girl, who reminded her of Jenny, in charge of a governness in spectacles. She smiled at her almost unconsciously, so spontaneous, so interwoven with her every mood was her love for children; but the little girl, being very proper for her years, did not smile back, and a stab of pain went through Virginia's heart.

"Even children have ceased to care for me," she thought.

At the door, where she waited a few minutes for her taxicab, a young bride, her eyes shining with joy, stood watching her husband while he talked with an acquaintance, and it seemed to Virginia that it was a vision of her own youth which had risen to torment her. "That was the way I looked at Oliver twenty-five years ago," she said to herself; "twenty-five years ago, when I was young and he loved me." Then, even while the intolerable pain was still in her heart, she felt that something of the buoyant hopefulness of that other bride entered into her and restored her courage. A resolution, so new that it was born of the joyous glance of a stranger, and yet so old that it seemed a part of that lost spirit of youth which had once

carried her in a wild race over the Virginian meadows, a
resolution which belonged at the same time to this other
woman and to herself, awoke in her and mingled like a
draught of wine with her blood. "I will not give up," she
thought. "I will go to her. Perhaps she does not know—
perhaps she does not understand. I will go to her, and
everything may be different." Then her taxicab was called,
and stepping into it, she gave the name not of a shop, but
of the apartment house in which Margaret Oldcastle
lived.

It was one of those February days when, because of
the promise of spring in the air, men begin suddenly to
think of April. The sky was of an intense blue, with little
clouds, as soft as feathers, above the western horizon. On
the pavement the last patches of snow were rapidly melting, and the gentle breeze that blew in at the open window
of the cab, was like a caressing breath on Virginia's cheek.
"It must be that she does not understand," she repeated,
and this thought gave her confidence and filled her with
that unconquerable hope of the future without which she
felt that living would be impossible. Even the faces in the
street cheered her; for it seemed to her that if life were
really what she had believed it to be last night, these men
and women could not walk so buoyantly, could not smile so
gaily, could not spend so much thought and time on the
way they looked and the things they wore. "No, it must
have been a mistake, a ghastly mistake," she insisted almost passionately. "Some day we shall laugh over it together as we laughed over my jealousy of Abby. He never
loved Abby, not for a minute, and yet I imagined that he
did and suffered agony because of it." And her taxicab
went on merrily between the cheerful crowds on the pavements, gliding among gorgeous motor cars and carriages
drawn by high-stepping horses and pedlers' carts drawn

by horses that stepped high no longer, among rich people
and poor people, among surfeited people and hungry
people, among gay people and sad people, among contented people and rebellious people;—among all these,
who hid their happiness or their sorrow under the mask
of their features, her cab spun onward bearing her lightly
on the most reckless act of her life.

At the door of the apartment house she was told that
Miss Oldcastle could not be seen, but, after sending up
her card and waiting a few moments in the hall before a
desk which reminded her of a gilded squirrel-cage, she
was escorted to the elevator and borne upward to the ninth
floor. Here, in response to the tinkle of a little bell beside a door, she was ushered into a reception room which
was so bare alike of unnecessary furniture and of the
Victorian tradition to which she was accustomed, that
for an instant she stood confused by the very strangeness
of her surroundings. Then a charming voice, with what
sounded to her ears as an affected precision of speech, said:
"Mrs. Treadwell, this is so good of you!" and, turning,
she found herself face to face with the other woman in
Oliver's life.

"I saw you at the play last night," the voice went on,
"and I hoped to get a chance to speak to you, but the
reporters invaded my dressing-room. Won't you sit here
in the sunshine? Shall I close the window, or, like myself,
are you a worshipper of the sun?"

"Oh, no, leave it open. I like it." At any other moment
she would have been afraid of an open window in February; but it seemed to her now that if she could not
feel the air in her face she should faint. With the first
sight of Margaret Oldcastle, as she looked into that
smiling face, in which the inextinguishable youth was less
a period of life than an attribute of spirit, she realized

that she was fighting not a woman, but the very structure
of life. The glamour of the footlights had contributed
nothing to the flame-like personality of the actress. In
her simple frock of brown woollen, with a wide collar of
white lawn turned back from her splendid throat, she embodied not so much the fugitive charm of youth, as that
burning vitality over which age has no power. The intellect in her spoke through her noble rather than beautiful
features, through her ardent eyes, through her resolute
mouth, through every perfect gesture with which she
accompanied her words. She stood not only for the ele-
mental forces, but for the free woman; and her freedom,
like that of man, had been built upon the strewn bodies of
the weaker. The law of sacrifice, which is the basic law of
life, ruled here as it ruled in mother-love and in the industrial warfare of men. Her triumph was less the triumph
of an individual than of the type. The justice not of
society, but of nature, was on her side, for she was one
with evolution and with the resistless principle of change.
Vaguely, without knowing that she realized these things,
Virginia felt that the struggle was useless; and with the
sense of failure there awoke in her that instinct of good
breeding, that inherited obligation to keep the surface of
life sweet, which was so much older and so much stronger
than the revolt in her soul.

"You were wonderful last night. I wanted to tell you
how wonderful I thought you," she said gently. "You made
the play a success—all the papers say so this morning."

"Well, it was an easy play to make successful," replied
the other, while a fleeting curiosity, as though she were
trying to explain something which she did not quite understand, appeared in her face and made it, with its redundant
vitality, almost coarse for an instant. "It's the kind the
public wants, you couldn't help making it go."

The almost imperceptible conflict which had flashed in
their eyes when they met had died suddenly down, and
the dignity that had been on the side of the other woman
appeared to have passed from her to Virginia. This dignity, not of triumph, but of a defeat that surrenders everything except the inviolable sanctities of the spirit, shielded
her like an impenetrable armour against both resentment
and pity. She stood there wrapped in a gentleness more unassailable than any passion.

"You did a great deal for it and a great deal for my
husband," she said, while her voice lingered unconsciously
over the word. "He has told me often that without your
acting he could never have reached the position he holds."

Then, because it was impossible to say the things she
had come to say, because even in the supreme crises of
life she could not lay down the manner of a lady, she
smiled the grave smile with which her mother had walked
through a ruined country, and taking up her muff, which
she had laid on the table, passed out into the hall. She had
let the chance go by, she had failed in her errand, yet she
knew that, even though it cost her her life, even though it
cost her a thing far dearer than life, her happiness, she
could not have done otherwise. In the crucial moment it
was principle and not passion that she obeyed; but this
principle, filtering down through generations, had become
so inseparable from the sources of character, that it had
passed at last through the intellect into the blood. She
could no more have bared her soul to that other woman
than she could have stripped her body naked in the market-
place.

At the door her cab was still waiting, and she gave the
driver the name of the toy shop at which she intended to
buy presents for Lucy's stepchildren. Though her heart
was breaking within her, there was no impatience in her

manner when she was obliged to wait so..ie time before she could find the particular sort of doll for which Lucy had written; and she smiled at the apologetic shop-girl with the forbearing consideration for others that grief could not destroy. She put aside her own anguish as utterly in the selection of the doll as she would have done had it been the peace of nations and not a child's pleasure that depended upon her effacement of self. Then, when the purchase was made, she took out her shopping list from her bag and passed as conscientiously to the choice of Jenny's clothes. Not until the morning had gone, and she again rolled up Fifth Avenue toward the hotel, did she permit her thoughts to return to the stifled agony within her heart.

To her surprise, Oliver was awaiting her in their sitting-room, and with her first look into his face, she understood that he had reached in her absence a decision against which he had struggled for days. For an instant, her strength seemed fainting as before an impossible effort. Then the shame in his eyes awoke in her the longing to protect him, to spare him, to make even this terrible moment easier for him than he could make it alone. With the feeling, a crowd of memories thronged through her mind, as if called there by that impulse to shield which was so deeply interwoven with the primal passion of mother-hood. She saw Oliver's face as it had looked on that spring afternoon when she had first seen him; she saw it as he put the ring on her hand at the altar; she saw it bending over her after the birth of her first child; and then suddenly his face changed to the face of Harry, and she saw again the little bed under the hanging sheet and her-self sitting there in the faintly quivering circle of light. She watched again the slow fall of the leaves, one by one,

as they turned at the stem and drifted against the white
curtains of the window across the street.

"Oliver," she said gently, so gently that she might have
been speaking to her sick child, "would you rather I should
go back to Dinwiddie to-night?"

He did not answer, but, turning away from her, laid his
head down on his arm, which he had outstretched on the
table, and she saw a shiver of pain pass through his body
as if it had been struck a physical blow. And just as she had
put herself aside when she bought the doll, so now she
forgot her own suffering in the longing to respond to his
need.

"I can take the night train—now that I have seen the
play there is no reason why I should stay. I have got
through my shopping."

Raising his head, he looked up into her face. "Whatever happens, Virginia, will you believe that I never
wanted to hurt you?" he asked.

For a moment, she felt that the strain was intolerable,
and a fear entered her mind lest she should faint or weep
and so make things harder than they should be able to
bear.

"You mean that something must happen?" she said.

Leaving the table, he walked to the window and back
before he answered her.

"I can't go on this way. I'm not that sort. A generation ago, I suppose, we should have done it—but we've
lost grip, we've lost endurance." Then he cried out suddenly, as if he were justifying himself: "It is hell. I've been
in hell for a year—don't you see?"

After his violence, her voice sounded almost lifeless, so
quiet, so utterly free from passion, was its quality.

"As long as that—for a year?" she asked.

"Oh, longer, but it has got worse. It has got unendurable. I've fought—God knows I've fought—but I can't stand it. I've got to do something. I've got to find a way. You must have seen it coming, Virginia. You must have seen that this thing is stronger than I am."

"Do—do you want her so much?" and she, who had learned from life not to want, looked at him with the pity he might have seen in her eyes had he stabbed her.

"So much that I'm going mad. There's no other end to it. It's been coming on for two years—all the time I've been away from Dinwiddie, I've been fighting it."

She did not answer, and when, after the silence had grown oppressive, he turned back from the window through which he had been gazing, he could not be sure that she had heard him. So still she seemed that she was like a woman of marble.

"You're too good for me, that's the trouble. You've been too good for me from the beginning," he said.

Unfastening her coat, which she had kept on, she laid it on the sofa at her back, and then put up her hands to take out her hatpins.

"I must pack my things," she said suddenly. "Will you engage my berth back to Dinwiddie for to-night?"

He nodded without speaking, and she added hastily, "I shan't go down again before starting. But there is no need that you should go to the train with me."

At this he turned back from the door where he had waited with his hand on the knob. "Won't you let me do even that?" he asked, and his voice sounded so like Harry's that a sob broke from her lips. The point was so small a one, all points seemed to her so small, that her will died down and she yielded without protest. What did it matter —what did anything matter to her now?

"I'll send up your lunch," he added almost gratefully. "You will be ill if you don't eat something."

"No, please don't. I am not hungry," she answered, and he went out softly, as if he were leaving a sickroom, and left her alone with her anguish—and her packing.

Without turning in her chair, without taking off her hat, from which she had drawn the pins, she sat there like a woman in whom the spirit has been suddenly stricken. Beyond the window the perfect day, with its haunting reminder of the spring, was lengthening slowly into afternoon, and through the slant sunbeam the same gay crowd passed in streams on the pavements. On the roof of one of the opposite houses a flag was flying, and it seemed to her that the sight of that flag waving under the blue sky was bound up for ever with the intolerable pain in her heart. And with that strange passivity of the nerves which nature mercifully sends to those who have learned submission to suffering, to those whose strength is the strength, not of resistance, but of endurance, she felt that as long as she sat there, relaxed and motionless, she had in a way withdrawn herself from the struggle to live. If only she might stay like this for ever, without moving, without thinking, without feeling, while she died slowly, inch by inch, spirit and body.

A knock came at the door, and as she moved to answer it, she felt that life returned in a slow throbbing agony, as if her blood were forced back again into veins from which it had ebbed. When the tray was placed on the table beside her, she looked up with a mild, impersonal curiosity at the waiter, as the dead might look back from their freedom and detachment on the unreal figures of the living. "I wonder what he thinks about it all?" she thought vaguely, as she searched in her bag for his tip. "I wonder if he sees how absurd and unnecessary all the things are that he does day after day, year after year, like the rest of us? I wonder if he ever revolts with this unspeakable weariness from waiting on other people and watching them eat?" But the waiter, with his long sallow face, his inscrutable eyes, and his general air of having petrified under the surface, was as enigmatical as life.

After he had gone out, she rose from her untasted lunch, and going into her bedroom, took the black brocade gown off the hanger and stuffed the sleeves with tissue paper as carefully as if the world had not crumbled about her. Then she packed away her wrapper and her bedroom slippers, and shook out and folded the dresses she had not worn. For a time she worked on mechanically, scarcely aware of what she was doing, scarcely aware even that she was alive. Then slowly, softly, like a gentle rain, her tears fell into the trunk, on each separate garment as she smoothed it and laid it away.

At half-past eight o'clock she was waiting with her hat and coat on when Oliver came in, followed by the porter who was to take down her bags. She knew that he had brought the man in order to avoid an emotional scene; and she could have smiled, had her spirit been less wan and stricken, at this sign of a moral cowardice that was so characteristic. It was his way, she understood now, though she did not put the thought into words, to take what he wanted, escaping at the same time the price nature exacts of those who have not learned to relinquish. Out of the strange colourless stillness which surrounded her, some old words of Susan's floated back to her as if they were spoken aloud: "A Treadwell will always get the thing he wants most in the end." But while he stabbed her, he would look away in order that he might be spared the memory of her face.

Without a word, she followed her bags from the room, without a word she entered the elevator, which was waiting, and without a word she took her place in the taxicab standing beside the curbstone. There was no rebellion in her thoughts, merely a dulled consciousness of pain, like the consciousness of one who is partly under an anæsthetic. The fighting courage, the violence of revolt, had no part in her soul, which had been taught to suffer and to renounce with dignity, not with heroics. Her submission was the submission of a flower that bends to a storm.

As she sat there in silence, with her eyes on the brilliant street, where the signs of his play stared back at her under the flaring lights, she began to think with automatic precision, as if her brain were moved by some mechanical power over which she had no control. Little things crowded into her mind,—the face of the doll she had bought for Lucy's stepchild that morning, the words on one of the electric signs on the top of a building, the leopard-skin coat worn by a woman on the pavement. And these little things seemed to her at the moment to be more real, more vital, than her broken heart and the knowledge that she was parting from Oliver. The agony of the night and the morning appeared to have passed away like a physical pang, leaving only this deadness of sensation and the strange, almost unearthly clearness of external objects. "It is not new. It has been coming on for years," she thought. "He said that, and it is true. It is so old that it has been here for ever, and I seem to have been suffering it all my life—since the day I was born, and before the day I was born. It seems older than I am. Oliver is going from me. He has always been going from me—always since the beginning," she repeated slowly, as if she were trying to learn a lesson by heart. But so remote and shadowy did the words appear that she found herself thinking the next instant, "I must have forgotten my smelling-salts. The bottle was lying on the bureau, and I can't remember putting it into my bag." The image of this little glass bottle, with the

gold top, which she had left behind was distinct in her
memory; but when she tried to think of the parting from
Oliver and of all that she was suffering, everything became
shadowy and unreal again.

At the station she stood beside the porter while he paid
the driver, and then entering the doorway, they walked
hurriedly, so hurriedly that she felt as if she were losing
her breath, in the direction of the gate and the waiting
train. And with each step, as they passed down the long
platform, which seemed to stretch into eternity, she was
thinking: "In a minute it will be over. If I don't say something now, it will be too late. If I don't stop him now, it
will be over for ever—everything will be over for ever."

Beside the night coach, in the presence of the conductor
and the porter, who stood blandly waiting to help her
into the train, she stopped suddenly, as though she could
not go any farther, as though the strength which had supported her until now had given way and she were going
to fall. Through her mind there flashed the thought that
even now she might hold him if she were to make a scene,
that if she were to go into hysterics he would not leave
her, that if she were to throw away her pride and her self-
respect and her dignity, she might recover by violence the
outer shell at least of her happiness. How could he break
away from her if she were only to weep and to cling to
him? Then, while the idea was still in her mind, she knew
that to a nature such as hers violence was impossible. It
took passion to war with passion, and in this she was lacking. Though she was wounded to the death, she could not
revolt, could not shriek out in her agony, could not break
through that gentle yet invincible reticence which she had
won from the past.

Down the long platform a child came running with cries
of pleasure, followed by a man with a red beard, who

carried a suitcase. As they approached the train, Virginia entered the coach, and walked rapidly down the aisle to where the porter was waiting beside her seat.

For the first time since they had reached the station Oliver spoke. "I am sorry I couldn't get the drawing-room for you," he said. "I am afraid you will be crowded"; and this anxiety about her comfort, when he was ruining her life, did not strike either of them, at the moment, as ridiculous.

"It does not matter," she answered, and he put out his hand.

"Good-bye, Virginia," he said, with a catch in his voice.

"Good-bye," she responded quietly, and would have given her soul for the power to shriek aloud, to overcome this indomitable instinct which was stronger than her personal self.

Turning away, he passed between the seats to the door of the coach, and a minute later she saw his figure hastening back along the platform down which they had come together a few minutes ago.

CHAPTER VI

THE FUTURE

A CHILL rain was falling when Virginia got out of the train the next morning, and the raw-boned nags harnessed to the ancient "hacks" in the street appeared even more dejected and forlorn than she had remembered them. Then one of the noisy negro drivers seized her bag, and a little later she was rolling up the long hill in the direction of her home. Dinwiddie was the same; nothing had altered here since she had left it—and yet what a difference! The same shops were unclosing their shutters; the same crippled negro beggar was taking his place at the corner of the market; the same maids were sweeping the sidewalks with the same brooms; the same clerk bowed to her from the drug store where she bought her medicines; and yet something, the only thing that had ever interested her in these people and this place, had passed out of them. Just as in New York yesterday, when she had watched the sunrise, so it seemed to her now that the spirit of reality had faded out of the world. What remained was merely a mirage in which phantoms in the guise of persons made a pretence of being alive.

The front door of her house stood open, and on the porch one of the coloured maids was beating the dust out of a mat. "As if dust makes any difference when one is dead," Virginia thought wearily; and an unutterable loathing passed over her for all the little acts by which one rendered tribute to the tyranny of appearances. Then, as she entered the house, she felt that the sight of the familiar objects she had once loved oppressed her as though the spirit of melancholy resided in the pieces of furniture, not in her soul. This weariness, so much worse than positive pain, filled her with disgust for all the associations and the sentiments she had known in the past. Not only the house and the furniture and the small details of housekeeping, but the street and the town and every friendly face of a neighbour, had become an intolerable reminder that she was still alive.

In her room, where a bright fire was burning, and letters from the girls lay on the table, she sat down in her wraps and gazed with unseeing eyes at the flames. "The children must not know. I must keep it from the children as long as possible," she thought dully, and it was so natural to her to plan sparing them, that for a minute the idea took her mind away from her own anguish. "If only I could die like this, then they need never know," she found herself reflecting coldly a little later, so coldly that she seemed to have no personal interest, no will to choose in the matter. "If only I could die like this, nobody need be hurt—except Harry," she added.

For the first time, with the thought of Harry, her restraint suddenly failed her. "Yes, it would hurt Harry. I must live because Harry would want me to," she said aloud; and as if her strength were reinforced by the words, she rose and prepared herself to go downstairs to breakfast; prepared herself, too, for the innumerable little agonies which would come with the day, for the sight of Susan, for the visits from the neighbours, for the eager questions about the fashions in New York that Miss Willy would ask. And all the time she was thinking clearly, "It can't last for ever. It must end some time. Who knows but it may stop the next minute, and one can stand a minute of anything."

The day passed, the week, the month, and gradually the spring came and went, awakening life in the trees, in the grass, in the fields, but not in her heart. Even the dried sticks in the garden put out shoots of living green and presently bore blossoms, and in the borders by the front gate, the crocuses, which she had planted with her own hands a year ago, were ablaze with gold. All nature seemed joining in the resurrection of life, all nature, except herself, seemed to flower again to fulfilment. She alone was dead, and she alone among the dead must keep up this pretence of living that was so much harder than death.

Once every week she wrote to the children, restrained yet gently flowing letters in which there was no mention of Oliver. It had been so long, indeed, since either Harry or the girls had associated their parents together, that the omission called forth no question, scarcely, she gathered, any surprise. Their lives were so full, their interests were so varied, that, except at the regular intervals when they sat down to write to her, it is doubtful if they ever seriously wondered about her. In July, Jenny came home for a month, and Lucy wrote regretfully that she was "so disappointed she couldn't join mother somewhere in the mountains"; but beyond this, the girls' lives barely appeared to touch hers even on the surface. In the month that Jenny spent in Dinwiddie, she organized a number of societies and clubs for the improvement of conditions among working girls, and in spite of the intense heat (the hottest spell of the summer came while she was there), she scarcely allowed herself a minute for rest or for conversation with her mother.

"If only you would go to the mountains, mother," she

remarked the evening before she left. "I am sure it isn't good for you to stay in Dinwiddie all summer."

"I am used to it," Virginia replied a little stubbornly; for it seemed to her at the moment that she would rather die than move.

"But you ought to think of your health. What does father say about it?"

A contraction of pain crossed Virginia's face, but Jenny, whose vision was so wide that it had a way of overlooking things which were close at hand, did not observe it.

"He hasn't said anything," she answered, with a strange stillness of voice.

"I thought he meant to take you to England, but I suppose his plays are keeping him in New York."

Rising from her chair at the table—they had just finished dinner—Virginia reached for a saucer and filled it with ice cream from a bowl in front of her.

"I think I'll send Miss Priscilla a little of this cream," she remarked. "She is so fond of strawberry."

The next day Jenny went, and again the silence and the loneliness settled upon the house, to which Virginia clung with a morbid terror of change. Had her spirit been less broken, she might have made the effort of going North as Jenny had urged her to do; but when her life was over, one place seemed as desirable as another, and it was a matter of profound indifference to her whether it was heat or cold that afflicted her body. She was probably the only person in Dinwiddie who did not hang out of her window during the long nights in search of a passing breeze. But, with the physical insensibility that accompanies prolonged torture of soul, she had ceased to feel the heat, had ceased even to feel the old neuralgic pain in her temples. There were times when it seemed to her that if a pin were stuck into her body she should not know it. The one thing she asked, and this Life granted her except during the four weeks of Jenny's visit, was freedom from the need of exertion, freedom from the obligation to make decisions. Her housekeeping she left now to the servants, so she was spared the daily harassing choice, of the market and the table. There remained nothing for her to do, nothing even for her to worry about, except her broken heart. Her friends she had avoided ever since her return from New York, partly from an unbearable shrinking from the questions she knew they would ask whenever they met her, partly because her mind was so engrossed with the supreme fact of her ruined universe that she found it impossible to lend a casual interest to other matters. She, who had effaced herself for a lifetime, found suddenly that she could not see beyond the immediate presence of her own suffering.

Usually she stayed closely indoors through the summer days; but several times, at the hour of dusk, she went out alone and wandered for hours in the streets that were associated with her girlhood. In High Street, at the corner where she had first seen Oliver, she stood one evening until Miss Priscilla, who had caught sight of her from the porch of the Academy (which, owing to the changing fashions in education and the infirmities of the teacher, was the Academy no longer), sent out her negro maid to beg her to come in and sit with her. "No, I'm only looking for something," Virginia had answered, while she hastened back past the church and down the slanting street to the twelve stone steps that led up the terraced hillside to the rectory. Here, in the purple summer twilight, spangled with fireflies, she felt for a minute that her youth was awaiting her; and opening the gate, she passed as softly as a ghost along the crooked path to the two great paulownias, which were beginning to decay, and to the honeysuckle arbour, where the tendrils of the creeper brushed her hair like a caress. Under the light of a young moon, it seemed to her that nothing had changed since that spring evening when she had stood there and felt the wonder of first love awake in her heart. Nothing had changed except that love and herself. The paulownias still shed their mysterious shadows about her; the red and white roses still bloomed by the west wing of the house; the bed of mint still grew, rank and fragrant, beneath the dining-room window. When she put her hand on the bole of the tree beside which she stood, she could still feel the initials V. O. which Oliver had cut there in the days before their marriage. A light burned in the window of the room that had been the parlour in the days when she lived there, and as she gazed at it, she almost expected to see the face of her mother, with its look of pathetic cheerfulness, smiling at her through the small greenish panes. And then the past in which Oliver had no part, the past that belonged to her and to her parents, that hallowed, unforgettable past of her childhood, which seemed bathed in love as in a flood of light: this past enveloped her as the magic of the moonbeams enveloped the house in which she had lived. While she stood there, it was more living than the present, more real than the aching misery in her heart.

The door of the house opened and shut; she heard a step on the gravelled path; and bending forward out of the shadow, she waited breathlessly for the sound of her father's voice. But it was a young rector, who had recently accepted the call to Saint James' Church, and his boyish face, rising out of the sacred past, awoke her with a shock from the dream into which she had fallen.

"Good-evening, Mrs. Treadwell. Were you coming to see me?" he asked eagerly, pleased, she could see, by the idea that she was seeking his services.

"No, I was passing, and the garden reminded me so of my girlhood that I came in for a minute."

"It hasn't changed much, I suppose?" His alert, business-like gaze swept the hillside.

"Hardly at all. One might imagine that those were the same roses I left here."

"An improvement or two wouldn't hurt it," he remarked with animation. "These old trees make such a litter in the spring that my wife is anxious to get them down. Women like tidiness, you know, and she says, while they are blooming, it is impossible to keep the lawn tidy."

"I remember. Their flowers cover everything when they fall, but I always loved them."

"Well, one does get attached to things. I hope you have had a pleasant summer in spite of the heat. It must have been a delight to have your daughter at home again. What a splendid worker she is. If we had her in Dinwiddie for good it wouldn't be long before the old town would awaken. Why, I'd been trying to get those girls' clubs started for a year, and she took the job out of my hands and managed it in two weeks."

"The dear child is very clever. Is your wife still in the mountains?"

"She's coming back next week. We didn't feel that it was safe to bring the baby home until that long spell of heat had broken." Then, as she turned toward the step, he added hastily, "Won't you let me walk home with you?"

But this, she felt, was more than she could bear, and making the excuse of an errand on the next block, she parted from him at the gate, and hurried like a shadow back along High Street.

Until October there was no word from Oliver, and then at last there came a letter, which she threw, half read, into the fire. The impulsive act, so unlike the normal Virginia, soothed her for an instant, and she said over and over to herself, while she moved rapidly about the room, as if she were seeking an escape from the moment before her, "I'm glad I didn't finish it. I'm glad I let it burn." Though she did not realize it, this passionate refusal to look at or to touch the thing that she hated, was the last stand of the Pendleton idealism against the triumph of the actuality. It is possible that until that moment she had felt far down in her soul that by declining to acknowledge in words the fact of Oliver's desertion, by hiding it from the children, by ignoring the processes which would lead to his freedom, she had, in some obscure way, deprived that fact of all power over her life. But now while his letter, blaming himself and yet pleading with her for his liberty, lay there, crumbling slowly to ashes, under her eyes, her whole life, with its pathos, its subterfuge, its losing battle against the ruling spirit of change, seemed crumbling there also, like those ashes, or like that vanished past to which she belonged. "I'm glad I let it burn," she repeated bitterly, and yet she knew that the words had never really burned, that the flame which was consuming them would never die until she lay in her coffin. Stopping in front of the fire, she stood looking down on the last shred of the letter, as if it were in reality the ruins of her life that she watched. A dull wonder stirred in her mind amid her suffering—a vague questioning as to why this thing, of all things, should have happened? "If only I could know why it was—if only I could understand, it might be easier," she thought. "But I tried so hard to do

what was right, and, whatever the fault was, at least I
never failed in love. I never failed in love," she repeated.
Her gaze, leaving the fire, rested for an instant on a little
alabaster ash-tray that stood on the end of the table, and
a spasm crossed her face, which had remained unmoved
while she was reading his letter. Every object in the room
seemed suddenly alive with memories. That was his place
on the rug; the deep chintz-covered chair by the hearth was
the one in which he used to sit, watching the fire at night,
before going to bed; the clock on the mantelpiece was
the one he had selected; the rug, which was threadbare
in places, he had helped her to choose; the pile of English
reviews on the table he had subscribed to; the little glass
water bottle on the candle-stand by the bed, she had bought
years ago because he liked to drink in the night. There
was nothing in which he did not have a part. Every trivial
incident of her life was bound up with the thought of him.
She could no more escape the torment of these associations
than she could escape the fact of herself. For so long she
had been one with him in her thoughts that their relation-
ship had passed, for her, into that profound union of
habit which is the strongest union of all. Even the years
in which he had grown gradually away from her had appeared to her to leave untouched the deeper sanctities
of their marriage.

A knock came at the door, and the cook, with a list of
groceries in her hand, entered to inquire if her mistress
were going to market. With the beginning of the autumn
Virginia had tried to take an interest in her housekeeping
again, and the daily trip to the market had relieved, in a
measure, the terrible vacancy of her mornings. Now it
seemed to her that the remorseless exactions of material
details offered the only escape from the tortures of memory. "Yes, I'll go," she said, reaching out her hand for the

list, and her heart cried, "I cannot live if I stay in this room any longer. I cannot live if I look at these things." As she turned away to put on her hat, she was seized by a superstitious feeling that she might escape her suffering by fleeing from these inanimate reminders of her marriage. It was as if the chair and the rug and the clock had become possessed with some demoniacal spirit. "If only I can get out of doors I shall feel better," she insisted; and when she had hurriedly pinned on her hat and tied her tulle ruff at her throat, she caught up her gloves and ran quickly down the stairs and out into the street. But as soon as she had reached the sidewalk, the agony, which she had thought she was leaving behind her in the closed room upstairs, rushed over her in a wave of realization, and turning again, she started back into the garden, and stopped, with a sensation of panic, beside the bed of crimson dahlias at the foot of the steps. Then, while she hesitated, uncertain whether to return to her bedroom or to force herself to go on to the market, those hated familiar objects flashed in a blaze of light through her mind, and, opening the gate, she passed out on the sidewalk, and started at a rapid step down the deserted pavement of Sycamore Street. "At least nobody will speak to me," she thought; but while the words were still on her lips, she saw a door in the block open wide, and one of her neighbours come out on his way to his business. Turning hastily, she fled into a cross street, and then gathering courage, went on, trembling in every limb, toward the old market, which she used because her mother and her grandmother had used it before her.

The fish-carts were still there just as they had been when she was a girl, but the army of black-robed housekeepers had changed or melted away. Here, also, the physical details of life had survived the beings for whose use or comfort they had come into existence. The meat and the vegetable stalls were standing in orderly rows about the octagonal building; wilted cabbage leaves littered the dusty floor; flies swarmed round the bleeding forms hanging from hooks in the sunshine; even Mr. Dewlap, hale and red-cheeked, offered her white pullets out of the wooden coop at his feet. So little had the physical scene changed since the morning, more than twenty-five years ago, of her meeting with Oliver, that while she paused there beside Mr. Dewlap's stall, one of the older generation might have mistaken her for her mother.

"My dear Virginia," said a voice at her back, and, turning, she found Mrs. Peachey, a trifle rheumatic, but still plump and pretty. "I'm so glad you come to the old market, my child. I suppose you cling to it because of your mother, and then things are really so much dearer uptown, don't you think so?"

"Yes, I dare say they are, but I've got into the habit of coming here."

"One does get into habits. Now I've bought chickens from Mr. Dewlap for forty years. I remember your mother and I used to say that there were no chickens to compare with his white pullets."

"I remember. Mother was a wonderful housekeeper."

"And you are too, my dear. Everybody says that you have the best table in Dinwiddie!" Her small rosy face, framed in the shirred brim of her black silk bonnet, was wrinkled with age, but even her wrinkles were cheerful ones, and detracted nothing from the charming archness of her expression. Unconquerable still, she went her sprightly way, on rheumatic limbs, toward the grave.

"Have you seen dear Miss Priscilla?" Virginia asked, striving to turn the conversation away from herself, and shivering with terror lest the other should ask after Oliver, whom she had always adored.

"I stopped to inquire about her on my way down. She had had a bad night, the maid said, and Doctor Fraser is afraid that the cold she got when she went driving the other day has settled in her lungs."

"Oh, I am so sorry!" Virginia exclaimed, but she was conscious of an immeasurable relief because Miss Priscilla's illness was absorbing Mrs. Peachey's thoughts.

"Well, I must be going on," said the little lady, and though she flinched with pain when she moved, the habitual cheerfulness of her face did not alter. "Come to see me as often as you can, Virginia. I can't get about much now, and it is such a pleasure for me to have somebody to chat with. People don't visit now," she added regretfully, "as much as they used to."

"So many things have changed," Virginia said, and her eyes, as she gazed upon the blue sky over the market, had a yearning look in them. So many things had changed —ah, there was the pang!

On her way home, overcome by the fear that Miss Priscilla might die thinking herself neglected, Virginia stopped at the Academy, and was shown into the chamber behind the parlour, which had once been a classroom. In the middle of her big tester bed, the teacher was lying, propped among pillows, with her cameo brooch fastening the collar of her nightgown and a purple wool shawl, which Virginia had knitted for her, thrown over her shoulders.

"Dear Miss Priscilla, I've thought of you so often. Are you better to-day?"

"A little, Virginia, but don't worry about me. I'll be out of bed in a day or two." Though she was well over eighty-five, she still thought of herself as a middle-aged

woman, and her constant plans for the future amazed
Virginia, whose hold upon life was so much slighter, so
much less tenacious. "Have you been to market, dear? I
miss so being able to sit by the window and watch people
go by. Then I always knew when you and Susan were on
your way to Mr. Dewlap."

"Yes, I've begun to go again. It fills in the day."

"I never approved of your letting your servants market
for you, Virginia. It would have shocked your mother
dreadfully."

"I know," Virginia said, and her voice, in spite of her
effort to speak cheerfully, had a weary sound, which made
her add with sudden energy, "I've brought you a partridge.
Mr. Dewlap had such nice ones. You must try to eat it
for supper."

"How like you that was, Virginia. You are your mother
all over again. I declare I am reminded of her more and
more every time I see you."

Tears sprang to Virginia's eyes, while her thin blue-
veined hands gently caressed Miss Priscilla's swollen and
knotted fingers.

"You couldn't tell me anything that would please me
more," she answered.

"I used to think that Lucy would take after her, but she
grew up differently."

"Yes, neither of the girls is like her. They are dear,
good children, but they are very modern."

"Have you heard from them recently?"

"A few days ago, and they are both as well as can be."

"And what about Harry? I've always believed that
Harry was your favourite, Virginia."

For an instant Virginia hesitated, with her eyes on the
pot of red geraniums blooming between the white muslin
curtains at the window. In his little cage in the sunlight,

Miss Priscilla's canary, the last of many generations, burst suddenly into song.

"I believe that Harry loves me more than anybody else in the world does," she answered at last. "He'd come to me to-morrow if he thought I needed him."

Lying there in her great white bed, with her enormous body, which she could no longer turn, rising in a mountain of flesh under the linen sheet, the old teacher closed her eyes lest Virginia should see her soul yearning over her as it had yearned over Lucy Pendleton after the rector's death. She thought of the girl, with the flower-like eyes and the braided wreath of hair, flitting in white organdie and blue ribbons, under the dappled sunlight in High Street, and she said to herself, as she had said twenty-five years ago, "If there was ever a girl who looked as if she were cut out for happiness, it was Virginia Pendleton."

"They say that Abby Goode is going to be married at last," Virginia remarked abruptly, for she knew that such bits of gossip supplied the only pleasant excitement in Miss Priscilla's life.

"Well, it's time. She waited long enough," returned the teacher, and she added, "I always knew she was crazy about Oliver by the way she flung herself at his head." She had never liked Abby, and her prejudices, which had survived the shocks of life, were not weakened by the approaching presence of Death. It was characteristic of her that she should pass into eternity with both her love and her scorn undiminished.

"She was a little boisterous as a girl, but I never believed any harm of her," Virginia answered mildly; and then as Miss Priscilla's lunch was brought in on a tray, she kissed her tenderly, with a curious feeling that it was for the last time, and went out of the door and down the gravelled walk into High Street. An exhaustion greater than any she had ever known oppressed her as she dragged her body, which felt dead, through the glorious October weather. Once, when she passed Saint James' Church, she thought wearily, "How sorry mother would be if she knew," while an intolerable pain, which seemed her mother's pain as well as her own, pierced her heart. Then, as she hurried on, with the nervous haste that she could no longer control, the terrible haunted blocks appeared to throng with the faded ghosts of her youth. A gray-haired woman leaning out of the upper window of an old house nodded to her with a smile, and she found herself thinking, "I rolled hoops with her once in the street, and now she is watching her grandchild go out in its carriage." At any other moment she would have bent, enraptured, over the perambulator, which was wheeled by a nurse and a maid, down the front steps into the street; but to-day the sight of the soft baby features, lovingly surrounded by lace and blue ribbons, was like the turn of a knife in her wound. "And yet mother always said she was never so happy as she was with my children," she reflected, while her personal suffering was eased for a minute by the knowledge of what her return to Dinwiddie had meant to her mother. "If she had died while I lived away, I could never have got over it—I could never have forgiven myself," she added, and there was an exquisite relief in turning even for an instant away from the thought of herself.

When she reached home lunch was awaiting her; but after sitting down at the table and unfolding her napkin, a sudden nausea seized her, and she felt that it was impossible to sit there facing the mahogany sideboard, with its gleaming rows of silver, and watch the precise, slow-footed movements of the maid, who served her as she might have served a wooden image. "I took such trouble to train her, and now it makes me sick to look at her," she

thought, as she pushed back her chair and fled hastily from
the room into Oliver's study across the hall. Here, her
work-bag lay on the table, and taking it up, she sat down
before the fire, and spread out the centrepiece, which she
was embroidering, in an intricate and elaborate design, for
Lucy's Christmas. It was almost a year now since she had
started it, and into the luxuriant sprays and garlands there
had passed something of the restless love and yearning that
overflowed from her heart. Usually she was able to work
on it in spite of her suffering, for she was one of those
whose hands could accomplish mechanically tasks from
which her soul had revolted; but to-day even her obedient
fingers faltered and refused to keep at their labour. Her
eyes, leaving the needle she held, wandered beyond the
window to the branches of the young maple tree, which
rose, like a pointed flame, toward the cloudless blue of the
sky.

In the evening, when Susan came in, with a newspaper
in her hand, and passionate sympathy in her face, Virginia
was still sitting there, gazing at the dim outline of the tree
and the strip of sky which had faded from azure to gray.

"Oh, Virginia, my darling, you never told me!"

Taking up the piece of embroidery from her lap, Virginia met her friend's tearful caress with a frigid and
distant manner. "There was nothing to tell," she said.

"Is—is it true that Oliver has left you? That—
that——" Susan's voice broke, strangled by emotion, but
Virginia, without looking up from the rose on which she
was working in the firelight, answered quietly:

"Yes, it is true. He wants to be free."

"But you will not do it, darling? The law is on your
side."

With her eyes on the needle, which she held carefully
poised for the next stitch, Virginia hesitated while the

muscles of her face quivered for an instant and then grew rigid again.

"What good would it do," she asked, "to hold him to me when he wishes to be free?" And then, with one of those flashes of insight which came to her in moments of great emotional stress, she added quietly, "It is not the law, it is life."

Putting her arm round her, Susan pressed her to her bosom as she might have pressed a suffering child whom she was powerless to help or even to make understand.

"Virginia, let me love you," she begged.

"How did you know?" asked Virginia, as coldly as though she had not heard her.

For an instant Susan's pity struggled against her loyalty. "General Goode told me that there had been a good deal about Oliver and—and Miss Oldcastle in the New York papers for several days," she answered, "and this morning a few lines were copied in the Dinwiddie *Bee*. Oliver is so famous it was impossible to keep things hushed up, I suppose. But you knew all this, darling."

"Oh, yes, I knew that," Virginia answered; then, rising suddenly from her chair, she said almost irritably: "Susan, I want to be alone. I can't think until I am alone." By her look Susan knew that until that minute some blind hope had kept alive in her, some childish pretence that it might all be a dream, some passionate evasion of the ultimate outcome.

"But you'll let me come back? You'll let me spend the night with you, Virginia?"

"If you want to, you may come. But I don't need you. I don't need anybody. I don't need anybody," she repeated bitterly; and this bitterness appeared to change not only her expression, but her features and her carriage and that essential attribute of her being which had been the real Virginia.

Awed in spite of herself, Susan put on her hat again, and bent over to kiss her. "I'll be back before bedtime, Virginia. Don't shut me away, dear. Let me share your pain with you."

At this something that was like a smile trembled for an instant on Virginia's face.

"You are good, Susan," she responded; but there was no tenderness, no gratitude even, in her voice. She had grown hard with the implacable hardness of grief.

When the door had closed behind her friend, she stood looking through the window until she saw her pass slowly, as though she were reluctant to go, down Sycamore Street in the direction of her home. "I am glad she has gone," she thought coldly. "Susan is good, but I am glad she has gone." Then, turning back to the fire, she took up the piece of embroidery and mechanically folded it before she laid it away. While her hands were still on the bag in which she kept it, a shiver went through her body, and a look of resolution passed over her features, making them appear as if they were sculptured in marble.

"He will be sorry some day," she thought. "He will be sorry when it is too late, and if I were there now—if I were to see him, it might all be prevented. It might all be prevented and we might be happy again." In her distorted mind, which worked with the quickness and the intensity of delirium, this idea assumed presently the prominence and the force of an hallucination. So powerful did it become that it triumphed over all the qualities which had once constituted her character—over the patience, the sweetness, the unselfish goodness—as easily as it obscured the rashness and folly of the step that she planned. "If I could see him, it might all be prevented," she repeated obstinately, as though some one had opposed her; and, going upstairs to her bedroom, she packed her little handbag and put on the travelling dress she had worn in New York. Then, very softly, as if she feared to be stopped by the servants, she went down the stairs and out of the front door; and, very softly, carrying her bag, she passed into the street and walked hurriedly in the direction of the station. All the way she was thinking, "If only I can see him again, this may not happen and everything may be as it was before when he still loved me." So just and rational did this idea appear to her, that she found herself wondering passionately why she had not thought of it before. It was so easy a way out of her wretchedness that it seemed absurd of her to have overlooked it. And this discovery filled her with such tremulous excitement, that when she opened her purse to buy her ticket, her hands shook as if they were palsied, and the porter, who held her bag, was obliged to count out the money. The whole of life, which had looked so dark an hour ago, had become suddenly transfigured.

Once in the train, her nervousness left her, and when an acquaintance joined her after they had started, she was able to talk connectedly of trivial occurrences in Dinwiddie. He was a fat, apoplectic looking man, with a bald head that shone like satin, and a drooping moustache slightly discoloured by tobacco. His appearance, which she had never objected to before, seemed to her grotesque; but in spite of this, she could smile almost naturally at his jokes, which she thought inconceivably stupid.

"I suppose you heard about Cyrus Treadwell's accident," he said at last when she rose to go to her berth. "Got knocked down by an automobile as he was getting off a street car at the bank. It isn't serious, they say, but he was pretty well stunned for a while."

"No, I hadn't heard," she answered, and thought, "I wonder why Susan didn't tell me." Then she said good-night and disappeared behind the curtains of her berth, where she lay, without undressing, until morning.

"This is the way. There is no other way to stop it," she thought, and all night the rumble of the train and the flashing of the lights in the darkness outside her window kept up a running accompaniment to the words. "It is a sin—and there is no other way to stop it. He is committing a sin, and when I see him he will understand it, and it will be as it was before." This idea, which was as fixed as an obsession of delirium, seemed to occupy some central space in her brain, leaving room for a crowd of lesser thoughts which came and went fantastically round it like the motley throng of a circus. She thought of Cyrus Tread-well's accident, of the stupid jokes the man from Dinwiddie had told her, of the noises of the train, which would not let her sleep, of the stations which blazed out, here and there, in the darkness. But in the midst of this confusion of images and impressions, a clear voice was repeating somewhere in her brain: "This is the way—there is no other way to stop it before it is too late."

In the morning, when she got out in New York, and gave the driver the name of the little hotel at which she had stopped on her first visit, this glowing certainty faded like the excitement of fever from her mind, and she relapsed into the stricken hopelessness of the last six months. The bleakness of her spirits fell like a cloud on the brilliant October day, and the sunshine, which lay in golden pools on the pavements, appeared to increase the sense of universal melancholy which had followed so sharply on the brief exaltation of the night. "I must see him—it is the only way," her brain still repeated, but the ring of conviction was gone from the words. Her flight from Dinwiddie showed to her now in all the desperate folly with which it might have appeared to a stranger. The impulse that had brought her had ebbed away, and with the impulse had passed also the confidence and the energy of her resolve.

At the hotel, where the red bedroom into which they ushered her appeared to have waited unaltered for the second tragedy of her life, she bathed and dressed herself, and after a cup of black coffee, taken because a sensation of dizziness had alarmed her lest she should faint in the street, she put on her hat again and went out into Fifth Avenue. She remembered the name of the hotel at the head of Oliver's letter, and she directed her steps toward it now with an automatic precision of which her mind seemed almost unaware. All thought of asking for him had vanished, yet she was drawn to the place where he was by a force that was more irresistible than any choice of the will. An instinct stronger than reason was guiding her steps.

In Fifth Avenue the crowd was already beginning to stream by on the sidewalks, and as she mingled with it, she recalled that other morning when she had moved among these people and had felt that they looked at her kindly because she was beautiful and young. Now the kindness had given way to indifference in their eyes. They no longer looked at her; and when a shop window, which she was passing, showed her a reflection of herself, she saw only a commonplace middle-aged figure, with a look of withered sweetness in the face, which had grown suddenly wan. And the sight of this figure fell like a weight on her heart, destroying the last vestige of courage.

Before the door of the hotel in which Oliver was staying, she stood so long, with her vacant gaze fixed on the green velvet carpet within the hall, that a suspicious attendant came up at last and inquired if she wished to see any one. Arousing herself with a start, she shook her head and turned back into the street, for when the crucial moment came her decision failed her. Just as she had been unable to make a scene on the night when they had parted, so now it was impossible for her to descend to the vulgarity of thrusting her presence into his life. Unless the frenzy of delirium seized her again, she knew that she should never have the strength to put the desperation of thought into the desperation of action. What she longed for was not to fight, not to struggle, but to fall, like a wounded bird, to the earth.

At the crossing, where there was a crush of motor cars and carriages, she stopped for a moment and thought how easy it would be to die in the crowded street before returning to Dinwiddie. "All I need do is to slip and fall there, and in a second it would be over." But so many cars went by that she knew she should never be able to do it, that much as she hated life, something bound her to it which she lacked the courage to break. There shot through her mind the memory of a soldier her father used to tell about, who was always first on the field of battle, but had never found the courage to charge. "He was like me; for I might stand here for ever and yet not find the courage to die."

A beggar came up to her and she thought, "He is begging of me, and yet I am more miserable than he is." Then, while she searched in her bag for some change, it seemed to her that the faces gliding past had became suddenly distorted and twisted as though the souls of the women in the rapidly moving cars were crucified under their splendid furs. "That woman in the sable cloak is beautiful, and yet she, also, is in torture," she reflected, with an impersonal coldness and detachment. "I was beautiful,

too, but how did it help me?" And she saw herself as she
had been in her girlhood with the glow of happiness, as of
one flying, in her face, and her heart filled with the joyous
expectancy of the miracle that must happen. "I am as old
now as Miss Willy was then—and how I pitied her!"
Tears rushed to her eyes, which had been so dry a minute
before, while the memory of that lost gaiety of youth came
over her in a wave that was like the sweetness of the
honeysuckle blooming in the rectory garden.

A policeman, observing that she had waited there so
long, held up the traffic until she had crossed the street,
and after thanking him, she went on again toward the hotel
in which she was staying. "He was kind about helping me
over," she said to herself, with an impulse of gratitude;
and this casual kindness seemed to her the one spot of
light in the blackness that surrounded her.

As she approached the hotel, her step flagged, and she
felt suddenly that even the passive courage which was hers,
the courage of endurance, had deserted her. She saw the
dreadful hours that must ensue before she went back to
Dinwiddie, the dreadful days that would follow after she
got there, the dreadful weeks that would run on into the
dreadful years. Silent, gray, and endless, they stretched
ahead of her, and through them all she saw herself, a little
hopeless figure, moving toward the death which she had
not had the courage to die. The thought of the familiar
streets, of the familiar faces, of the house, of the furniture,
of the leaf-strewn lawn in which her bed of dahlias was
blooming;—all these aroused in her the sense of spiritual
nausea she had felt when she went back to them after her
parting from Oliver. Nothing remained except the long
empty years, for she had outlived her usefulness.

At the door of the hotel, the hall porter met her with
a cheerful face, and she turned to him with the instinctive

reliance on masculine protection that had driven her to
the friendly shelter of the policeman at the crossing in
Fifth Avenue. In reply to her helpless questions, he looked
up the next train to Dinwiddie, which left within the hour,
and after buying her ticket, assisted her smilingly into the
taxicab. While she sat there, in the middle of the seat, with
her little black bag rocking back and forth as the cab
turned the corners, all capacity for feeling, all possibility
of sensation even, seemed to have passed out of her body.
The impulse that was carrying her to Dinwiddie was the
physical impulse that drives a wounded animal back to die
in its shelter. Even the flaring advertisements of Oliver's
play, which was still running in a Broadway theatre,
aroused no pain, scarcely any thought of him or of the
past, in her mind. She had ceased to suffer, she had ceased
even to think; and when, a little later, she followed the
station porter down the long platform, she was able to
brush aside the memory of her parting from Oliver as
lightly as if it were the trivial sting of a wasp. When she
remembered the agony of the last year, of yesterday, of
the morning through which she had just lived, it appeared
almost ridiculous. That death which she had lacked the
courage to die seemed creeping over her soul before it
reached the outer shell of her body.

In the train, she was attacked by a sensation of faint-
ness, and remembering that she had eaten nothing all day,
she went into the dining-car, and sat down at one of the
little tables. When her lunch was brought, she ate almost
ravenously for a minute. Then her sudden hunger was followed by a disgust for the look of the dishes and the
cinders on the tablecloth, and after paying her check, for
which she waited an intolerable time, she went back to her
chair in the next coach, and watched, with unseeing eyes,
the swiftly moving landscape, which rushed by in all the

brilliant pageantry of October. Several seats ahead of her, two men were discussing politics, and one of them, who wore a clerical waistcoat, raised his voice suddenly so high that his words penetrated the wall of blankness that surrounded her thoughts, "I tell you it is the greatest menace to our civilization!" and then, as he controlled his excitement, his speech dropped quickly into indistinctness.

"How absurd of him to get so angry about it," Virginia thought with surprise, "as if a civilization could make any difference to anybody on earth." And she watched the clergyman for a minute, as if fascinated by the display of his earnestness. "What on earth can it matter to him?" she wondered mildly, "and yet to look at him one would think that his heart was bound up in the question." But in a little while she turned away from him again, and lying back in her chair, stared across the smooth plains to the pale golden edge of the horizon. Through the long day she sat, without moving, without taking her eyes from the landscape, while the sunlight faded slowly away from the fields and the afterglow flushed and waned, and the stars shone out, one by one, through the silver web of the twilight. Once, when the porter had offered her a pillow, she had looked round to thank him; once when a child, toddling along the aisle, had fallen at her feet, she had bent over to lift it; but beyond this, she had stirred only to hand her ticket to the conductor when he aroused her by touching her arm. Where the sunset and the afterglow had been, she saw at last only the lights of the train reflected in the smeared glass of the window, but so unaware was she of any change in the utter vacancy at which she looked, that she could not have told whether it was an hour or a day after leaving New York that she came back to Dinwiddie. Even then, she would still have sat there, speechless, inert, unseeing, had not the porter taken her bag and accompanied her from the glare of the train out into the dimness of the town, where the crumbling "hacks" harnessed to the decrepit horses still waited. Here her bag was passed over to a driver, whom she vaguely remembered, and a few minutes later she rolled, in one of the ancient vehicles, under the pale lights of the street which led to her home. In the drug store at the corner she saw Miss Priscilla's maid buying medicines, and she wondered indifferently if the teacher had grown suddenly worse. Then, as she passed John Henry's house, she recognized his large shadow as it moved across the white shade at the window of the drawing-room. "Susan was coming to spend last night with me," she said aloud, and for the first and last time in her life, an ironic smile quivered upon her lips.

With a last jolt the carriage drew up at the sidewalk before her home; the driver dismounted, grinning, from his box; and in the lighted doorway, she saw the figure of her maid, in trim cap and apron, waiting to welcome her. Not a petal had fallen from the bed of crimson dahlias beside the steps; not a leaf had changed on the young maple tree, which rose in a spire of flame toward the stars. Inside, she knew, there would be the bright fire, the cheerful supper table, the soft bed turned down—and the future.

On the porch, she stopped and looked back into the street as she might have looked back at the door of a prison. The negro driver, having placed her bag in the hall, stood waiting expectantly, with his hat in his hand, and his shining black eyes on her face; and opening her purse, she paid him, before walking past the maid over the threshold. Ahead of her stretched the staircase that she would go up and down for the rest of her life. On the right, she could look into the open door of the dining-room, and opposite to it, she knew that the lamp was lit and the fire burning in Oliver's study. Then, while a wave of despair, like a mortal sickness, swept over her, her eyes fell on a telegram that lay awaiting her on the hall table, and when she had torn it open, she read:

Dearest mother, I am coming home to you,

HARRY.

THE END